Cheyenne Crossing
The Journey

By
F.R. Paris

PublishAmerica
Baltimore

First printing

At the specific preference of the author, PublishAmerica allowed this work to remain exactly as the author intended, verbatim, without editorial input.

ISBN: 1-4241-1733-X
PUBLISHED BY PUBLISHAMERICA, LLLP
www.publishamerica.com
Baltimore

Printed in the United States of America

DEDICATION

This book is dedicate to the love of my life, my wife Peggy, to our family Jane, Ken, Pam, Oren, Mike, Nancy, Shelley, Beth, Leon, Tim and Rhonda, all of whom encouraged me, and in their own way contributed to this story. Thanks to my Mother and Father for telling me, what it was like way back then and for instilling a love of history in my life. A special thanks goes to Doctor David C. Evans whose thoroughness saved my life. Finally to Pamo without her insistence and continued encouragement this story might have went untold and most likely be lying in some drawer, gathering dust.

FOREWORD

Partially hidden by a stack of firewood Ty watched the closed door of the sod shanty. Small seams of light showed between the cracks of the crudely made entryway. From time to time, the streaks, broken by the shadow of something moving inside, led Ty to believe that it was someone pacing back and forth. Occasionally he could hear the angry voice of a man talking to someone or to something. Ty thought, "It can't be a dog or it would have picked up my scent by now it's got to be another person but how many?" He remembered Rocky's warning, "Just take it a step at a time."

The rising moon threw just enough light for Ty to see the entire area around the shack. Rocky was behind the building hoping to find a window to look into. While he waited his worries came back to him, was this really the right cabin? The rider-less horse had led them here but did he stop on his own or did some homesteaded catch him and place him in the corral? Who was inside, the raw-hider's partners or innocent homesteaders just having a disagreement before preparing for sleep?

Damn the raw-hiders anyway, they would still be alive if they had just left well enough alone. When Ty and Rocky left the Landing in the middle of the night, Rocky figured that the two in the saloon would follow. The weather was in their favor, the blowing snow helped cover their tracks and with a couple of direction changes, they hoped that they would lose them. After riding through the night and the following day, they set up their camp at the edge of a small pond.

Spreading their bedrolls, Ty fell to sleep while Rocky took the first watch. The moon had slowly moved across the black sky and was disappearing under the western horizon, when a low growl from Tuff caused Ty to come awake. Lying there, he could hear the sounds of Rocky sleeping. Tuff continued to sound an alarm with a growl that told Ty things were not right. Moving quietly to Rocky's side and placing his hand over his mouth to keep him still while he woke him up, "Tuff thinks there is something out there, heard a rustling myself, don't think it was the wind."

Without a word said by Rocky, but using a hand signal, he motioned Ty back toward the pond and using his finger pointing at his eyes, indicating, to stay alert. Returning to his bedroll, with his shotgun ready, his wait was not for long when two shots rang out he felt rather than heard a bullet pass close to his head. He fired one barrel at the flash where the shot had come from and for a very short period a man, illuminated by the blast of the shotgun, Ty heard a grunt and then the sound of the man falling.

A shot from Rocky's Hawkins rifle sounded, and then there was nothing but silence. After a short time Rocky asked, "You alright?"

"Ya, are you?"

"Missed me, did you get your man?"

"Think so, thought I heard him drop."

"I'm sure I hit the one I was shootin' at but can't be positive. I heard my shot hit and heard a grunt; we'll just wait a while and see who can out wait the other."

An eternity went and they could hear a slight rustle from time to time and then there was the sound of a running horse.

"At least one got away, most likely the fella I shot. Let's not be in to big of a hurry to check on the other varmint if he ain't dead now he will be."

"The way the dog is actin' its over."

"The mean son of a bitch just earned his keep; I didn't think he was in camp when we shut it down. By the way, I'm sorry as hell about fallin' to sleep like a damn old greenie, I sat here and before I knew it, I must have gone over the edge. Without old Tuff, we most likely would be dead by now but then on the other side I wouldn't have to talk about me fallin' to sleep. If it had been you that didn't keep up your watch I would have been a mad son of a bitch. Guess it's your right to cuss me ifin' you want."

"Hell were alright ain't we, let's forget it." Then as an after though he said, just loud enough for Rocky to hear, "The damn kid has a lot to learn, hope I'm up to it."

The smiles while not seen were on both set of lips, but they were there.

At first light, they walked to where Ty thought he had shot his man. The dead man's left chest, blown away as he lay in a puddle of dried blood that the flies had already claimed.

"That's one of 'em from the saloon, guess I had 'em pegged right."

The second one had also been hit, but apparently not killed. A trail of blood led to a shallow spot where two horses stood, a riding horse and the other a packhorse. The pack was larger than the ones their horses carried, but not put together as well. "Didn't take long loadin' this critter, it's a wonder that they got this far."

A hole, dug just deep enough to bury the man and just before placing the body into it's new resting place, Rocky bent down and started to go through the mans pockets.

"Damn it Rocky what are you doin', he's dead, you can't steal from a dead man."

"Lookin' to see if he's got a name on him can't say words over him ifin' we don't know his name, now can we?

Rocky removed a piece of wrinkled paper and handed it to Ty. Carefully opening the folded paper, he read the names, first to himself and as he did, he looked up and said, "Son of a bitch I know this here name, it was on a wanted poster I seen after the war. Plunket—William Plunket, he was one of 'em that was wanted for murder with Mr. Casey."

The dirt pushed back onto the body and Rocky said, "Watch over this here sinner—Amen."

"Thought you said that needed to tell the Lord his name."

"The Lord knows us all son, he knows us all."

As they rode north, following the tired horse, Rocky's voice interrupted Ty's thoughts. "You thinkin' about the dead man or just the shootin'?"

"The shootin', it seemed too easy. Before hand I wasn't nervous and afterwards it didn't bother me one way or the other, is that the way it is?"

"You were protectin' what was yours, some son of a bitch wanted it, and you said no. The shootin' was goin' to happen; it was bound to. Just as soon as those two decided we were easy pickin's, they were dead. You shoot a man for what he is and what he is wantin' to do to you; you can live with that, you shoot a man for any other reason, that's a different story that is murder, plain and simple."

Half the day passed and Tuff appeared, running back showing more excitement than usual. They rode a short distance further and found the second man lying in the short grass. The darkened blood on his shirt, high upon his right chest, showed where Rocky's shot hit him. The way the blood caked his lips and chin, it was safe to figure the bullet went through the lung, blowing it away.

Ty walked off a few paces, looking at the tracks left by the now rider-less horse it had never stopped when the body had fallen to the ground. This seemed odd and he asked Rocky about it.

"Most likely had the reins tied to his saddle and as hard as he was ridin', the horse is worn out don't know or gives a damn that he lost his rider.

Going through the pockets of the dead man reviled one hundred and seventy eight dollars and sixty cents, in gold and coin together with a note, written in pencil that even Ty had to study. "Think this part is talkin' about two wagons and this word I think is harness, the last part is eight mules. There is something else wrote here but I'll be damned if I can make it out. Written in big numbers are 230, most likely means dollars, who ever wrote this never had much learnin'."

Handing the piece of paper to Rocky, "that's pretty cheap for two outfits, ain't it?'

"Depends if you buyin' or sellin', this gent must have been sellin', seein' as he had most of the money in his pocket. Some poor damn family or maybe two, is most likely dead layin' out there somewhere with their bones picked clean. These scavengers made their livin' doin' what they were goin' to do to us. Ty if you add the other bastard's money to this and what do you get?"

Waiting for Ty to finish he went on, "No one is goin' to miss these damn bastards or the people they killed. If some one stumbles across the bodies of those innocents, which ain't likely, everyone will figure the injuns did it, they always do.

The man in the cabins voice brought Ty out of his thoughts. He could not hear all of what he was saying, but every other word was a cuss word of some sort. The longer he talked the louder he got and the more it convinced Ty that this was the raw-hider's cabin.

Rocky was still nowhere in sight, maybe he had found a peak hole in the sod. "Dammit if I got to shoot another person, I want to be sure who it is, not just think I know."

Concentrating on the shadows surrounding the dirt shack, a thought crept into his mind. He had completely forgotten about his backside. Quickly Ty looked back over his right shoulder, studied the darkness for an instant, and in doing so remembered what Rocky had told him. 'A hell of a lot of men I knowed thought they were walkin' into trouble and then got shot in the back before they ever got there. You got to remember to watch all four sides at once, takes some doin' but it can be done.'

Ty then remembered more of what Rocky had told him back at the Landing. They were sitting in the saloon and Ty had asked what the Indians were really like. Rocky, between drinks of rotgut whiskey started to tell him.

"Don't know where to start; their life is like nothin' I had ever seen, it's a hell of a lot different than on this side. There ain't no fightin' amongst the people of the tribe but meaner than hell to their enemies, just like us, they protect what is theirs. In every tribe that I ever seen they watch over one another just like family. Hell back home you might of had a dozen neighbors not many livin' within earshot. In the tribe, everyone is a neighbor lived right next to one another all their lives."

"The young is their future and they know that. When it comes to the youngins, it's hard to separate 'em, you know like brother or sisters. As I was sayin', in the tribe its one big family, a few squaws might have to watch every damn kid in the village while the other squaws do their thing. The youngins they listen to their elders and it makes no never mind ifin' they're blood related or not, an elder is to be paid attention too."

"A council helps the Chief run things and they have a damn sight fewer problems than the so called civil people. Justice is fairer too, ain't no gettin' around something just cause you got more than someone else. They have survived forever in what most folks would call the wilderness. I'm thinkin' that till the white man showed up it was a damn sight better than now."

He talked about the French trappers that were there before Louis and Clark even started their westward journey. He talked about them bring trading goods that the Indians could use; he also told about the firewater and disease that they brought.

"The damn mountain man and trappers weren't much better than the

French. The tribes, they took 'em in treated 'em like they were one of their own. The ones that came back to the civil life told stories that made others follow, hell, whole wagon trains of people headed west, the more that came the worse it got."

"The injuns see this and know there ain't nothin' they can do to stop it, short of war; to them, the writin' is on the wall, they know this is there last chance and they know that they are fightin' a loosin' battle but it's their way of holdin' on a little longer. After thousand of years of livin' like they do, we can't expect 'em to change over night. God Dammit, who said our way was the right way, their way is more to my choosin'."

Rocky leaned back in his chair, on his face was a big smile. "You wouldn't believe these people, you've got to remember they have survived since the beginin' of time with nothin' but knives and arrows to protect and provide for themselves. They know the land like no one else ever has, or maybe ever will. Their lives depend on it and taught from birth how to hunt, what they can and can't eat. Plants that we take for weeds are medicines to them. They cook their meat over fires started from flint and steel, hell, I have even seen 'em start a damn fire by rubbin' two sticks together it ain't easy to do, but it works."

"Another thing when you see an injun warrior on a horse you don't know where the horse begins and where the rider ends. At a full gallop, they can ride sittin', standin' or hangin' from the side. They use their knees mostly, the leather chin strap is really a hackamore and is used more to hold the horse than for ridin'."

"With their sharp eyes and ears and them knowin' the country like they do, few injuns are ever surprised or caught off guard. No better hunters or tracker ever lived. They can track a snake across water and tell you how long and what color it was. They can sneak up to within inches of a deer or rabbit, hell; they can walk up quiet like to a fella and steal the horse right out from under him, he won't know it's gone till his ass hits the ground."

Again, Ty's thoughts returned to the cabin, the man's voice was silent; the place was deathly quiet. Without warning, the door opened and a big man stepped out carrying a rifle. The snarl of Tuff and then you could see him sprint across the clearing.

Before the dog could cross the open ground, a shot rang out. Swinging his eyes back to the door, the man framed by the shadowy light, was raising his rifle again, preparing for another shot at the charging animal.

Nothing more than a reflex action, brought Ty's rifle to his shoulder. The kick of the rifle and the sound of the bullet hitting flesh told Ty that he had shot another man.

As the man fell, he heard the wild screams of a woman, the sudden flash of Tuff entering the doorway, then nothing but silence.

CHAPTER 1
Spring 1865

There is a lot of time to think when you're walking behind a mule and staring at its butt. Ty O'Malley had followed Buck all morning plowing a field that had been overgrown with weeds and grasses for the last three years. The overgrowth was just one of the things that made the job more difficult, together with the rusty plow with weather, cracked handles, which were splintered and hard on the hands. It seemed as through instead of gaining he was losing ground with each pass. Looking behind him all he seen was the rough furrows of freshly turned soil. The thought entered his mind that the plowing would be the easy part; breaking up the brisling clumps that looked like porcupines, would be the challenge.

Plowing was a tiresome task one that he did not like to do, Ty thought that is was the part of farming that seemed to destroy rather than create. Even after the ground had been broken up previously it still did not appear right.

Ty had heard of big places in the south that plowed up hundreds of acres of virgin ground each year and planted cotton. Of all the things that a farmer could plant, why would you plant cotton, it was hard to grow and harder to pick, you need to have a lot hands to grow cotton. The worst part is after you have raised it and harvested what good was it, you sure as hell couldn't eat it.

Folks up here in the northeast part of Missouri farmed to survive. Surplus eggs, vegetables and sometimes livestock feed was sold to city folk for cash money to buy the necessities; otherwise you raised what you needed.

Stumbling, nearly falling behind the plow his previous thoughts vanished and soon new one's replaced them. It was a hot day for the middle of March no clouds, not even a trace of a breeze, sweat had soaked his shirt and plastered it to his body. Visions of jumping in the stock pond crossed his mind; the cool water of the pond fed by a natural spring was only a stone throw away. Ty swam there last evening, first wearing his shirt and pants hoping to soak the dirt and grime out, he then stripped down to the buff and hung his clothes on a tree limb to dry.

As usual, his thoughts turned to the far west mountains, the very ones that folks had talked about ever since Louis and Clark had made their historic trip up the Missouri and to the big ocean beyond. They told stories of Indians, their ways, their villages and their nomadic travels. Of wild animals that roamed the plains and mountains. They told of the bear, mountain lion, deer and elk that were in abundance, the hugh herds of buffalo that blacken the prairie and of the number of wild horses that belonged to no one. All this talk was exciting to Ty, it was a lot more exciting than staying home and working the farm.

Some said that Lewis and Clark never made it to the ocean but others said that if they did not see it how did they know it was there. Mountain Men that went later said that the ocean was there all right, along with more mountains, rivers and tribes of Indians than Lewis or Clark could every imagined.

They told stories about a place called Coulter's Hell where water and mud shot out of the ground for hundreds of feet and boiling hot. Other places the mud and water just bubbled up from the ground, never stopping and letting off steam that smelt so bad it made you gag. It was a spooky place even for the old-timers that had seen it many times. It was a safe haven for mountain men who needed a few days of rest or to avoid bands of Indians that were out to cause them harm. The Indians believed it was haunted and entering it would take them away from the protecting hands of Mother Earth and bring nothing but evil to their lives.

The two or three mountain men that Ty had heard tell their stories spoke in a language different than most. Some mountains they called the little mountains the others just the big mountains. The little mountains avoided by most; were sacred to the Sioux Indians that lived on the plains near them. The big mountains were the place to be, they were so big that you might not see another human in a whole year; most had to wait until rendezvous time. They would tell theirs stories about leaving the civil life for the mountains and use words like crossing over, which Ty found, had two meanings, the first one meant crossing the great Mississippi River. At one time, the only people beyond the river were the mountain men and the Indians. The other was when someone died; they crossed over to the other side, heaven or hell or maybe to the happy hunting ground. They spoke about keeping their hair, loosing their parts and referring to their rifles and knives by name and treating them as near human. When referring to themselves they said this child or this old son. They used nicknames when they spoke of friends or acquaintance they had met, they seldom used real names for whatever reason. Not many returned to the civil life some married Indian women and raised families and many were killed by Indians or wild critters; no one knew how many or by who.

All the stories that Ty had heard made the life more interesting and the danger that much less. He spent most of his time listening to tales told by travelers or to folks that seemed to have any knowledge about the west. At every opening Ty would ask questions about the mountain life how did they live, how did they talk with the Indians and how did they survive in the wild? What did they do when they ran low on powder and shot? Questions that Ty hoped would aid him when the time came for him to cross over. It was an adventure never far from his mind; He knew that it was just a matter of time before it would happen. Everything that he could learn would prepare him for the time when he would cross over. Ty was determined to learn as much as he could about how to live and survive on his own.

He thought about the war and all of the hardships it had caused. The very reason he was working for Mrs. Casey was the war. It seemed all the men in northeast Missouri were fighting in the damn Civil War, along with Kevin and James, Ty's brothers. They had signed on in 1861 with the Missouri Regulars. Ty was thirteen years old, soon to be fourteen when they left. Both of the boys, along with many of their friends, were convinced that the war would be over before they got there; the Johnny Rebs would have given up and headed home.

It was an exciting time the hubbub of recruiting and the talk of what everyone was going to do if the Rebs still wanted to fight. "Us Missourians would show 'em a thing or two," the recruits would say. They expected be gone for just a short while; little did anyone know or imagine that four years would pass before some would come home and many more would not.

The boys left for war leaving their mother and Ty to run the farm. Ty often thought about what it must be like fighting in a war that meant killing other people. Now that he was old enough he wondered how he would react under fire, He knew that he would be scared but did not think that he would turn tail and run. He was sure that he could learn to ride with the best of them; he already knew that he could out shoot most any man.

Hunting squirrels, rabbits and opossum made an excellent marksman out of him even if he was shooting an old flintlock rifle. The war would have to wait or come to him, Ma and the boys were counting on him to stay and do what needed done.

After the long winter, his Mom and he had just gone through Ty wonder why people farmed. With blizzards that ripped out of the northwest drifting snow up to six feet deep, sub zero temperatures and making life damn miserable. The usual odd jobs normally handled in the winter, this year went undone. Fences went un-repaired; barns and chicken coops neglected, folks just didn't go outside if they didn't have to. When it was as cold as it was the livestock did not leave the barn except on the few days that the wind and snow permitted. The neighbors did not hire out any work when times were this bad; cash money was tough to come by.

When you farmed for your lively hood money was never far from your mind. Mom worried that if something unexpected came up would there be enough money in the bank to pay the taxes or for that mater whatever else might come up? They would need to wait and see what the crops were like this year before she would relax, before she started to worry again. Would the nearly worthless wartime green backs that she had stashed away be worth anything, she had kept them as a part of her support for President Lincoln; it was her part in financing the war effort.

True they would have the handwork Ma had made this winter and the pelts Ty had cured from his hunts this past season but would it be enough to last until fall harvest? This job, gotten so early in the spring should ease some of his Mothers concerns.

As Ty follow Buck down the furrow, his feet hurt, his boots were just too small for his growing feet and new boots were out of the question until wars end. He might be able to trade them at the cobbler's shop next time he was in Jamesville, if he could stand it that long. He had plowed many a furrow bare

15

footed in the past but the weeds and dried stubble in this unused field would cut his feet to ribbons if he tried it now. Many fields in northern Missouri were in the same shape no one to plow them; most people did not have money for the seed.

Not only were Ty's feet growing, he also had shot up like a weed over the past year. His rough hands darkened by the sun and callused by farm chores hung at the end of his long arms, he had outgrown his shirtsleeves some time ago. His neck, shoulders and chest had also doubled in size with the riggers of farm life. At age seventeen, he was a shade over six foot tall and weighed a little over one hundred and eighty pounds. Muscle had replaced what was left of his child like body fat. When he moved, he moved with a cat like grace deliberate and with a sense of purpose. Like the cat, he was quick on his feet and lightning fast with his hands. Those that did not know him and looking at his size would think of him as a slow moving oaf.

While Ty was daydreaming, Buck had come to the end of the furrow and stopped. It was the mule's way of saying that he needed a drink to clear the dust from his throat. Ty unhitched the traces and took a hold of the bridle strap, while talking to Buck he led him first to the small patch of shade near the fence. It was where Ty had his water jar, hoping that the shade would keep the contents cool. Picking up the jar and still gripping Buck's bridle he headed for the stock pond. Filling the jar, he took a long drink, paused and took another drink, then poured the rest over his head. While Buck took his time satisfying his thirst, Ty took off his shirt and soaked it in the pond, it would be cooler for a time, but would not last long. After drinking his fill, Ty filled; the jar again, latched on to Buck and placing the jar in the shade, reattaching the traces, began the next furrow.

In another two weeks, school would be letting out for the summer and most folks would be starting their gardens. The size of the garden would depend on the number of kids there were to prepare the ground for planting and the amount of seed the family had carried over from last year. Potatoes, corn, squash, pumpkin, carrots, cabbage, beans, dill and tomatoes were the common fare, with cucumbers, beats, peas and lettuce if the seeds were available.

Thinking about how it used to be when school ended brought a smile to Ty's lips. The joy of being out of school was a freedom that didn't last long.

The routine of farm life could not wait; it was not long before Ma reminded him that chores needed doing.

Ty thought about how hard his Mother had worked to keep him in school. He remembered the fighting and his arguing with her about going to school, but as usual, Ma won out, she had insisted that at least one of her sons was going to get some real schoolhouse learning. She had failed with her first two sons because of the death of her husband. Kevin was in his second year and James in his first when their father died. Ty was just two months old and his Mother could not do all of the chores it takes to keep a farm going, the boys had quit school to help.

Mom's Bible used for prayer time and to teach the boys how to read, was the only book she owned. Kevin and James were not in the least bit interested and could see no reason for learning but Ma didn't give Ty a choice, he went to school. When the boys had gone off to the war, he stopped to help his mother, as his brothers had done earlier.

He remembered the book of Genesis, which his Mother had read to him since he was old enough to pay attention. It told about how the Lord had made heaven and earth on the first day. On the second day, he made night, day, morning and evening. The earth he made was to come forth and bring seeds, grasses and trees. Finally, he made man and all of the animals and creatures on the earth. God was pleased with what he had done and so on the seventh day he rested.

Ty thought that it sure would be nice if a fella could rest on the seventh day as the Lord had. It seemed as though he would have to kill himself trying to catch up, working the home place, plowing, planting, and taking care of the three cows, a dozen hogs, chickens, and old Buck seemed like enough.

Now Mrs. Casey needed help, with the chance to make extra money, he could not refuse her. She lived alone while her husband was off to the war. Last month she had broken her arm and there was no way to get her crops and garden in without help. A neighbor of the O'Malley's told Ty that Mrs. Casey would pay twenty cents an acre to plow and harrow her ten acres of ground. Hoping that he would get there first, Ty rode Buck over to her farm.

Distance was a problem Mrs. Casey lived fifteen miles from the O'Malley's. Ty could sleep in the barn, he had done that before, or outside if need be. Not knowing what he had to do or what shape the fields were in, there was no way of knowing how long it would take. Ten acres was not very big, his own fields he knew, these he did not.

Arriving at Mrs. Casey's he discovered that the fields, over grown with weeds, the result of not being touched for three years. The weeds and old oat stubble had taken over the field; it needed turning over completely, before he could harrow it. Ty explained to Mrs. Casey of the problems and she agreed to pay an extra fifty cents, hard cash, no green backs. Accepting the job, he went to work hitching Buck to a rusty old plow that had seen better days.

Wilma Casey, standing at the door of her cabin, watched Ty working in the field. She couldn't help picturing her husband, Charles, walking behind the plow. Charles was the same height and built similar to the young man; she missed him so much and for four of her five years of married life she had been living alone. Charles had been twenty-two and she was nearly seventeen when they married in July of 1860. They lived in Johnstown, Illinois, where Charles worked for a feed and grain company. Within a few months of their marriage, Charles's widowed Mother died, leaving an inheritance of three hundred and sixty four dollars. Land out west was there for the taking. Buying a Conestoga wagon and four draft horses, they sold what they had and headed for Kansas.

After crossing the Mississippi River at Hannibal, Missouri, they headed west. The third day, after the crossing, Wilma had a miscarriage and lost the baby she had carried for nearly two months, she was hemorrhaging so severely that Charles could not control it. Swinging into the nearest farmyard, he rushed to the house for help. Luck was on their side, a midwife happened to be there; she helped stop the bleeding and probably saving her life. Wilma was slow to recover from the ordeal and Charles refused to go further until her strength returned.

Hearing of a small farm of thirty-seven acres that included a cabin and barn Charles decided to buy it. The owners were moving; they hoped to homestead in Kansas and in that way stay clear of the war. Charles bought the farm for twenty-five dollars and traded the Conestoga wagon for the livestock that they could not take with them. With the purchase of the chickens, pigs and two of their milk cows, with a little luck they would be able to stay here until Wilma's health returned and could continue on their western trek.

The previous owners had planted a garden but did not provide for a cash crop. Charles planted a late crop of oats; his thinking was that if it did not head out, he would feed it this winter to his stock. This was the summer of 1861; the War Between the States had just begun.

The barking of a dog caught his attention, looking back; he could see Mrs. Casey standing at the edge of the field, with what he hoped was his lunch. She carried something tied up in a towel and carrying a larger cloth in the other hand.

Ty was nearly finished with the furrow that he had started, and continued to the end before stopping. Disconnecting Buck from the plow, tying the traces up to the harness and removing the bridle from Buck's mouth, he then walked with Mrs. Casey to the stock pond. Buck graze on the abundant grass that grew near the pond while Mrs. Casey spread the cloth under the trees that would shade this area during the summer months. Ty washed up and joined Mrs. Casey as she opened the bundle that contained his lunch, there appeared to be more than what one person could eat and she said, "Do you mind if I eat lunch with you, it would be nice to have someone to talk with for a change. Except for church on Sunday, weather permitting, I rarely get a chance to visit."

Ty, slightly embarrassed and caught off guard, could only nod his head up and down.

They sat down; Ty crossed his legs and Mrs. Casey gracefully sat on her right hip. She straightening the skirt of her dress so that it would cover her ankles, "You've had a long morning, I bet that you are hungry and ready for a rest."

There were thick bacon slices, fresh bread and jelly. Two slices of pumpkin pie and a jar of fresh cool milk, wrapped in wet burlap.

Handing Ty a tin plate she told him to help himself. At home, Ty would have forgotten the plate and just placed the bacon between two slices of bread but he didn't want to act awkward in front of Mrs. Casey, so Ty just waited for her to make the first move, and then he would do the same. Mrs. Casey smiled, "I thought we could eat our pie without spoon, pumpkin pie isn't very messy."

It was Ty's turn to smile; she seemed to be a very nice woman.

As he bit into his sandwich, he studied Mrs. Casey for the first time. She didn't appear very old, older than Ty of course, maybe in her early twenties. Her hair was dark and hidden under a kerchief; she had a very thin face that went with the rest of her body. She was tall, about five-foot-eight or nine and she couldn't weigh more than one-hundred-and thirty pounds. Each time Ty had seen her she wore a big smile and her eyes fairly lit up her face.

The dog was a very large mongrel with medium length coat, slightly bigger than a collie, with a broad, muscular chest, a huge head and a pointed nose. His dirty looking coat was gray and white and scars were visible on his hips and shoulders. He was definitely a one-person dog, he barked or growled every time Ty moved or looked at him. As they ate lunch, the dog laid and watched from a vantage point a short distance away. Mrs. Casey had informed Ty on the day of his arrival, that the dog was overly protective of her. "He is just a big bag of wind, he won't hurt you, I don't think, he just puts on a good show. He stayed when his owners moved west. Charles and Tuff, as we called him, never got along very well. The poor dog rubbed my husband the wrong way, it's the only time I ever seen Charles beat an animal. The more he was beat, the meaner he got towards Charles. He likes me, we get along just fine."

Watching the dog as he ate, Ty started to talk to him in a very low tone, saying the same words repeatedly; there was no meaning to most of what he was saying. After a while, Tuff raised his head and looked at Ty, as if wondering what in the hell was he talking about. He watched for a few minute, then laid his head down and proceeded to watch them eat. Ty took a small piece of bacon and placing it at arms length, offered it to Tuff. In the same low tone he said, "Take it boy, go ahead and eat it." Tuff didn't move a muscle, but continued to watch his every move. Taking the bacon and tossing it closer to the dog, "It's yours. You can eat it." There was no response at all. Standing up slowly, Ty took a step toward the dog, which brought on a low growl from deep in his throat. Tuff raised up on his front paws curled his top lip, showing his long fangs and warning Ty not to come closer. Ignoring this jester Ty knelt down, trying to put himself the same level as the dog. He held the bacon in his hand and reaching out, continuing to speak softly, he held the meat to within inches of the dog's mouth. Cocking his head to one side, he took the bacon. Ty then gave him a piece of his bread and had a friend.

Setting down he said, "Come here boy, no one is going to beat you." Tuff, his head still cocked, moved closer and laid down between Mrs. Casey and Ty, with his nose just touching the spread cloth.

"That is remarkable; I've never seen anything like that before. You're the first to feed him and have him eat it, except for me of course. You do have a way with animals; I would never have thought that anyone could get that close to Tuff this soon. I do think that you have made a friend."

"Animals have always been important to me. They all have a purpose in life, one way or the other they're all here to help us, some are here to feed us and some are here to make our work easier. Others are here to protect us and to amuse us. Tuff just got off to a bad start, but I bet that he is a good dog."

Conversation came hard for Ty, and apparently for Mrs. Casey. Think as he might, he did not know how to start another discussion. He hoped that Mrs. Casey would ask a question or say something to break the tension. Finally, she did break the silence by commenting about the weather, specifically about the heat and wondering if this was what our summer was going to like. Ty agreeing, "It is warmer than normal, but we still have some cold days to look forward to and just maybe some more snow."

"Have you lived here all you life?" Ty shook his head up and down, forgetting that his mother had always told him that is was not proper to do when talking to someone. Ty hurriedly answered that he was born just east of here.

Mrs. Casey, looking off to some distant point, "I came here with my husband just a few months before the war started. We came from Indiana, we were on our way to Kansas when I got sick and we had to stop. We bought this place in April 1861 and my husband got called to the Army in August, I haven't heard a word from him since."

"My brothers and your husband must know each other; they left in August of '61 too, maybe at the same time, you never know."

"Have you heard from your brothers since they have been gone?"

"We heard from James, he is the younger of the two. When he was in a hospital in Pennsylvania, he had someone write a letter to Mom, just to tell us that he was wounded, but not bad and that he was going to be all right.

That was in '63 but she hasn't heard anything since. We never did hear from Kevin, we just hope that he's all right."

Tears began running down Mrs. Casey's cheeks and the silence came back. Ty sat there helpless, wondering how to handle this, he had never encountered this happening to anyone but his mother. With her, he would just put his arms around her and hold her tight until she stopped crying. Mrs. Casey was something different; did she expect him to offer his shoulder to cry on or something? Some people just had to cry things out and get them out of their system; they don't want anyone to console them, so Ty decided to wait. After a few minutes, she apologized, explaining that she was sorry that she had made a fool of herself, "I know that crying doesn't help, it's such a silly thing to do."

In the very next breath she added, "Mr. O'Malley what do you know about growing corn?"

Mr. O'Malley, no one had ever called him that before and it set him back for a minute, "We've planted it for as long as I can remember."

She told him that this field was going to be corn; she had heard that the army would buy all of the corn you could grow. Continuing she said that for four years, she hadn't grown enough to get by. She had to supplement her needs by using the balance of the money left from the inheritance, and then she started to sell whatever she could to raise money. The smaller team of draft horses went first; most of the small tools next, then some of the pigs and chickens. The last too go were the remaining team of horses. Without the horses, she had no need for the light spring wagon, so it went as well. She had kept the plow, the harrow, a drag that she did not know what it was used for and some hand tools such as hoes and shovels.

"How we spent that money, I'll never know, when Charles left for the war we had less than forty dollars to our name."

She desperately felt that she had to hold on to the farm, whether Charles returned or not. To do this she had to have a cash crop this year. With her last sale, she had bought enough seed corn to plant ten acres, if this failed, she did not know what she would do.

"Will this ground grow corn?"

"I don't know why it wouldn't, but it's sure going to take a lot of work.

This is good soil and it will grow just about anything that you plant. Do you have the seed here; I didn't see it in barn?"

"Yes, I have it in that small building next to the chicken coop. I don't know much about planting and such, but I would like to learn, will you help me, can you teach me?"

"It don't take a lot of know how to plant corn, you just, sort of, put it in the ground, hoe it to keep the weeds down, pray for rain and trust in the Lord."

"It does take a lot of work; do you think one person can do it?"

Ty didn't know how to answer her right away, he wondered if that one person was her. He didn't want to hurt her feelings and he knew that it wasn't as simple as he had said.

"After the plowing and harrowing, you have to hoe ridges about six inches high, about eighteen inches apart and then you plant your seed on the ridges about ten inches apart. When the corn starts to grow, you have to hoe in between the ridges to keep the weeds from stealing all of the moisture and you have to keep hoeing most of the summer; it's a lot of work."

"Ma'am, it may not be my place to say this, but if you are thinking about planting this field by yourself, I don't see how you can. With your broken arm, you can't hoe, that is the first thing you'll have to do after I get this field plowed and harrowed."

"Is there anyway, well—I mean, is it, possible that you could help out, if we'd share the money that we make on this crop? I have the seed and all we have to do is plant it, my arm will heal soon so that I could help."

Wanting to help her, but knowing he couldn't, he tried to think of an easy way to say no. He had Mom's place to take care of, and that would take all of his time.

"Isn't there any neighbors nearby that would help you out now and again, maybe a couple of youngins or some friends?"

"I don't know of any."

"Have you thought of asking the congregation of your church for help?"

"My husband always said that you shouldn't be beholden to anyone. If you can't do it by yourself or hire it done then it probably doesn't need doing."

"But don't you think that your husband would understand and be grateful to you if you got this crop in?"

Tears came again, this time harder and lasted longer. A thousand things were going through Ty's mind; there must be a way to help. I guess she is just going to have to come down from her high horse and ask someone, other than me for help, the problem was how to convince her.

Today is Friday and I won't be done here until late Saturday or early Sunday, I wonder if she will go to church come Sunday morning.

Ty waited for her to dry her eyes, "Do they have church this week?"

"Yes, they have it every Sunday, at least I think so, why do you ask?"

"Well I haven't been to church in some time. Mom and I go whenever we can; it has been a while since we last got there. Problem is, I ain't got any extra clothes, and I would have to wash my clothes Saturday night." Ty did not tell her that he only had one other shirt to his name. "Are you planning to go?"

This caught her by surprise and she hesitated before she answered. "I haven't given it much thought; it's been last fall since I've been there. The church is three miles away and we would have to walk."

"Do you know what time it starts?"

"Yes, early, at eight o'clock, I think."

"If it's all right with you I think I will go, you're welcome to come with me if you want too."

"I think that would be nice, it may turn some heads, me with such a young man and all."

"Old Buck is going to stiffen up on me if I don't get back to plowing. That was a mighty fine lunch you fixed but I was just wondering how you made the crust. Mom uses a rolling pin to make her piecrust but that takes two hands, you've only got one good one."

"I patted it flat and hoped that it wouldn't be too tough."

"Well ma'am it sure wasn't tough, it was mighty good."

She started to pick up the plates, placing them back in the dishcloth, "Mr. O'Malley, I'll see you at supper."

"Please, Mrs. Casey, just call me Ty, I don't seem to answer very well to anything else."

"All right Ty and if you want to call me Wilma, you can, my Charles called me Willie; I haven't heard that name spoken to me in a long time."

"I think I had better just stick to calling you Mrs. Casey that is what my Mom would want me to do."

As she went toward the cabin, Ty gathered Buck and his freshly filled water jar and he went back to plowing.

Surely if the Minster of her church knew of her plight, he would try to find her help. True most of the men were gone to the war but there were older men and strong youngsters about that could help. Even women would, if they just knew of her situation. He would go to church Sunday, speak with the Minister and see what he could do. If they got enough people to come on one day, say a Sunday, they could hoe and plant the same day. After the seed was in and her arm had healed, she might be able to stay ahead of the weeds, if she worked at it every day.

Late Saturday afternoon the sky darkened, the winds pick up and rain was almost certain. Ty had completed the plowing and had started the harrowing. The turned earth laid in large clumps from the plowing, a musty odor rose from the fresh turned ground, three years of decaying weeds and neglect was apparent. Buck was a big mule but it still was with great effort that he pulled the heavy harrow across the rough furrows. If Buck held up and the rain stayed away, he should be done late tomorrow morning. The appearance of the sky showed very little chance of that happening.

During Bucks break for water and rest, Ty looked around the barn for something to add to his bed in the loft. For three years, no hay or fodder had been stored in the hayloft. The last two nights Ty had gathered up whatever he could find to supplement the blanket that Mrs. Casey had given him. Mostly burlap bags that once had held corn or oats.

The roof of the barn neglected for the last few years, had holes in it the size of bushel baskets; it would be damn hard to find a dry spot to sleep if it did rain. In his searching of the corner of the barn for more sacks, he found a harrow that Mrs. Casey had not told him was there. Looking it over he'd seen that it was made of a steel frame about five-foot across and four feet deep. There were steel pins that looked like railroad spikes, positioned six inches apart, each row off set from the first; the pins were adjustable for depth. If this would break the clumps of earth, held together by years of root growth, it would be quicker and easier on Buck.

Attaching the traces to the harrow, he found that this worked far better than the flat bottom drag that he had been using. It would take several passes to get the clumps of soil broken up; however, it would take a lot fewer than with the other one. He had drug the field twice when the rain started, at first, just a slow drizzle and by the time Buck was safely in the barn, it was coming down in sheets. Mrs. Casey was standing at the door of the cabin trying to get Ty's attention, waving her arm and trying to yell over the noise of the rain. When he finally noticed her, she motioned for him to come to the cabin. Waiting for a let up in the rain, Ty climbed to the hayloft to find a dry place for his bedding looking around he could see everything was wet. Carrying his blanket and the burlap bags, he went down in the barn itself. He found that by now the loft floor was leaking about as bad as the roof. Placing the blanket and burlap bags in a feeding stall, under the manger, he made a dash for the cabin.

Standing on the small stoop, Ty stomped his feet, tying to shake off as much mud and rainwater as he could. "You're all right, come on in out of the rain. You can wipe your feet on that rug it will not hurt anything. Here sit by the stove till the chill is gone."

"It's raining cats and dogs out there, and it doesn't look like its going to let up soon. I put Buck in the barn; it's not much drier in there. I rubbed him down real good so he'll be all right. I wished he had some oats or some corn to eat, he's had a long day."

"I found a steal harrow and it worked a whole lot better than that drag I started with. I would have been done this afternoon if I had known about it sooner."

"I'm sorry that I didn't know we had one, it must have come with this place. I'm sure that Charles never said anything about it, maybe he didn't know himself."

"Supper will be ready in a few minutes; just sit down there at the table, at the end would be fine."

Ty looked around the small cabin, really for the first time. He had only been inside once before and for a brief time at that. They had eaten all their previous meals outside, under a giant maple tree, its branches just starting to bud. Tonight there was no choice but to eat inside, the rain seen to that.

The main room consisted of the cooking stove, a few wooden packing crates, nailed to the wall. There was a handmade table with four crudely made chairs. A sideboard that held containers marked with names such as, flour, sugar, coffee, all most likely empty, cornmeal, salt and pepper. In the corner were jars of canned tomatoes, carrots, corn. There were a few jars of canned meat; it looked like mostly chicken. There were two windows, one in the east wall and one in the south wall. Covering the windows were slips of feed sacks that had seen better days. An opening, probably to the bedroom partially covered with a blanket held back by a nail. The floor of the cabin was rough ash with gaps between planks a quarter of an inch wide. The only item that appeared somewhat new was a dusty double-barreled shotgun that hung above the door.

Cooking on the stove was a kettle of beans. Mrs. Casey opened the oven door from time to time to check on something, most likely cornbread.

"The beans smell good; I'm hungry enough to eat a horse."

"I hope you like cornbread; I made a whole tin full."

"Mom always makes more than we can eat, at one setting, we both like it in cold milk. A lot of times we eat cornbread and milk for breakfast or at noon time."

"How much of the field did you say you had left to do?"

"After I finish the next pass, I'll change directions. One more round should do it."

"The way it's raining now I doubt that it will be dry enough to finish tomorrow. I'm sure that you are in a hurry to get home and see your mother. I hate to see you go; it is going to be lonely again around here after you are gone. When you are by yourself all the time, it makes the days very long, after a while you start talking to yourself, just to hear the sound."

"Don't you visit with your neighbors; there are cabins all around your place and not very far away. I saw a woman and a youngster working in the fields just south of here, I waved and they waved back, they seemed friendly enough."

"We used to visit but I got embarrassed and felt uncomfortable, when we saw one another. They knew that things were not going well for me and they always offer to give me things that they thought I needed. Charles was always a proud man and wouldn't accept handouts so I didn't want to either."

"They were only being neighborly I'm sure. Over at our place, we help our neighbors and they help us. We don't think a thing about it; Mom says that is what neighbors are for."

"It is just that I am so ashamed that I cannot give anything back. The last year has been real hard for me, it was just easier for me to stay at home and not visit."

"Neighboring ain't like that. It's not what you can give that is important; it's being there for each other, at least that is what I think. A neighbor is just— just there in good times and in bad. Mom says that sometimes you're just there to console when it's a grieving time and you're there for the happy times too. Maybe it's no more than holding a sick baby or feeding the livestock. Our neighbors are like that, just there."

"You're going to need help with the planting and your neighbors are your best bet. You might have to kill a couple of chickens and boil up some beans to feed 'em but they won't ask for more."

She got up and opened the oven door with a piece of broom straw and she tested the cornbread. "It's done, we can eat now, and it will only take a minute to get it on the table."

You could hear the rain beating against the window; it wasn't letting up. The sky was darker now than when Ty had first come into the cabin. "It looks as if it's going to rain all night; don't look like it's going to let up at all. I don't think I'll be working the field tomorrow, Church might be out of the question as well."

"I'll set the candle on the table; we'll probably need it before we're though with supper. I wish that I had some onion for your beans, Charles ate them that way?"

Mrs. Casey sat two tin plates and cups on the table, and then added a knife and two spoons. She said to Ty, "Will you step out on the porch and get the milk jar; it's in the rain barrel by the door, it should be nice and cool after this rain."

Lifting the kettle of beans by the bail on the pot, she sat it on the table; she turned and retrieved the cornbread from the oven. "It's not much; I hope that it will fill you up. I have some applesauce for dessert; I just put it up last year."

Filling his plate and buttering the cornbread very lightly, for he did not know how much butter she had left, he proceeded to eat. The beans, seasoned with bacon rinds and the taste of the hickory smoke gave them a fine flavor. Neither spoke until Ty took his second helping of beans, "These hot beans sure taste good on a night like this and your cornbread tastes just like Mom's."

"Well thank you; there is not much to making it. You know its kind of funny, cooking I mean. In the winter and sometimes in the early spring you have fresh meat with nothing but dried or canned fruits and vegetables. Then in the summer and early fall you have canned meat, sometimes a fresh chicken but all of the fresh vegetables and fruit you have grown. I don't know what time of the year I like best."

"Guess I don't either, the winter is the hardest time for both man and the stock, just to survive is a real test. Then we have a winter like the last one and you wonder how anything makes it through. Spring is a good time, grass turning green and flowers growing. The birds come back and the smell of the ground, it's like no other. Summer is hot; the heat makes the days seem longer and there are the storms that come twisting down from the sky picking up everything in their path. Then you're always worrying about the rain, are we going to get too much or not enough and the biggest worry, are you going to get it when you need it. Fall is harvesting time, canning, butchering, smoking hams and getting the house ready for winter. Spring and fall are my favorites, I guess. I like the outdoors, but this last winter was two long. I never cut so much firewood and mended so much harness in my life. Mom spent her time knitting and reading the Bible, mending what needed done."

Eating only a small plate of beans and two pieces of corn bread, Mrs. Casey continued the discussion about the seasons. She agreed that winter was the hardest, especially when you are by yourself, as she had been. Keeping the fire going and carrying wood at least kept her active. She had started a diary of what she did and of what she thought. Laughingly she said that she would have to keep it hidden from Charles, it would embarrass her if he read it.

After eating his fill, and sliding the plate to the center of the table, she asked, "Would you like some applesauce to top off this fine supper that we just ate? It's a little tart, I was short on sugar when I put it up, but I hated to waste the apples."

"I'm about to bust, I ate too much; let's wait on the applesauce for now."

Mrs. Casey cleaned up the table and did the few dishes. Leaving the remaining beans in the pot, she placed them on the cooler end of the stove. She placed the cornbread back in the oven. "I wish I had a pipe of tobacco to offer you, I know that men like to smoke a pipe full after eating."

"I don't smoke anyway. I have chewed some until Mom threatened to kill me if I ever done it again. Kevin and James both smoke and chewed, I guess Mom never scared 'em much."

"Mr. Casey and you haven't had much time together since you got married, have you? It's too bad that you couldn't go back to your family when the war started, I guess it would have been too far to go by yourself, all that distance?"

"I haven't any family to go back to, except for my aunt and we didn't get along that well. My folks are both dead, they died when I was eleven years old, in a fire; my Aunt Millie raised me. When I was sixteen, I got a job in a mercantile store that is when I met Charles. He was so handsome and all the young ladies would just flock to him. When there was a dance, he never sat down someone was always there to dance with him. I was very shy and did not have the nerve to ask him for a dance. One night he walked right up to me and said, "How come you dance with everyone else but never with me?"

"Sir you have never asked me." I said.

"Will you do me the honor and dance the next reel with me?"

"We danced the rest of the night together. When we finished he walked me to my boarding house. One month later, we were standing at the altar getting married, it was so grand."

"Charles was very independent and some folks thought that he was mean. I never knew him to be that way; he was always good and very kind to me oh, he got upset when things did not go his way. He would yell and holler and turn red in the face for a while but he would get over it fairly soon, then everything would be back to the way it was."

A gust of wind pelted the rain against the windows, rattling the glass panes as if to knock them out of the frames and beneath the door, water was saturating the rough wooden floor. At times, the wind would whistle through the small opening around the door and windows so loudly, causing interruptions in their conversations. Other than the constant dripping of the rain down the chimney pipe, the roof seemed dry.

Night had fallen sometime ago and the candle slowly was disappearing into the holder, indicating it was time to call it a day.

Ty stood up, stretched, "I think it's time for me to head to the barn and get some sleep, it's been a long day."

"You're not going out in this rain you would get soaked to the bone and most likely get pneumonia. You can sleep right here on the floor in front of the stove, I have more blankets and a quilt you can use, you will be more comfortable than out in that wet barn."

"Mrs. Casey, I don't think that would look right, me and you staying in the same house at night together I'll be all right out there, don't worry about me."

"It may not look right, but I will not let you go out in this rain and that is final. Besides who is going to know that the two of us were here together tonight and not the last two nights, nobody that's who. We're grown people and I don't care what other people might or might not think, I'll get your bedding and help you make your bed."

Ty shrugged his shoulders and was quiet; he really wasn't that fond of trying to find a dry spot in the barn anyway.

Moving the table further from the stove, she placed the heavy quilt on the flour between the stove and the table. "Here is a blanket to cover up with, I'm sorry but I haven't got a pillow, I hope that you can sleep without one?"

"Sure I can, I'll probably be asleep before I hit the floor anyway."

She picked up the burning remains of the candle and went into the bedroom, "Good night Ty."

"Good night Mrs. Casey, see you in the morning."

Taking off his shirt and boots, but leaving his pants on, Ty laid down. Covering himself with the blanket, listening to the rain and the wind he fell to sleep.

Something stirred and Ty came awake. Thinking that he was dreaming he started to close his eyes again, and then sensed Mrs. Casey standing over him. The blackness of the night made defining objects of any sort impossible. Without a word, Mrs. Casey knelt down, raised the blanket and crawled into Ty's bed. "Hold me Ty, please hold me, I'm so lonely."

As she moved next to him, pressing her body to his, taking his face in her hands, kissed him.

31

CHAPTER 2

Waking up, Ty felt her lying next to him; she was sleeping with her arm across his chest. Knowing now that it was not a dream but a reality, what was he to do or say? He lay very still, not wanting to wake her just yet. He needed time to think, how did this happen and why did he let it happen? This was not his first time, but with another man's wife it was, no way could he justify but what is done, is done. How was he to explain to her that he was sorry that it happened, Ty thought, she is in my bed isn't she it can't be only my fault.

She stirred next to him, and opened her eyes; a blush caused her face to turn to a rosy glow. She smiled as she looked at Ty and said, "Good morning Mr. O'Malley, did you sleep well, I certainly did. Before we get all apologetic and ashamed, I want to tell you that I'm not sorry that this happened. I am sorry that I took advantage of you; I hope you will forgive me. This was not planned, it just happened; please don't think the worst of me."

"If you took advantage of me it is because I let you. I didn't do anything to stop it and I guess I'm glad. It must be hard to live like a widow, not knowing if your man is dead or alive. I am sure this war will be over soon and we all can get back to a normal life. Not knowing is real tough, but it will get better. I think that the best thing is to forget that this happened, don't you?"

Lying on her side, with her head resting on her hand, she looked at him for the longest time, not speaking, just watching his face. Blinking her eyes and showing a small smile, "I suppose your right I didn't want the night to end, it was easier to pretend in the dark" Suddenly, seeming embarrassed she stood up and turning her back to the bed, put her nightgown on. As she walked to the bedroom to get dressed, Ty got up, he quickly dressed but what happened last night was still on his mind.

The wind had stopped but the rain continued to fall. A breakfast of fried eggs and some of the cornbread sat on the table. Without speaking they ate their breakfast and Ty slid back his chair saying, "I'd check the field" and stepping to the door he looked out at the water puddles standing in the yard, "By the looks of the yard we're done for at least two days and maybe more. We had at least two inches of rain, the yard looks like a lake. If it's all right with you, I think I will head for home and get some of the chores done that need doin'. I want to see how Ma is doing and if we don't have anything that pops up, I'll be back on the second day after the rain stops. As I go by the church and if I see the minister, I'm going to talk to him about trying to get you some help with the planting, is that all right with you?"

"I hate to ask for help, but I don't see any other way. I feel embarrassed to ask now, after all this time, I hope they will understand. Please don't let on to the Minister that I'm completely helpless or that I'm irresponsible, please. Wait until I get my money Ty; I want to pay you now so that it will be taken care of. I know that you will be back, I'm not worried in the least about that." Going to the sideboard and removing a small pitcher from behind some empty glass jars, she counted out two-dollars and fifty cents and then she remembered the extra fifty cents she owed him. She replaced the remaining coins back in the pitcher and returned it to its place in the sideboard.

"Mrs. Casey I wish that you would keep the money until I come back to finish the job. I'd feel bad if for some reason I couldn't get back, at least keep the fifty cents until I'm done but she insisting that Ty take the money and she placed it in his hand.

Mounted on old Buck, he looked back and waved. She stood under the maple tree wrapped in a blanket, shielding her face from the rain as best as she could and returning his wave with her good hand. She looked as if she wanted to call out or beckon him back, but she did neither.

Nearing the church, he could not see any sign or indication that anyone was at the church. It was still early, not yet eight o'clock and gambling that he might find the minister there this early, he dismounted and went in. A large man in a black suit was straightening the benches that the congregation would sit on when services started. Ty stuck out his hand and they shook hands. You could tell about a man just by his handshake, a firm grip and a hearty shake was a good sign. Ty introduced himself, asked if he was the minister of the church, and asked if he had time to talk for a minute.

"My name is Reverend Koppleman and yes I am the spiritual leader of the congregation, what can I do for you?"

"Reverend do you know of a Mrs. Casey, her husband is named Charles, he is off fighting the war?"

Reverend Koppleman thought about it for just a second and said, "Yes—yes I do, she comes to church occasionally but I haven't seen her recently. I am sure it's due to the weather, if I remember correctly she always walks to church."

"She lives by her self about three miles west of here on a small piece of ground that she is trying to farm. She broke her arm in a fall last month and has it in a sling. I hired on to get her field ready for planting but I got my own planting to do and I can't stay to help with hers. Mrs. Casey needs to get this crop in; she already has the seed corn."

"What would you have me do?"

"Well I was hoping that maybe some folks in your flock could lend a hand and help her out. She is a very shy, a kinda quiet woman from what she told me and not too many people even know her. I just met her couple of days ago, myself; she seems like a very nice person."

"All of my flock are farmers; I can't imagine when anyone could find the time to help, even if they wanted to."

"By the look of these benches you must have quite a few folks coming to church. Men folk is scarce I know because of the war and all, but women and youngsters know what farming is about. I think that just about everyone likes to gather at church socials, picnics and such. I was thinking about a picnic next Sunday, maybe right after church, at Mrs. Casey's place. The hoeing and planting wouldn't take long, less than a day if enough showed up. Folks would have to bring their own hoes and maybe each one could make a dish of something to share."

Reverend Koppleman looked away and thought for a moment. "Not many folks know Mrs. Casey, that's true but then again the Lord never said we should help only the ones we know, now did he? We all get in a bind at times and need some help from our neighbors and friends, sounds like this is Mrs. Casey's time. As you said, she is a shy, private person and probably

34

never had to ask for help before. As I remember when asked to take part in church happenings, she never did for whatever reason. When she comes to services, she seems to be in a hurry to leave, as if, she were scared of making friends. Do you think she will be in church today?"

"She had planned to be, but the rain is going to keep her away."

"I like your idea of a picnic, very much. After the winter we have just gone through maybe an early spring outing would be just what the Lord ordered. This morning I'll ask the members what they think about this idea and we'll see what we can do to help."

"I'm headed home till the rain lets up then give it a couple of days for the ground to dry and I'll be back to finish the field. If it's anywhere near the end of the week you can count on me to stay over and help."

"Does Mrs. Casey know about your plan to ask us for help?"

"I talked to her about her needing help and she was to shy to ask herself, so I said that I would. Her biggest problem is what her husband would think about her asking. She said that Mr. Casey didn't want to be beholden to anyone, she wants to please him more than anything I guess."

"Depending on the answer we get from the members, I'll take a ride over there this week and I'll tell her of our plans; I am convinced that all will want to help."

"Thank you Reverend, I'll be back as soon as I can, but while I'm here can I ask a favor of you?"

"Certainly."

"Would you say a pray for my brothers and for Mrs. Casey's Charles? Ask the Lord to watch over 'em and bring 'em home safely. I'm hopin' that this war will end soon."

"I pray for all of the men fighting in this ridiculous war Mr. O'Malley. Today I will say a special prayer just for you. Take care of yourself, young man and have a safe ride home."

Ty arrived home drenched from his head to his toes; the closer to home he got the harder the rain fell and the wind seemed to blow it right into his eyes. After putting Buck in the barn and rubbing him down with a dry sack, he gave him some hay and a handful of oats. Taking time to dry the harness as best he could, he hung it across the railing of the stall to finish drying.

Checking the stalls where the cows were, he'd seen that they had plenty of feed and the water pails were full. There were no new calves yet, what were they waiting for. "Girls you can start anytime now, I'm home. You two young ones might just need my help seeing as how this is your first try at being mothers. You're not planning to have at 'em at the same time are you?"

Entering the house, he immediately removed the coat and hat, shaking them hard to knock the water off, before hanging them on the wooden pegs beside the door. His Mother was sitting in her rocking chair, mending a sock. The smell of bread baking in the oven brought a smile to Ty's face, "Hi Mom, you all right, you must have figured on me bein' home today?"

"I figured that the weather would drive you home, thought you would be here earlier than this did the rain slow you up?"

"No, I just got a late start then I stopped and talked to the Minister that took a while, the rain didn't help either."

Ty told his Mother all that had happened, leaving out a couple of things; she did not need to know. Explaining that he had to go back to finish it and that he might even help with the planting if everything went well. Adding that it depended whether or not the minister got some help.

"I am glad that you're home, this rain makes everything so gloomy, I hope we get sunshine tomorrow. There are things that need to be done before we get to the planting but I guess if we had everything in the ground we wouldn't be complaining about the rain, would we?"

"As hard as it is raining now it might have just washed the seed out, I think we're lucky that we waited besides it's not even the first of April yet."

"Anyone stop by while I was gone?"

"Not a soul, I did see some strangers on the road Saturday, heading east. Looked like a whole family, with most likely everything they owned in that ox cart. Headed for Hannibal to find work I'd guess."

Ty got up, reaching into his pants pocket, took out the money and gave it to his Mother. "She insisted on paying me now, even though I wasn't completely done. She even paid me fifty cents more because the fields laid dormant the last three years. I tried to talk her out of paying me now, but she said that she wanted it taken care of and instead of hurting her feelings, I took the money. She is a very nice person; I think she would trust most anyone."

After counting the money, she handed it back to Ty; "You know where my bag is. Thank you son this extra money is going to come handy, there is always something that you need that you don't count on"

Walking to the stove, she opened the oven and removed two pans of bread. One pan contained a loaf and the other was what Mom called finger rolls, Ty's favorite. Setting each pan on the right side of the stove, she placed lard on a clean rag and coated the top of each loaf of bread with a thin layer of it, giving it a bright shine. This would keep it from drying out.

"We'll let the bread cool for a minute then I'll spoon you up some beef stew and we'll eat. The root cellar is getting in bad shape, eventually we're going to have to clean it out and replace the straw, best we get rid of whatever is tainted; some of the apples and carrots are getting mushy. I am hoping we can stretch what we have left to get us through the summer; I know it's going to be nip and tuck. Get the butter crock and the milk, will you Ty?"

Normally the butter was kept in the well house but when it was cool, it was kept in the rain barrel right next to the door. Mom used the rainwater out of the barrel to wash the clothes in and a pail sat right next to it in case you needed water in a hurry.

"I'll get it when I come back; I have to go out back." Putting on his wet coat and hat, Ty went around to the back of the house where the outhouse was sitting. Relieving himself, he made a dash for the door, getting the butter and milk containers, went back inside.

Turning to close the door Ty said, "By the look of the sky, I don't think it's going to let up at all but least the wind is not howling like it was Saturday night, I thought it was going to blow the house down. After all the snow we had this winter, this just might be the start of a wet spring."

"Most likely, it always seems to be that way, wash up and we'll eat."

Sitting at the table Ma said grace as always, she asked the Lord to watch over the boys and see to their safety. At the end of the prayer, with their heads bowed, they each prayed silently. Tonight Ty prayed for Mrs. Casey as well as for his Mom and his brothers. As they ate the stew, they talked about the taxes on the farm and having to go to the courthouse at Willow Springs to pay them and a stop in Jamesville to restock the items that they were out or short on.

Sliding his bowl to the center of the table he said, "The stew was good and the bread was the best I ever ate, good dinner Ma."

"You always say that, I never know whether to believe you or not. You've done that ever since you were a boy, do you really mean it?"

"Of course I mean it; you're the best cook I've ever known."

"How many have you known in your short lifetime?"

"Maybe three, but that's enough to know that you're the best."

Leaning back in his chair, feeling full and warm, not wanting to think about tomorrow and what laid ahead of him. There were always things that needed done when you have a farm. You could put them off for a day or two, but you always had to do them eventually. On bad days like this, you could fix harness, repair tools and equipment, or clean out the barn. All winter long, he had mended the harness and small hand tools. Prior to calving, the cows stall would need cleaning, so he might as well start on that, in the barn it would at least be dry.

"Tomorrow I'm going to work in the barn and get ready for the new calves. I want to separate the cows anyway and clean up some. Is there anything else that you would rather have me doing?"

"Nothing I can think of, not in this weather."

Monday morning arrived and was no different than Sunday. On Tuesday, it stopped raining about midday; the sky was clear and bright blue, not a cloud in sight. The warm rays of the hot sun touched the wet earth and the world was healing.

The first of the two cows that were to calve gave birth to a heifer calf on Tuesday. The second one gave birth on Wednesday, a set of twins, one a female and one a male. All three seemed healthy as they tried to stand on their wobbly legs. Surprisingly neither young heifer had any trouble calving. The older cow would not calve for about six weeks; they staggered the breeding in this way so that they would always have fresh milk.

Noon Wednesday, the rains returned, not heavy and not continuous. It would rain for a while and then a beautiful rainbow would appear. Shortly the rain would stop, only to have it start up again, just enough to keep the ground sloppy. Ty could not work in the fields so he repaired leaks in the roof of the barn and he mended what fence that he had rails for.

He couldn't keep his mind off Mrs. Casey, his thoughts were on Saturday night and as hard as he tried not to, kept reliving it over in his mind. It wasn't right, he knew that, but it happened. To be honest he had wondered what it would be like to go to bed with Mrs. Casey. This thought was on his mind while they were eating their lunch under the trees and the thought crossed his mind before he went to sleep that night. It wasn't so much Mrs. Casey or even the fact that she was lonely; it was just what young boy's thought about when they saw a pretty girl. Ty never thought it would do any harm just to think about it, but now that it happened, what should he do? She was lonely and I was curious what was wrong with that? What about next time, what was going to happen then, if you could justify it once why not a second time? Oh my god, what happens if she gets pregnant? If Charles returns and finds her pregnant, what is he going to do, kill me? If he does not return, I will marry her but what is going to happen if the war is still going on when it is her time, Dammit, I should have known better. I'll talk to her when I get there, if I ever do. This damn rain could stop anytime now; we've had enough.

Ole' Saul came out Thursday morning, shining like you wouldn't believe. The rain was gone for now, another day like this and the fields would be ready to work.

Suppertime Friday Ty told his mother that he thought that he would go over to Mrs. Casey's tomorrow morning. "The fields are drying out and I feel bad about not going over there sooner. I know that there was nothing I could do about it but I got her money and I feel that I owe her something extra."

As the sun peaked over the eastern horizon, Ty was well on his way, astride old Buck, with his mind racing ahead with the thought of seeing Mrs. Casey again. Of coarse, he would first stop and see the Reverend and find out what arrangement he might have made to help, if any.

Nearing the church, he saw Reverend Koppleman raking a patch of ground in front of the church, a flower garden most likely. Anxious to find out what the Congregation had decided to do Ty rode into the churchyard.

"Good morning Reverend, how are you?"

"Why Ty, it's good to see you on such a fine day."

"I don't mean to sound too abrupt, but I am curious to find out what happened last Sunday in church, what did they have to say about helping Mrs. Casey?

"The congregation thought that a picnic would be grand, they all agreed to meet at Mrs. Casey's house after services on Sunday, they said that helping her was only being Christian like. Right after the services on Sunday, we will meet at her farm and they were certain they would get the crop in before the day was spent."

"Now comes the strange part, I took a ride over to her place on Wednesday, between the rain showers; I could not find anyone at home. I waited and looked around but couldn't find a thing out of place, so I left. The following day I went to her house again and again found it vacant. I have no idea where she might be or where she might have gone, did she say anything to you about an impending visit or errand she had to go on?"

"No, by all reckoning, she has no family and wasn't neighborly with anyone at least not that she mentioned. Are you sure that she wasn't in the barn or maybe in the chicken coop, did you go inside to see if she was sick or something?"

"I opened the door and called out to her but there was no answer, I felt uncomfortable just going in the house, not knowing her all that well. To be honest I never thought that she might be sick, I'm worried now do you mind if I go with you to her house?"

Reverend Koppleman went around behind the church, got his horse and buggy, "Why don't you tie your mule to back of the buggy and ride with me?"

Ty could not imagine where she might have been when the preacher was there. Suddenly an idea came to him, "Do you think that she might not have recognized you and was scared to say anything, I think that maybe she is alone so much she gets frightened easily. Been tryin' and tryin' to think of where she might have gone, I can't think of a place or a thing that would keep her away."

"I do remember that when I opened the door and quickly looked in there were dishes on the table, more than one I think."

The ride to the Casey's didn't take long, but seemed forever to Ty. His mind was traveling so fast and in so many directions, trying to come up with a reason why the Preacher didn't find her at home. The more he thought, the more confused he became.

"Relax Ty, we'll get to the bottom of this, I'm sure there is probably a good answer to why I didn't find her at home; everything will work out all right."

Arriving at the small cabin nothing seemed out of place as Ty remembered. From the barn, the sounds of the mooing cow and the squealing pigs filled the air. Walking up to the door and knocking, there was no answer; again, he knocked, only harder this time, still no response. Slowly opening the door, he stepped inside. He saw that on the table were dirty dishes, and the nearly empty pot of beans. The remaining beans in the pot were hard and crusty; they had been there for a while. There were three dirty plates one on one side and one on at each end of the table. The chairs sat turned and back from the table and muddy tracks were on the floor beneath them, by the size of the footprints, men made them.

Going to the doorway of the bedroom, he pulled back the blanket that covered it and looked in not knowing what he would find but Mrs. Casey was not there either.

"It looks normal enough to me", the Reverend said, "Do you see anything that looks out of place?"

"I never saw her bedroom before, so I can't say but the dirty dishes and the mud on the floor don't look right. When I ate supper here last Saturday, the floor was so clean that you could have eaten off of it. As soon as we finished eating, she got up and washed the dishes saying that if she puts off doing 'em right away, it was harder to do 'em later."

"Do you see anything that is missing?"

"I was only in here the one time that was for supper. There is something that I saw that night that is missing, there was a double barrel shotgun hanging above the door. I remember that because it was the only thing that appeared new or nearly new in the whole cabin. It was dusty and looked like it hadn't been used lately."

"Did she ever talk to you about hunting rabbits or birds?"

"No, we never talked about it. She didn't say anything and I never asked besides, with her broken arm I don't think that she would be out shooting a shotgun. Someone was here and she fed 'em, I'm thinkin' that she knew 'em, nothing is tipped over or knocked down like if, there had been a fight or something. When they left they took the shotgun with 'em and maybe Mrs. Casey too."

"They must have left in a hurry, seeing as how the dishes are not done up and put away. Those beans have sat there for a while, three or four days, Ty who do you think they were?"

"She told me that she had no family and her husband is off to war. She also told me that she didn't know if he was dead or alive she hadn't heard from him since he left."

"If you want we can check out the out building, the barn and chicken coup. If we find nothing, we can talk with the neighbors; I know most of them they go to my church."

Starting out the door Ty stopped, and said, "I just thought of something, Mrs. Casey paid me when I left on Sunday she got money out of a pitcher in the sideboard let's see if the money that was left is still in the pitcher."

Moving two glass jars from in front of the pitcher Ty shook the container and it was empty, the money was gone. Knowing that she had returned some coins to the pitcher after paying him, but where was it now? Mrs. Casey must have removed it and out of habit placed it back in the sideboard, she sat the jars back as they were. Anyone else would have just taken the money and left the pitcher out in the open.

"She left with 'em I don't know why, but she did. Reverend lets go check the other buildings I don't think we will find anything but it won't hurt to look."

In the barn, they found where at least three and maybe four horses had spent some time stabled. The droppings were several days old and in the grain box, there were traces of fresh oats. Ty knew that there was no oats on the place, whoever it was they brought their own. The cow stood at the manger rail not milked and was apparently hurting from the lack of attention. There was no hay in the manger the water bucket was empty, hungry, thirsty and the pressure of the full udder caused her to moo constantly.

Ty said, "I'll go ahead and milk her now if you want to look around some more, maybe checking the chicken coup and down by the stock dam. I'll feed the milk to the pigs I'll bet that they haven't eaten in sometime either, we're going to have to find someone to take care of the critters until we come up with a better plan."

As Ty approached the pigpen smelling the fresh milk, the squealing pigs nearly trampled each other getting to the feed trough. Attempting to pour the milk into the hollowed out log, which served as the trough, the milk spilled over their heads. It was eaten in no time at all and Ty knew it was not enough to fill them but it would have to do for now.

Looking around the entire place, there was no sign of Mrs. Casey. Other than the neglect of the stock, there was nothing out of the ordinary. The chickens still penned up and the eggs not gathered, they had been there for several days and a couple of the hens had started to set.

Going back to the cabin, they looked around again and then got into the buggy, "I'll just tie Buck to the maple tree we can pick him up on our way back."

The Garrett family living just south of Mrs. Casey's remembered that just before bedtime on Monday night they had seen three or four people on horseback heading south. What had brought their attention to the road was the barking of a dog that sounded very excited. "I couldn't see the dog and couldn't tell who the riders were but one of the riders kept yelling at the dog, telling it to go home."

"Mrs. Garrett could you tell if one of the riders was a woman, maybe if one was being taken away against their will" the Reverend asked.

"I couldn't tell it was dark and there was a light rain falling. If the dog had not been barking we would have missed them completely. There was a smaller animal following I think it was a packhorse or maybe a mule I don't really know."

"We will have to inform the Constable tomorrow in the mean time Mrs. Garrett would you and your son Joseph, find a way to provide for the livestock at the Casey place?"

"Of course Reverend Koppleman it would be no problem for us, we had offered our help to Mrs. Casey before but she always turned us down. She was such a sad person by herself and all, too much time alone I think."

Of the five cabins visited, only one could remember seeing some riders. It was disappointing but no one could add to Mrs. Garrett's account.

Ty asked, "What should I do about finishing the field, Mrs. Casey paid me already and I think I should do it even if she is not there. I would hate to have her return and find that I didn't keep my word."

"The way it looks I don't think she will return very soon. It looks like she just left and did not worry about the stock, the cabin or the chickens. I wouldn't worry about the field anymore if I were you; we've most likely seen the last of Mrs. Casey."

The thought of not seeing her again suddenly hit home. Ty felt that something very important had entered and left his life all too soon. He felt lonely and sick he wanted to see her again just to be sure that she was all right.

He wanted to tell her how he felt about her, find out why she left, and if she left of her own free will or did someone force her. Maybe I should go back to her place and spend the night, just to be there if she should return.

Ty did not want to go home, if he went home now could he tell his mother what had happened without sounding so attached to Mrs. Casey? He was sure that his mother would be able to tell that something was amiss and ask for an explanation.

"Reverend Koppleman last time I asked a favor of you and you agreed now I have one more. There is no way that I can go looking for Mrs. Casey, as bad as I want to and I can't stay here to see if she comes back. Will you somehow get word to me if she does return?"

"I'll do that Ty, of course I will, I will need to have a better description of where your place is at but I will get a message to you. I will get word to the Constable tomorrow and tell him what we know, someone has to provide for securing the cabin and taking care of the stock, he can provide for that and perhaps he will be able to shed some light on this mystery."

After giving the preacher a detailed map of how to get to the O'Malley farm Ty mounted Buck and turned for home with the disappearance still on his mind; Ty rode as if he were in a trance, his only thoughts were of what happened to Mrs. Casey. Just hours ago, he was worried about what he would say when he saw her, now he might never see her again. His biggest concern was that she was so frail and with her arm the way it was could she protect herself if need be? For some, reason he could not explain how, but Mr. Casey had to be involved he just felt it in his bones. For no other reason would she leave her farm without him, she had been determined to save the farm for her husband's return; no, she just wouldn't leave without Him.

CHAPTER 3

The sun had set and the moon was not yet showing in the dark sky when Ty arrived home. The light from the kitchen window caught his attention and broke his chain of thought. He realized that Mrs. Casey had completely occupied his mind from the time he left the church until now. A growl from his gut reminded him that he hadn't eaten since morning and he was hungry as a bear, his breakfast consisted of fried eggs and mush. I wonder what Mom had made herself for supper, knowing Mom; it would be very little, her appetite was not what it had been the older she got, the less she ate.

To let her know that he was home, he rode up near the house and said, "Ma I'm home I'll put Buck away and then be in."

Not waiting for an answer, he turned Buck's head toward the barn but before Buck could take a step, Ma was at the door, "Leave Buck there for now and come in here right away, I have something to show you."

Dropping off the mule's back, Ty headed for the door his only thought was that Mrs. Casey had found her way here. "What is it Ma, what's happened?"

"Just get in here boy."

Taking his mother's arm, they stepped into the kitchen. A man sat with his back to the door and waited for them to enter. When he stood up and turned to face Ty he said, "About time you made it home, makes a fella wonder if he ain't welcome."

"James is that you?"

"Who else would it be little brother, the boogie man?"

Their eyes met but before Ty could get a good look at James they were together, a huggin' and cryin' with tears running down their cheeks and poor

Ma caught in the middle. For the longest time they stood, holding one another, no one spoke.

As they stepped back, Ty noticed the dirty rag sling that supported James's left arm, "Your arm is hurt, what happened, is it broken?"

James' answer was slow in coming, he said, "It's broke all right, along with my collar bone, that's what got me out of the war. The Doc told me that my arm may never heal straight; most likely will be useless. It was the second time that they hit me in this arm, seems to take longer to heal this time. The first time I sent word to you that I was wounded, did you ever get the letter?"

"Yes but what about Kevin, do you know when is he coming home?" Ty asked.

"He doesn't know where Kevin is they were separated early in the war; James has no idea of his brother's whereabouts."

Tears streaked Ma's face as she told Ty about Kevin, "James said that a lot of the men from Missouri got sent to other companies to fill in for their losses. He said that this war killed a mess of people."

"Are you home for good, you don't have to go back do you?" Ty asked.

"I'm home to stay I never want to leave again. I just want to sit here with Ma and you and together we'll wait for Kevin's safe return but for the time bein' I won't be of much help to you farmin'. There are some things I can still do, feedin' the chickens and gatherin' the eggs will be a nice start. I won't have to carry no rifle or duck every time I hear a noise, that's goin' to be different."

"How did you get home, where were you when you got hit, what battles were you in?" All these questions and more, Ty wanted answers to.

"Hold on here for a minute," Ma said, "There is plenty of time for all those questions after I feed you supper. I'm going to fry up some eggs and make a stack of pancakes for you boys. I got two men to feed now, sounds good to just to say that. Ty you go take care of Buck and check on the calves and such, button everything down for the night."

"Wait Ty, I'll go with you give me a chance to jump in the water trough and wash some of this road crude away. Ma do you have a bar of soap and a dry towel, it will feel strange to be clean for a change."

"I'll get you Ty's clean shirt and a pair of pants. Your first supper home will just have to wait till you've washed up, now don't take to long I just got you back and I don't want you out of my sight for long."

"Ma, I'm goin' to be home for a long time I don't plan on goin' anywhere soon. Right now I just want to clean up some, and besides nature is callin'."

"All right but hurry, I ain't going to hold supper for long."

Getting the lantern down from the peg, Ty walked to the stove, taking an ember, he lit the lantern. They left the house and walked to the barn. Buck hadn't waited for them; he was already in his stall. Ty was taking care of Buck removing the harness and placing hay in the manger. He filled the water pail, and rubbing Buck down with a hand full of dry hay. James was washing himself in the water trough. When the bath and the chores were finish, they talked while they looked at the horse that James had ridden home. It was dark bay, with a white face and four white stockings. Ty said, "What is his name or does he have one?"

"Ain't had time to name him, I just call him horse. He sure carries himself well. Smooth and gentle, like ridin' in a rockin' chair. He has some speed when you need it, I'm sure that he was a cavalry mount."

Looking over at the new calves James said. "That is a sight for a change watchin' these calves, knowin' they are goin' to grow up, instead of dyin'. In the war, we fed ourselves on what we could scavenge or take sometimes it was cows and calves just like these. Hard workin' people, who didn't do anything to start this war, lost everything they had, the army just took whatever they wanted and then some; if we couldn't eat it or used it; we destroyed it so the enemy couldn't have it. We burnt houses, barns and crops still growin' in the fields it made most of us sick to see the mess we made of peoples lives."

As they finished up in the barn James said, "Ty, I don't know where Kevin is or if he is alive, a lot of men have died in this war, young and old ones alike. I wish I was convinced that Kevin is goin' to be all right, but I ain't. When we talk about Kevin and Ma will, just go along with what ever I say Kevin is a survivor and I am bettin' that he is alive; at least I'm hoping so. If there is any way in hell that he can make it home, he will, I don't want to lie to her but I don't want to hurt her either."

"I don't see how you got separated; you went in the same time, wouldn't they let you stay together if you would have asked?"

"One day we were called to formation the officer in charge asked the first two ranks to step forward and marched 'em away. Kevin was in the first row and I was in the fourth one we didn't know that we were bein' separated until that night when the first two squads didn't show up for supper; I never saw him again and in askin' around no one knew where that group went. The rumor was, to Tennessee, the company that I was in left the next day for Virginia."

"Didn't they know that you were brothers and wanted to stay together?"

"All they worried about was bodies and gettin' people where their needed. The army was fightin' on so many fronts and so many men were dyin' they couldn't keep up with the requests. We never understood their thinkin' a lot of people from Missouri went to the Potomac River region near the Capitol. Units from eastern Pennsylvania was sent to western Tennessee it just didn't make sense to us."

"Boys what's taking you so long, the cakes are done and I have started on the eggs. How many do you want James, and you Ty?"

"Just fry up three or four for me." James answered. "I'm not used to eatin' to much at a settin'."

Ty responded with the same number and added, "We will be there in just a shake were about done out here."

"We had better get in there, or Ma will be coming to get you. She is so excited that you are home at last she won't let you far from her sights for a good time to come."

The table was ready when they walked into the house, a stack of pancakes sat in the middle of the table that under most circumstances would feed an army. Ma was putting the eggs on our separate plates and on the stove was a pan of hot syrup.

"Took you boys long enough, I was beginning to think that you weren't hungry. Maybe it's my cooking that you don't like, it probably don't taste like army fixin's."

Ma watched her two sons as they ate but her thoughts were of her remaining son, wherever he was. She said a prayer for Kevin asking the Lords help in bringing him home safely, adding thanks for getting James back.

"When was the last time that you sat at a table and ate your supper, Son?"

"I don't rightly know Ma, but it's been some time ago. As I think on it, it would probably be this very same table. When I was in the hospital, we ate where we were, in bed or squattin' on the ground. Out in the field they didn't have any tables to sit at either."

Ty could not keep from watching everything that James did or keep his eyes off of his face. It had been so long since he had seen James, realizing that he was not as big as he remembered, or as young. The happy, take it or leave it smile was still on his face, his hair was long and matted, still wet from washing it in the trough. There were streaks of gray showing at the temples; his once sparkling eyes were replaced with a sad longing pair, looking just at you and not beyond, with help, the sparkle would return and match his smile once again. He looked a lot lighter than when he left home, but that was only natural. Ma would put some weight on him now that he's back. The one thing that looked normal, as Ty remembered, was the size of his hands, Ma always said that James' hands were like his fathers, huge and big enough to fight a bear with a stick.

"How long have you been here James?"

"Not long, just before sunset. I put my horse up in the barn before I came to the house to see Ma, I didn't want to scare her so I waited a little while to see if you would show up. Then it dawned on me that you might not be stayin' here at all, thought you might be fightin' in the war by now. Ma was just gettin' the lamp lit and I waited for her to put it down on the table before I opened the door. I thought she was goin' to faint or something, we just kind of looked at each other for a while, and she said, "O sweet mother of God, it is you James you've finally came home."

"Then we ran to one another and held on for dear life, we both cried till you got home, you don't know how much I missed you both and how I worry about Kevin. Kevin will find his way home, he always has and he loves us all too much not to. He will first have to do his duty to the army, as dumb as the fightin' is but he'll be here as soon as it's possible."

"Where did you come from, I mean when they told you that you could come home?"

"I was in a camp in Pennsylvania, for men with wounds and such. I was pretty damn sick for a spell; I had lost a lot of blood and had a fever that wouldn't stop. They had me on a table, ready to cut my arm off, when I woke up. I asked what they were doing to me and they said that my arm had to come off so it wouldn't get infection in it, they called it gangrene poison. I asked 'em, do I have it now and they told me no. Then leave my arm alone you can cut it off when it's full of that shit, sorry Ma, and not until. I tried to get up off the table but fell instead; I guess I was too weak to stand. I passed out and when I came, too I still had both arms. I found out later that a man from Ohio stepped forward, put a rifle barrel on those butchers and told 'em to forget it. "Better do as I say, killin' ain't new to me." He said. At least that is what I heard. I never did find out what his name was or for sure where he was from. I stayed in that camp for another two or three month. When I didn't get any worse they gave me some papers and said I could go home."

"I don't know what you folks heard about a big fight in Pennsylvania called Gettysburg. It was a God almighty battle as you ever heard of, they say that two hundred thousand men fought there. Half fought for the union and the rest for the Rebs. We fought for three days and they say that fifty thousand lost their lives, half on each side. Ten thousand or more were taken prisoner, it had to the bloodiest fight of the war."

"We were dug in on the high ground and I think that is what won the battle for us. The Rebs would charge us and damn near break through, but each time our lines would hold. Bodies of dead soldiers were lying on top of each other and when the next charge came, they would step on the dead bodies to get to us, it was god almighty awful."

"I was in the cavalry under General John Buford, we moved from one place to another, wherever they needed some back up troops. We lost about half of our company and most all of our horses on the first raid of the confederate's cavalry. One thing that has got to be said about 'em, Southerners are good riders. They came a stormin' up that first afternoon, like fleas on a dog. There were so many of 'em that I can't, to this day, figure out why they backed off when they did. We heard that they were waitin' for reinforcements from their General Longstreet. They pushed us around pretty good that day and we thought that we were done soldiers for sure, but they let us regroup that saved our lives and maybe the war, so I've heard."

"After Gettysburg we all headed south to attack Richmond. This time we screwed up, waiting for reinforcements before we attacked their headquarters. That's when General Stonewall Jackson and his troops hit us and drove us all the way back to Pennsylvania. I got hit in that battle, didn't know it then but now their calling it, the battle of Seven Pines."

"I headed home sometime in February, a foot. These papers they give you to show that your done fightin' are right important to have. There is a lot of deserter's leavin' the army for any number of reasons, cowardice, murder and thievery. Some are just homesick and just want to be home. Obeyin' orders when the odds are that you won't make it, was pretty damn tough. Some just stole away in the night and never was seen again."

"I hadn't been on the road but a week, sure as hell not makin' very good time. When one night I'm layin' in the woods, to damn tired to sleep, and I heard something or someone crawlin' though the dead leaves and grass. By the sound, I figured it to headed right at me so I laid my knife, aside of me and my rifle pointed at the sound. All of a sudden, they let out a howl and came for me I shot the one through the chest and grabbed for my toad sticker just as he was headed belly down on me. All I had to do was to turn my wrist and he landed on the point. He didn't die right away; I found out that it was my papers they wanted."

"Come mornin' I scraped a hole in the ground and buried 'em together. Ma, I did say words over 'em, they was just young ones and probably scared to death. Durin' the night I thought that I heard a horse pawin' the ground and I checked I found two mounts tied just fifteen rods from where I was sleepin'. Those boys didn't need 'em anymore so I just borrowed 'em, I sold one in Ohio, for fifteen dollars, so I could eat. It is mighty tough to hunt with just the one arm and I was gettin' hungry."

"I rode the rest of the way but took it mighty careful, I didn't want to fall into any groups and maybe have my papers taken. I stayed by myself pretty much the whole way, it took longer but I'm here in just about in one piece."

Ma said, "Son you must be very tired what you need is a good night's sleep in your old bed, what do you say we call it a night and start again tomorrow? We will have all the time in the world to hear about the war and all, in the days to come."

Going to bed that night Ty thought of Mrs. Casey for the first time since getting home. The excitement of James return had wiped all else from his mind. Come tomorrow, he would ask if James knew of Charles Casey, if he did, what had happened to him?

After breakfast of bacon, eggs and fried mush, chased down with a glass of cold milk, the conversation turned back to James.

Between questions and answers, Ty spoke about the missing woman and of the strange circumstances about her disappearance. Of the riders that were seen by Mrs. Garrett and the livestock that was just left to fend for themselves, the dirty cabin and the missing shotgun. The muddy tracks and the way the money jar was put back as if nothing was amiss.

"Reverend Koppleman will get word to me if she should return but the Reverend is convinced that she is gone for good. I'd like to know why she left and where she has gone, it just doesn't seem right that she would leave without a word to someone."

"James when you and Kevin joined up did you know her husband, a man by the name of Charles Casey? He lived about fifteen or twenty miles west of here, his wife said that he left in August the same as you."

"I might but the name don't ring a bell, what did he look like?"

"Close to my size and weight, I'm guessing, dark hair, but on that I'm not sure."

"Still it don't trigger any one right off the top of my head, they were takin' men just about every day, when we joined up. Being strangers, they pretty much looked all the same, no reason to take any special notice. Maybe he left at a different time than we did."

"From what Mrs. Casey told me he must be pretty good looking, a woman's man."

"Hold on, there was a man that thought he was better than most, he was a royal pain in the butt, complained all the time about any little thing. As I remember, he was headed for Kansas when the war started; the description you gave me fits him all right"

"Yes Mrs. Casey told me that they were on their way to Kansas when she became sick."

"I'll bet you that was him all right; he thought he was really something he didn't make new friends easily. If you're asking where he went, all I can say is that he went east with the same group that I did. I don't recall when I last saw him, I'm sure it was before Gettysburg."

"Well now I guess it is of no matter anyway, seein' as Mrs. Casey is gone. The only person other than me that might be interested would be Reverend," Ty said.

The days of April were good days, sunshine with bright skies with just enough rain to help set the seeds and very little wind. The crops were mostly in, except for the potatoes that would be planted in the dark of the moon. A second crop of tomatoes, green beans, peas and some cooking herbs would be planted later to extend the freshness throughout the summer.

All this time James was getting stronger and working his arm some. The collarbone was healing, it was just his arm giving him trouble and he tried to use it as much as he could. At times when he would forget about his injured arm, you could hear him cuss a half a mile away. The arm remained crooked and bent, but his grip and hand strength was returning only the heaviest of jobs would slow him down and rarely would he ask for help from Ty.

Rumors were circulating from across the fences and from people that were passing by, that the war was ending. The middle of April brought word that an actor named Booth shot President Lincoln in a theater and that the South had surrendered to General Grant somewhere in Virginia. Emotions were hard to suppress, people were sad and damn mad that an actor had killed their president and on the other hand, that if the reports were true that the war was over it was a time to celebrate. The word had started to spread around that the troops were being discharged and could be home soon. James was sure that the dismissed men would have to find their own way home; the army was done with them and cared less what happened.

Ma said, "The war is still on until Kevin returns home there is no sense in getting excited. When he comes across the door jam, I'll know then that the war is over and we can get our lives back to normal."

Confirmation came from the local Constable, Mr. Drake. He rode out to advise Ty that there was no news about Mrs. Casey. He did say the proceeds from sale of the livestock and the chickens and the land itself would go to the county for taxes and such. If there were any moneys left over, the county will mostly credit it to the Casey's account.

"Mr. Drake, what have you heard about the war ending, is it over for good?"

"They say it is; I haven't got any thing in writing or nothing official. The telegraph messages their getting at the Post office says that it is and I sure as hell hope so."

James said, "Do you get any notices tellin' about the men that are missin' in action, or maybe about the prisoners that were kept in those rottin' camps?

I know after a battle or a skirmish the names were posted on the company bulletin board tellin' who didn't make it and the like."

"From time to time they send a package of papers with names and descriptions of people that the Army is looking for. To be honest I never looked too close at 'em. I can't say for certain, but some of the ones that I took the time to look at, were about murders and deserters. I think there were some men wanted for rape in there too. The names didn't ring a bell they weren't from around here so I didn't do anything with any of it."

As Ty talked with the constable, James went up to the house where Ma was doing some mending. Ty could hear his Ma sobin', they were happy tears but tears with fearful overtones attached. Now that the war was over either Kevin would come home or we would never see him again, there was no reason for him to stay away if he was alive.

"Do they send these lists by where they are from or just all together?" Ty was thinking of Kevin but could not help but to include Mr. Casey in his concern.

"I've never paid a whole lot of attention to any of the names. If I told folks about these lists, you all would be asking questions everyday, I would never get my work done."

"Are the lists still in your office, did you keep 'em?"

"Most of them are there I guess, I don't recall throwing any away."

"Mr. Drake if I came to your office on Saturday, would you let me look at those papers, they just might have something about Kevin in 'em."

Listening to Ma's sobbing was very painful, she was a strong person but the pressure of not knowing was stronger.

"I wouldn't bother you, just sit and look."

"Don't see how that would hurt, I'll be waiting come Saturday.

Preparations for the trip to Jamesville on Saturday began on Wednesday. The wagon moved out of the shed, swept out and scrubbed down. All four wheels removed and the hubs packed with fresh grease. The fresh oil on Buck's harnesses made them shine as if they were new and the brass decorations on the neck collars and the bridles, polished to glisten like gold.

Late in the afternoon Ma came out to inspect the progress. "Ty do we still have that can of red paint in the barn, the spokes need painted. It wouldn't hurt to touch up the trim around the box and seat too. Make it look better if they had some bright paint on them."

"We do but I wouldn't bet on it being very good, it's been there a long time. It's been two or three years since we had that can open, that is when we painted the wagon last. Why do we need to paint any ways, the wagon looks good enough as it is?"

"It's been nearly four years since I rode into town with two of my sons a riding with me. I want people to notice when we come into town. I want them to say, why there are the O'Malley's and James is with them. The only thing that would be nicer is if Kevin were here too. But you know boys; I have a feeling that it won't be long before we're all going to be together again, I can't tell you why but something in my bones tells me that Kevin is all right and will be home soon."

"I hope your right Ma, it would be something to see the old scudder and hear him laugh like he use to. Do you remember Ma when we use to work all day and wrestle half the night away? We would take Ty and throw him between us like a bag of potatoes; he would laugh up a storm and Ma, you would yell for us not to hurt him. We just did those things to Ty to get under your skin, make the kid grow up faster. When we was pickin' on him, we was only trying to make him tougher we knew that he would need to be someday. Look at him Ma, he is bigger than Kevin and me ever was and most likely stronger to, the only thing he ain't is better lookin'."

With that, James gave Ty a shove and laughed. "Kevin and me were a handful for you, weren't we Ma?"

"That and then some, but a lot of the times you thought you were pulling the wool over my eyes, I knew what was happening. Like the corn squeezing you made the corn whisky out of and hid it in the hayloft, it was right good; I had a taste of it myself. Then there was the time you and Kevin went to the dance at the grange hall and came home all bruised and battered, did you really think that I believed that you rode into a low branch and fell off your horse like you wanted me to? I figured that you had a fight I just didn't know with who. That big boiling kettle you found along side of the road, on my birthday no less. I know that you were hiding away some of your pelts to buy it. You three would go hunting, come home empty handed time and time again. I knew better, my boys were better hunters than that, Oh I saw through most of your pranks all right, but as long as they didn't hurt anyone except yourselves, I didn't say anything. I still loved you even if there was a white lie or two."

Saturday morning every one was up earlier than usual. Packing eggs in a box, layered with straw to protect them from breaking. Mom had a crock of butter, wrapped up in wet burlap. Ty had bundled and tied the pelts he had gathered over the winter. There was fewer than last year, but Ty thought they were better quality because of the cold weather. Ma had placed her knitted baby caps, shawls, along with baby blankets and booties in a paper package. Fancy crocheted table and back covers, were her pride and joy, she placed them in a separate package, a lot of time and effort had gone into the making of these items. She knew that both Bentines and Andersons would accept them; she had worked all winter on them and had a good number to sell or trade to the stores in Jamesville. James had wanted to sell his horse there was no need to feed an animal unless there was work that critter could do, an ex-cavalry horse did not fit on a working farm. Ty had grown fond of the horse he called him Duke and had talked James out of selling him.

Leaving the yard Ma said, "Did you throw in a piece of canvas just in case it rains, I know that it doesn't look like rain now but this time of year you never know."

"Yes Ma, we got the canvas." They said in unison and added, "We threw in a couple of blankets just to be safe."

"Ma you look so pretty this mornin', if I didn't know better I'd say you were out looking for a beau. Wantin' us to clean all up, paint the wagon and even curryin' old Buck. Have you got someone in mind?" James asked.

"If I did, I wouldn't tell you heathens about it, you both have a big mouth, neither of you could ever keep a secret anyway." Boys I don't know why but I'm so excited to be going to town, I feel like a young girl. It seems like forever that we have been there, when was it Ty, do you remember? I think that it was over six months ago that I was there, you went about Christmas if I remember right."

Ty agreed with his Mother and said so. He added that he had last been to town in the middle of the week and no one was there, it would be different today.

Buck kept up a steady pace, slowing for the upgrades, but making good time otherwise. They saw many other families going in the same direction, some on foot and others in wagons or buggies. The weather was pleasant and with spring came the need to replenish much of the goods that they used last winter. If folks had their choice, they would always come to town on Saturday, for nothing else just to meet their friends and hear all of the gossip. Besides, on Saturday there were more people to trade with and more goods to choose from. The more folks that were in town meant more sales for the merchants and the better deals they would give in return. Bartering was a way of life for most farm folks, they used cash only to pay fees, taxes and on occasion, to hire work done.

The morning chill had left the air when the buildings of Jamesville came into sight. Already you could see people moving from store to store, not that there were that many stores in the whole town. Jamesville was typical rural town with most everything that the surrounding community needed to survive. There was the livery barn, with the blacksmith shop along side of it a mercantile store that sold soft goods such as cloth, boots and shoes, ready-made shirts and dresses, most any thing that you would need to clothe your family. Two saloons that also doubled as hotels and eating establishments. A General Store that sold farm supplies, house wares, patented medicines, staples such as salt and pepper, butchered meats, milk and eggs and whatever a person needed for that matter. There was a cobbler's shop and a millinery shop.

There was the City Court house, which housed the Constable office and jail. The law office of Attorney Malcolm J. Sterns and beside that was old Doctor O'Toole's office. Located right in the middle, on the south side of the street was the Goodnight Bank. Directly across from the bank was the Post Office. The schoolhouse sat on a small rise a short distance north of the Main Street. Two churches served the tiny town, a Methodist and a Baptist. They sat at either end of the street, and on Sunday morning folks heard the bells miles away. The large building south of town was the Grange Hall, the meeting place of the community, dances along with holiday observances and special celebrations that were too large for anywhere else. Scattered along side of and behind the businesses; were the homes of the merchants and the city folks. The more prosperous homes had carriage houses behind the neatly painted buildings with their fenced yards.

"The town hasn't changed much since I last saw it, maybe not quite as busy as it was back then. That was four years ago and it seems like a hundred. Do you still sell your pelts to Gill at the livery?" James asked.

"Ya, he still is a trapper at heart." Ty replied.

"There hasn't been many changes in last few years, as a matter of fact I can't think of any changes. Gill still has the livery and Anderson has the General Store. We have a new blacksmith his name is Robertson. He came from over by Hannibal a couple of years ago, seems to be a nice enough man, I don't know if he is married or not. Ty had Buck re-shod when he was here last, did he say if he was married?"

"He is married all right, or at least he had better be, he has a woman and three kids that I know of. He is not all that old, I wondered why he was not in the Army, and so I asked. Seems as through he got shot up pretty bad and they sent him home. That is when he came here; he had heard that we had a need for a smithy."

Turning at the Baptist Church, Ty said, "Where do you want to go first, Anderson's or Bentines? We'll let you out with your knitting and such. James and I will go to Gills and see to my pelts, it shouldn't take long and we'll come back with the eggs and butter."

"Stop at Bentines I promised them first pick of my stock last time. They take good care of me; let's see how they do this time. Unload the eggs and butter there too I'm thinking that Bentines will buy them."

"Come to think about it, I'll send James back with the wagon and I'll go see Mr. Drake. I shouldn't be to long; I'll meet you at Anderson's."

As Ma got down from the wagon and an old friend greeted her, who she had not seen in a long time. Ma turned back to the wagon, "You remember my son James don't you Hazel, he just returned from the war with a hurt shoulder and arm. He is home to stay now; it will be wonderful to have him under my feet."

She continued to talk with Hazel and others as they walked toward Bentines Store. James and Ty went directly to the livery and sought out Gill, a tall lanky Norwegian, with blond hair. He came slowly up to the wagon, "What can I do for you Ty; say is that you James, I'll be damned if it ain't, when did you get home? He stuck out his hand to shake James's and notice the sling on James arm. Got shot up did you, Is it going to be all right, can you use it?"

James responded, "I got back a couple of weeks ago I guess you haven't changed much you old Swede."

"By golly you know that I'm not a damn Swede, you always say that, you know that I am an honest Norwegian." Gill was laughing and still shaking James hand.

"Gill; you look great, how is Mary and the kids and you had better stop shakin' my hand or you just might break it too, one arm broke at a time is enough?"

"Come on back in the barn I've got a bottle there that needs to be opened." Gill lead the way to a back stall. Out from under the hay in the manger he produced a bottle of clear liquid. "I know this is good, cause I made it myself." He pulled the cork and handed it first to James who took a hefty swallow and handed it back. Gill then handed it to Ty.

Ty looked at James, then back to Gill, placing it to his lips took a drink. With out blinking handed the bottle back to the Norwegian, who in turn took a very long pull from the bottle.

"Hell Ty, I didn't know you were experienced with the hard stuff, where did you get a taste for it?" James said jokingly.

"You and Kevin should have found a better hiding place for the jug you left behind. I found it a while back and decided to try it, found that it wasn't all that bad. I had to stay away from Ma most of the day, so I hid out in the corn crib and slept."

Anxious to get to the constable office, Ty asked if he was still buying pelts. "I've got some good ones this time, rabbit, fox, coon, some deer hides, mink and otters. The cold winter made for some heavy pelts, are you interested?"

"Lets take a look at what you got, did you trap 'em or shoot 'em?

"Trapped some and shot some. The ones I shot didn't hurt the pelts none, I was careful to hit 'em in the head for the most part."

Spreading the skins out on the wagon bed, Gill picked each one up, felt it, and blew on it to check for thickness, he then smelt each one for mold or decay.

"Fine pelts you got here but the rabbit skins aren't selling well this year,

I guess there is too many of 'em. I'll tell you what I'll do; I'll give you twenty dollars for the whole lot."

Knowing Gill and his fondness for haggling over the price Ty stubbornly said, "Make it twenty eight and it's a deal."

"Dammit Ty, you know that I can't make any money at that price. I'll make it two and a half dollars more but I can't go higher."

"I'll settle for twenty five and you throw in a bag of oats for old Buck, if you see your way clear to do that, we got a deal."

"You drive a hard bargain I won't make a damn dime on this deal and you know it. I did get a good deal on some skins from old man Hopkins, so maybe I'll break even." Extending his hand he said, "It's a deal."

Leaving the Livery with a smile from ear to ear, James said, "You handled your self as if you knew exactly what Gill was goin' to offer you and what he would end up payin'. Where did you learn so much about haggl'ng, me and Kevin were never that good."

"Have you ever watched Ma when she takes her little fancy hand work in and barter for supplies, she is the best that I've ever seen? She shows 'em the best that she has got that gets 'em real interested and then it's up to her to set a price, they will usually end up giving what she asks for. Then on the other end, if Mom is buying, she starts by offering a fair price. Then starts to point out any problem with what ever she is buying, a snag in the yarn or too much mold on the round of cheese. She buys and sells at her own price most every time, she's a sharp one Ma is."

As the wagon came to the Constable Office, Ty gave James the pelt money and told him to give to Ma and he hopped off the wagon, "I don't know how long this will take, but I'll find you when I'm done."

Seeing Mr. Drake, sitting at his desk, Ty walk into the small room. He looked around for the first time, never having a reason to be in here before.

"I see that you made it never doubted that you wouldn't. Come over here to this old table and I'll get you started." Handing Ty a stack of paper about two-and a half inches high, "Here's the latest ones that I got, the older ones are over there in the corner. If you see anything that I should know about just leave it out and I'll study on it later."

Ty started through the letter sized paper one at a time. Reading mostly the names, but occasionally he would get wrapped up in the story of the offense.

The majority reports were missing in action or of the death of a soldier. After about an hour, finding nothing, he began to wonder, just what is it that I'm looking for?

Inside he knew that he was more interested on information concerning Charles Casey than Kevin. If Kevin was dead Ty did not want to know about it, it was better to have the dream of his returning some day, than to know that he would not be coming back at all.

Nearly completing the first stack, Ty was about to give up when the next flier caught his eye. There were no pictures but there were several names listed on the one piece of paper.

****

WANTED FOR MURDER, DESERTION and ESCAPE

CHARLES I. CASEY Hannibal, Missouri
PETER G. HOWES Stockville, Indiana
WILLIAM K. PLUNKET Westbend, Ohio
OLIVER A. PRICE Burke, Michigan
JAMES JOHN WATTERS Sandburg, Indiana

The above listed men are wanted for desertion and
escape on January 17, 1865 from the United States
Army Depot at Harrisburg, Pennsylvania to avoid
being tried for murder of Major John Barry Lewis,
an Officer in the Fourth Volunteer Regiment of
Pennsylvania. Major Lewis murdered on
November 22, 1863. A $500 reward is offered for the
apprehension of these men, dead or alive.

****

Ty just sat there and looked at what he had just read; he couldn't believe that was the same Charles Casey. The flier did say that he was from Hannibal, more than likely all the men from around here had their homes listed as

Hannibal. What were the chances that there was more than one Charles Casey from the same place? Deep in thought Ty sat there, wondering if the person that took Mrs. Casey, could have been her own husband Maybe the other men on this list was still with him.

"Mr. Drake I've got something here that I think you should look at. You might be able to come up with another explanation, I certainly hope so anyway."

The Constable leaned back in his chair as Ty handed the flier to him. "What did you find son I hope its not bad news about your brother."

"No it's not about Kevin but it has Mr. Casey' name on it, I can't believe what it says."

Slowly reading the notice, shaking his head from side to side, he looked at Ty, and then read it again. "Do you suppose that there is a mistake here, I can check with the Army Office in Hannibal, but it will take a couple of days. In the mean time, I wonder if we should keep this to ourselves, no sense in spreading it around if it's not true."

"Do you think that is who Mrs. Casey left with; do you suppose he came back for her? They left in dark, about nightfall, according to Mrs. Garrett, that seems strange, don't you think?"

"Now hold on for a minute." He paused, "Catch your breath son let's give some thought to it. The escape was in the middle of January, so that would give him enough time to make it this far even if he were moving slow and easy but I can't picture a man that is wanted for murder coming back to his home territory where he might be recognized"

"The Casey's weren't here all that long and they weren't very friendly with their neighbors and such. I'll bet that only a very few people in the whole county would know him by sight. His wife was here for four years, never did get friendly with her neighbors, and never even tried to become part of the church doings. Mrs. Casey told me that her husband did not want to be beholden to anybody, said if you couldn't do it by yourself it didn't need doing, they were loners."

"Well son you put together a mighty fine story, I can't disagree with you. I'll look into this come Monday and if I get some answers I'll ride out and tell you but in the mean time I think it's better not to say what we've uncovered, do you agree?"

"It is going to be tough not to tell James and Ma, they will probably figure out something is bothering me, and ask questions."

"I don't see any harm in letting your folks in on this, just tell them after you leave town today. Tell them not to repeat it till they hear from me, can you do that?"

Shaking hands, Ty headed out to find Ma and James. He saw Buck standing at Anderson's hitching rail eating the oats that Gill had provided. The nosebag was tied to his bridle so that he could eat at his leisure. James was standing talking to a group of men discussing the war. "Ty, did you find what you were looking for, was there anything about Kevin?"

"No, not a thing, I went through a pretty big stack of notices most were about deserters and such, not very exciting."

"Where is Mom, in Anderson's?"

"No she walked across the street to the bank, to check on something with the banker. She made her deals with Bentines and Anderson's and I'm bettin' that she came out ahead. I was to wait here and help Mr. Anderson load the wagon. The way it sounds we're goin' to have a hefty load goin' home; I hope old Buck is up to it."

Ty reached into the wagon, breaking off a piece of cheese that they had brought with them. "Looking at those papers took longer than I thought I was developing a pure hunger for something to eat. Guess I will walk over to the water tank and wash this cheese down. Has Buck taken on any water or just been eating those oats?"

"He drank his fill before I gave him the oats what do you think, I forgot that oats will swell up when he takes on water, I waited awhile and then tied the nose bag on,"

"We had better wait on the rest of the oats till we get home. We'll water the old cuss just before we leave." Taking the nosebag off, Ty said, "We'll save the rest of these for later boy."

"James, did Ma check at the Post Office, I don't know for what but you never know?"

"First place she went after leavin' Bentines, didn't have any mail though, I think she was hopin' for something from Kevin."

About that time Mr. Anderson and a young man, that Ty didn't know, started carrying out Ma's purchases. There was huge sack of flour, cornmeal, and a large bag of sugar, a box containing salt, pepper, baking soda and matches and a five-gallon can of kerosene for the lamps. It surprised Ty to see a round of cheese bigger than a dinner plate, wrapped up in cheesecloth, Ma never bought cheese before. Many smaller items wrapped up in brown paper and tied with white string. To Ty it had always been like Christmas when you got home from town, not knowing what was in those wrapped up packages.

Thanking Mr. Anderson for his help in loading the wagon. "Appreciate your fairness to our Mom." He led Buck across the street to Bentines, stopping to water him at the tank. Careful not let him drink his fill; they would water him again before they left.

By the time Ma had completed her business at the bank, the balance of the goods were loaded on to the wagon. It was getting late in the day and Ma was acting kinda strange, quieter than normal. She only said, "I think I have had all the excitement I can stand for one day, let's go home."

Crawling into the wagon, Ty with the reins and Ma setting beside him, they heading Buck out of town. Riding in the wagon box behind them, James said, "Ma, what took you so long at the bank, for what little money we have I didn't think we needed to store it in a bank."

"Well we haven't got much, but I always thought that to be safe we should keep it in the bank now I'm not so sure."

"Why, what happened to change your mind?"

"James you never knew Mr. Goodnight he came here after you and Kevin left. He seems to be a very nice person; I never had any trouble with him until today."

"What kind of trouble did you have?"

"Well, when I got to the bank, Mr. Goodnight was alone; his clerk was nowhere to be seen. I walked up to his desk and told him that I wanted to put some money into our account and while I was there I'd also like to check on what we already had in it. We talked for a few minutes, about the end of the war and this past winter and such. He counted my money, "Thirty six dollars, is that right?" he asked.

I agreed that it was correct. He got up and went to the little file box that is used for the statement sheets. He looked through the papers and turned around, "I can't seem to find your ledger sheet, Arthur, that is my clerk, must have missed filed it. He will be back the first of the week and I will ask him about it, in the mean while I'll give you a receipt for your deposit and add it to your account on Monday."

"I didn't know what to say so finally I said if it's not in that file, just where could it be?"

"Arthur has been over to Willow Springs paying the taxes on the property that we care for, he must have taken yours by mistake or perhaps it was stuck to another statement. It happens some times don't worry about it; our bank is not big enough to loose customer's records, Arthur will know where they are when he returns. We will correct your account promptly; you can be assured of that."

"Well, Ma, if you know the man and trust him with your money, what is the problem you got the receipt don't you?"

"No I haven't, I didn't take it, and I kept the money instead. I'll not be giving any bank more money if they can't tell what is in my account. I told Mr. Goodnight that when he showed me the statement, then I would deposit it."

"What bothered me the most was the way he acted, it was like he didn't want to find our account statement. He was hiding something. I know he was."

"We have to go to Willow Springs to pay our taxes anyway; we might as well go this next week. We can stop and check on our money then." James said.

Thinking about what Ma had said about the banker, and wondering what would happen if they didn't find the records. Ty asked, "Who would want our little dab of money, if Mr. Goodnight or Arthur wanted to steal money I think they would go after more than what we got."

"I think that we should give the bank a chance to find our records and make it right, I'm sure they will."

"You're probable right, James, I worry too much don't I Ty?"

Slapping Buck with the ends of the reins, just to remind him that they were headed for home and not to dally around.

All three were quiet, listening to the quickening steps of Buck and watching the sunset.

Ty was restless trying to decide when to tell them what he had found out about Mr. Casey. Waiting until they were well down the road to home, he started by saying, "I found out some bad news concerning Mr. Casey. We, the Constable and me, don't know if it is the right person, so he is going to check on it as soon as he can. He said that there was no sense in saying anything about this just yet, he's going to keep it quit till he can contact the Army."

"There was a flier in those stacks of papers about five men that are wanted for murdering an Army Officer and for escaping from the stockade in Pennsylvania. Charles Casey's name was on it, it said that he was from Hannibal. We can't believe that there would be two men with the same name both from Hannibal. We think it is what happened to Mrs. Casey he came home and they left at night. There is a $500 reward posted for him."

"Ty, I'm glad that if that is the case, you weren't there when he showed up, no telling what he would have done." Ma said leaning her head toward Ty and laying it on his shoulder.

James chimed in with stories that he had heard about men pushed too hard and never told what was going to happen or why. "Some men couldn't take the strain and went crazy. They didn't all kill their friends or officers, but I know for a fact that it did happen."

Small talk invaded the conversation about Mr. Casey and many questions that couldn't be answered, someday they might be. They talked about what Ma had got for her fancies, and what she had received in return. She was very pleased with the whole day. Happy for what Ty's pelts had brought and proud of her haggling with the merchants and the chance to meet old friends.

The ride home seemed longer than the one going to town. All three were tired and knew that they still had to unload the wagon, milk the cow and do the rest of the chores before retiring for the night. Turning into the lane that lead to the house, Ty abruptly pulled up on the reins and brought Buck to a stop.

"There is a light on in the house, we've got company, someone is in there or was, James you take the reins and I'll drop off here. I'll go the rest of the way in the shadows you and Ma just take it easy and go slow, hold back a ways till I give you the sign."

Ty dropped off the wagon and disappeared in the shadows. James started Buck forward at a very slow pace, keeping his eyes on the house.

They had hardly gone fifty feet when the door opened a man stepped out. "O'Malley's is that you?"

Ma screamed like I had never heard before and slumped into the wagon seat as James shouted, "Is that you Kevin?"

"Now who do you think it is, the boogie man, of course, it is me I've been waitin' for you to show up for over half a day."

By this time, the boys were on the ground and running at one another. Ma had recovered and was trying to get out of the wagon yelling, "Kevin get over here and help me you scoundrel, are you all right? With tears, streaming down her face Ma held him for what seemed like an eternity. She was kissing, hugging and saying, "Thank you Lord, Thank you Lord, My prayers have been answered my boys are home, all of them. Thanks be to the Lord."

While the boys unloaded the supplies and completed the chores, Mom prepared a meal that left everyone leaning back and rubbing their stomachs. They sat and talked long into the night, Kevin sitting next to Ma and Ma holding his hand as if she would never let it go again.

Life in the O'Malley house would start over again, just as the rain renewed the fields so did the love renew the bond of separation of these last four years.

CHAPTER 4

Ma wrung the necks of two young roosters, fried them and made baking powder biscuits. For the boiled potatoes, she made rich, creamy, white gravy. She then sat down to feed her three sons for the first time in four years. For dessert, she cut up some apples and with the rest of the biscuit dough, made apple dumplings that were ate warm with fresh cream poured over them. Kevin ate as if there was no tomorrow.

"These fixin's are what kept me going the last four years. When I was tired and hungry, it always made me feel better just thinking about your cooking, Ma. I could smell your bread baking all the way down to Louisiana. Every cold biscuit I ate reminded me of how much better your biscuits were and I wished for your sausage gravy at every stop along the way. You don't know how I missed you all, if the truth was known I think I worried about James the most, that I'd have to admit, seein' as how I always took care of him and kept him out of a lot of scrapes. Without me to watch over him, you just never know what mess he might get into. Look what he done to his arm, I'll just never understand you boy."

"What about us, Ma and me, didn't you worry some about us?"

"Once or twice is all." Kevin looked down and you could see a tear in his eye. Wiping it away with his thumb, "There were times that I never thought that I would see you again. I prayed to the Lord that everything was all right and that you were safe. At times, I was so scared; you can't believe it, war ain't pretty and it sure taught me how stupid killin' and fightin' is now I don't want to talk about the war anymore. I just want to get back to farmin' and livin' the good life again, sleepin' on a bed, eatin' at a table, and crawlin' in the water trough when ever I want to."

"Well today you're going to just sit around and do absolutely nothing, talk if you want or sleep if you have a mind to. It's going to be so grand to have you all together; I want to cry when I think about it. God has been good to us and we should never forget it, some families aren't as lucky as we are."

Monday morning, during breakfast, Kevin heard about the situation at the bank, and the need to go to Willow Springs.

"All the way home I heard about folks from up north, carpetbaggers they call 'em, takin' over lands that the taxes hadn't been paid on. Hell they just run folks off their places for no cause except that someone wanted their land. The Law down south is nothin' but northerners, appointed by the people in Washington. They have no concern about elections or that some Rebel had lost his land and along with their land, they lost everything along with it. If a Carpetbagger finds a place or some property that they want, the taxes are raised so that no way in hell can the owner pay 'em, them they declared 'em in default and some northerner buys it. There will be some of that up here, if the folks haven't kept up with their taxes, or can't pay 'em. The war made some people damn rich, they're lookin' for ways to spend it and they don't care who they might hurt in the process."

"I can't see that happening here folks at the courthouse and the constable knows everyone that lives in the county; we're all hard working, and honest. So maybe some didn't have enough to pay the taxes, they will make good after the first crop comes in."

"We'll just have to wait and see Ma, you might be right."

That night the boys teased Ty about having his own bed. "You always were spoiled from the day you was born, now that we're home, you'll probably want to keep your own bedroom and we will have to add on. For now, I'll just tell you, that if you snore or fart, James and me will put you out in the barn to sleep, we promise, right James?"

"Without so much as a blanket."

"We will just have to see about who will put who where. You had better rest and build up your strength before your little brother whips you both."

"It for sure is goin' to have to wait for the mornin', tonight I'm to damn tired," Kevin answered.

Monday was a full day for the O'Malley's chores neglected the past two days were finished. It was different today Ty thought with all three boys working the chores went fast. There was time to talk and make plans for projects that they would do in days to come. Ma could not stay away from the boys, she was underfoot and always in the wrong place. She followed Kevin from chore to chore and late afternoon she went to the house to start supper, but continued looking out the doorway ever chance she got.

As darkness fell, the O'Malley's sat outside; watching the stars slowly appear. Occasionally one would make small talk about some item of equipment they wanted to improve the operation of the farm, now that all three boys would be working it. Disappointment hit Ty when James suggested they trade Duke for two more mules. Ty knew that made sense but he had become real attached to that horse. He wished he could come up with some other way to get the mules.

Wrapped in a shawl to ward off the late evening chill, Ma sat between Kevin and James listening to what they had to say. "Ty you have been quiet tonight, don't you have anything to say, you, better than anyone know what we are going to need? Your say is as important to what happens to this place as any ones. You kept it going when the boys were away and did a find job of it; I'm proud of you and I know that your Pa would be too. Boys, most of the time the oldest son takes charge of a place when there is a change of leadership, I want all three of you to run this place. If there is something that you can't agree on, then I will be the final say."

James, bending forward to look at Ty, "Is it the tradin' of Duke that has got you lathered up?"

Ty knew that there was no other way to get what they would need next year, without using the horse for barter. "I know we are going to need the extra mules. We'll need some extra harness and another plow, but they can wait till spring, there is no need to feed two more mules all summer. Come fall we can break ground in all three fields. One of 'em hasn't been touched for two years. While you were gone I rotated the fields trying to keep the weeds down and keeping the earth broken up so the rains could soak in and not run off."

"You've got a point I think that we should wait and see what opens up. A few of the farms won't be doing much, if the men folk don't come home. We can probably get some pretty good deals if we wait." Kevin agreed.

Ma got a tear in her eye, "We aren't going to take advantage of no widow women just cause her man got killed in the war and she can't farm the land, I won't permit that."

Putting his arm around her shoulders, Kevin said, "Ma we aren't like that, we will be fair you know that"

Tuesday morning a horse stomped out in the yard. Ty got up from the table to see what or who it was. "Well good morning Mr. Blake come on in we're just finishing up with breakfast, Ma can set a plate for you."

"No thank you I ate my breakfast on the move today."

"It's pretty early for you isn't it, I didn't expect you till later in the week, did you check out that flier?"

Mr. Drake nodded that he had confirmed the names on the poster; it was Charles Casey all right. Using the new telegraph machine that had been installed at the Post Office, he wired the Army Depot at Hannibal. Confirmation came back a short while later warning that Charles and his bunch was dangerous. "We was warned that they should be approach them damn cautiously. Charles and the others had tried to rob a Military Paymaster. When they caught 'em, they killed the Officer in charge and when they escaped, they nearly beat the guards to death, left 'em unconscious in the jail cell. Later one of the guards died and the reward went to $750. They abandoned their stolen horses in Pittsburgh. The Army believes that they may have worked their way down the Ohio River and if that's the case, he could be headed home all right. When they raised that reward, it tells me that they want those boys real bad. The uncle of the Officer killed is a Senator or something, he is offering another $250 reward, hell, he's even hired the Pinkerton Detective Agency to look for them. The Army said that they would pass on the descriptions of the others as soon as they got it from Washington. When I hear, I'll let you know and one more thing, Ty if I was you I wouldn't be trying to find them by yourself, that would be plain foolish, they sound like a mean lot."

"You haven't seen the Reverend Koppleman, have you?"

"No, I got the wire late yesterday afternoon. I headed out here early so as I could see you and get back. Now that the war is over there seems to be a hell of a lot more to do, I really opened a bag of worms when I contacted the Army. They sent me a dozen messages yesterday, before I got the one about Casey, I think I made a mistake letting them know that I was interested."

"I'll ride over and tell him what we have found out, is there anything more that I should tell him?"

"I don't know what it would be. I really haven't had time to think this one out. Son I want you to know that you showed me a thing or two about bein' a good detective and I thank you for that. I would never have looked in that box of fliers, probably just throwed them away. I'm going to look at the rest of them just as soon as I have time thanks for your help."

As the Constable rode off Ty said, "James can I borrow Duke to ride over to the Reverend's house, think I should tell him about Mr. Casey, the sooner, the better."

"Sure go ahead and take him but start him slow; he hasn't been ridden much here of late."

Ty felt like a million dollars riding Duke, his gait was smoother than Bucks and he stepped out real brisk. The horse had no problem keeping up the pace, at this rate he would be at the church before he knew it.

He found Reverend Koppleman working at the church, repairing a screen door. When he seen Ty he stopped and welcome him with a hand shake and asked how he had been. They sat on the steps of the church and Ty informed him of the Armies flier about the murder and all.

"That is a surprise to me I never would have expected to hear anything like that of one of ours, and then again, I never knew him all that well. Strange things happen in war it changes a lot of things, not just people. They say that war is hell and I hope that we never have to go through another one."

"Mr. Blake told me about the livestock being sold and the place was taken by the county for back taxes. I never gave a thought about her not paying her taxes but from what she told me she never had any money may not of even known that they had to be paid."

"The way she left her place, I don't know what to think. I feel sorry for what happened and nobody ever wants to see someone's home taken away. Which reminds me, when Mr. Blake was out this way, tending to the Casey business, he served an eviction notice to the Garretts, did he tell you that?"

"No it must have slipped his mind, with the news of Mr. Casey and all."

"He said that their taxes were in arrears. He also said that the place had been sold to the same outfit that bought the Casey's land, you remember the Garrett' place, it joins up with the Casey's land. The Garretts swear that they had kept their taxes up to date, the bank at Jamesville was suppose to be taking care of that for 'em, or so they say. The problem is the Garretts don't have a receipt to prove it, so there is little they can do. The constable can force 'em off any time the new owner wants. The land sold to a Land Company that I never heard of, the G. R. Land Company, of Hannibal. It's probably going on over where you live too, talking to members of my flock, it's apparently happening all around us."

Shaking hands again, Ty mounted Duke and the Reverend said, "That's a fine looking horse your riding."

"James rode him all the way from Pennsylvania, a fine riding horse, makes you fell kinda special setting up here, I called him Duke, he is like royal blood and I like he way he holds his head up and steps out like he is better than most."

"If there is any more news, I'll get it to you some how, take care of your self Reverend."

The ride back went faster than Ty wanted for riding Duke was like sitting on a cloud. The thought crossed Ty's mind, of just heading west and not looking back, he knew that he would never do that, but it was fun to dream.

Ma was just putting supper on the table when Ty rode in, washing up, they sat down to eat. After the prayers, they all ate in silence, it was obvious that something was bothering James.

When supper was finished, Ma said, "Out with it James, you look like you're about to bust, spit it out, lets hear it."

"The crops are lookin' good right now, the rain showers are hittin' us at the right time and the corn grubs ain't a problem yet. If ever thing goes well we will have a decent harvest. I just hope that were not in for a big surprise come fall. I'm afraid that the prices are goin' to drop bad and the cost of everything is goin' to go through the roof."

"Why do you say that, James people are going to buy things that they couldn't get during the war? In most cases, there will be more help on the farms and in the shops. People will be raising larger crops and there should be all kinds of bartering and trading going on. True they won't have much money this year but they still will be willing to make deals on better times to come. The price might drop a little from what it is now, but we can handle that."

James repositioned his chair and started by saying, "We've just went through a war that cost a lot of lives and money, who do you think is goin' to pay for this war? I know. It's goin' to be the little farmer, the small shopkeeper, and the people just scratchin' out a living. Our taxes and our prices are goin' to go up so high that you will choke on 'em. Then people will start losin' their farms and homes because they can't pay their taxes. Like Kevin said about the south, there will be money people from back East standin' in line to buy up the property for a little of nothin'. They will combine the small places with one another and make big places that will be more profitable. There won't be family farms anymore, just moneymakin' places like down south. The blacks won't be here to provide free labor but there will be plenty of poor, white folk's willin' to work for nothin' just to survive. I'm so sure about this that I would bet everything that it's goin' to happen."

After listening to James, Ty then told the family what the Reverend had said about all the places that were going back to the county. Then about the Garretts situation, "It seemed to the Reverend that only one company was buying up the land, The G. and R. Land Company of Hannibal."

Ma said, "Kevin, you mean to tell me that they could take your land right out from under you without giving you a chance to hold on to it, I don't believe that. Another thing I don't believe is that they can make us pay for a war we didn't want in the first place. That doesn't appear to be right, we scratched and did without these last four years and did the praying that the war would end and you tell us that we're going to have to lose our farm. I'd fight for this land, your daddy and I was the first to settle on Doanes Creek, oh, we had some neighbors, but they were a distance away. Besides all you boys were born here, this is your home and when I'm gone, the land is yours. I'd rather die first than see this ground change hands that way."

Kevin said, "Ma, how are we doin' on the taxes anyway, are they up to date or do we owe some on 'em?"

"The taxes are up to date; we made sure of that, we did without just to keep them paid. They are due now but we're going to Willow Springs the end of this week to pay them. We'll stop in Jamesville and check on the bank situation. Mr. Goodnight had offered to pay them out of our account like he was doing for some other people but I wanted to pay them myself, just to ease my mind, wanted to know that they were taken care of."

"The Garretts had done that same thing; Mr. Goodnight said that he would take care of their taxes too. The Reverend said that they didn't even get a receipt, to show that they had paid 'em. When they asked Mr. Goodnight said that he knew nothing about it."

"Boys, up until last Saturday I wouldn't of thought that Mr. Goodnight would say that he would do something and then not do it? We've known him at least for two or three years and we've never had a reason to distrust him before, he always has treated us fair. Besides, why would any friend or neighbor want our little farm bad enough to cheat us out of it?"

Mom was beside herself, not wanting to believe anything bad about an old friend. She continued to ask question of the three boys and thought on their answers. "Ty you know that last fall we put our crop money in the bank, it should still be there, now why would a man like Mr. Goodnight suddenly change?"

James spoke again, "Greed, Ma if there is a chance to make money, who would know it sooner than most, the banker. He also knows what places have the best land and has plenty of water. Besides and more importantly, he probable knows what places are behind on their taxes."

"When we get to town, we had better be careful about how we handle this; there really might be a good reason why he couldn't find your ledger, Ma."

"In all my born days I never thought that a friend, even if he is a banker, would think about stealing from us, we ain't got anything. I remember your Daddy saying that he hoped that we never got rich, cause then you had to worry about keeping it, if you stayed poor you could just enjoy life for what it was."

"Not to be nosy, but how much money was there in the bank." Kevin asked.

"There should be a little over forty-nine dollars, the taxes are, as I remember, eight dollars and some odd cents."

Early the following day they headed for town and as they rode toward town, they all were thinking the same thing, what if Mr. Goodnight couldn't find the ledger sheet and what if there was no money in the account, what would they do then?

Kevin spoke to no one special, "You haven't heard of the bank havin' trouble, have ya or maybe hear anything about some trouble that he was in before? I have a funny feelin' about this, way down in my bones, I'm sure that it will work it's self-out in the end but Damn it sure is strange that they only have one record of a person's money, it don't seem right somehow."

"The damn bank could have burnt down yesterday, we would never know unless someone thinks that were interested and rides out to tell us. I agree with Ma, who would want our little bit of money, sure it is a lot to us, but wouldn't be much to most people. There ain't enough to talk about, let alone brag about it." Ty answered.

No one wanted to confront Mr. Goodnight directly with their concerns so they decided that Ma would ask if he had found the account sheet, and they would go from there. If he produced it then there would be no problem, if not an explanation would be demanded. Silently they all hoped that everything would work out and a confrontation with Mr. Goodnight would not have to happen.

Tying Buck up at the hitch rail, in front of the bank Ma noticed that the door of the bank was standing slightly open and the closed curtain, which had closed "written" on it.

"That's strange; I've never seen that before the door has always been shut and this time of day the bank should be open."

James holding his hand up to stop the rest from going any further said, "Lets not rush into this, till we know what is goin' on in there, stay here while I check."

Approaching the open door very warily, he looked inside, seeing nothing, he then stepped inside, just as he entered the bank, James could hear load voices from behind a door with a sign identifying it as the office. Turning, he held his finger to his lips and signaled the rest to come into the bank.

Two voices, one much louder than the other, were angrily discussing some deal that they screwed up and why. The louder voice said "—brain in your god damn head. What in hell made you file on the Garretts place this soon, we talked about waiting and doing it all a once. I know that Drake is dumber than a jackass but he is smart enough to ask questions about why the taxes weren't paid. If the rest of the idiots that thought we were paying their taxes hear about this, there are going to be so god damn many questions asked, that Blake won't have to think. You dumb son of a bitch next time you check with me first, no there won't be a next time; we have to move now before this gets out. Financially we're not ready, but we got to salvage something, it's better than loosing it all."

"Roscoe you know that there was talk about the Garretts selling out when her old man didn't come home and I didn't want their place to be the only one we couldn't lock up. If we waited, the buyer would have found out about the taxes being due, there would have been questions that we would have had a hell of a time answering. It's her word against ours, she don't have a damn leg to stand on, no receipt, no written agreement, nothing."

Kevin, motioning for them to leave the bank, shut the door quietly behind him. Whispering he asked them to follow his lead, "Ma will introduce us, all but Ty of course and ask about her account, dependin' on the response, I will go one way or the other but I will get the money we got due us, that is for damn sure"

"What about the Garretts place, can we do anything to get their place back?" Ty was worried.

"We'll see about that too, just follow Kevin."

Knocking on the door softly at first and waiting a short time he knocked harder. As the door swung open, a man large enough to fill the entire doorway stood there with a smile on his face and a cigar in his hand. He greeted them with a slight bow, and apologized for not removing the closed sign.

"Mrs. O'Malley, come in." gesturing with his right hand. He went straight to his desk beside the teller's cage. He apologized again, this time for the cigar, "It's a nasty habit, but I can't seem to break it." Putting it out in a standing ashtray next to his desk, he invited her to set down.

Kevin looked around and not seeing a second man, figured he must still be in the office staying out of sight most likely, but listening sure as hell.

"I have good news for you we found your ledger sheet, it was just misplaced, I can show it to you if you like." Opening the drawer of the desk, he took out a yellowed card and handed it to Mrs. O'Malley. Ma looked at it momentary, and handed it to Ty.

While Ty looked at the card Ma said, "I would like you to meet my sons, you know Ty, this one is James and this one is Kevin they both were away fighting the war, but are now safely home."

Standing up he extended his right hand to them, "I knew that one of you had returned home but not both of you. I want to thank you for fighting this ridiculous war and protecting our civil rights. Who knows what would have happened if them Southerners would have won, thank you both again."

Looking at the calm appearing banker, Ty said, "There must be a mistake here it only shows that we have $4.54 cents and we know that is not right, we put more than that in here last year and we already had some in here from before."

"Let me see that ledger card."

Handing it to Mr. Goodnight and watching him study it while small beads of perspiration started to show on his forehead and upper lip. Twisting in his chair, he began his explanation of the history on the account. "The first deposit you made was in October of 1862, for twenty three-dollars correct?" Looking up he continued, "In April of last year you withdrew nine-dollars, correct leaving a balance of fourteen-dollars, for taxes as I recall." Ma silently agreed with the shake of her head, "Then in September of last year you again deposited thirty-five-dollars and fifty-cents bringing the new total up to forty-nine-dollars and fifty-cents. The last entry is a withdrawal for forty-five-dollars in January of this year, which accounts for the balance shown here."

Ma spoke very quietly when she responded to Mr. Goodnight's explanation by saying. "There was no withdrawal in January. Everything else is right except for the four cents, where did that come from and did someone sign for that with drawl? Don't someone have to sign for the money when it is taken out?"

"Why Mrs. O'Malley the four cents is the interest your money has earned and in a small bank as this, we never felt that we needed to request a signature for these maters. This is Arthur's writing; we will have to wait for his return to ask him he should be back later today."

With that Kevin, standing by the office door reached over and jerked it open exposing the man hiding there. Before anyone could say anything, Mr. Goodnight said, "Arthur what are you doing here your supposed to be in Willow Springs, explain yourself."

Caught completely unexpected, Arthur did not know what to say, he just stood there with his mouth open trying his best to come up with some logical answer, but he couldn't.

Grabbing Arthur's coat jacket, Kevin pulled him into the main bank. "I think this game has gone on long enough we know about the Land Company and some of your swindles. Even about your cheating of the Garretts and the others. Ma says that there should be forty-nine-dollars in here that is hers and I've never known my mother to tell a lie in her life, are you going to call her a lair now, I'd think on that one if I was you."

"Turn loose of Arthur this minute or I shall call the Constable, I know nothing about what you say. I resent the fact that you would even think it, Mrs. O'Malley. There might be a discrepancy with your account but there is no need to get violent, let us discuss this civilly."

"Are you tryin' to tell us that you're runnin' a clean bank here? What would you say if we told you that we overheard your argument, just now with Arthur? Do you remember what you said about Mr. Blake's intelligence, something about being a jackass; do you want to hear more?" Kevin growled.

Next, it was James turn, who slammed his knee against the desk drawer, just as Goodnight was pulling something out. Emitting a shallow scream, you could hear something heavy drop back into the drawer, his hand trapped inside. Cursing aloud, he said that he would charge them with bank robbery and angrily said that they would not get away with it.

"All we want is what is rightly ours. The way I see it you have two choices, give Ma her money now or we will shake it out of you, what is it goin' to be?" James asked as he slowly released the pressure on Goodnights hand.

"I'll give you your money, but don't ever come into this bank again or I will charge you all with extortion, is that clear?"

"You have our word on it," responded Kevin.

Speaking to the still shaken Arthur, Goodnight said, "Bring me the cash box so we will be rid of this rift raft." Counting out forty-nine-dollars and fifty-four-cents, he placed it on the desk in front of him, "Here is your money, now be damned."

As she stood, she asked if he would hand her the money, as she had when she entrusted it with him and she turned her palm up waited for the banker's response. She smiled as he picked up the money and dropped it in her hand.

James, still standing slightly behind the desk, told his mother to leave one dollar on the desk and wait outside for them. He said that he wanted to talk privately with Mr. Goodnight. As the door shut, James said, "Before we leave the bank today we will have a quit claim deed dated last week for, what was their names Ty, the Garretts? We heard you talkin' to Arthur so you know who we are referrin' to?"

Thoughts were racing through his mind like a summer windstorm, as Roscoe tried to think of a way out of this. Threats didn't seem to bother these people and with his only means of force was taken away he would do as they said; give them a quitclaim deed for the Garretts place, then as soon as they were gone he would run to Constables office and report a robbery. Finding a paper with printing on it, he proceeded to fill in the blanks; he signed it and started to give it to James. Before he could do it, Kevin reminded him that he needed a seal to make it legal. Frowning, he pressed it with his seal and handed it to James.

Looking it over James gave it to Ty and said, "Read this little brother and see if it says what it is suppose to."

Not knowing what to look for, Ty read the form aloud. "Quit Claim Deed" was the header. He seen it made out to the Garretts with a land description and signed by Roscoe Goodnight, President of the G and R Land Company. "Looks all right to me but I've never seen one before."

"I'm sure that Mr. Goodnight would not be so stupid as to make a mistake, now would you sir?"

Reaching for the deed, James said, "Ty, run down to Mr. Blake's office and fetch him over here right away."

"Now hold on here, there has got to be a way we can solve this without the law. Isn't there?"

With his face flushed and sweat rolling down his hound dog cheeks, he was now desperate; all of his plans were falling apart. "Boys would you like to make lots of money; I could see that it happened. Everything is in place for us to be the richest men in Missouri just a little more time and I will have enough money to buy a quarter of the state, you can join Arthur and me, there is no limit to what we will control. Think about it, no more dirt farming and no more living from hand to mouth, plenty of anything you ever wanted. Give it some thought."

"We will think on it while Ty here goes for the Constable, don't dilly dally kid."

The sound of the door closing was a death toll for Roscoe. Arthur looked at his boss for help but all he could see was a white handkerchief wiping the sweat from the broad forehead of a man trying desperately to salvage his life.

"Most of the places around here are to small to ever make a profit. If you could add these small pieces together, you could make a farming empire. Do you understand what I am saying, you could be part of it and the cotton plantations down south would be nothing to what we would have, money, power and respect, all of this could be yours you can't turn it down."

James feeling sorry for the damn fool standing there shook his head in wonderment, "Why would you steal from Ma, she didn't have much and what she had would be missed, you should have known that?"

"The war nearly broke me. The deposits just weren't enough to keep the doors opened. I started to borrow from some of the accounts that were more solvent, and then I got in to deep. Your Mom seems like a good manager I didn't expect her to need her money not till after I had time to return it, I never intended to keep your money it was sort of a loan."

"It's easy to say that after you been caught, I'm wonderin' what would have happened if you got to be as powerful as you expected; I'm thinkin' that Ma would have been out her money."

Arthur, white as a sheet stood there sobbing, saying repeatedly, "I knew that this wouldn't work, I trusted you and look what a mess you got us in."

"Shut up God Dammit keep your mouth shut."

"It was his idea from the beginning I never stole so much as a dime till I met him. This was a foolproof plan, it couldn't go wrong, could it you son-of-a-bitch? If we would have kept another set of records, like I said, we would not be in this mess now."

The door opened and Ty walked in, followed by Mr. Blake and then Ma.

The Constable looked first at Roscoe and then at James. "The boy here tells me that something damn wrong is going on here, Roscoe; can you explain what it is?"

"Thank god your here Blake these people, Roscoe pointing to James and

Kevin, were here to rob my bank at gunpoint, and in plain daylight. They were about to help themselves to all my money."

"Whoa now, slow down, who's got the gun?"

Kevin holding both hands palm up said, "The only gun you will find here is in his desk drawer he tried to use it on us after he admitted to stealin' Ma's money."

"I want to see my barrister before I say another word."

"Would that be Malcolm Stearns, or someone in Willow Springs?"

He started to say Malcolm, but remembered that his account was short too.

"Mr. Wainwright in Hannibal, I will send a courier to request his assistance immediately, he should be here no later than tomorrow and he will remedy this problem in short order. Upon his arrival, I will bring him by your office, you can be assured."

"Mrs. O'Malley are you going to charge Roscoe and Arthur here with bank fraud?"

"I certainly am, they're both crooks and should be locked up for a long time; it's not just us that they swindled, it sounds like a lot of other folks too. Anyone that trusted Mr. Goodnight, most likely got cheated."

"Roscoe, you too Arthur, come with me you're going to have a stay in my jail, I'll send word today to Mr. Wainwright by the telegraph wire. Lock up your bank and you may want to leave your personal items here in the bank that goes for your money, stick pin, and rings."

The expression on Goodnights face and the fear in his eyes had him frozen to his seat, he tried to speak but nothing would come out. The more he tried, the redder his face got and the more he stuttered, finally, he blurted out that he didn't want to go jail and begged for mercy. "I'll be ruined, I'll lose everything, isn't there some way we can work this out so that I can stay out of jail? I got some money that I could give to you; I could even make you partners in the bank, all of you. We could just forget that this happened and no one would be the wiser." Tears streaming down his face and slobbering at the corners of his mouth he added, "I can't stand to stay a day in jail, it would kill me, I can't stand small places."

"I think that is something that should have been thought out before you decided to screw people out of their life's work. You knew sooner than later that someone was going to find out about what you were doing if you didn't, you should have. I'm tired of talking, let's go."

"You're throwing away a fortune, help me, we can still make a deal."

Looking whipped and showing defeat, he got to his feet and said just loud enough for Ty and James to hear, "If I ever get out, you bastards are dead."

Walking to the Constable's office, Ty said, "What is going to happen to the people who have money in the bank, now that it is closed?"

"I don't really know since I've been constable no bank has ever went closed before. I guess that the State will come and take over, at least check over the books and such. They will probably figure up all the loss's and pay any honest bills then most likely, the State will have a sale and will divide the remaining money to the depositors, everyone will most likely lose some money. Thank God, I didn't have more than a few dollars in the place; I never trusted banks or bankers. How much does he owe you folks?"

"Just a dollar but that is enough to hang the son of a bitch ain't it?"

"I guess it is we'll find out won't we?"

"By the way Mr. Blake we found a Quit Claim Deed on his desk signin' it back to the Garretts. Can you get the deed to 'em, don't forget to tell 'em that it has to be recorded."

"I'll be damned; I know that the son of a bitch would not have signed this deed on his own and if I were smart, I'd asked how it came about that it was just lying on his desk. I might some day but for now, I'm just to damn busy. It will do me proud to tell Mrs. Garrett that she won't have move, it hurt me bad to serve it on them in the first place, thank you boys."

Placing the bankers in the only cell of the tiny jail, the constable handed them a sack. He told them to empty their pockets of everything that they might have forgotten. After the bankers had complied, they were searched for anything that they may of missed or refused to give up voluntarily. Mr. Blake even took Roscoe's cigars and matches.

"Why can't I keep my cigars are you going to smoke them yourself, you son-of-a-bitch?"

"Hell, after that I might just smoke them all. I really was more concerned about you burning the place down, it's been done you know."

Having a prisoner was not a common thing in Jamesville and Mr. Blake was making sure that everything was all right before he left the prisoners, to get some water for them. Outside he thanked the O'Malley's for what they had uncovered, "The community will thank you when the word gets out."

"Hell if that is the case lets head for home before a ruckus starts I don't want to be here when all the questions and thank you start," Kevin said as he looked at Ma and his two brothers.

Grabbing the reins and swatting old Buck on the butt, trying to get away before the whole damn town found out that their Banker was in jail. It didn't take long to be free of the town and alone on the road home.

"As I think on it the more it scares me what might have happened." She fell silence for a while and then as if nothing had happened said, "We'll have to make a trip to Willow Springs in the next day or two to pay our taxes, when should we go?"

The spring days passed, and the summer days began. Work on the farm grew tiresome, as it always did. The remaining cow had given birth to a female calf. Six head of cows, "Hell, we about got us a herd," Ty said. With Kevin and James helping, things went smoothly and there was time for horseplay and goofing off. It was just plain fun to have someone to talk and laugh with. Mom was a new person, her eyes sparkled and she had a sense of humor, a side of his mother that Ty hadn't seen very often in the past few years. With the three of them working the fields there was time to swim, wrestle, box and fix the little things that never got done? Ty was sorry now that they hadn't planted more acreage. James' arm was getting stronger; he could now do most anything.

The trip to Willow Springs completed and life had gotten back to normal. An occasional visitor would stop by; thank them for what could have been a disaster for the small community if they had not stopped it. Everyone that stopped wanted to know everything that had happened and the standard answer was that as soon as he knew that he was caught he confessed, that was all there was to it.

It was the middle of the summer and the heat was unbearable. The three boys were swimming in the pond when James said to Ty, "What do you want to do the rest of your life, I can tell it in your eyes that you don't want to spend it here, what would you do and where would you go, be honest with us?"

Ty thought that this is the time to tell them about his dream to go west. They had brought it up so it wouldn't be like he was running out on them. He had been thinking on this every since Kevin had gotten home. He wanted to go as far as he could and see whatever there was to see, if it meant only going as far as the City of Kansas or St. Joseph, he still wanted to go. He hoped to see the mountains, but they were a long ways off and he didn't know if he could stay away that long, he knew that he would miss Mom and the boys, but he really would like to try it.

"Well I've been thinking about going west, maybe to the City of Kansas or somewhere. I'd like to see some of the country west of here, the grasslands beyond the Missouri sound so unreal. They say that you can see for miles and never see a tree. There are buffalo herds you can't see the start or the end of and can't even see to the other side of 'em, do you believe that, can that be true? I'd like to go see for myself what is beyond here. You boys have been east; south and can tell all about them places, I want see what lies west of here. I've been thinking that this might be the right time to go, we short planted our fields this year and you two should have no trouble in harvesting it by your self, hell Ma and I did it for four years. The only problem is that Ma just got us all three together not so long ago, will she let me go now.

"Are you plannin' to be gone a long time or just go look around and come home trip."

"James, if you were me, could you just go look around and say, I'll be back in a week, I don't know how long it will take me. It's not that I don't love you guys and Ma, it's just that I hear these stories and I got to go look for myself."

"Boy, we don't want to see you go but it sounds like you've given a lot of thought to this here trip. We'll handle Ma for you, don't worry; just give us time to set it up." Kevin smiled and winked at James.

Ma was still not sure that her baby son was ready to go out on his own. Not knowing where he was going or when he would be back, for that matter if he would be back. She tearfully agreed to let him go, and gave him a five dollar gold piece. James offered him Duke and after much discussion, Ty agreed. With the urging of all three, he accepted James army rifle and knife, Ty planned to leave early the following day.

After a breakfast of eggs, bacon and fried potatoes, Ty was busy saddling Duke when Mr. Blake and four riders rode into the yard. The four riders stayed in the saddle while the Constable dismounted to speak with Ty and his brothers.

"Morning boys, is every thing all right out this way?"

"Ty is gettin' ready to go see the world, but the rest of us is fine what brings you out this way so early?" James asked.

"Goodnight broke out of the Willow Springs jail last night and some of the folks thought they seen him leaving Willow Springs and headed for Jamesville. We figure that he had some money hid out somewhere, probable in his house, we found his jail clothes there and the horse he rode from Willow Spring in his shed. Some folks in Jamesville thought that they had seen him ride out of town heading west but knowing he was in jail, they assumed that it couldn't be him. If we can take their word for what they thought they saw, then we think he was riding a big bay horse from Hanson Livery, Gill was out getting a load of hay and wasn't going to be back until late. Long here, said that he remembered the horse, Gill had just traded for him about a week ago. It was to dark to pick up any tracks, so we waited till sun up. Seein' as he holds you fellers responsible for his trouble, I thought I would stop and see if you had seen anything, wanted to warn you to be on the watch for him. We think that he is most likely on his way to St. Louie or there-abouts."

"How did he break out?"

"Old man Peterson was taking him to the out house when the son-of-a-bitch jumped the old jailer and took off. Peterson's in bad shape but still holding on, at least he was this morning. Be on the watch for him, I think he is crazy."

"Did I hear right Ty, you leaving, if I might ask where to?"

"West, I don't know how far yet I'm just going to look and see what life is like somewhere else, I'll be back, I'm sure of that." Looking at his mother and choking back a tear.

"Well we're headed that way you can ride with us as far as you like, right boys?" asking the group gathered behind him.

"I'll do that; just give me another minute or two Mr. Blake it's a little hard to leave when you've spent your whole life here. I didn't think that it would be this tough."

"We'll head on out and you can catch up when your ready."

Ma and the boys stood just outside the barn door, as Ty mounted Duke.

The tearful good-byes said and the only thing left was to turn and ride away. It had sounded so exciting just moments ago, now that the time had come, it was difficult to turn away. Knowing that you were leaving those that you loved and heading out into a world that was unknown to you.

Pulling Duke's head around, waving goodbye, trying desperate not to cry Ty rode from the yard. Mom was shouting after him to be careful, and to come home soon and Kevin yelled that they loved him and to watch out for himself.

Riding slow, trying not to catch up with the rest until the lump in his throat disappeared. Without looking back, he raised his left arm, gave a final wave and speaking to Duke, he said, "Well old horse we're on our way to somewhere, we just don't know where. It's going to be just you and me and I'm dumber than a stick on what you can handle day in and day out. You'll just have to let me know some how, what you can take and what you can't. I think the two of us are going to be a good team. Do you s'pect we should pick up the pace, got to catch up with Mr. Blake and the rest of the posse, I guess there is no going back now, is there?"

Mr. Blake and the Constable from Willow Springs, Mr. Adams, rode in the front and behind them rode Bill Webster, Adams' deputy; Jack Long that worked for Mr. Blake, bringing up the rear was Ty and Duke. With the plodding of the horses and the squeak of the saddle leathers, Ty could hear very little that the others said. That was all right, he was just riding with them until either they caught Mr. Goodnight or his trail turned from the west to the south or north. Ty was not committed to the entire chase, it was only that they were going in the direction, when that changed they would part company.

CHAPTER 5
Spring 1866

The sun its winter brightness concealed by clouds of snow had not been seen for two days. The relentless, freezing, northwest winds hurled the snow with a biting force against the frosted windows. The snow caked its self on everything it touched including a man's skin and clothing. If a person happened to be caught outside in a storm like this, it was akin to committing suicide and visibility was impossible. The blizzard winds beat against the side of the house, leaving small deposits of snow on the inside corners of the loose fitting windows.

Ty had found refuge in this small but clean room, of the Simpson's boarding house. The bare walls of the room were barriers from the freezing cold winds that shook the entire building. The lone frosted window, hidden behind a curtain of gaudy red material, gave Ty something to do. To pass the time, in the lonely room, he would scratch small holes in the frost with his fingernails until he could peer out of the small opening. After the ridiculous effort, he could see nothing but the blowing snow. The cold crept into the tiny room and for additional warmth; Ty draped the bed quilt over his shoulders. He saw his breath as a small vapor cloud, every time he exhaled. Sitting on his bed, he wondered if the storm would ever end, the cramped quarters were all right for a night but this was too long. He ate his meals downstairs with the other tenants. Mostly sales representatives, they sat around the potbelly stove, talking about nothing and questioning everything. Ty avoided them by spending his time alone in his room.

The storm had held off just long enough for the completion of the railroad from St. Louis to the City of Kansas. People still preferred calling it by its original name, Westport Landing, the name City of Kansas just didn't ring right. With the exception of the pro-slavers who wanted the city to be part of the state of Kansas.

The storm had given him a few more days to think about his future, to go west with Rocky or play it safe and work for Mr. Perry. The talk had been that the tracks would continue on to St. Joseph but the expense of building a bridge over the Missouri River had dampened that idea for now. Mr. Perry had offered him a job in Illinois when this one was finished and the money he could save would help at home, if he ever made it back.

A nagging thought came back; did he really want to partner up with Rocky and was he ready? If he went west, would he ever see his family again, would they ever know if he was alive and living his dream? The decision was easy but making it was another story, he still had to convince himself that he was ready.

Railroad work had been hard, working seven days a week and each day lasted from first light to dark. You were up before sunrise and didn't eat the last meal of the day till well after the sun had set. After working all day and eating whatever fare they served, everyone scrambled to find a place to spread his bedroll. The tents provided by the company were little more than filters to keep out the rain and snow. All but a few of the men had spent their weeks pay on blankets along with waterproof ground covers, the ones that didn't certainly did the following week. Nothing could keep the cold from penetrating through the blankets, ground sheet and your clothing didn't seem to help either. Like rain, the snow, as it melted, ran under the walls of the tent and soaked everything lying on the ground. On real blustery nights, you were lucky if you could find a boxcar to sleep in, the more bodies that the car held, the warmer it was. The smell of the dirty unwashed made you forget about the cold. Huge metal barrels, along side of the tracks, were kept burning all night, they were hand warmers primarily, but did provide some light.

The days were different; the mere effort of doing your job warmed you. The Superintendent made sure that there was no loafing once the day's work started. The rail grade laid out and shaped in warmer weather then the ballast, ties, and the rails placed last when the temperature had little effect on the material used. Working through the winter was hell but with the warmer days of spring, things went smoother and you could see progress made. The last trestle, just outside of Westport Landing, delayed by the weather and everyone was surprised when it was completed just as the tracks arrived.

The snowstorm had stopped construction on Friday, just as the main track was to tie into the switchyard. The crews lined up and paid their wages, thanked for sticking around to see the job completed and some received a bonus. Ty was one of the lucky ones and received ten extra dollars.

It was Sunday afternoon and no sign that it was going to break soon. Duke worried him, although he knew that he was safe in the stable behind the boarding house where there was plenty of feed and water. He felt thankful that Mr. Perry had let him keep him in the railroad corral as the tracks moved steadily west. It saved Ty a lot of worry and he could see Duke from time to time.

Loneliness had never bothered Ty but being laid up in this room, with the walls closing in and the smell of the stale air was getting to him. The cost of the room was not much but he was using up money that he was saving to outfit himself. If he crossed over, he would need a packhorse, packsaddles and all the vitals that were necessary to get him started. He figured that it was better to spend the twenty cents a day rather than be out in the cold, struggling to survive.

The hard-core railroad workers didn't mind at all they just held up in the nearest salon drinking and eating, to stay warm. They would remain there till it was time to find another job or they went broke.

They fought at the drop of a hat, brothers against brother and best friend against best friend it didn't matter. The fighting came natural to a railroad man; it just went with the job. There was three ways to get a better job on the railroad, work your ass off, and hope that your boss would see what you accomplished or with just a few dollars, paid under the table; you could buy a better job. The easiest way was to fight your way to the top with your fists. If a man had a job, that you wanted and if you could whip him, the job was yours. Ty had learned very fast that your hands and feet was your ticket to a better job, whipped twice was enough. Fair fighting was not going to cut it, everything went hands, feet, clubs, tricks and the one that caught Ty off guard was the biting. Ty had learned the hard way, and now even the old timers didn't mess with him.

The last one that challenged him was a young man maybe four years Ty's senior. He was heavier than Ty, by fifty pounds and he was about three inches taller, a Tennessee boy by the name of Zack Taylor. He was from the riverbank area known as the Muddy Hell and had been fighting all of his life.

After a series of advancements, most with the aid of his fists, Ty was in charge of the inventory of rails and ties. Ma's determination that Ty get a schoolhouse education helped here, this job you needed ciphering, reading and writing to inventory the supplies.

Zack, prodded by his friends to go after Ty's job, walking up with an air of invincibility and said, "O'Malley you've had this job too damn long it's made you soft. I think that I will trade jobs with you, is it mine?"

Ty nervously shuffled his feet; he dropped his eyes, as if to give up instead brought his right fist straight up from the ground, right in to Zack's lower jaw. As the blow landed, Zack's head rocked backwards, with a loud crack causing Ty to think that he had broken his neck, but he knew better. Zack let out a roar, spit blood on the ground at Ty's feet, but before he could recover Ty had hit him with his left and again with his right hand knocking him down.

Rising up on one knee, he picked up a four-foot length of wood used to keep the rails separated when they were stacked. Swinging at Ty's head and missing, Ty again landed two blows to Zack's midsection, you could hear the wind rush out of his lungs and by all rights, and the fight should be over.

Squatting on one knee, he spit out another mouth full of blood. Rubbing his jaw said, "You shouldn't have done that boy, now I'm going to cut you up real bad." As Zack stood up, he reached behind him and drew a knife from his belt. He pointed it at Ty's gut and began to circle to his right staying in a low crouch ready to spring at any opening that Ty gave him.

There was encouragement yelled to both men. In the excitement of the event, half of the spectators were yelling for Zack "To gut the son-of-a-bitch, stick him good." The remaining men were yelling to Ty that he had a knife, "Watch out for the flip," they cried. Ty knew that the flip was when you tossed the knife from hand-to-hand to confuse the other man on where the strike would come from.

A stocky man wearing a buckskin shirt, held up a knife of about equal proportions, and flipped it to Ty. He caught it by the grip and whirled around to see Zack hesitate only for a moment, as he glanced over his right shoulder, wanting to be sure of his footing.

Having never being in a knife fight before Ty thoughts reminded him that he should not get to excited, take it easy, and let him make the first move, concentrate on his eyes." With that, thought just about out, Zack lunged at Ty's stomach. The point of the sticker only inches away, Ty side stepped, and brought his knee up to make contact with Zack's arm. At the same time brought the heel of his knife down, pinching Zack's forearm between the knee and the knife. The impact made a sickening sound as the bone snapped, breaking the arm, just above the wrist. The cracking of the bone sounded like a rifle shot and Zack fell to the ground, letting out a blood-curdling scream. "You son of a bitch, you broke my God damn arm, damn you to hell it hurts god damn bad, I've got to get to the Doc, son-of-a-bitch it hurts."

Unable to move his arm across his chest gingerly he walked away, holding his broken arm with the other hand, leaving his fallen knife where it lay.

The crowd had turned silent as they witnessed the end of the fight. One man near the front of the group said, "Kill the son of a bitch, give him the same medicine that he was going to give you. Any bastard that would pull a knife on another should be gutted out like a God damn hog."

Ty turned slowly looking at the man with obvious disgust, a look that froze the man and he lowered the knife then as an after thought, he lifted the weapon and examined it for the first time. It was remarkable similar to James's, it was about twelve inches long, with a blade of two inches. From the hilt, it curved gracefully to a point and sharpened like a razor. The top four inches also honed into a cutting edge. It seemed important not to damage such a weapon by dropping it. He located the owner and reversing his grip handed it back then realizing he had been holding his breath, he exhaled and said, "Thanks."

Looking at the stunned crowd, "The fights over, the man needs some help." The fight had lasted less than three minutes and Ty walked away as if it was no big deal.

He moved over to a stack of wooden ties, as if to go back to work but when he was safely out of sight, he started to shake; he didn't think he would ever stop. This had been his first taste of a knife fight, but some how he knew that it would not be his last.

A voice said, "You fought a damn good fight son, fightin' don't appear to be new to you?" The voice was that of the leather shirt, he carried the knife tucked in his belt while carrying Zacks in his left hand. As soon as the stranger spoke, the shakes ended, Ty was his old self again. "Just a warnin', I would watch my back trail real close if I were you, I think you made an enemy."

"I fought some as a kid, mostly with my two brothers but never felt that I was fightin' for my life till this time." Looking the stranger over from leather boots to his coonskin cap, he went on, "I had to learn to fight for real when I went to work for the damn railroad. Either you learn to fight or you're married to the handle of a spike mall the rest of your life. Thanks for the use of your knife; my brother had one just about like it. When I left home he gave it to me but I didn't think that I would be needin' one today."

The two men stood, facing one another each one sizing up the other. "Why do you think I made an enemy, he called me out and lost that is all there is to it. It has happened before and will happen again don't see why this one is any different. I've been in other fights since goin' to work for this railroad, when they were over we just went along as if nothing happened, this won't be any different, everyone will forget about it by tomorrow. Thanks again for the use of your knife and the warning, guess I had better introduce myself, I am Ty O'Malley from east of here."

"My name is Seth Buntrock, most call me Rocky. Son you made that fellow look like a greenhorn, he won't forget that. He never landed a punch or so much as scratched you, he won't forget that either. To some people and Zack is one of 'em, bein' the big man means everything. They win a few fights and suddenly it turns them into bullies, a damn pain in the ass to everyone, watch him; you ain't seen the last of him."

"The sound of your voice tells me that you're not from around here, it's none of my business but are you Irish?"

"I sure as hell ain't a goddamn Mick, no offense O'Malley; I'm Scottish to the bone, by birth, but mountain man at heart. I've tried both sides of the river, civilized and the out yonder; I sure as hell like the last best by a damn sight. As soon as this job is over I'll be headed back to them wild and beautiful mountains, I don't belong on this side of the river anymore, never did, I guess. As soon as I get my poke together and my supplies lay in, I'm a gone child, too many people around here to please and cater too."

Ty's eyes got wide and the excitement showed in his voice as he accepted Seth's apology about the Irish. Anxiously he asked Seth, "How far west have you been?"

"I've been north to Fort Pierre and spent some time in the Sioux country even went to their sacred mountains that they call the Paha Sapa. Then up to the start of the Yellowstone and into Blackfoot territory, south to the salt-water lake that Jim Bridger found and came back to Westport Landin' by the way of the Plate River. I covered a lot of ground in the three years I was out there but there still is a lot I ain't seen, I intend to see it all some day, if I can keep my parts together."

"They tell me that it's not what it used to be out there. Some that I've talked to even says that it's getting to crowded and all tore up. I've always thought about going west, out into a land that I've heard tell is as big and wild as anything you ever could dream possible. I want to go where there is no folks, to clutter up the countryside, is there any places left like that Rocky? I heard about the Dakotas and the stories about the big mountains, I want to see what living out there is all about, you know just to get lost in the grass and mountains. It must be different being alone and having only yourself to account for hell, I know that it's got to be a damn hard life, but I'd like to try it."

"Oh there's still land that is not been trodden over but it's not like it was. It wasn't long ago that when you crossed over the Missouri, you was alone, not anymore, times have changed." As he stopped and looked away, you could see the sadness in his eyes of something that was gone forever.

The silence seemed eternal and Ty thought that the conversation was over. He still had questions that needed answered and hoping to keep Rocky talking Ty asked, "What would a man need if he was to go up to the Dakotas, or maybe the high mountains?"

Rubbing his chin and winking at Ty he said, "I guess that you would have to be a little crazy like me. I've been to both, the high mountains I liked the most. Ain't no way of tellin' a man how it is, you got to experience the feeling yourself. Oh, I guess that every man probably sees and feels 'em different but to save my soul, I can't figure why I ever came back to this side, times were changing and I guess it was because I was kinda scared and maybe a little lonesome. I had a run in with the Blackfeet Tribe and it didn't sit well so I came back to see if I was missin' anything, found that I was the mountains."

"Blackfeet Injuns don't take kindly to strangers that horn in on their huntin' grounds as a matter of fact they get down right mean about it." Again, the faraway look crept into his eyes, and you could all most see his thoughts, as he relived the past in his mind. A smile crossed his lips and he continued, "They get just about as mad when one of their lady folk takes a shine to a white man that was about all of me that they could take, so they decided that I wasn't welcome anymore."

"That is another story, a long one at that, I'll hold back on that one till we have more time, I best be getin' back to work, if I want to keep this job. If we have time some day and ifin' we cross trails, I will tell you all about them Blackfeet."

Laughingly he slapped Ty on the back "Take care of yourself and watch your backside."

Turning to walk away, Perry the track supervisor, interrupted. "I guess I missed the fight but looking at you, I'd say that it wasn't much of one, there isn't a mark on you O'Malley I'm thinking that the other guy looks worse—right. Buntrock, what in the hell are you doing here, you're not going to test old man O'Malley here are you? I hope to hell not, cause one fight a day is all this crew can stand, we still got to get the job done. Besides, I saw this man here get whipped twice before, when he first came to work and I don't expect to see him get whipped again so don't waste your time Buntrock, get back to work."

As Buntrock walked away, "Do I look like a pilgrim to you; it was good talkin' to you O'Malley."

Before Ty could get started on his way, the Super said, "Ty I want to talk to you, in the next few weeks, work on this railroad will wind down and I'll head north. I have a job waiting for me in Illinois it will run through the rest of the spring and well into the fall, I'm not working any more winter jobs, I'm getting to old I guess. What I need to know is if you want to go with me, you're welcome too. I like how you're put together and I know where I stand with you, how about it? You can call your own shots and you would be working directly for me, kinda like my trouble shooter."

Ty thought for a length of time, knowing all along what his answer was, but not wanting to hurt the mans feelings. "Mr. Perry, I would if I hadn't made other plans. I plan to go west as soon as this job is finished and I can get my gear put together. If things don't work out, I'll let you know. I thank you for asking, it makes a man feel good that you thought of me."

That evening after eating his supper Ty went looking for Rocky, as he strolled by the burning barrels, men would yell at him with various comments about how he handled himself during the fight. One man stood up, offered his hand and said, "In all my forty six years of living I ain't ever seen a fight like that, son you fairly well kick the shit out of that bully, and he had it coming too. With only one working hand, he'll probably not be cutting such a wide swathe for a day or two." Ty shook his head in acknowledgment, and continued on his way. The thought went through his head wondering what Zack would do now that he couldn't work for the company anymore, with one hand; there wasn't much he could do.

Seeing the broad back encased in the fringed leather shirt, and knowing that he had found Rocky, he began to think about how he was going to approach the subject of going west with him.

Rocky was standing at a burning coal barrel, trying to keep his hands warm, talking with two other men that Ty did not know. Seeing Ty, Rocky stepped aside saying, "Hello O'Malley, there is room right here, you will have your back to the wind and the smoke won't be in your face. Ellis Brink and Tom Cassidy, this is Ty O'Malley."

"Saw you today, sure glad that it wasn't me you took your hurt out on. That was some fight to bad Ellis here didn't get to see it, he was back getting a load of ballast."

"Things always happen when I'm not around, damn it anyway, I wish that I could have seen it."

"It wasn't something that I was looking for, I never thought of myself as a fighter. Grow'ed up with a pair of brothers, both bigger than me, helped some. Right now I would just like to forget that it happened and go about my business."

Rocky scratched his head and with a glint in his eye said, "What is on your mind Ty, it wouldn't be more questions now would it?" Not waiting for an answer, but lowered his head, when he looked up he began to talk, "Men have there own reasons for goin' west its nobodies business what those reasons are, some go just to get lost; others go to find their place. I would guess that most go for the excitement of doing what others haven't done. If it's the excitement you're looking for, I can help you with that, where ever I go, excitement seems to go with me."

Tom asked, "Is this a personal conversation, if it is we will leave?"

"No need for that, I just meet Rocky today and found that he has been west to the mountains and that is what I aim to do when this job is finished. He was telling me about why he left 'em and came back to this side. That was before we got interrupted this morning, I was hoping that he would tell me more."

"I told you that the Blackfeet had a mean disposition didn't I, well to go along with their disposition, they got rules and laws that everyone has to follow, hell they will run their own kind off, if they mess up. Man or woman caught or accused of being unfaithful gets marked up really bad, have to carry the sign the rest of their lives. They got other laws about hunting, attending councils and even what place you fall in when you move camp.

I screwed up when I spent the winter held up with one of the war chief's daughter, she was a good one, Evenin' Star was."

You could see a look of sadness flood his eyes, as he stared deeper into the burning barrel. What he saw, I'll never know, when he looked up again, the corner of his eyes were moist, momentarily reflected the red and orange flickering flames. With a slight brush of his hand, they disappeared and he went on with his story. "Shortly after spring had come, her and me, was packing up to go and that's when her pappy decided I wasn't good enough for his daughter but really it was cause I didn't have any horse's to trade for her. A woman like her would bring seven or eight, and maybe a couple of buffalo robes."

"They didn't ask me to leave but they do have a funny way of saying goodbye, those Blackfeet do, there is no chance of a second visit. They strip you down, to your bare skin, moccasins too, run you through a gauntlet all the while; they beat you with clubs, switches and anything that's handy, the Squaws do the most damage, they beat me good, they thought that I was dead and so did I."

"They must have dragged me some distance from the camp, how far I'm not sure. I'm a guessin' that I laid there for the rest of the day, and part of the night. The next thing that I know'ed is the rain hittin' my face and a coyote or a camp dog a sniffing around me, probably thinkin' that they had an easy meal. I guess that when I moved, it scared 'em off."

"I tried to sit up and couldn't, just rollin' over on my stomach took a lifetime. I finally got my head up and seen the camp fires off in the distance. I know'ed that they would check for my body, come mornin' and I didn't want to be here if they did, one gauntlet was a plenty, I had to find me a hidey hole and soon."

"I couldn't sit up or stand, so I started to roll and crawled away from the fires. I know'ed this country pretty damn well, knew that there were ravines and creases off in the direction that I was headed. If I could get to a deep one, it just might give me enough cover to hide. I was at it for what seemed like hours then I started to slide rather than roll, must of fell for ten or fifteen feet. Think I either passed out again from the fall, or maybe from exhaustion. Later I found that I was in a fairly deep ravine full of brush and sharp rocks."

"The rain was falling harder, and I knew that was good, anything to slow them damn savages up. My muscles were starting to come around. I crawled and pulled myself into a thick patch of plum bushes, tried to make myself as small as I could. It wasn't long before I dozed off for a time and woke up sudden like; the water in the crease was risin', and moving damn fast."

"The only thing that was keepin' me there was the bushes and I figured it was worth the gamble to get further away, so I crawled out and let the water carry me downstream. It was a ride akin to the gauntlet, the rocks and the branches cuttin' at my skin, till I was as raw as fresh meat."

"Something brought me to an abrupt stop, weeds and bushes must have formed a dam. I decided that I wasn't going any further, I hurt so bad that death sounded good right then."

"Pullin' myself to the side, I tried to cover up with what I could dig out with my hands and hopin' that the mud would stop some of the bleedin'."

"I fell asleep, and was awakened by the voices of the Blackfeet warriors, they was lookin' for this child. By the sound of it, they were all on horseback, riding as the young braves liked to do, racin' back and forth and havin' more fun showin' off, than findin' me."

"They must not of felt that I was worthy of an all out search and that didn't hurt my feelin's a damn bit. After a short while, they rode off laughin' and talkin' about how full the wolf was that dragged me off and ate me."

"I first felt the top of my head and found that my hair was still there, last thing I remembered for the rest of the day, must have passed out or fell asleep, I don't rightly know which one. That night I made my way down the now muddy draw, sleepin' in the daytime and movin' at night. I came on a stream that I figured would run into Yellowstone. I spent the most part of two days braidin' wild grapevines into ropes that I could use to tie a couple of dead trees together for a raft. I found a tree that had been hit by lightning and broke off a piece for a paddle."

"I barely had the strength to get the logs into the water, but when I did, there was no holdin' back. I sure as hell didn't need to paddle, so I used it to keep me headed down river and not just spinnin' in the current."

"The Yellowstone moves mighty quickly, in those narrow canyons but thank god, Fort Mackenzie sets on a big old slow bend of the river."

"When I came around that big bend and seen old Fort Mackenzie I yelled and sent up a holler that a painter cat would be proud of."

"Old Mac took me in and gave me some whiskey and fed me till I past out from eatin'. He said that I slept for two full days then woke up hungry as a horse and wantin' to eat again, just like I never missed a beat."

"It took me a bit of time to heal up, big old scabs covered my body and when I moved, they cracked open soakin' the old leathers that Mac had given me, damn near turned 'em red. Later on, he gave me a rifle and a broke down horse and I headed for Fort Bridger, down on the Platte, with two other gents, we had it in our minds to headquarter there. When we arrived, we found old Jim was gone, he heard that someone found gold in Montana territory, on the Ruby River. Folks were outfittin' themselves and heading north all wanting to be the first there and make their fortunes."

"We knowed what this would do to the tribes up there, the Crow, Flatheads and the Blackfeet weren't goin' to look to kindly on white's trespassin' on their lands, muddyin' up their streams, rivers, and such. Gold Miners crawlin' over mountains and draws, like bugs on a shit pile, we didn't want no part of that, and we'd learned that kind of gold ain't worth it. The miners went north and we headed down the Platte for St. Louie, with what pelts the gents had."

"That is about it, I needed to put together a new pack, so I took this here job, needed money for what it is that I would be takin' with me. I'm headed west as soon as this railroad is built and when we hit Westport Landin' all you're going to see is my elbows and my ass a headed west."

"When you crossed over was it by yourself or did you go with a party?

What is the best way, overland or by river boat?"

"Hell, now you can just sign on with a train of wagons headed for Oregon, safer and you will have company, get off whenever you like. It's not my cup of tea, but I can't speak for everyone. We went overland some on horse back and some on foot. I was about your age when I made my crossin', there was fourteen of us and we were out to make our fortune in gold and furs. We knew that the fur market had dried up, but we figured that it would come back, there was a lot of talk about gold in the mountains, and seemed right at the time. We figured that if we didn't find the yellow stuff, we could always bring home a load of furs. Not beaver and such, but fox, mink and the like. Were we in for a surprise, we weren't but a week out when the boys afoot called it quits; it was hard to keep up with us on horseback. With 'em carryin' all their provisions in a backpack was to damn tough, so that left just eight of us to go lookin' for our fortune."

"Why didn't you go up the river on one of those boats I heared about, Tom and me were talking about 'em just a day or two ago?"

"If you get on a paddle wheeler, it's to damn expensive and a flat bottom won't sail upstream so you have to drag it, too damn much work, besides we all wanted to see and live off the land."

"What about the rest of your bunch did they make to the mountains?"

"All but one, poor son-of-a-bitch's horse got scar't by a little old rattlesnake and throwed him, he broke his neck. We laid him in a washout and caved in the bank about all we could do."

"Did you stick together after that?"

"Till we got to what's called the Bighorn River country. Three of our bunch decided that is as far as they wanted to go, wanted to put their stamp on them there mountains and they didn't want to go no further. It was what they were lookin' for all a long and they knowed it. Strange how different things jump up and bite a man. Those three had come a long way and knew that River was what they was lookin' for. The four of us was still lookin' toward the high mountains, could see 'em in front us and we were goin' to get to 'em, come hell or high water."

"After we left the Bighorn River we skirted the mountains, on the north side. Not knowin' it then, we missed a place what they call Colters Hell. Seen it later and parts are pure spooky, the stories we heard didn't do it justice."

"You got to understand what stops one man makes another look harder. The beauty of them damn mountains do different things to men, some want to claim something and call it theirs but it won't ever be theirs, the land belongs to everyone. Others figure that if it's this pretty right here what is it going to be up higher; and they was right. By the time we got to Fort Mackenzie, only an older man that went by the name of Cutter was with me. From there we went our separate ways never saw him again."

Ty listening intently, "When you head that way again are you going by yourself or are you looking for a party to go with?"

"Most likely by myself, lessin' I find a seasoned crew to go with, the problem with that is if they are goin' where you want to go. Goin' with a greenie is to damn hard, thinkin' for 'em and all. The country is big and there is a hell of a lot of ways to find trouble, even if your not lookin' for it."

"I know what a greenie is; it's me, ain't it? I learn fast and follow orders good; I can get what I need and take care of what I get. I won't be a bother to you I know it, you tell me once and I remember. I know that I got a lot to learn, but I'm willing to listen and find out. Just talking to men that's been there, makes me wonder, what I can believe and what can't. I want to hear what is out there from someone that I can trust, someone that won't lie to me."

"Didn't say it was you, didn't say nothin' of the kind. I got to tell you though, you got to ask yourself why you are a goin' and what do you hope to find when you get there? If you're goin', just to go lookin' at the country, hell that's ok but you will come back to this side. If you want to be, part of something big, bigger than you can picture in your mind, then that's the place for you. Want to help open up the country for pilgrims that want to follow and don't want to lead now that's a reason for goin' too. You mentioned you've dreamed on this along time, well son there is a bunch more to know about before you make up your mind to go across. I will tell you what I know and you will have to fill in the pieces. Besides why do you think that I won't lie, you don't know me from shit on a stick?"

"Well the way I see it is, it would be damn foolish and just down right dumb to lie to your new partner."

"Whoa, hold on here a minute son; you're takin' a hell of a lot for granite. Don't I have any say in this? You're askin' a bunch of questions and I'm trying to answer 'em. I guess to start with I'd tell you that it ain't a life cut out for just anyone, what makes you think you can cut it, a hell of a lot of other men have tried it and didn't fair out so well. They were lucky if they had words said over 'em let alone be buried."

"There is dangers that you ain't never even thought of, hell, you might drown crossin' a river, you never know. If you make it across, a rainstorm like you ain't never seen, with lightin' and wind and hail as big as your fist might do you in. After one of those lightin' storms, I have seen grass fires that burns for miles and miles. I ain't never seen one myself, but they tell me that a buffalo stampede is the worse thing that can happen to a man and his animals. They say that you can hear it comin' for half a day before you know which way to run and hell, I ain't even got to winter storms, or the floods, and critters out there that can eat you alive, wolves, painter cats, bears, and snakes as big as your arm. If you're still in the interested, in crossin' over, then I'm willin' to talk but it's on my terms, or not at all. You think on it some and let me know, I ain't goin' nowhere till this here railroad has got to where it's headed."

"Until you convince me differently, I am ready to go, when can we talk again?

"Like I said, think on it and ask your self some questions, before you take the leap, it's a hell of a big step."

Two men with a wagonload of coal, rolled up to the barrel and with a shower of sparks, they replenished the fire. An empty bucket sitting near the heating barrel was filled, and off to the next warmer they went, with never so much as saying hello.

Extending his hand, first to Ty and then to the two men he said, "It's gettin' late and damn cold, I think I'll turn in and try to get some shuteye. I'll be seein' you again O'Malley, think on it." With that, Rocky turned and disappeared into the night.

The knock on the door brought Ty out of reminiscent mood with a startle, it was as if he had been asleep but he knew he hadn't been. Sitting up in his bed, he inquired who it was and heard the voice of Mrs. Simpson reminding him that dinner was ready and that he had better hurry if he wanted anything to eat.

Downstairs wasn't any warmer than in his room, the other boarders were sitting at the table with their coats on, buttoned up to the neck. Sitting between two huge men, with just enough room to breath, Ty helped himself to the potatoes and gravy then asked for the eggs and sausage. As he placed two eggs and a piece of sausage on his plate, he could see Mrs. Simpson watching closely, being ever watchful that he not take more than his share. There was bread on the table but no butter. A lonely jar of something, probable apple butter, sat at the far end of the table.

Everyone must have been very hungry or talked out. The only noise heard was the grating of the eating utensils, and the grunting sounds of men that were eating to fast. Ty thought, I wonder if all fat people eat like these two, afraid that there would not enough to fill their cavernous bellies.

Breaking out of his thoughts, it dawned on Ty that he could not hear the wind blowing or the windows rattle. Hoping that the storm was over, he walked to the door and looked out, "Hey folks, the storm is over and the wind has gone down, I don't see any more snow falling. I'm going to get my coat and check on my horse, Mrs. Simpson do you have a shovel, I'll clear the snow drift away from the front door?"

Taking the steps two at a time, he rushed into his room. He hung a scarf around his neck and hurried, pulling his coat and wool cap on. Leaving his room, he literally bounced down the stairs, to be clear of his restricting room and the confinement with the others was exciting to Ty besides that he would get to see how Duke withstood the storm.

Shoveling a path as he went, he opened the side door to the barn. A low growl escaped in the cold air and froze Ty in his tracks. He did not remember seeing a dog when he put Duke in his stall and filled it with hay. Standing just out side of the door Ty decided that if the dog were mean, Mrs. Simpson surely would have told him about it, wouldn't she. Slowly pushing the door open, a warning growl greeted him; it was coming from Dukes stall. Worried about Duke, Ty stepped into the barn, speaking slowly and quietly at the dog, he could not see. Suddenly a movement from within the stall and emitting a soft whimper, a large dog moving at a slow creep, came toward Ty. As the dog entered the fading sunlight that was showing through the doorway, Ty recognized Tuff. Dropping to one knee and taking the dogs head in his hands, pulled it to his chest, "How in the hell did you get here, Tuff?"

Feeling his rib bones through his matted fur, Ty thought about what Mrs. Garrett had said the night Mrs. Casey disappeared, a barking dog was following the riders and someone telling it to go home. "You followed Mrs. Casey all the way here didn't you, I wish you could tell me where our friend is now, old dog it would sure take a worry out of my mind; I wonder if she is close by. You taking shelter here could mean that she is."

While Ty was talking, a figure standing in the doorway, cast a shadow across the floor of the small barn. Tuff's lips curled up, exposing his teeth and his neck hair ruffled, a low growl erupted from his throat and every muscle in his body tightened a warning to the stranger, to stand his ground.

Looking over his shoulder, he saw one of the guests that he had spent the last two days with, the man stood motionless, obviously to scared to enter or to run away.

Talking in a low soft voice and patting the dog's back, Ty assured the man that is was all right. "I've got a hold of him he ain't going to do anyone harm. I know the dog from a long time back but I'll be damned if I know what he is doing here."

"The son of a bitch sounds meaner than hell, are you sure, it's alright? I just want to check on my horse, and see to his needs, it won't take long, hang on to the hound; I'll be gone in a minute."

Forking some hay into the manger and filling the water pail, he headed for the doorway, "I'll warn the others about this mutt but you had better get rid of him before he chews some one up. Chain him up or lock him in the grain bin, he scares the shit out of me."

Rubbing the dog's ears, Ty thought about Mrs. Casey. "I wish you could tell me what happened to your mistress. If you could only talk, I know that you would tell me where she is and why she left home, come to think about it, how did you find me, you were never around Duke. Unless you just crawled in here to get out of the storm, that's what must of happened, just a freak of luck on our part, right dog. Now I've got to figure out what to do with you tonight, I can't let you get up and leave on me without me being able to follow you, you just might lead me to Mrs. Casey. I hate to tie you up or for that mater lock you up. Sure as hell, Mrs. Simpson won't let you sleep in the house and I don't want to sleep out here in the barn. Come to think about it, it might be warmer out here."

Looking around for some place that he might confine Tuff, but finding nothing, Ty turned loose of the big dog to look for a chain; he would just chew through a rope. As Ty rose up, the big dog went into Dukes stall and lay down, as if to say, don't worry about me, I'll be right here, I won't go anywhere.

Scratching his head and wondering if he read the dog thoughts correctly said out loud, "You don't want to be locked up or tied to a post do you? It looks as if you plan to stay the night with Duke, I'll just warn the rest of the folks that you're out here, they won't disturb you in the least, I'll bet on that."

Finishing with Duke, and rubbing him down with an old sack, he patted him on the neck and said, "You two can spend the night getting better acquainted, I have a feeling you are going to see a lot of each other in the days to come. I'll see you at first light and we'll see where you lead us, old dog."

Returning to the house where Mrs. Simpson was washing the dishes. "Mrs. Simpson may I talk with you, I know you're busy, but this won't take long."

"If I can keep working while we talk, it won't hurt anything, what's on your mind?"

"When I went to the barn to check on my horse, a big old dog challenged me. I think I recognized him from back home, do you know where he came from or how he got here?"

"Is he a dirty colored gray, with a low growl that freezes you in your tracks, teeth about so long," she held up two fingers a little over an inch apart "And about hip high, a real mean looker?"

"That is him all right"

"Some months ago, late in the fall anyway, a big talking man and who he said was his wife, showed up looking for a room. He said that it was only for a short while, until they could find a place of their own. They had come up from St. Louie with two other men, where they went I don't know. After ten days or so, I asked them to leave; I haven't seen or heard from them since."

"Their dog now, is another matter about a week after I ask them to leave, the dog started to show up here for a day or two at a time. At night, he would stay in the barn but during the day, he would just disappear. We wouldn't see him for a few days and sure enough, here he was back, like he was lost or looking for someone."

Mrs. Simpson had stopped doing the dishes and was sitting across the table from Ty. Smiling, more to her self than to Ty, she went on, "I liked the dog and he seemed to like me but let any man come near him, he was a different dog, mean and ugly to them and gentle as a lamb to me. It scared me that some young boy might be hurt or harmed, so I started running him off. I hadn't seen him for several weeks now; it doesn't surprise me that he is back."

"These people that stayed here with the dog, do you remember their names?"

"I couldn't forget them if I wanted to, Curtis Conway was his name and if you think that dog looks mean, you should see Mr. Conway. The way he treated that woman was a shame I never heard her say a word all the while she was here, he spoke for her. He called her Sarah but I still don't think she was his wife, not in the real sense anyway, I've never seen another person as scared as she was of him. When I heard him slapping her one night I said that was enough and I asked them to leave the next day. She could have stayed and I told her so but when he left, she went with him, I've often wonder what became of her."

"Was she a small woman, a little shorter than you, small of bone with a thin face, dark eyes that seemed to twinkle and a smile just waiting to happen?"

"The first part is right but I never seen her smile and her eyes were tearful and red for the most part, living with that man I could see why."

"Did you ever hear 'em mention a Charles Casey or a Wilma, maybe the name Willy, anything about Hannibal or going to Kansas?"

"No, not that I recall Conway talked some about St. Louie and I first thought that he was a lawman, from what he said, he talked of wanted posters, rewards, and such. When those other two showed up, the three of them would sit out on the front porch and whisper, Lord only knows what about. One day I heard Mr. Conway say to the others that it was a sure thing and that they would be rich within the year. Whatever it was he said, they would never be missed just disappear, with no questions asked. I have no idea what they were talking about but I would bet that it was of no good."

"Do you know how they arrived, did they have horses and could you describe 'em?"

"Yes, they kept them in the barn along with a mule and that was another reason that I wanted them gone, I asked them if they would keep the animals in the corral and the big man told flatly, no. Oh' they paid extra for the use of the barn, but there was no room for my regular boarders, it wasn't helping my business."

"The horses were branded on the left hip with the letters U. S., both were bays, and not very well kept. All the while they were here, I never seen them curried, or their manes brushed. The mule was small, looked like skin and bones how it stayed alive, I don't know."

"You've ever seen 'em since?"

"Not even once and I say good riddance. I felt sorry for the women but she had a chance to stay here and she wouldn't, maybe she liked to be slapped and bossed around, I don't know."

"Well thank you Mrs. Simpson for the information I certainly appreciate your time. Would you tell the rest of the guests that the dog is in the barn, I wouldn't want anyone too get bit or something, I'll have him gone the first thing in the morning. I won't stay for breakfast, but thank you for the room and the fine meals. If you should run across the Conway's be careful I think they are dangerous, goodnight."

CHAPTER 6

The white drifts of snow glistened as the first rays of the sun crept over the rooftops of the sleeping town. Standing in the doorway of the barn and not hearing the expected snarl of Tuff, convinced Ty that the dog had went his own way. Going directly to Dukes stall, he saddled the horse, and thought that his only hope of finding the whereabouts of Mrs. Casey had disappeared with the dog.

Closing the door, before mounting up, Ty heard a sound behind him. He was surprised to see Tuff sitting with his tail wagging so hard that it was brushing the snow from side to side. Kneeling down, he scratched the dog's ears and thanked him for sticking around, "Had your breakfast, I see, whose chicken was it, Mrs. Simpson's? Let's see where you're going to lead me this bright day, to your mistress, I hope."

Tuff started toward the main part of Westport, dodging the deep drifts and looking over his shoulder from time to time wanting to be sure, that Ty was following.

Saloons, boarding houses and stores of all types lined the streets. The boarding houses were located next to the saloons and most likely used for one-night stands. There were gunsmiths, leather goods, saddler shops, and every kind of store you could think of; it was a long way from Jamesville. As early as it was, people were already on the move, eight or nine wagons pulled by as many as twelve braces of oxen loaded with goods, from where Ty had no idea, were lined up a long the street. Several teamsters were standing together, waiting their turn to unload their supplies. Riding closer Ty seen that there were two Freight offices side by side, one named the Santa Fe and the other the River Freight Companies, they seemed to share the same yard

Merchants were busy shoveling and sweeping snow from their

storefronts; some were busy unloading boxes and bags from ox carts placing them next to the doorways. Stocking up for the summer, when the demand of wagon outfitters would be the greatest. At that time huge wagon trains would form, loaded with immigrants, heading west in hopes of starting a new life.

Near the river were large corrals filled with horses, mules and oxen. Outside the fence, rails were huge stacks of hay and wooden bins most likely full of oats or corn. The drifted snow, piled high, made everything look larger than it really was. The forges in the blacksmith shops, stoked and made ready for the day's work ahead. Wagon wheels were stacked vertical in sets of four some waiting for the steel rims to be attached and others ready to be placed on the axles of the completed wagons.

Two large yards of nearly finished wagons, one on the east and the other one on the west side of the street. Near the front, closer to the street, stood wagons ready to sell, all except for the canvas and single trees, which was the last thing placed before the wagons left the yard. Signs above the gates identified one as the Studebaker Company and the other as the Conestoga Wagon Company.

Ty was amazed that so much activity was taking place this early in the day. He had never seen anything as big as Westport Landing; he wondered where all the people had came from.

Trying to see everything and keep track of Tuff, at the same time was difficult the dog was a hundred yards out in front and seemed to know exactly where he was going. Speaking to himself, Ty said, "I had better pay attention, just in case you turn and I don't, your not leading me on a wild goose chase are you, old dog?"

A short time latter, the docks of Westport Landing came within view. Tuff walked up to a vacant gangway and laid down with his head on his paws. Two men made a wide swing to avoid coming to close to the dog, as they passed, one mumbled something to the other the words Ty could not make out, they appeared to know the dog and stayed clear of him.

For a short while, he watched him lying just a few feet from the walkway, looking out across the water and not moving a muscle.

"If this where you camp out during the day, must makes for a pretty easy life, it's what folks would call leading a dog's life. Dammit, if you could just talk, I bet that you would tell me that Mrs. Casey got on board a boat right at this spot, and left you behind."

Tying Duke to the gangway, he said. "I'll be back after I talk with those fellers over there, don't go anywhere."

The men were busy weaving a new loop into end of an old line. One was complaining, "This is damn foolish to try and fix such old ropes, hell all that is going to happen is that it will break again they always do."

"Excuse me, but I was wondering if you fellas could tell me who owns that dog over there."

The talker and the bigger of the two looked up, "Most likely he belongs to the god damn devil, and you can't get close to that son-of-a-bitch he'll take your leg off. He won't even take food from any one just wants to chew a fella up. I don't know how he made it this far without someone shooting the bastard, he is mad at the world about something, he sure as hell is. Been laying in that same spot here every day that I've been here, what would you say Clint, most of the winter anyways?"

Clint said, "Long damn while Ben, about the time the Yellerstone made her last trip north last fall."

"The Yellerstone", Ty knew that it was the Yellowstone, but not wanting to correct them he said, "Where is she now?"

"Up river."

"It's pretty early for the boats to be going up stream isn't it, didn't think they would leave before the end of spring."

"Depends on the freight, with that new railroad their building across the territory, west of Council Bluffs, its keeping them damn boats real busy; be a long summer with all that freight going north. This early, Counsel Bluffs is about as far as they can go without running into ice or maybe Sioux City at the most, some will wait there for open water and then go on north. Some years the ice is so bad that they can't leave till April but we've had a good winter, except for the last two-three days. Next week all this snow will be gone and all we will have are the memories."

"Were you here when the Yellerstone left?"

"When."

"The last couple of times she left."

Looking at each other, Ben said, "In this same spot."

"Do you ever pay attention who boards the boats when they leave?"

"Most of the time no, were to damn busy to stand around and watch. When the Yellerstone pulled out last fall, there was a ruckus that caught my attention, only reason that I looked up, remember Clint?" The smaller man kept working on the rope shook his head yes, apparently he didn't talk unless he had too.

"Was there passengers on that trip?"

"Some, I didn't see 'em all just the ugly mean bastard and a couple of the injuns that he was given hell to. He sure acted like an asshole shoving 'em around like he did."

"Do you remember seeing three men and a lady board her, they might have taken their horses and a small mule?"

Scratching his chin whiskers and looking at his friend, he started to shake his head from side to side. He finally broke the silence with a quizzical look on his face, "You a law man or something?"

"No just looking for some friends of mine that might of went north."

"No horses that I remember. The Injun youngsters, probable just out of sister's school and the man I told you about. If I recollect right, there was two or three men, maybe more, standing at the rail. One was dressed in buckskins as I recall I didn't know any of 'em".

"If the ticket office was open you could check with 'em, they would know." Pointing at a weathered building, a short distance from the dock, "They keep a record of all the passengers that go on the boats."

When do they most generally open the place up?"

"Not till the Yellerstone gets back and that could be a day or two or maybe a week or might be longer."

"Where would I find the boss or someone that would know about them records?"

"You might check over at the River Freight Company, Gus owns that too."

Thanking them for their help, Ty turned and walked toward Duke, then he stopped, "What's this Gus look like, and what is the rest of his name?"

"Sails, he is a small man, wears a suit, glasses and most likely be in his office." Both men laughed and shock theirs heads, like Ty should know that all ready.

"Old dog were going to the Freight office are you coming or staying?"

Mounting Duke, he headed back toward town. Glancing down he was happy to see the dog walking at Duke's heals. "Your welcome too stay with us old friend if that's what you want."

The freight office blocked by the very wagons and big two wheel carts that Ty had seen earlier, some pulling away and others taking their places, operating like a well-oiled clock. Wagon Masters were shouting orders and pointing to which he wanted put where. Some went to one Company, and the balance to the other. Men were bumping into one another, in their rush to get the job done.

A little man in a suit and wearing little round glasses was busy writing on a stack of paper.

Tying his horse to rail, across the street and out of the way, he approached the small man.

"Are you Mr. Sails?"

"I'm paying fifty-cents a day if you want to work, get to it, what name do you go by?"

"It's not work I'm looking for, I'd like to ask you a question, if I may."

"Come back later, maybe Wednesday, I'm to busy now."

"It's about some friends that might of went up river on the Yellowstone, a man, his wife and two other men, name of Conway, do you remember?"

"Conway, yes I've heard the name, don't know where, now leave me get back to my work."

"Could you check your records at a later time, if I return?"

"Yes-yes, not earlier than Wednesday, now be gone."

Visiting one saloon after another, he finally found Rocky sitting at a table drinking whiskey right from the bottle. The table was empty except for Rocky, his bottle and a long barreled Hawkins rifle leaning against a chair. Without moving his head or his eyes, he said, "Where you been holdin' up son, I've been sittin' here a waitin'. Figured you find me sooner or later do want a drink of this here rotgut, I've tasted better at the gatherin's but this the best these damn people have."

Lifting the bottle, and taking what looked like a long pull, he then pretending to swallow. He sat it down and making the damn awfullest face, saying, "That is the worse shit that I've tasted in my lifetime, how in hell can you drink it without puking?"

"Just you wait old son when you've gone without, anything that burns will cut the craving. Mind my words son, just you wait and see."

"When do we plan to head west and what am I going to be needin', I've made up my mind."

"Let's talk on it some."

"You've told me about the bad of it now tell me what I'm going to need and when were leaving."

"We'll get to that soon enough but there's rights and wrongs that has got to be agreed to. I'm the lead; I told you before that it is my way and no other way. When we leave Westport Landin', every mistake you make, you will hear about it. It will be for your own good so listen up. I'll tell you what you done wrong and what to do to fix it. When I give an order like stop, run or shit, anything you hear me say, don't argue just do it, understood? It might be my life or yours at stake and we might not have time to talk about it."

"When we decide to leave, it is nobodies business but ours, so keep your mouth shut. Leavin' before sun light is what most do, we'll be different were leavin' when I say so. Keep your rifle oiled and loaded it could be anytime."

"Who's going to care when we leave, are there Indians this close to the river or for that matter here in town?"

"Most likely not right now, our biggest worry is the damn scavengin' white man, worse than the injuns they are. Track ya, kill ya and steal your horses and pokes, that's our first concern, Injun's come later."

"Let's talk about men, our kind and the rest. I ask you, can you tell an honest and trustworthy man, white, black or red, by just looking at him, hell no, you learn to trust him as time goes by. You walk around Westport here and as soon as people find out you got ten-cents in your pockets, you will have more friends that you can shake a stick at. Some will cut your throat for no reasons so don't trust anyone you don't know. Keep your valuables out of sight and don't make any show of brag, keep your mouth shut. Watch behind you, as well in front and at night walk away from buildings, in the street is the best; be ready to defend what's yours. Nine out of ten men are all right, it's that one you've got to watch. Some will steal pennies from a dead man they don't give a shit, they don't care who they hurt, it's their way of showin' how mean they can be. To them killin' and stealin' is easier than doin' a honest days work."

"The first week or so out, we will watch for signs of shod ponies. Gangs will lay in wait for small groups and jump 'em, most generally hit at night, when they're camped and asleep. Most folks don't worry about runnin' into injuns till there well away from the river, they don't expect trouble that soon."

"The bastards take anything of value, your gear, horse, rifle, saddle, knife, wagon, livestock and provisions, anything that can be resold, they're worse than any heathen you will ever cross paths with. They bring their bloodied goods back here or some other town and sell it pennies on the dollar. Killin' your own kind and takin' away their futures is damn rotten low, hangin' 'em from theirs balls, is too damn good for 'em."

Taking a drink of rotgut, and then offering the bottle to Ty, "No thank you, it ain't to my liking."

"If the white man is so bad, why do we hear what devils the red men are, sounds to me like your calling 'em saints or something. Why do we hear how mean and sneaky they are and why are they so worried about a few intruders that want to live in their country, are they that much different than us?"

"When you get right down to it, Injuns are no different than white men, oh—they live different than we do in buffalo skinned tipis and such. They have their own huntin' and campin' grounds just like we have our own places. If you take something belongin' to a white man and if it's important enough he'll fight to get it back, same way with the Injuns. You take their land, their buffalo and their way of life, they will fight to keep you out. If you treat, a white man kindly and you've got a friend, same way with the Injun. If we make it that far you'll find whole tribes that will take you in and some will let you winter with 'em and treat you like one of their own but you will also find some mean sons of bitches that will take your hair in a wink of an eye."

"What turned 'em against the white's so, from what I hear there is plenty of land beyond the river for everyone. I've heard that a feller can goes days, sometime for weeks, without seeing another human being, it don't sound like it's to crowded out there."

"Not by a long shot but they have reason for fightin' the Whiteman; they're comin' into their home territory and they have had some bad experiences with our kind. They welcomed us at first and then told us to leave, when they found out what we were like."

"We just take what we want; we tear up their lands with our plows and drive off the game. We shoot the buffalo and take only the hides and the tongues, the rest of the meat we leave to rot."

"All the stories I hear is that the Indian is the cause of the problems, nobody ever blames us."

"They should, it's just easier to make it right if we can convince folks that it is them that is attacking us."

"Now tell me if you owned a piece of ground and some son-of-a-bitch tried to take it away from you, what would you do?"

"I'd fight back, most likely, anyway I could."

"The injuns no different, he wants to keep what's his, and always has been his since he took it away from some other tribe. Hell boy, wars have been fought over land since before Jesus Christ. Back in the old country, where my folks come from, land has changed hands hundreds of times, first one clan and then the other, they loose it back to the first and so forth, it never ends."

"The injun just don't look at it that way. They forget that they fought to win their land and huntin' ground, by pushin' someone else off it. He sees this rush of white men as a final, unstoppable war against the injun people and he sees it as his last hope to hang on. Wagon trains have been going west for years now, the injun sees this and he is scare't, all he can do now is fight."

"All that land out there and there is not enough room for people to mix, why is that?"

"I guess that the French can be blamed for some of it, they was first to come lookin', some even before Lewis and Clark. They came down from Canada trappin' for fur or lookin' for their place. They started tradin' with the Tribes, bringin' goods that the Injun needed and some that they didn't need at all. Whiskey and disease came with 'em and they shared both with the Natives. The Injuns liked the whiskey and many tribes were damn near wiped out by the white mans disease."

"Once the Natives got a taste for rot gut whiskey, which they couldn't handle cause it was new to 'em, they would just go crazy when they drank it. They couldn't get enough and that was the beginnin' of bad times for the Injuns. Some traders started to trade more whiskey and less goods like blankets, bright cloth, beads, cookin' pots and trinkets. When the supply of whiskey went dry for any reason, the Injuns went to raidin'. He went to killin' to get whiskey, firewater, as they called it, like I said they couldn't get enough. Up until that time, the traders had a pretty good life the Injuns had accepted 'em as friends, and shared everything with 'em. When the trappers started to loose their hair, they figured out what they did wrong."

"Mountain Men followed the French Canadians into the high mountains. They came first to explore and lookin' for fortunes in furs and gold, ended up lovin' the beauty and the spaces. They just plain got hooked on the life out there, a lot of 'em, I'm thinkin', was strong-minded and couldn't adjust to life on this side of the river. It's lonely, but a wonderful kind of loneliness for some, a hell for others. You've got to be able to provide for yourself, regardless of the weather or the circumstances. They didn't put down roots, moved from time to time, never in the same place for long and lived out in the open for the most part. Built dugouts with logs and covered 'em with dirt for the cold times. Some wintered with friendlies, and even married Injun squaws. As it turned out, the damn mountain man and trappers weren't much better than the French."

The more Rocky drank, the more he repeated the last couple of words of each sentence. Between drinks and long thoughtful pauses, it gave Ty a chance to think. Rocky must really miss the mountains and his encounters with the Indians. There was a love there that he could not be hide. It made Ty think that not only the Indians were afraid that their world would change, but so was Rocky.

"Now the writin' is on the wall," he started to say, "They know that this is their last chance and they know that they are fightin' a loosing battle, it's their way of holdin' on just a little longer. After thousands of years livin' their lives like they do, we can't expect to change 'em to our ways over night. God damn it, who said our way was the right way, their way is to my choosin'."

For a few minutes the two sat there, not saying a word, but thinking about what Rocky had said.

"Tell me about what the Indian life is like, I've heard stories that they go around naked, winter and summer and that they eat their meat raw. Is there any truth to the story that they eat dog? Indians, I been told, ride bare back with just a piece of leather for a rein, are they as good horsemen as I've been told?"

Smiling, Rocky leaned back in his chair, "You wouldn't believe these people but you got to remember that they have survived since the beginnin' of time. They know the land like no others ever has or maybe ever will their lives depended on it. They're taught from birth how to hunt, what is edible, and what is not. Plants that we would take for weeds are medicines to 'em. They cook their meat over fires started by flint and steel and other times they might start it by rub two sticks together. Dog is a delicacy, eaten at special times when they are trying to please a guest or a visitor of big importance."

A quiet Rocky sat there thinking, and with a slight smile, he went on. "The tribes that I came across all had councils that ruled the tribe. From where and when they moved their camps, to who got rewarded for bravery for doin' something special. They were the judges, the court, and the jury. The difference between their laws and ours is that they go for all the tribe members. Our laws are for some of the people, the ones that can afford it can find a way around the courts. Other words they buy their way through the trouble they get into, not with injun justice. The Chief has the final say and they all listen to him, he earned his job with what he has done and by showin' that he is a leader."

"You've seen the leathers that I wear, the injuns taught us that, they don't tear; keeps you from gettin' cut and scraped up so bad walkin' or ridin' in the brush country. Water don't seep through like when you're wearin' cottons, or wool. The greasier they get the more water that they shed and the best part is that a new suit of clothes is a shot away."

"Why is there so much fringe and hangie downs on the sleeves and leggins, is there a reason?

"In battle you want to look as big and as fierce as you can the fringe blows and moves around, makes you look bigger. Like a dog, when you get him riled up, his neck hairs stand up and make him look bigger than he is. A war chief also told me, that it confuses wild animals, they don't know where your leg or arm is, all that extra hangie downs might cause 'em to miss if they attack you."

"Never thought of that, I had guessed that it was just for looks. I don't know that I can get use to a breechcloth, I would think you would feel undressed."

"It's better than gettin' caught with your pants down."

"Another thing, when you see a injun warrior on a horse, you don't know where the horse begins and the rider ends. At a full gallop, they can ride sittin', standin' or hangin' on the side. Knees and heels they used to control the direction and speed, the leather chinstrap is more to hold the horse with than to use it for ridin'. When they go on the warpath, they paint their faces and their horses in their own special pattern and color. Hopefully this will scare the hell out of their enemies maybe make 'em turn tail and run. The paint and the patterns is also a spiritual thing it's their way of prayin' and askin' for help in battle. Injun braves are straight up fighters; it makes no difference what tribe you're lookin' at. Now with a white man, if threaten by danger will shoot first and try to take the advantage for himself. A warrior brave will try to get as close to you as he can, touchin' you if he can. Young braves can make a name for himself by countin' coup it shows the elders how brave and fearless he is. Takin' coup proves that he is a leader too. After the battle or fight, the braves are given eagle feathers for their deeds. Sometime if they show their bravery many times over, they will get appointed to the tribe council. It's a big honor to sit by the council fire, and decide what the tribe is to do next."

"With their sharp eyes and ears and with 'em knowin' the country as they do, few injuns are ever surprised or caught off guard. No better trackers or hunters live. They can track a snake across water and tell you how long it was and they can sneak up to within inches of a deer or a rabbit. For the most part, you could be standin' next to one and never know that there was one within a mile of you. Whatever you've heard about an Indian on the warpath is most likely true. Durin' the war, if the North or the South had the Sioux, Cheyenne, or the Crow as their Calvary; they would have won the war and made it a hell of a lot shorter."

The effects of the whiskey were starting to take its toll, the slurred words and he paused a long time between sentences. Talking one minute and then throwing his head back and laugh so hard that tears came to his eyes. Ty was beginning to wonder if anything he said was true or maybe was he just pulling his leg.

"Rocky, you talk about the Crow and Sioux and such, how many tribes of Indians are there?"

"I don't think anyone knows for sure. There is tribes down south and further west than I've been. Stories I've heard from old timers is the Apache and the Comanche are mean bastards. They claim the land south and east of here. Meaner than the Blackfoot or the Sioux, I can't picture."

"Before you drain this bottle, and order another one, you might tell me what I'm going to need, if you are too drunk to move, then I can at least go looking to find what I need."

Sitting up straight and looking Ty in the eye, "Son I'll be the judge as to when I had enough, you remember that. I've never been told when to start or when to stop, if I want, God Damn it, I'll drink all day. When it's time, we'll go lookin' not till then."

Looking straight into Ty's eyes, for what seemed like minutes, with a look that backed up his words. Turning his head away and looking at the bottle, slowly he reached out and shoved the nearly empty container away. When he had finished, he smiled as if nothing at all had happened and continued, "Sure in a hurry to dust this place, ain't ya child."

"Yes."

"So am I, old son lets make council and get on with it."

Rocky's change of character, baffled Ty, from laughing and slurring his words one-minute, to a very serious tone the next. It's a mystery how his mind must work, he acted so damn drunk and for so early in the day, Ty was ready to write him off. Wonder if I know enough about this man, to partner up with him, up until now, I didn't give it a second thought. Hell I've got a couple days to think on it, I'll just have to play it by ear.

The chair made a grating sound as it was shoved away from the table bringing Ty back from his thoughts, "Where do we go first or is it what do we do first?"

"Lets get clear of this stinkin' saloon, and put our minds together on what we got and what we are goin' to need."

With his rifle in his right hand, he looked every inch a mountain man, more so than Ty had thought. It suddenly dawned on him that Rocky needed to be wandering somewhere west of here; the civil life was not for him.

A bench sitting along the outside wall of the Post Office was to the liking of both men. Fresh air is what Rocky needed, with no bottle to distract him.

"Lets figure out what you got and what you'll need."

"I got a horse and saddle, a knife and a Canfield rifle that my brother James brought home from the war, the rest I'll have to buy."

"What kind of knife you got one like mine.

"No not as big as the one you let me use that time but damn near, James and I have skinned a lot of animals with it."

"Can you cut down a small sapling or protect yourself in a fight with it, does it keep an edge, one that you could shave with it and not have it go dull on you before your done?

"In a fight I guess if I had my druthers, I would have one like yours and I never tried to cut down a tree with it I just always used a ax for that. As far as the edge goes it is a good one."

"Might want to get to get one like mine it just might save your hide someday."

"That's alright with me, I can still keep the one I got, a second one won't hurt me none."

"That your horse over there?" Pointing at Duke, "That long legged bay?"

"Ya, his name is Duke, I brought him from home."

"Looks like a horse built for speed, where were goin' you don't need speed, you got to have a horse that will last. One that can go all day and through the night if need be. The bay beside him is what I mean, he won't win any ribbons at the county fair but I bet he has grit and does what's asked of him. Would the thought of tradin'—Duke, say for something more suited for the wild country, ever cross your mind? You're goin' to need a second horse for packin' and spellin' your ridin' horse. Duke would bring you both and pack equipment to boot, what do you say?"

Surprise and disappointment struck Ty at about the same time, he was proud of Duke and he thought of him as the finest horse he had ever seen and he was his last tie to his folks and home. He had never given thought to anything but riding him forever.

"What makes you think that Duke won't fill the bill, for a highbred horse, he has a lot of bottom, you'll see. I'll buy a packhorse and saddle, I've got the money, but I'll keep Duke."

"Son I just told you that I'm the leader of this outfit and the first thing I tell you, you want to argue about it. Said I wouldn't go along with such and I won't. I've seen plenty of that kind of horse, last for maybe a week or so, and then their legs go. They ain't worth the powder to put 'em down, its better you listen to me on this one, it's for the best."

"You just said that you can't tell what a man is made of, at first glance and I say the same goes for horses and dogs, you get to know 'em first, and then decide. If you knew what is inside of Duke, you wouldn't question him, if it's a choice between my horse and you, I'll take my horse, I know him better."

With that said Ty got up, turned around and extended his hand to Rocky, "I'll find my own way west, thank you for all that you've told me, I appreciate it."

Holding on to the hand that he had just shook and gripping it tighter he said, "God Dammit son hold on there, wait just a damn minute, when you make up your mind, you do it in a hurry. I'm pleased that you were listenin' to me, I didn't know if you were. We can talk about your horse, I'll give ground if you will, is it a deal?"

"It depends on the deal."

"You keep Duke, over there, but I get to pick your second horse. After we're on the trail and if he can't keep up the pace we trade him or leave him, understood?"

"Where would we trade him after we leave West Port, some homesteader?"

"There or at a tradin' post you won't get as much for him out there, but he is tradable, a good horse is worth something anywhere."

Feeling the tension leave his body, he replied, "You won't have to look for a place to trade him, he'll out last any horse you pick."

It was time for the mountain man to break into a big grin, "Old son lets get movin', maybe, just maybe, you will teach me something about horses."

"That dog layin' over there by your horse, is yours too?"

"No."

"Sit back down here and we will start makin' our list. First things first, we will buy our own stuff, what's mine is mine and what's yours is yours, agreed. I'm goin' to need a ridin' horse and we both will need a packhorse or a mule. If we play our cards right, we'll get 'em to throw in a couple pack saddles too."

"What about a riding saddle for you?"

"Mine is at the livery over yonder," Motioning with a twist of his head. "I left it and some of my gear there when I sold my horse. That livery is a good place to start lookin' for our stock the owner goes by the name of Cheek, seems to be a fair-minded man, one I think we can trust."

"Tough little Injun ponies is what we want, if we can find um, they're the best for what we got in mind. They can find their own feed and go forever on just a sallow of water."

Chuckling Ty said, "How do we tell a Indian pony from the rest, do they look different, like wear feathers or something?"

Trying to look serious and wearing a straight face he answered, "It's the way they whinny, they all sound different dependin' on the tribe that raised 'em. Some don't make a sound, those the Indians used for night raids and sneakin' up on folks, you'll know when you hear or don't hear one."

After a thoughtful moment, both men broke out laughing, Rocky threw back his head and started to slap his leg so hard that with each slap it sounded like a rifle shot. Ty laughed so hard that tears came to his eyes and had to hold on to the bench to keep from falling off. Every time they slowed down and looked at one another, the laughter was renewed.

Keeping his eyes closed Ty said, "I think I will just let you pick out the horses, you seem to speak their language better than I do." The laughter started all over again.

Finally catching their breath, Rocky said, "If you will let up for a minute I'll tell you the truth, an injun horse is short and kinda stocky. He has a lot of what some folks call plain old guts. For a hundreds of years no one messed with their breedin'. Mixed and uncontrolled breedin' means that the traits best suited for survival is carried forward with each generation, not necessarily the fastest or the best lookers, just the toughest. There is a tribe that breeds their horse's special like, the Nez Perce. Now they have bred a mountain horse that has the prettiest markin's you will ever see. Spots on their butts, for the most part singles 'em out. Each one is different and prettier than the other. Once you've seen one, you'll never forget what they look like. Ownin' one makes you a damn special person. They're a prize all right."

"You ever own one?"

"Hell no son, the only ones I ever did see'd with a horse like that was a

War Chief of the Blackfeet, called Fire in Mouth. One of those horses was worth ten, maybe twelve of any other kind."

Trying to move Rocky along Ty said, "After the animals, what then?"

"You'll need some leathers, we'll nose around for some as we gather the goods were goin' to need. If we're lucky we might find some Injun made, their the best. We sure can't leave with those clothes you've got on, won't last the first week on the trail."

Interrupting Ty said, "I see that you carry a Hawkins, had it long?"

"Got it at Bridger's tradin' post on the way out of the mountains, it's a good one."

"Ain't the new breach lock rifles with the cartridges better, or maybe the new Henry repeater?

"Not where we are goin'. Out there, most everyone carries shot and powder. Cartridges might be hard to find and I don't trust 'em. Anyways they get wet and if you don't dry 'em right away they turn green. Durin' the war many men lost their lives just for that reason. The green ones will jam in your rifle. There's a place to use 'em all right and I intend to take one with me. Shotguns are different, the paper cartridges are all right, they stay dry cause there is a wax that covers 'em. They are faster to use when you're fightin' in close and they are handy for putting meat on the table. I never had a need for one, but a lot of men do. I don't see anything wrong with the Henry, if you want one; just carry a hell of a lot of cartridges."

"We'll take a couple of those new hand guns with us and hope we don't shoot our selves in the foot, you ever shoot one of 'em?"

"No."

"They say it is like pointin' your finger at what it is you want to hit. Hell if it was that easy the war would of been over a long time ago. If we don't like 'em we can always trade 'em for something."

As they stood looking at the pen full of horses, Cheek, the livery owner was pointing out the horses that were not for sale. Some belonged to customers and others were unbroken or green.

Taking his time and watching the horses move around the enclosure, Rocky asked Cheek what he knew about the black pinto, the one with the white face.

"Traded for him just this spring, three years old, I'd say, Frank Talburt brought him in along with three others. I know Frank and he knows horses, said he was a good one and I believe him. Quiet horse; don't mix much with the others and likes to be out in the weather."

Crawling through the fence and walked up to the pinto, all the while talking softly, so as not scare the horse but it did not work, the pinto shied away, moving to the other side of the pen. Rocky's movement across the enclosure spooked the other horses. The pinto stood his ground till the last moment and then started to side step away from him again.

"Spooky, bastard ain't he?"

"Never took notice of it before," Cheek said.

"How the hell do you get close to the son-of-a-bitch, shoot him?"

Cheek said, "I guess you got to show him whose boss, he is pretty much a loner."

"Ty, throw me that rope, I'll ketch the bastard."

Shaking out a loop in the well-used rope, he approached the elusive mount. Repeating the words, "Easy boy, easy now, ain't goin' to hurt you, stand still you ugly bastard."

Edging closer and still talking in quiet, low voice, the paint suddenly laid his ears back, lowered his head and charged Rocky. Stepping aside, he laid the loop over the horse's head and with the other end quickly wrapped it around a snubbing post at the center of the pen. With no slack remaining in the rope, the wild horse came to an abrupt stop falling ass over teakettle. Rising to it's feet but still groggy it stood spread legged as Rocky pulled the slack out of the line. The horse, shaking his head to clear it, stumbled closer until he stood next to the snubbing post. A wild look was in his eyes and snot was dripping from his nose and mouth. Out of wind and taking great breaths of air, trying to get his lungs full again but there still was an air about the horse as if to say, "You haven't beaten me yet."

Leaving him tied to the post, Rocky walked up to where Cheek and Ty was standing. "I think I got his attention, now I've got to convince him of that."

"How you going to that?"

"Son you just stand here and watch you might learn a trick or two."

"I'm watching."

"Cheek, you ever ride this horse?"

"No."

"Has he been ridden?"

"Frank might of, he didn't say, he said he was broke."

Taking the saddle blanket in one hand, he walked toward the pinto. As he grew near, the horse tried to pull away from the post. Curling his lips and showing his teeth, he wanted desperately to scare Rocky off. Approaching slowly and talking as he had before, giving the scared horse time to smell and get use to his odor. Holding the blanket close to his flaring nostrils, he edged closer and brushed it cross his nose. The first several times the horse snapped at it with his teeth, failing to jerk it out of Rockys hands, he appeared to give up. As he held the blanket with one hand, Rocky began to stroke and scratch the side of his head with the other. Moving up to his ears and then to his neck, the pinto stood quietly.

Backing away a few paces, he moved around the pinto, constantly talking. Facing each other again, Rocky approached showing the blanket and repeating what he had done before. This he did several times in the next few minutes, each time moving gradually closer to the mounting side.

The next step was to place the blanket on his back. Time after time, he promptly shook it off. Attempting to strike out with hooves was impossible because of the short lead the pinto was left with the shaking of his head, sideways and up and down, trying to use his teeth, nothing worked.

Speaking in a low voice, just for the horse to hear, "You done actin' up, bronc, you and me are goin' to get along damn-it, were two of a kind, remember that."

Twisting his head back over his left shoulder, the pinto softly snorted.

Walking back to the railing he said to Cheek, "You think there is hope for that son-of-a-bitch."

"You never know about horses. I'd give him back to Frank if he was around, the son-of-a-bitch left the country might never see him."

Wrinkling his brow, Cheek said, "Sure you don't want to try again, I'd give you a good deal if you could get him to come around."

"I'll think on it."

"You want to look at another?"

"Nothing else caught my eye."

"Got a couple in the barn that's got some run left in 'em, want me to bring 'em out?"

"No, Ty can go take a look; I'll turn loose of the devil horse."

Duke stood at the hitching rail with Tuff was lying at his feet. As Ty entered the dark barn, the blackness within the barn appeared deeper; it was quite a contrast with the bright sun light of the street. Momentarily blinded, Ty did not see or hear the two men just inside the door.

He heard a deep growl on his left and the deathly scream of a man in pain. Starting to turn toward the sound but interrupted by a blow to his right shoulder. Twisting as he fell to the ground a second blow glanced off his back. Looking up all that Ty could see was the legs of a person coming toward him. Lurching forward and grabbing both legs in a bear lock, he threw him violently to the ground. Jumping to his feet, just as the other man regained his, Ty with his right arm nearly useless, struck out with his left. He connected with a solid blow to the side of the man's face, staggered, but still standing, he missed with a left hook. He followed it up with a wild right hand, just missing Ty's chin. This opened up the whole right side of his face, and Ty didn't miss. Hitting the ground like sack of grain, he laid there, as he started to rise up on one knee, he fell back again, not moving a muscle.

With his eyes now adjusting to the light in the shadow of the walls, Ty knew that the fight had gone out of the man, motionless, he was still lying crumpled next to the doorway. Turning his attention to the cursing and screaming to his left, he could see Tuff had the arm of the second man locked tightly in his jaws. "Ok, let him go old friend, I'll take it from here."

The words barely out of his mouth, a roar of a gun and the sound of a bullet passing close to his head, caused Ty to drop to one knee just missing the man that Tuff still held. Patting the dog's head and telling him to turn loose, Tuff sat on his haunches, holding the man's arm in his mouth, still ready if needed.

The man was yelling, "Get this damn dog away from me, he's a goddamn killer, son-of-a-bitch someone get him off me."

"Who's your friend that is shooting at me?"

"Go to hell."

"If you don't want more of the dog, you had better start talking."

"Ty are you all right in there?"

"I don't know, better stay out of sight; some bastard is shooting at me, I can't tell from where."

Turning loose of the man's shirt he said, "Get your ass out of here and take your friend over there with you."

Not rising completely up and holding his arm across his chest, he moved his still unconscious partner outside.

"We got the two cut throats," Rocky shouted.

"Son," it was Cheeks voice, "There's a loaded shotgun just to the right of the door if you need it,"

"You ain't going to get to it, you can try if you've a mind to, but I'll kill you before you can get there."

Another shot rang out and buried it self in the framework of the door. "O'Malley I said I would get you, bastard, and I aim to."

Straining his memory and trying to recognize the voice, but couldn't, "Why don't you throw out your gun and face me, I'm not armed?"

"Your friend outside is"

"He won't interfere, I'll see to that."

"He did once and I sure as hell ain't going to trust him now."

"Zack is that you, you chicken shit coward?"

"It's me all right and you're a dead son-of-a-bitch, like you should of been the first time."

Splinters tore from the wall just above Ty's head. It didn't sound like a flintlock or a rifle; probably one of those handguns that Rocky was taking about.

Edging around the wooden partition, trying to get closer, a forth shot sounded. As Ty moved so did Tuff and with his hands, he was asking the dog to stay, but the dog continued.

"You all right son, do you want me to go around back?"

Not wanting to give away his position, Ty never answered. Still crawling on his stomach and taking advantage of all the cover he could. Suddenly stopping he said to himself, "Hell I can see better than that bastard. I'm looking at the dark end and he is fighting the sun light coming in the door just a little closer and I'll rush him, hope to hell he don't move."

With the straw and hay covering the dirt floor, and made crawling much easier. Stopping to, listen from time to time assured Ty that Zack hadn't moved. He was sure that he was next to the wall at the end of the barn; he could hear Zack breathing as he crawled closer.

Ty stopped, sensing a movement in the dark then another shot sounded, followed by a flash of light from the gun barrel, brought him up and charging at the flash. Crabbing Zack and trying to get hold of the gun he twisted Zack's right arm, letting out a scream Zack swung the gun at Ty's head, missing, he dropped the weapon. Crabbing the first thing that he touched, a hay hook hanging on the wall, ripped at Ty's arm. As Ty's left fist racked him along side of the head, and with Tuff hanging on to his leg, he fell back into the wall. He let out a blood-curdling scream and for a short minute just stood there, then slumped to the floor.

Leaning against the horse stall and catching his breath he yelled, "He is down, come on in."

At the same time, the rear doors of the barn opened and sunlight streamed in. Rocky with the Hawkins to his shoulder stood there. The sun lit up the area where Zack laid, blood was slowly forming in a pool at the base of his neck.

Looking at the wall that Zack had fallen against were several long spikes or nails that held shovels, pitchforks and other items uses in a livery stable. Zack had fell back on a spike that had gone deep into his neck. The weight of Zack's body had bent the nail and let the body fall to the floor.

Rocky and Cheek turned the body over and found the hay hook stuck in his right side, "What away to die, stabbed by your own self and a rusty god damn nail killing you."

Hearing a sick sound just out side the barn, Rocky stepped out and saw Ty throwing up, he was shaking all over.

Standing behind him he said, "Son I know how you feel, I felt the same way after I killed my first man. About the same situation but mine was a young injun out on his first war party. You just have to think what it would be like if it was the other way around. He was out to kill you anyway, he could. The other two men were suppose to beat you so that Zack could kill you himself he was a crazy bastard. Most likely cost old Zack here some money, he didn't get much out of it, now did he?"

Straightening up and wiping his face on his sleeve he saw that his sleeve was torn from his elbow to his wrist, Zack had missed by a hair. He turned to Rocky and Cheek, "I didn't want to kill him just talk some sense into his head." Tears were still running down his dusty cheeks as he stood there in a fog, shaking his head from side to side.

"Why did he want to kill me, I fought him fair and beat him fair too, why couldn't he just leave it alone, now he is dead and I did it, damn it to hell, I didn't want this."

Placing his hand on Ty's shoulder Rocky started by saying, "Not that it makes any difference now, but I told you that a bully like Zack can't turn loose of these things. They wear on 'em, thinkin' about it all the time. If not now it would have been later."

Regaining his composure, Ty remembered Tuff, looking around saw, him lying near the outside wall of the barn. Walking over to him, he knelt down rubbing his ears, he looked for any cuts or signs of his being hurt, and none were visible. Ty thanked the dog by burying his head in the matted fur of the dog, "How did you get there so quick, if it hadn't been for you, I might be dead, thank you Tuff."

Rocky looked at Cheek and asked, "You know whose dog that is?"

"Seen him around, mostly just up and down the street. The word is that he is a mean mutt not to be messed with."

"Ty, you sure you don't know that dog, he sure as hell saved you at least a beatin', if nothin' more?"

"Ya I know the dog, but I don't own him, nobody owns him that I know of."

"He seems to have taken a likin' to you and Duke."

"I knew him from back home, we run across one another last night."

"Then he is your dog."

"No he goes where he wants and does what he wants, today, thank god, he followed me; tomorrow he might go another way. He is free to do what he wants."

"I think his mistress left him here when she went north on the Yellowstone, she was about the only one that could handle him. The way I was told, was that her husband and the dog didn't get along very good. That's most likely the reason that he is still here, her man wouldn't take him, the dog never cottoned to men much."

By this time, the City Constable and a half a dozen others had showed up. Two men with badges were holding the two men that had jumped Ty at the barns entrance, "Which one of you killed this son-of-a-bitch?"

Ty stepped forward, "I didn't do it on purpose he was shooting at me, when I caught up to him, he fell on that nail there and died."

Knelling on one knee he first looked at the imbedded hay hook then rolled Zack over and looked at the neck wound. "You were not shooting back just him shooting at you, right?"

"I had no way of shooting at Zack I didn't even have my rifle with me; I was just coming in the barn to look at a couple of horses that Cheek told us about."

The constable and another man spent some time looking over the body then the lawman started to ask Ty some questions.

"How did it happened did you know the man, was there bad blood between the two of you?"

Ty explained as best he could, about the fight an he answered all of the constable's questions.

Ty asked, "Did you talk with the other two and what did they say?"

"About the same as you, it looks like they were out to get you all right, the dead man paid 'em each five-dollars to bring you to him. They say that they didn't know that he was going to try to kill you. Not much, I can charge you with, self-defense I'd call it but do me a favor and stay out of trouble we don't need it around here."

Shaking Ty's hand, he apologizing for the rough treatment in his town and to the coroner said, "Let's see if there is enough in his pockets to pay for his burial, then you can haul him away."

Catching Rocky's eye he said, "Lets get finished here and get gone, the sooner the better."

"Cheek, before all of this excitement, we was talkin' horse tradin', you come up with any better offers."

"The gray and the short tailed bay, I'm going to need no less than thirty-five-dollars. I ain't figured out what you want the pinto for you can't ride him, you said so yourself. Can't see him being a packhorse, he won't take a blanket, let alone a saddle but I guess that's your problem. Give me forty-five-dollars for the three and it's a deal."

"You drive a hell of a bargain, but if you throw in a couple of pack saddles and halters with lead ropes it's a sale."

"God damn it man, I'm loosing money on the pinto as it is, if I throw in the other shit you ask for, I might as well close up."

"That's my offer, take or leave it."

"If you can get that pinto out of here without tearing the place up, it's a deal."

Placing halters on the gray and the bay was no problem. Rocky hoped that he had read the pinto right, he would know soon enough.

Still snubbed to the post, Rocky started toward him and with the same lingo as before. As he walked up to face the horse, he reached up, scratched his ears, and rubbed the horse's cheek. He untied the rope from the post and waited for the pinto's reaction, the horse stood there. Rocky led the horse out of the pen and it followed like a pet dog.

"How in the hell did you do that?" Cheek asked.

"I just had to remind him that he was broke and that I wasn't goin' to hurt him. I figured that it's been awhile since he has been rode, forgot what it was all about and I don't think he likes strangers much."

"Hells bells, you think you can ride him?"

"I wouldn't have bought him if I didn't."

"He tried to bite and kick you and wouldn't even let you put a blanket on his back, what makes you so sure you can ride him?"

"It took me a while to figure out that he was just playin', it was a game to him."

With that, Rocky halted the horse and with a grip on the pinto's mane, he swung his leg over the horses back. He sat there watching Cheeks face, his mouth was open and his chin had dropped to his boots.

"You ain't got a bridle on the bastard just a goddamn rope and he is standing there as big as hell, you screwed me damn good and I won't forget that." Breaking into a low chuckle and shaking his head from side to side, "Yes sir you sure enough screwed me, here I am running a horse barn and thinking I'm a good horse trader as there is and you showed me that I don't even know my own horses, shit I deserve to be taken. A mountain man took me for a green horn and I fell for it. Now you'll ask for a free nights stay and feed for what you bought and after a screwing like what I just got, it's yours I got that coming to me, yes sir but just one night."

"We've got to keep 'em somewhere might as well be here."

"One night is all, you pay for the rest."

"We might just stay the week and let the snow melt."

"Put 'em in the barn, and drop some hay down, we'll settle up whenever. If you want that devil shod, you had better stick around and help, the others won't be a problem."

"Can we get new shoes on him now; we got some runnin' to do?"

"Take him over to Big Daniel's and tell him we need it done right now, he'll do it."

Leaving the horses at the smithies, and after helping with the pinto, they went about their business.

The rest of the day went fast buying his first leathers and a new double barrel shotgun, along with a buffalo robe and a Hudson Bay wool blanket, canvas, ropes, and provisions to get them started on their journey. The storeowner agreed to accept James's old rifle as a trade in a new Henry long rifle and four boxes of cartridges.

Ty thought that they went over board on coffee and sugar but Rocky reminded him that they would be on their own once the side of bacon and beans ran out. "I like my coffee with lots of sugar, makes short rations taste better."

"What else we going to need?"

"We got about all we can carry don't need nothin' more that I can think of." That serious look crossed Rocky's face and he scratched at his beard, "Maybe one more thing, a bottle for tonight and a couple for the road, oh not for drinking mind ya, just for medicinal use, case we get bit by a snake or a mad skunk. We might use it for tradin' too you never can tell."

"As I recall, what you buy is yours, I don't need a bottle. I've got some money left and if I don't need all of it, I'll send some home."

"Where we're goin' you won't need much lessin' we need some at a tradin' post. Keep a little silver and if you got a couple of gold pieces, that should do it."

"I'll go to the Post Office now and get the rest of it on its way to Ma. Hell if I don't I might spend it on women or something crazy like."

"I'll just walk over there with you don't want to loose you this late in the game."

Purchasing a money order and writing a letter to Ma and the boys, telling that he was all right and was headed for the mountains. He said that he was going with Rocky and that he would see them sometime in the future and not for them to worry.

For an extra nickel, the Post Office in Jamesville would deliver it right to Ma's door.

Wiping a tear from his eyes, so that Rocky wouldn't notice, "Done all that I need to do, when are we leaving?"

"See what the weather is like in the mornin' and decide then, I don't want to be caught out in the open if we should get another storm."

"You got a place to stay the night?"

"That drinkin' establishment that I was at when we met up is most likely where I'll be, come sunup. One last drunk before the big country, it will have to last me a long time I'm thinkin', don't plan on bein' back this way again."

"I sure as hell don't want to sleep in a chair all night, I'll find me a bed somewhere and gather you in about sunrise."

"Cheek said that we could sleep in the loft of his barn, if we had a mind too."

"That's good enough for me, I'll tag along with you and get me something to eat, while you start on your drunk."

"We'll go back to the livery and finish puttin' our packs together and check on the horses new shoes, kinda in a hurry to get to the saloon."

Rocky ordered a bottle for drinking, and three for takin'. "You can haul these to the barn when you go, if you've a mind to."

Ty ordered a plate of stew and a mug of beer and finished by wiping his plate clean with the last of the bread. "If you're going to stay and suck on that bottle, I'm going to call it quits see ya come sun-up, right?" Waiting for Rocky to answer seemed forever and when he did speak, all he said was, "Put them jugs in my pack will you old son?" Then with a wave of his hand, went back to his bottle.

Ty watered the horses and finishing closing up the canvas wrapped packs making everything was ready to go. The packs didn't seem to have been disturbed; it was as they had left it.

Stepping outside of the barn and around to the side, relieved himself. After crawling up the ladder to the loft with his blanket and ground sheet, he preceded to make his bed.

Before he had a chance to fall asleep, he heard Rocky calling his name, just a whisper ever so softly. Shaking the blanket from his body, he went to the loft opening, "It can't be morning yet, what's up?"

"Get your stuff, were leavin' now and be damn quiet doin' it."

With his blanket rolled in the ground sheet, he joined Rocky in saddling the horse and loading the packs. The two packhorses, the gray and bay, stood quite while they placed the heavy loads on their backs. The black and white horse Rocky called "Satan", his bay packhorse; he just called him "Horse". Ty had chosen to name his new horse, "Pat", for no reason except that he liked the name.

Within minutes, they headed west out of Westport Landing, with nothing but the glistening snow and the early evening stars to guide them.

CHAPTER 7

Within an hour, the wind had picked up and the biting snow crystals hit their faces like pellets. Pulling his new fur cap tight to his chin and mouth, he squinted his eyes for a little more protection while he followed Rocky.

They had started southeast and as the blowing snow covered their tracks, they changed their direction, heading straight west. Ty was confused but trusted Rocky to know what was right, he would ask questions later. When they made the move to the west, was when the snow nearly hit them head on. Riding with his face turned to the left and urging Duke to stay close to Rocky, trying for all he could to keep the painful snow from his face.

Riding west for what seemed like hours, Rocky stopped and dismounted. Immediately checked his horse's legs and removing his fur hood, listened to the breathing of both animals.

Following his lead, Ty did the same. The check completed, Ty moved up to where Rocky was standing, on the down wind side of the pinto, "Everything all right has one of 'em pulled up lame?"

"No, their fine, after you've ridin' a horse that's been hold up for a while, you got to be sure you ain't pushin' 'em too far, to fast. I don't want to ride 'em into the ground, how's Duke and the Gray holdin' up?"

"They feel and sound alright to me."

"This wind is the best thing that could happen to us it makes for damn miserable ridin' but the snow is fillin' in our tracks and that's good, damn near makes trackin' impossible."

"Someone following us?"

"Just a hunch but you never know."

"Did you see or hear someone behind us, or are you just being careful?"

"Careful mostly there was two gents in the saloon that was damn interested in when we were leavin' and real interested where we were headed."

"After you left, I got kinda loud, with my drinkin' and all. These two gents asked if they could share my company and my table, they said that they had their own jug. I told 'em that if it was talk they were after, they had better find someone else to sit with, if it was a drinkin' they wanted, go to it."

A few drags on the bottle and the questions started. "Heared your headed west it's none of our business but when you planning to leave?"

"Your right, it's not any of your business."

"Hold on there partner, were just being friendly, as long as were sharing this here table thought I would be sociable, I didn't mean nothin'."

Slapping Ty on the arm and pointing to the wind side of Duke, laid Tuff, "It looks like the dog that don't belong to anyone is followin' us."

"Looks that way, go on with your story."

"Well they bought another jug and we proceeded to drain it, I wasn't drinkin' as much as they thought I was. One of 'em started to test me, talkin' about my rifle and askin' dumb questions, I went along with 'em and started pourin' my guts out to 'em. Told 'em we was leaving first thing in the mornin' headed for the Santa Fe Trail, and was going as far as Bent's Tradin' Post, then north to the high mountains."

"You've been there before?" they asked.

"Never that far south, but I hear there is gold in them mountains and I aim to get some."

"Going across injun country alone ain't smart, you're better off to sign on with a wagon train that's headed for Mexico."

"Were hopin' to tie up with one at the Cottonwoods just southwest of here. We'll just set there and wait for one to show up don't figure that it will be too long. Seen a bunch of carts bein' unloaded today they should start back south pretty damn soon, can't see 'em wait too damn long. If we can't sign on with one, we'll wait for another."

"Got a greenie with me, most likely slow me up some but hell; I've never been in a hurry in my life till now I've got to shit so bad, I can taste it. Watch my bottle; I intend to drink till sun up, how about you boys?"

"With that I got up grabbed my rifle, went out back and headed for the livery. They may have waited twenty minutes, not much longer, wouldn't take 'em long to figure that I had passed out, fell in the shitter or just plain took off. They will come after us all right, in this weather we'll be tough to track. They think were stayin' on a southeast route direct to the cottonwoods so they will most likely swing around and try to get in front of us. Try to ketch us flat footed."

"What did you tell 'em anything for, you said to keep our mouths shut."

"Them two were going to go after us anyway, I told 'em believable shit, it was a lie, but believable. As drunk as they thought I was, helped to convince 'em."

"Besides, this pinto I'm on has been sold twice to Cheek, last fall and again this spring, the Smithy told me. Them two folks in the saloon, sounded like the pair that brought 'em in, nice of the Smithy to warned me about it."

"Cheeks crooked; I would have a hard time believing that he sounded honest."

"Hell you can't blame Cheek he might of been told a good story when he bought him the second time, I still think he is honest, but maybe a little greedy."

Taking out one of the bottles in his pack, he pulled the cork, and took a healthy shot. Handing the bottle in Ty's direction, "Takes the snap out of the wind some and the bite out of the cold, it won't hurt to prove me right take a swallow."

What the hell, he would try a small shot; he reached for the bottle in Rocky's out stretched hand, took a swallow and was amazed how fast he warmed up.

"It ain't no better than before." A sudden shiver over took his body and disappeared as soon as it had come. "It does have a quality to it, don't it?"

Laughing Rocky crawled in the saddle and head out, never looking back. Pulling up beside of his partner, "How late we going to ride?"

Yelling over the wind he answered, "You gettin' tired?"

"No."

"I thought we would go the night out and maybe some tomorrow. It's just as warm ridin', as tryin' to sleep. If you start to freeze up, we can walk along side the horses; put new life in your legs and save some on the horses too."

They rode in silence for a long time, giving Ty a chance to think. This wasn't how he had picture his trip would start, in the middle of the night with no one to watch as he rode out of sight, for that matter, no one knew he was even gone. For some reason he was reminded of the crowd of people in Hannibal when James and Kevin left for the war. Grinning to himself he thought, who in the hell would be interested in my where abouts anyways?

A thought crossed his mind about Mrs. Casey. He hadn't had a chance to follow up with the Riverboat people on Mrs. Casey's trail, things just happened to fast. If he did find that she went north what could he do about it, there's a lot of country out there. I'd never find her, don't even know where a person would start?

Every so often, the riders would get down and lead their horses, circulation would return to their legs, and the horses would shield them from some of the raw wind.

Ty thought the night would never end. Hours after they left Westport Landing the struggling sun forcing its way through the fog and overcast sky, it lighten the horizon and permit Ty to see the country he was riding through. As the sky grew brighter, the wind let up and the only shadows seen were theirs. For as far as Ty could see, there was not a tree to be found, just rolling grassland partially cover with snowdrifts. A ground wind, hardly noticeable, gently moved the snow from one drift to another.

"We'll hold up in that low ground and build us a fire. Have a biscuit and a cup of coffee."

Ty looked ahead and to each side but could not see a draw, a gully or a damn thing except grass. "What low ground you talking about?"

"Just ahead of us son, use your eyes, give 'em a chance and they will show you things that most people won't see. Start lookin' at the grass just ahead of your horse and keep raising your eyes, real slow till you see a break in the grass. See a thin line that looks out of place and the grass beyond is a lighter shade, do you see it. The closer we get, you lose the line, but you can see the ground slopin' down. Not much protection from the wind but at least we can get the horses below the skyline, might even find us a buffalo waller to camp in. Put us even further below the line of sight be less noticeable to eyes that might be lookin' this way."

"Hell I see it now, never paid no mind before. I sure have got a lot to learn."

"We'll keep workin' on that, it takes time out here to ketch on to all of the tricks, just take 'em one at a time and remember what you see. Don't expect to learn 'em all from me, cause I don't know all the tricks, I'm still learnin' myself."

The depression wasn't deep, maybe a quarter mile wide. The ground wind still persisting to blow snow from one spot to another. The snowdrifts were larger and deeper, covering most of the ground. As soon as they dropped below the skyline, Rocky reined to the left. They rode another half mile before drawing to a halt in a shallow depression, about fifteen or twenty foot across. Stepping down from the saddle, Rocky looked at Ty, "Gather up some of those buffalo chips, the dry ones burn better. If you choose right you won't get your hands covered with buffalo shit." Rocky pointed off to his right where the ground was clear of snow.

Shaking his head from side to side, "We going to burn buffalo shit to cook our coffee, I heard of that but I never thought that they really did it. How many do we need and how do I tell if they're dry enough?"

Laughing under his breath Rocky replied, "The ones that have a lot of worm holes in 'em, and ain't green. Bring an armload, we might rest the horses a little longer let 'em feed on this new grass; they've had a long night too."

Feeling something amiss, he looked around and realized that Tuff was nowhere to seen. Carrying an armload of chips back, nearing Rocky he asked, "Did you see Tuff follow us in, I can't see him anywhere."

"He was here, the last I seen him he was headed up the draw, he'll be back most likely scoutin' around."

Stacking the chips in the area that Rocky had cleared with his feet, Ty stepped back and watched Rocky take out his powder horn, sprinkled a few grains of powder on one of the lower ones and using a small piece of flint and his knife to create a series of sparks, in seconds he had a fire going. It amazed Ty how hot it burned, hotter than wood by a long shot and no smoke.

Snow placed in the coffee pot, when it began to boil, they added the ground coffee. The smell of the coffee boiling in the pot brought visions of home to Ty. During the war, it was nearly impossible to get coffee and served only on special occasions. When the brew was ready and removed from the fire, Rocky added a handful of snow, to settle the grounds.

Cold biscuits and hot coffee was just enough to spark their appetites, bacon would have been their first choice, but they would save it for later.

After the sparse breakfast was finished, they leaned back on the packs. They watched the horses while they grazed on the new sprouts of grass. Rocky had made it clear that they not bunch up, so Ty sat on one side and watched up the slope while Rocky located himself to see the other. "This way a person can't get the drop on one and still watch the other, that's why we ride a distance apart." Rocky reminded him.

"What made you turn to the left and not to the right when we rode in, any reason?"

"If we was being followed, we don't want to be surprised. If they follow, our tracks into this here draw without thinking and we can see or maybe hear 'em first, we're down wind and the wind carries sound real good."

"When I was out gathering the chips, I seen more of these holes that were camped in, are these wallers?"

"Boy, you are green, don't even know a buffalo waller when you see one. You sure as hell do have a lot to pickup on."

With a piece of wheat grass in his mouth and scratching his check, he started to explain. "You see in theses swales, like were in, when it rains the water washes in dirt and fine dust. You seen a pig waller in the mud, well a buffalo wallers in dirt to get rid of bittin' bugs and fleas and stuff. When one buffalo is done wallerin' another takes over and then another, all the time diggin' the hole deeper and deeper. The bigger ones fill with water and the buffalo, deer and varmints of all kind drink from 'em. Injuns hide in 'em when they are out huntin' just like us, were hidin' in one?"

Ty pulled a long stem of grass and looked it over before using it as a tooth pick. "If I lay here much longer I'll be sleeping before you know it."

"I'll see that you don't, were not out of the woods by a damn site them two don't look like they would give up easy. They know by now that we ain't headed for the cottonwoods. Maybe something else will ketch their eye, but I'm bettin' that they will figure out we turned west."

After a short while, Tuff showed up carrying a dead rabbit in his mouth, he laid down a distance from the campsite and proceeded to eat his breakfast.

"I'll be damned," Rocky said, "He sure knows how to fare for himself, don't he now."

"I guess he is used to it, the morning we left, I seen him with chicken feathers on his muzzle, probably hasn't been fed by anyone since he lost his mistress.

Neither said anything for several minutes until Ty broke the silence. "This is what I was told it was like nothing but grass as far as you can see. I really didn't believe them stories I'd heard, figured there had to be trees. Why do you think there aren't any, the soil looks like it would grow most everything?"

"The Buffalo has been on this land for, Christ I don't know how long. The herds have broke down everything that they couldn't eat, the trees never had chance to grow. Now that the herds are smaller and moved further west the trees will come back in time."

"When will we run into the big herds?"

"If we went straight west, we would see 'em probable tomorrow. But were gonna head northwest when we leave here. I'd figure that we will come across the smaller bunches in two or three days."

"Why are we going to change course, it seem like it would be smarter to keep going like we are."

"I want to head for the Platte, just west of what they call Omaha and follow it to the forks. Then go north, get away from the wagons and such goin' to Oregon."

"What about the Indians, that would put us pretty close to the Dakotas, won't it?"

"West of 'em some if we don't screw up but the Injuns I hear are quiet now, at least till we get north of the Platte, that is when I figure we got to start worryin' some. Not that there ain't any between us and the river, there is but a hell of a lot more a little farther west."

Rocky's thoughts seem to vanish from his mind as his gaze moved to the northwest. Just as abruptly, he started again. "If we can get across the Platte, we'll keep headed North by West. We can see the big mountains, in say, middle of next month. I'm damn ready to get to Blackfoot country maybe I'll find Evenin' Star. She is most likely married now, might even have a batch of youngins." That far away look and sound had returned to Rocky's voice. The same sound that Ty had heard that night at the burning barrel. He just sat there with his eyes looking out toward the endless grass.

Suddenly sitting up straighter, with an attempt to change the subject, he said, "West of here the grass is a hell of a lot shorter than here, they call it Buffalo grass. If they want to get full, which I don't think they ever do, the buffs have to keep moving. This leaves some grass for the ones that follow behind. As short as it is, it grows all the time, except in the winter." Pausing and pointing his right ear into the wind, sat for a moment before saying. "Must be damn fine grass, you never see'd a thin buffalo. What are you thinkin' about, you look a million years away?"

Ty looked down at his feet and hesitated before saying, "You suppose that if in' those two show up we'll have to have it out with 'em?"

"If you want to keep what's yours and that includes your life. When they show up it's because they want what we got and they're ready to do what it takes to get it. We'll have to do what we got to do to keep it, that is why I told you never go anywhere with out your rifle or that there shotgun you got now, never forget it."

After a spell, they both raised up, started to say, at the same time, that it was time to move on. A chuckle and a big smile crossed Rocky's lips, "We might just make a good pair, we seem to think the same or at least at the same time."

Placing the packs and the saddles on the rested horses, they continued up the draw. After a short distance, Rocky said, "You keep ridin'; I'm goin' to check our back trail." And with that flipped the lead rope of his packhorse to Ty, rode slowly up the right bank. As soon as his head appeared above the horizon, he stopped and surveyed the trail over which they had come. Riding back to where Ty was he said, "Didn't see a sign but we still had better be damn careful. They might have gotten in front of us, I doubt it but you never know.

Several deer and a lone coyote was kicked up as they rode, they seemed to have come from out of nowhere and without asking Ty figured that they must have been hiding in a waller. Rabbits and prairie chickens seen from time to time and again Ty decided against asking what kind they were, he would find out soon enough.

They rode most of the day and staying as low as possible. Toward evening Rocky abruptly pulled up and dismounted, "We'll camp here and eat some, while I get things started, you picket the stock."

The saddles and packs removed, and the horses placed on a short length of rope, staked and let to feed. Rocky had gathered the chips and the fire was hot as he placed the coffee pot to one side. He laid four slices of bacon in a small iron skillet and he started to prepare supper.

"Won't they smell the coffee and bacon, the smell could pull 'em right in or at least it will tell 'em where we are."

"We won't be here that long."

"What do you mean we won't be here, were set up for the night ain't we?"

"For the time being but we won't be sleepin' here tonight. We set up and make every effort to convince, who ever might be watchin' that we're here for the night. After dark, we pack up and move on a ways, there's water just west of here we can water down the horses and find us a nice little hole to throw our robes in. We'll muzzle the horses to start with and let 'em graze toward mornin', now make yourself at home."

"Damn it Rocky you think of everything, maybe I'll learn a thing or two."

"I still got my hair."

"How in hell do you know that there is water where you say it is? I don't see no trees or anything else that would tell that there is any near here, are you guessing?"

Watching Rocky's headshake from side to side, either in wonderment or disgust, Ty didn't know which, but he knew that he would find out soon enough.

"Damn it boy look around and pay attention last couple hours there has been sign a plenty, if you would just heed 'em. See anything different about the goin's on now than earlier?"

Thinking hard, wanting to please his teacher, Ty could not come up with one thing that was different except for the late part of the day. "Hell it looks all the same to me it's getting later and the sun will set before long, what is it that I should see?"

"I see that I'm goin' to be hard pressed to teach you enough for you to make it on your own. This time of day, watch the birds and small game that we see, nine chances out of ten they're looking for water. A bird is goin' to go straight for the water, drink it's fill and head straight back to it's nest. Hell, even Tuff knows that much, he headed that way as soon as we set up camp. You got to keep your eyes open and see all that is happenin' around you. All them creatures are tellin' a story you just got to listen and watch. See a flock of birds up all at once; something flushed 'em, hear 'em go quiet something is near. Watch out the sides of your eyes for the deer and other grass eaters will tell you what direction to be lookin' in. They all run away from what spooked 'em. Its going to take time I guess, but you will ketch on or you most likely won't make it far."

Both were silent and Ty was thinking, there was so much to learn and the damn dumb part was he had known this back home just didn't need it that much then. "You know Rocky; I might be smarter than I think I am, damn it I knew those things before, thought it would be different out here I guess."

"Use you head son, and the rest will come easy."

The bacon eaten and the coffee still warm in the tin cups, they wiped up the grease with cold biscuits. They laid back with their heads resting on their saddles. "When do we move out?"

"When it is good and dark and the moon is still down. We will change directions a couple times then find us a cozy hole and get some sleep we both need that. The stock needs their fill of grass and water it's been slim pickin's since we left."

Shortly after the sun had set and before the moon had risen, the horses were loaded and off to the north they went. Ty thought to himself that when we left the camp the water was just west of us, we are headed north and Rocky said that they would change directions a couple of times. I've got to think and pay attention I can't rely on Rocky's sense of directions forever.

Riding up, along side of his partner Ty, whispering to hold the noise down, he asked if he could take the lead and see if he could find the water on his own. With just a motion of his arm and a slight pull of the reins Rocky fell behind Ty's packhorse and they rode in silence.

After an hour or so and several direction changes later, the water hole appeared right in front of his nose. Smiling and feeling pretty damn good about his feat, he waited for Rocky to complement him. Rocky just went about removing his pack and saddle., then led the horses to the small pond of water. He thought to himself that this water would dried up before summer then muzzling his horses, he picketed them near the new campsite. Following his lead, Ty did the same and only then, did they spread his ground sheet and placed his buffalo robes on it. Using their saddles for a pillow, they laid their heads back.

"I'll keep the first watch least till I can't stay awake any longer and then it's your turn. This way we will both get some sleep even if it is in short spurts, all right with you O'Malley?"

"Sounds good, I'm not sure that I could take the first one."

"I won't last long, get what sleep you can."

Closing his eyes and wondering where Tuff was, he fell asleep.

Something brought Ty awake, opening his eyes but not moving, he then heard Tuff's low growl. The dog lay next to Ty and was telling him that things weren't right.

Rolling out of his robe, still gripping his shotgun, he crawled, slowly to where Rocky's bedroll was. As he neared the spot, Ty could hear the slow breathing of a person asleep. Afraid to startle the sleeping man, he placed his hand over Rocky's mouth, and was amazed how fast his eyes opened, without so much as a twitch of his body.

Whispering he told him, "Tuff figured that something ain't right." With his hand, he pointed to the north, the direction of the dog's attention.

Rocky, now alert motioned for Ty to move in the direction of the water and to keep low. As he was doing this, he pulled his handgun and placed it on top of the bedroll. He then picked up the Hawkins that had been across his legs.

As Ty moved, so did Tuff, finding a spot next to the shallow bank, he directed his attention to a shadowy area, north of the camp. The only sound was off to the east where the horses stood hobbled and muzzled.

The hair on Tuff's neck stood up suddenly and Ty was sure that the moment was near. In the murky moonlight, Ty saw a movement, then a flash of light and just seconds later; he heard the sound of the gunshot followed by a second shot, off to his right. Rocky's answering shot followed the second and without a thought, Ty pulled the first trigger of his shotgun. The blast seemed to light up the area and Ty could see the first shooter jump backwards, and then it was silent.

Watching the spot that the man had been for only a minute, he turned to the second man, at that time Rocky said, "You get your man?"

"I think I did he ain't never move since I shot him, what about yours?"

"I know I hit him, heard the lead hit and heard him grunt. We will just sit here for a spell and see who can be quietest, us or them."

An eternity went by and you could hear a slight rustle from time to time, then there was the sound of a running horse.

"At least one got away, most likely the feller I shot. Lets not be in to big of a hurry to check on the other varmint. If he ain't dead now he will be, O'Malley, sure you're all right?"

"I'm ok, the way the old dog is acting it's over."

"The mean son-of-a-bitch, just earned his keep, I didn't think he was in camp when we shut it down. By the way, I am sorry as hell about fallin' asleep like a damn old greenie. I sat here and before I knew, it I must of went over the edge. Without old Tuff, we would most likely be dead by now then on the other side, I wouldn't have to talk about me falling asleep. If it had been you that didn't keep up his watch, I would have been a mad son-of-a-bitch, I guess it's your right to cuss me ifin' you want. "

"Hell we're all right ain't we, lets forget it." Then as an after thought, he said, just loud enough for Rocky to hear, "The damn kid has got a lot to learn, hope I'm up to it."

The smiles, not seen on either set of lips, but they were there.

"We might as well take the muzzles off the animals now and let 'em eat their fill, I think the worst is over, that feller won't be comin' back this way not tonight anyway."

Ty took the next watch and Rocky relieved him a couple of hours before sun-up. As the sky lightened, they walked to the spot where Ty had shot at the first shooter. He lay there with his left arm and shoulder nearly detached from his body.

Ty showed no sign of getting sick, looking at the body he could see where the pellets had entered the man's chest and tore through his heart and lung. Next to the body in a pool of blood laid a short-barreled repeating rifle.

Rocky said, "That's one of 'em from the saloon I guess that I had 'em pegged right. I don't think that the other one will be there, but let's see what he might of left." pointing to his right.

The second one also hit but not killed, a trail of blood led to a shallow spot where two horses stood, ground reined and chewing on their bridle bits, one a riding horse, the other a pack animal. The pack was larger than the ones their horses carried, and not put together as well. "Didn't take much time loadin' this critter, it's a wonder that they got this far." Rocky said as he tugged on the ropes holding the pack together. "I'm just guessin', but it don't look like they were goin' back to the Landin', now does it?"

"Don't look that way, what do we do now?"

Rocky answered, "We'll let these horses drink, do some eatin' and then scratch a hole in the ground for that dumb son-of-a-bitch over there. Has no right to it but if we don't he might just poison the buzzards that will feed on him."

A hole just deep enough to bury the man was dug and just before placing the body in it's new resting-place, Rocky bent down and started to go through the dead mans pockets.

"Damn it Rocky what are you doin', he's dead; you can't steal from a dead man."

"Lookin' to see if he had a name on him, can't say words over him ifin' we don't know his name, now can we?"

In his search, one pocket turned up fifteen dollars in gold and a small hand full of coins. Counting the coins Rocky said "Seventeen dollars and sixty-two cents rich bastard, wouldn't you say?" Rocky placed them in the pouch that hung from his neck. Another pocket hid a plug of tobacco, and a knife that had seen better days and finally, Rocky handed a sheet of folded-yellowed paper to Ty, "O'Malley can you read this, I'm not good with writin' and all."

Carefully opening the folds of paper, he read the names, first to himself and as he did, he looked up and said, "Son-of-a-bitch, I know this here name, it was on a wanted poster I seen after the war. Plunke—William Plunket, he was one that was wanted for murder with Mr. Casey. There was a reward for him and four other men you thinks it's still good?"

"I don't give a damn if it is good or if it was for a thousand dollars or more I ain't goin' back to claim it. Now you being a young feller and still lookin' for his place could do it but I'm headed west and goin' to keep headin' that a way."

"Hell it would be my luck that the reward ain't good anyways, I guess I'll just keep going the same way you do."

The dirt was pushed back onto the body and Rocky said, "Lord watch over this here sinner—Amen."

"I thought you needed to tell the Lord his name."

"The lord knows us all son, he knows us all."

Breaking camp was completed and the packs were loaded, Ty was reaching for his saddle when Rocky suggested that Ty take the saddle off the rider less horse. "It's sure not going to be missed and besides these Mexican saddles are a lot easier on your ass than that wooden McClennon son-of-a-bitch you're using now. You can move from side to side on one of these and not pinch your balls off."

"Duke here never has had a saddle like that on his back that I know of, think he is going to like it as heavy as it is?"

"He won't know the difference after ten minutes a chinch is a chinch to a horse."

"You think we should follow these tracks and see how far that critter gets besides I kinda want to know where he is. We know he is a son-of-a-bitch but what we don't know is that if he is dead or still up and about."

With the new horses bringing up the rear, they started north at a steady pace, Tuff ran out in front and soon was out of sight. Ty's thoughts were on the shooting, how damn easy it was to pull the trigger. Why didn't he feel some sort of sorrow, at least remorse? If he had seen the man's face first, he wondered if it would make difference. Kevin and James said that they had to learn to kill. Then it was just shooting and hoping you hit the Reb first before he hit you. They said that it was nothing personal, just war; there were no faces on the men they shot and they only remember the sounds of the rounds fired at them.

Ty remembered that he was not scared lying there waiting. He remembered that he had told himself repeatedly to fire only one barrel at a time and don't rush my breath' in, keep it normal. Thinking back, he amazed himself that he was as calm as he was; would it always be this easy? With Zack, Ty thought I didn't really kill him; he did it himself, the stupid bastard.

Rocky's voice interrupted his thoughts and he wasn't sure what he had said, "What did you say; I had my mind somewhere else?"

"Are you thinkin' about the dead man or just the shootin'?"

"The shootin', it seemed too easy, before hand, I wasn't nervous, and afterwards it didn't bother me one-way or the other. Is that the way it is?"

"You were protectin' what was yours, some son-of-a-bitch wanted it and you said no. The shootin' was goin' to happen it was bound to, just as soon as them two decided we were easy pickin's they were dead. You shoot a man for what he is, and what he is wantin' to do to you, you can live with that, you shoot a man for any other reason, is a different story, that's murder, plain and simple."

Changing the subject Rocky said as he pointed to the ground, "Don't see as much blood but his horse is slowin' down, not followin' a line. Tells me that he is in bad shape, his horse is goin' where he wants, we will come across the bastard soon."

Before the sun had hit its peak, Tuff came trotting towards the pair of riders. Turning around two or three times as if to say, follow me. "Think he found somethin' up a head."

"Sure acts like it."

Riding only a short way, dismounted and walked slowly to where Tuff now laid. The body of the second man lay in the grass; shot high in the right chest. The way the blood caked his lips and chin, it was safe to figure that the lung was blown away.

Ty walked off a few paces looking at the tracks left by the now rider-less horse. It had never stopped when the body had fallen to the ground, this seemed odd and he asked Rocky about it.

"Most likely had the reins tied to the saddle, as hard as he was ridin' the horse is wore out, don't know or gives a damn that he lost his rider."

Going through the pockets of the dead man, Rocky found one hundred and seventy eight dollars and sixty cents, all in gold and coin. Together with a note written in pencil, that even Ty had to study on, "Looks like it says 2 wagons, this word I think is harness and the last part is 8 mules. There is somethin' else wrote here but I'll be damn if I can make it out. There is a number, 230 don't know if its dollars or maybe it means something else. Guessin' with what money he had on him it most likely is dollars, who ever wrote this never had much learnin'."

Handing the piece of paper back to Rocky, "That's pretty cheap for two outfits ain't it?"

It depends on if you're buyin' or sellin'. This gent must of been sellin' seein' as how he has most of the money in his pocket. Some poor damn family or maybe two is most likely dead, layin' out here somewhere with their bones picked clean. These scavengers made their livin' doin' what they was goin' to do to us. You add the other bastard's money on to this and you got what?"

Waiting for Ty to finish adding, he went on, "No one is goin' to miss theses damn bastard or the people they killed. If the bodies of them innocents are ever found, the injuns will be blamed, they always are."

"The way I figure it totals $195 and what ever the change was, that's not near to the $230 the paper said."

"Theses bastards most likely came to town broke, they spent some of the take to get drunk, get laid and most likely had to stock up on powder, supplies and such. Yes sir theses boys were raw hiders all right."

Digging in his pouch and retrieving the $17.62, placing with the $178 dollars, he handed it Ty, "Split this up into two piles, one for me and one for you."

Jerking his head up and staring into Rocky's eyes, "I don't want any dead mans money, it ain't right the way I see it. Hell we don't even know if this is their money, it just don't seem right."

"Well old Son, if you don't want your share, you can just bury it with this here bastard. That way who ever owns this money can find it and dig it up, or then again, maybe this old son can use it in his after life, we don't know much about that now do we."

After saying his piece, he looked at Ty. "O'Malley, this here gold ain't goin' to help no dead man but it might come in handy to some one that is still kickin'. Put your share in your pouch, if you still don't want, it give it to some homesteader when we meet one. Besides, it's more money than you have ever seen at one time in your life and you may never see that much again."

Turning to get the short handle shovel off Ty's pack, Rocky began to dig a shallow grave. As he finished they placed the body into its resting-place and again Rocky said the same words as before.

Moving away, a short distance they built a small fire and ate dried jerky while they drank the hot coffee.

"Does anything strike you funny about this whole thing Rocky or am I just tainted in the head."

"No, just two ornery Raw hiders that got what they had comin'. They're most likely warmin' their feet at the fires of hell about now."

"No, I mean about the last one, the one that was wounded. He headed damn near straight north, into nothin' or nowhere. Here is a man who knows that at the most he is a day and a half out of Westport Landing. The man knows he's hurtin' bad, he could use some doctorin' for damn sure but he still rides north and look at the trail that his horse is still on, headed North, straight as hell. My guess is the horse is headed home and the gent knew that it was closer than the Landing, he knows that he can get help there."

"Hell O'Malley you just might be catchin' on, it all makes sense to me, suppose we should follow that old horse for a ways and see where he leads us."

Shifting in the saddle and adjusting the lead rope, "Let's think on that a spell."

Neither man spoke, sitting on their horses and looking out across the northern expanse of grass. "We got no way of knowin' for sure that the horse is headed anywhere but north. He could be standin' just over the next rise or ten miles from here. Do we care, or is there somethin' I am missin'."

"We care if we want to quit watchin' our back trail."

"See what you mean."

Ty answered, "I knew it wouldn't take long, you seem to be a fast learner and all."

"Now hold on you scrawny little shit, ain't I the teacher and ain't you the student?"

"Hell if we're careful we just might learn somethin' from one another."

Nodding his head in agreement, Rocky smiled and to himself said, "He's goin' to come around, it's just goin' to take time."

"How far do you 'pose it is to where that gent was headed?"

"Some place near water and closer than a day and a half, I'd think."

Rocky seemed to agree and followed with, "If you was sittin' and waitin' for some one to show up, and when the rider's horse shows up by its self, most likely with blood on the saddle, what would you do?"

Rubbing his chin, then scratched his head and sat up straighter in his new saddle said, "Well if these two were raw hiders like you think they were that money was to be brought back here and divided up." Looking to the trail that the horse left, he continued on, "I guess that I would saddle up and backtrack that horse, see if I could find out what happened, most likely I'd be damn worried about the money."

I can't argue with that, most anyone would do the same. Now if we are trailin' the horse from this here direction and whoever and how many is trailin' back towards us, we'll meet head on, won't we?"

The look on Ty's face showed that he had not thought they might run into them unexpected, not until Rocky had put it the way he had. In Ty's mind, he hadn't given any thought that there may be more than one person waiting for the men's return.

"If we don't follow the trail, we'll loose it unless we cut, back and pick up the trail from time to time it will be damn slow work."

"I think I got a better idea that horse knows where it is goin' and knows the shortest way to get there. We move down wind a might or two, far enough to be out of sight that way we won't run into whoever comes a lookin'. I'm a bettin' that wherever that old horse is headed, there be a shack or a camp there either one will for sure have a fire goin' on a day like this. Downwind we can smell the smoke and come in from the other way, how does that sound?"

Ty shaking his head in agreement added, "We can study on the situation thata way and know what we are facin'; as a mater of thought, why are we interested in findin' these folks. We can ride away and head for the mountains most likely save ourselves a lot of trouble?"

"Son, stop and figure what will happen when those men are found by their Rawhidin' friends. The two will be dead and the money won't be there. Whoever is left will want that money, you can bet on that. Come a lookin' for us and six horses make a damn good trail to follow, won't be hard to find us. Now I don't know about you but I would like to know what I am up against and when it's likely to happen, before it hits me."

"See your point, it was just a thought that entered my head and stayed. I never thought all that much about the money, or what would go through these gents mind, they sure as hell can find our trail easy enough."

"Sittin' here doin' our thinking is keepin' us from followin' that horse. We turn east now and it won't look like we are trackin' after it. Before they do any trackin' of us, they will go back to their camp and start from there, lay in a biscuit or two and some coffee."

"We had better keep our talkin' down some and keep our eyes and ears open don't know where they might come from."

Turning east, they rode for a time before cutting back to the North. They rode the biggest part of the day and the knots in Ty's stomach were twisting tighter and tighter. To himself he figured that a bite to eat might help but Rocky showed no sign of stopping.

The terrain was changing as they continued north, the shallow swales turned into deeper draws and for longer periods, they would be below the skyline. A distant line of trees came in and out of sight as they rode the rolling plains.

Slowing coming along side of Ty he quietly said, "Must be a creek or a river up ahead, do you see the trees?"

Without speaking Ty shook his head and went on searching the endless grassland for any sign out of the ordinary.

Just before dusk, Rocky pulled to a stop, looking at Ty and holding his nose in the air, made the sign of smelling. It wasn't necessary because at the same time Ty smelt the invisible smoke.

Motioning Ty to come up along side, he whispered, "We'll move on past the camp and get into those trees up there then move back on foot to take a look see."

Tying up their horse's as deep into the trees as they could and leaving them saddled and ready to go if they were needed, the men squatted down and tried to put together a plan. Tuff stayed back, near the horses and ate his supper of freshly caught prairie chicken.

"This stream curls back to the Southwest and that's where were goin' to find 'em, right on the bank and in the trees. My bet is that we won't be able to see the camp till were right on it, stay apart ten, twelve feet and move slow. If they have been here long and don't have a shit house, they will be using this area downwind of the camp for relievin' themselves." Smiling to himself he said, "Might catch one with his pants down, you never know."

"If they are there, what do we do, start shootin' or invite ourselves in for supper? How we goin' to know if they are raw hiders or settlers, I don't want to go shootin' no good folk."

"When the moon is full up and we can see some, it won't be hard to figure out what they is. Remember Ty, were just lookin' to start with no need for 'em to even know we're here. I'm bettin' that there will be only one or two others here and at the outside three. We'll check the horses for a count that should give us an edge up on the situation. Now go slow, if you see anything, let me know by hand sign. Keep a watch on me and I'll do the same, let's go careful like."

"Hold on, I think I had better take that rifle and leave this shotgun here, seein' as how I don't know what kind of shot I might get."

"Now you're thinkin' like a true mountain man."

The rifle in the crook of his arms and a pistol tucked away in his deep coat pocket, Ty crawled on his belly toward the suspected camp. The smell of burning cottonwood hung in the air and livestock making their restless sounds was not far away. Sensing, more than seeing or feeling Ty knew that Tuff was close. The dog moved silently as if he was stalking his supper, Ty wanted to make the dogs return to their own camp, but knew that it was useless to try.

After what seemed like forever, Ty seen Rocky's arm moving back and forth, indicating him to stop. Squinting, his eyes and looking slightly off to his right, he could just make out the square shape of a small building. Crawling to his right and closer to the clearing he heard and then seen the horses in a wooden rail corral. The corral stood to the front of where Rocky lay, separating him from the shack.

Ty could see nearly the entire front of the sod shanty, a streak of flickering yellow showed the location of the doorway. Who ever was in there was most likely moving around the movement, blocking the light from reaching the cracks in the door. There appeared to be no windows on the front or eastside and most likely there were none on the other sides.

Turning his attention to the corral Ty saw four horses and a cow. Scanning the clearing, he saw a small roughly built outhouse, it was no more than twigs and branches stacked to a height of four and a half or five feet. It didn't appear to have a roof and from where Ty lay, no door. A stack of wood piled near the shack; he pictured, rather than saw, an ax and a chopping block near by.

A movement on his right caused his heart to race, out of reflex action; he raised the rifle as he turned. A hand reached up and stopped the movement of the gun at the same time; he heard Rocky's whispering. "Let's move back a ways and talk this out, you go first and I will follow a bit later, want to be sure we weren't heard just now."

Waiting for Rocky, Ty thought what a damn fool I could have shot my partner and not even known it was him, this is spooky but damn it to hell I know better that that. Hell I've been in the dark before, this ain't no difference

I should have known that when Tuff didn't sound off, I was safe. Where is that dog anyway, still up there watchin', I'm guessin'.

Rocky's arrival was as quiet as the slight breeze that was blowing. He got right to it, "If one of those horses belonged to our dead Raw hider that leaves, at the most, three more inside. Did you notice that there were no signs of homesteadin', just ridin' stuff on the rails, at least on this side of the shack? The shit house didn't take long to build, put together with damn little privacy in mind, most likely no women folk here anyway. It looks like whoever is in there, ain't workin' for a livin'."

With his head swimming with what's and ifs and why, Ty did not know what to say. Thinking about what Rocky had said and from what he had seen with his own eyes, he answered, "I see it the same way but I've been thinkin' that we should wait for mornin'. If they plan to track us, they won't start till daylight. By that time we will know how many there is, it ain't like we got to do it now, is it."

Giving Ty time to put what other thoughts together, Rocky just sat back and waited, he knew that killing didn't come easy for the boy hell, it don't come easy for me, he said to himself. It's better to get these things done with than to wait for the other fellers to get an upper hand, do it at your choosing not theirs. The boy will come to this on his own if I give him time.

Fiddling with his knife and with his thumb, tested the edge; he picked up a stick and sliced it in half. Putting one end in his mouth, he started to whittle the remainder into fine shavings.

"Your right, we should get this done one way or the other. They are feelin' mad as hell right about now, plannin' on gettin' their money back. I sure as hell hope they ain't thinkin' that we're out here waitin'.

"We got a pretty good look at the layout, the corral, wood pile, the door and those trees that are out a ways?"

"There wasn't much more to see, a tree or two in front of the house that was all I see'd."

No sooner than saying it, Ty thought to himself, hell I'm starting to talk like him too."

"I sure as hell would like to see the other side of that shack before we go bargin' in there. O'Malley, here's what I think, one of us could work our way over to that woodpile, that way we would have the door covered, the other one work around to the back. If it's clear, I will come back to this side of the shack. Wait for my signal and then throw a stick at the door that should bring 'em out, from there on we play it by ear."

"It sounds to me like I go to the wood pile, why don't you just tell me that and not rattle on so? It's goin' to take you longer to get in place than me, what happens if they show themselves before were ready?

"All I can tell you is you're on your own, I won't be far."

Without so much as a handshake, they headed out; Ty worked his way back to the spot that he had left Tuff. Not seeing, but feeling that the dog was nearby, he moved to his left, creeping toward the nearest tree. His only cover was the two trees and then another forty or fifty step to the woodpile.

Arriving at the tree, he looked to see if he could pick out Rocky. To his surprise, the man was standing straight up and walking through the corral. The horse's heads were turned to watch but they stood calm, not at all excited. Seeing Rocky crawl through the far railing, he started to the second tree.

The thought of Tuff entered his mind, wondering where the damn dog was. Stopping dead in his tracks, for from the shack he could here a man's voice, yell at someone or something. "If it was a dog, it would have raised a warning long ago, it had to be another person, that makes at least two," he said to himself.

Squatting at the woodpile, he watched for Rocky's signal, he could no longer hear the man's voice the place was quiet. Without warning, the door opened and a big man stepped out. The snarl of Tuff, and then you could see him sprint across the clearing.

Before the dog could cross the open ground, a shot rang out. Swinging his eyes back to the door, the man, framed by the shadowy light, was raising his rifle again, preparing for another shot at the charging animal.

Nothing more than a reflect action, brought Ty's rifle to his shoulder. The kick of the rifle and the sound of the bullet hitting flesh told Ty that he had shot another man. As the man fell, the wild screams of a woman could be heared and the sudden flash of Tuff entering the doorway, then nothing but silence.

CHAPTER 8

Rocky stepped out of the shadows and as he did, he held up his hand, warning Ty to stay put. Slowly working his way to the opened door, kneeling as he peaked inside, making sure of what was in the sod shanty before relaxing the grip on the handgun. Slowing rising to his feet, he said, "It's clear now, only a woman and that damn dog of yours."

He knelt next to the body, and turned it over, the man was dead before he hit the ground, the bullet had struck his heart dead center. A faint smile crossed his lips, he quietly said, "Old horse remind me to never get in a shootin' match with the youngin', he's damn good. Then he added, "He won't be seein' any more tomorrows you shot him deader than hell."

Stepping away from the woodpile, he started to lever another round into the chamber then remembered that he had already done that. As soon as he had fired, an action that even he was not aware of, had told him to be ready in case others were in the shack looking for trouble.

Slowly walking toward the shack, his thoughts went to Tuff, the dog appeared to go after the man, but it was something inside that he was really after. Shaking his head in confusion, he stopped and looked at the dead body. He had been a big man and the clothes he wore were as dirty as the ground it's self. He stepped over the dead body and entered the small sod shack, to see Tuff licking the face of the crying woman. Looking again and staring through the dim light he said to himself, "For Christ sake that's Mrs. Casey."

Moving a step closer he asked, "Mrs. Casey it's you ain't it?"

Looking at her eyes, as she shook her head no, Ty knew it was her, eyes did not lie. She was dressed in men's clothing an old shirt and a pair of wool pants that were obviously much too big for her. Her feet were bare and covered with mud but the most striking thing that Ty seen was her hair, it was cut shorted than most men's, the ends sticking straight up.

In an instant, she had lowered her face toward the ground and rocked back and forth, still petting Tuffs matted hair.

"Wilma I know that it's you, was that Charles that we shot?"

She stopped rocking and she shook her head yes, raising her head and looking straight at Ty. Her wet eyes were burning with a meanness that surprised him and she continued to shake her head yes.

Thinking that it was Rocky and himself that caused the anger, he said, "I am so damn sorry, we thought that he was a raw hider, Rocky and I had a run in with a couple of 'em today. We followed one of the horses here at least we thought we did, Rocky did we miss somethin'?"

Waiting for an answer from Rocky that didn't come, Ty reached out to touch her hand. She jerked her hand away, so fast that Tuff growled at him. Assuring Tuff that it was all right, he tried again, this time her hand remained where it was and as Ty touched, it tears fell on his hand from closed eyes.

"It's going to be all right Mrs. Casey, we didn't know."

The tears turned to sobs, she began to shake and shiver while the sobs grew louder. All Ty could do was to pat her hand and wish that there were something else that he could do. He remembered another time that he felt helpless when she cried but it seemed so long ago.

Rocky standing behind Ty said, "Reckon she ain't a stranger to you, son."

"She's the one that owns old Tuff here, the one that I was tryin' to find back at the Landin'."

"Mrs. Casey are you all right, can I help you, I wish that there was somethin' that I can do." Picking a blanket up that was lying next to her he covered her shoulders, and waited.

Tuff had not moved his head, it was still on her lap with his eyes closed, not a sleep, but content just to lie there.

After what seemed to be forever, Mrs. Casey, rubbed her eyes dry on the corner of the dirty blanket, she blew her nose and spoke for the first time, still avoiding Ty, keeping her eyes down. "Yes I am Wilma Casey and yes the man that was shot was my husband Charles. He was a different man than the one I told you about so long ago, Mr. O'Malley. He was everything that

I knew he couldn't be." As she spoke, she had to choke back her tears, wiping her eyes repeatedly, without looking up.

"Charles and two other men have been stealing and killing since the last time we met. He was a vile, ugly, the meanest man that I have ever known. The war did things to him that I can't explain and I'm glad that he is dead, I hope his soul is burning in hell right now."

"The other two went to sell the wagons, the mules and everything else that they could get a dime for. One of their horses came in this afternoon, riderless and upset Charles, afraid that he would lose his filthy money. He was waiting for morning to start to backtrack the animal; he didn't care about the men that were missing, just the money. I am ashamed that you have to see me this way, Charles didn't care much about neatness."

Hearing a noise behind him, Ty turned and seen Rocky dragging the body away from the door.

"How did you find Tuff, the last I seen him was outside of Westport Landing. Charles never liked the dog and Tuff didn't like him, bad blood between them from the very start. The night that Charles and his friends arrived at the farm, he tried to get a rope on him, but old Tuff thought different and kept just out of Charles's reach. He said that he would have shot the poor dog, but he didn't want to make any noise, they were being followed by the U.S. Army, or so they said."

The sobbing had stopped and she could look Ty right in the eye and as she did so, she worked on her hair, trying to pat it down, but to no avail.

"Your husband must of got there a day or two after I left for home? The Preacher and me looked all over for you, knew somethin' was wrong with the stock left unattended. We asked the neighbors if they had seen or heard from you, a couple had seen some riders and heard a dog barking, thought that there was four riders all together."

"Charles and two of his army friends showed up on Tuesday just after dark you were to return after the rain stopped. He walked straight into the house I was so surprised and glad to see him but that didn't last long. He had changed, he acted like a wild man, crazy like, told me to get what money I had and roll up the blankets, and we were leaving that night."

"Mrs. Casey you can wait and tell your story later if you want, you must be tired and need some sleep."

"No! I don't want to sleep, I am afraid I'm dreaming now, just waiting to wake and find Charles still here, I hated that man."

"Do you want some coffee, or somethin' to eat I can fix it."

"Some coffee maybe, there is a little left in the can on the shelf over there, pointing at the only shelf in the tiny room. We were about out of everything Charles blamed me for that, the son-of-a-bitch, excuse me Mr. O'Malley, but I am not the same woman you knew back then, living with him and the other two has changed me."

Rocky moved to the warm stove and as he added wood to the dying embers, he quietly said, "It will be a minute but I can handle it just give me time to get this stove fired up."

"All I wanted to do was to get away and in West Port Landing, I just about got up enough nerve. A lady at the boarding house where we stayed knew something was wrong and invited me to stay with her. Charles would never let me do that; he would have killed me right on the spot and most likely Mrs. Simpson too. That was the nice lady that owned the boarding house."

"I stayed at the same place, just before coming west." It sounded so strange to say that. All of his life he had wanted to goes west, and now he honestly could say that he was. "That's where I met up with Tuff. Mrs. Simpson describe a couple who had been there earlier to me and I knew it had been you. She didn't know where you went, but I guessed it was by the river. I went to the docks but couldn't get into the Riverboat Company to find out, it was closed; Rocky and I left the same night"

Taking the tin cup of hot coffee handed to her by Rocky, old manners returned as she nodded her head and said, "Thank you." Her composer regained and apparently, the need to talk about what had happened drove her on.

Sipping the hot coffee, she continued, "When we showed up here a nice family had built this Soddy, a man and his wife who was expecting a baby. All they wanted to do was to farm and stay alive. Charles and his cohorts killed them, for no reason, just for this place. Charles and those other two could have built their own shack in a day. They were just mean and cruel, lazy as there ever was, that bunch. They let that poor woman cook and feed them then they took them outside and shot them, I can still hear the screams, then the shots and Charles laughing. It makes my stomach turn when I think about it and all I could think about for days, no weeks, is how long that baby lived after his mommy was shot."

Tears were rolling down her checks and she could no longer speak. Sobbing, she rocked back and forth, reliving the carnage that had taken place.

The change in Mrs. Casey brought Tuff's head up, turning it to one side, he crept closer and her arms went around his neck. Her sobbing continued to grow louder and minutes passed before the silence was broken. "Tuff, you were the only one that stayed loyal. All the days and nights that I talked to you about my Charles and what it was going to be like when he returned. I should have saved my breath he was not worth worrying over. Better he was killed in the war; there would be many people still living. You tried to tell me that he was no good I should have listened. People had told me that he had a mean streak, but never, till after his return, could I see it, you seen it right from the start, didn't you old friend?"

Feeling as sad as she sounded, Ty hesitated before saying that he thought that she should finish her coffee and get some rest.

Slowly shaking her head from side to side, she raised her head and said, "I don't think I could sleep another night in this shack, memories of the past still haunt me more at night than in the day. Mr. O'Malley there are things that I have seen done by Charles and his cutthroats that make me gag. I lived with it because I was afraid to leave, he would have came after me and beat me to within an inch of my life. I know now that he wouldn't kill me, he just wanted hurt me bad. Now that he is dead but I am still scared, I don't know why, you are sure that the other two are dead, are you positive, a 100 times positive?"

"They are dead and buried, cold and laid out on the flat land south of here, long before we got to the brakes of this here river, they were rottin' in hell. They ain't about to bother you none now, lessin' you believe in sprits and such. You just lay here, covered with these blankets, till mornin' and things will be better, Tuff will stay at your side I am willin' to bet. Old Rocky here and me will sleep just outside your door. The sunlight will make everything look and feel better."

"I will go get our stock and supplies won't be gone long."

"Who is he, can he be trusted, I couldn't stand being around another man, just waiting for his time, never again."

After Rocky left the small room, Ty said, "He is a good friend I met him a while back when I was workin' on the railroad. I would trust him with my life you can trust him too. He is a Mountain Man and is takin' me west with him, wants to get to Montana and meet up with a certain tribe of Blackfeet. He left a woman there a couple years back and he misses her in the worse way. Enough for tonight, lets get you settled in and we can talk more come sun-up."

"I don't want to stay in here, not for another minute, I'll take my bedroll outside, Tuff and I will bed down under the woodpile, I've done that before. We will be all right, Ty I just can't stay here."

"You would be warmer and at least have a roof over your head, in case the weather turns bad. It will be the last time, come sun-up we will decide what direction to go."

"No, I'll not stay here."

"Got your fussy side up, guess I know when to back off, all right Mrs. Casey, we will find a spot that is to your liking but I wish you would stay in here."

Grabbing a tattered buffalo robe and a blanket that had seen better days, she followed Ty out of the door, never minding to shut it.

In the dark shadows, with nothing more than the sheltered candle, they found a break in the stack of wood. "This was my bedroom when things got bad. When Charles and the others were so drunk that they didn't miss me, I slept out here."

On her hands and knees, she placed the old robe on the ground and then the blanket, shoving it in the opening, crawling in and with a ruffle of Tuff's ears, she pulled the robe in and around her. Looking carefully you could just see her face peering out.

Tuff laid down, with his back toward Mrs. Casey.

"I don't think that he will move till mornin' he is your dog for sure Good night Mrs. Casey, we will be close at hand."

Rocky laid out his bedroll on the far side of the fire, Ty placed his near Tuff, but far enough away so that if Mrs. Casey had to get up in the night she would not trip over him.

The cold night sky with it's twinkling stars brought his mind right back to Mrs. Casey. Saying to himself, "She must have been through hell the way it sounds not the life that I thought she would have had. It sound like the two of 'em had it going right, till the damn war came along. The war seemed to change everything; it affected everyone in some way or another."

"No telling what she might want to do I guess that whatever it is, I will face it when it comes. Can't see her going on west and I can't figure that she will want to go back to the Landin'. She is so damn scared no telling what might be in her mind."

This early in spring, the nights got damn right chilly and Ty rolled up in his robe, hat on and thought about the last few hours. What was the chance that he would find Mrs. Casey, in all of these thousands of miles, in this huge land, in this lonely spot?

The killing of Charles and the other two had been too damn easy. "Damn it Ty," he said to himself, "What is the rest of my life goin' to be like. In the last week four men had died; Zack, Charles and the other two that had pushed him and Rocky to far. Damn it, the taking of another's life was not right and he remembered again, what James and Kevin had told him that in war you didn't shoot at faces; you just shot back at those that were trying to kill you. The men that was killed was just bodies."

When sleep finally came, wrapped up in his robe, with his head lying on the new saddle that just today had became his.

There was nothing like the warmth of a good robe, for thousands of years it was probably the reasons that the Indians had survived. The buffalo had fed them, their hides used to build their tipis, winter clothing, war shields and sleeping robes. It would protect them from the snows of the winter cold and shield them from the rains. The hides also used to make travois's for carrying most every possession the nomadic people had. Without the buffalo what would they have done, would they have survived, Rocky didn't think so.

According to Rocky, there was not a part of the buffalo not used. He said that they even kept some of the innards, didn't waste anything. Not like the white that killed, took what he wanted and left the rest. We could learn a lot from the Indians.

At the first sign of light Ty was awake, he followed Rocky's advice of laying still and checking the area around him for danger. Sure, of himself, he threw back the robe and sat up surprised seeing Mrs. Casey placing pieces of wood for a fire near the shanty. He hoped that the new day would remove her fears of the past night.

"Morning Mrs. Casey, up early ain't you?"

"Not really you're the last to rise; your friend was up before I was. He is at the corral, checking on the stock, I wanted him to bring back a bucket of milk. When this fire gets hot we will have some flapjacks, hot cakes or pancakes, what ever you want to call them."

Shaking the robe and rolling it into a neat bundle, he tied it with a leather thong and placed it with the packs, all the while he was thinking, "How in the hell did they get up without me hearing them, they must of been damn quite or I sleep too damn heavy."

One of the newly acquired packs lay open and the contents placed on the canvas that had covered it. There was dried beans, cornmeal, sugar, coffee, a couple of sides of bacon, and a sack of flour. Off to the side were a small stack of plug tobacco and six bottles of rotgut whiskey. There were four packages wrapped in brown paper, the contents Ty could not guess.

Having to relieve himself, he headed for the stock pen, just around the corner of the shack would do, it was more private than in the outhouse not far away.

Ty seen Rocky squatting down beneath the only cow in the corral, with a bucket held between his knees, the sound of milk hitting the metal bottom made a steady swishing sound. The cow would move and Rocky would cuss and follow it until it stopped, Rocky did not look like a farmer in his leathers and fur cap. Ty let out a chuckle that brought Rocky's head around, "Son of a bitch boy don't go sneakin' up on a feller that away I about dumped the bucket. I sure as hell don't want to do this again, but the thought of flapjacks was hard to refuse. Mrs. Casey had already got the eggs."

Approaching Rocky, leaning on the rail fence, he waited until he thought the time was right. "Rocky, I want your thinkin', before I talk with her. I have spent some time thinkin' on what she might want to do and I don't have any of the answers. I know I can't just leave her here, I know that. If Mrs. Casey wants to go back I can't send her alone and for the life of me I can't figure what she might do out west."

"It's been in my mind since last night when I got the connection between you too, I know'ed then that it was going to mess up our plans some. Son, I can't go back, head out again, I miss the mountains, and the thought of seein' Evenin' Star again has got me tied up in knots. I left her once and for these past two years, I've wondered what happened to her. She was worth dyin' over, I know that now. There is just some things I got to do, and one of 'em is to see what happened to her. I'm sure she has a Buck by now most likely a high power one lookin' after her, but damn it to hell, is she happy, I got to find it out or die tryin'. You can't leave her here, I know that and so do you, if she wants to go on to another settlement, North or West of here, then we can take her. Goin' back, Son, I can't you will have to do that, I'm damn feelin' bad, but I just can't help you that-a-way."

The silence hung in the air for what seemed like forever neither man looking at the other both of them understood the others problem. The thought of going their separate way nearly brought tears to their eyes.

With an ever so light sniffing sound Ty said, "Rocky I sure don't want to give up on my plan to go to the mountains. I understand your thinkin' I know and you know that the only thing that can change it is Mrs. Casey. I owe her a safe trip to where ever she wants to go, she has had a damn tough life since the war broke out now I have to do what she wants."

Staring into the bucket of milk, Rocky slowly raised his eyes and looked at Ty. "Let's wait and see what direction we head, you never know what might happen."

Carrying the bucket, they returned to the small fire. In no time, the breakfast was ready a stack of cakes six inches tall was handed to Ty and a like one to Rocky. The tin plates were hot to the touch and had to be sat on a piece of firewood next to the fire. Homemade maple syrup had been lavishly poured across the cakes and brought an apology from Mrs. Casey. "Sorry we have no butter but then again if you hadn't brought the supplies in we wouldn't have had the maple syrup, there was a block of maple sugar in the packs." As an after thought, she said silently, "Charles always liked maple syrup."

Mrs. Casey was down at the creek cleaning the plates and the bowl, Ty and Rocky sat sipping the hot coffee, both men quiet, each man off on his own thoughts. Finally, Rocky said to Ty, "You take them whisky bottles and put 'em somewhere?"

"No."

"They sure as hell look gone, don't they? If you didn't take 'em and I didn't do it, kinda leaves Mrs. Casey or some spook, right?"

About that time Mrs. Casey returned to the fire and poured herself a cup of the hot coffee, sat down and without hesitation said, "I know your both are concerned about my well being but I will be fine, I plan to stay here for the time being and later I will decide what to do."

"Yesterday I thought that my life here would never end, I wanted to run away but didn't know where to go that Charles would not find me. Now that he is gone, I don't know what to do, I hate this place, it has been a living hell. You don't know what humiliation he put me through, I know now that he never loved me like I did him. After I lost our baby he never forgave me."

Hanging her head, she began to cry first in a whimper and then could not hold it back. Ty moved to her side and placed his hand on hers. He thought, I have never been good at this shit, Damn it, what do I do. The crying continued for several minutes, shaking and rocking back and forth then suddenly it ended as fast as it began, wiping her eyes and looking at Rocky, "Would you mind leaving us for a short while, there is something that I have to tell Ty. If you hadn't noticed, I destroyed the whiskey, I have no need for it, and I have seen what it does to men."

Placing his cup on the ground, he rose and said, "I'll go and find a spot for Charles do you have a choice or a place you want him in?"

"No, just out of sight."

Waiting for Rocky to disappear around the soddy, she seemed to be in deep thought. Gazing at the huge cottonwood trees and seeing the fresh buds of spring she said, "You're the only friend that I have had since my marriage, it is strange that you found me. Last night I was ashamed to have you to see me this way and trying to go to sleep last night, I remembered the last time we were together. The Maple tree at our farm was just budding out as these trees are, they remind me of a young man and a lonely woman who took advantage of him."

Ty started to say something, but she continued. "It was so lonely on that old farm not knowing from day to day, wondering if things were going to be all right and how I was going to survive. Thinking about the return of my husband, was he alive or had he died? If he did not return, where would I go, what would I do?"

She lowered her head for just a minute and then began again. "Ty, I am not a old woman but I do not feel like a woman of my age should. Before the return of Charles, I had three moments in my life that I thought that I would treasure forever. My marriage, when I knew that I was to have a baby and when I met you that spring day, only two remain. I did want to be a mother, most all women do, a person always wants to share a part of themselves with others, mostly with their off spring. Ty, I am happy that I had the time with you, but what happens now, what happened last night, as bad as it sounds, was not a sad time. It lifted a weight off my body. After the shock of knowing that Charles was dead, the tears that I shed were tears of joy. Joy because my husband was dead, his friends were dead and I could start all over again. No one would ever know what I was forced to do or how I had to live."

"Charles was mean; I don't think that it was ever just the money that he killed for, it was the pleasure of killing. His so-called friends were afraid of him and he knew that they would never cross him. They did his bidding, drank with him, killed, stole from poor un-expecting people and—," Looking Ty directly in his eyes said, "Shared his wife."

As soon as she had said that, she got up, bent over, kissed Ty on the cheek and walked to the door of the sod shack.

Ty sat there not knowing what to do. Looking at the soddy, he'd seen her enter and close the door. Tuff scratched at the closed door and when she did not respond he gave up, stretched and laid down.

Letting her have some time to herself, it would also give him time to figure out what to do. He poured another cup of coffee and waited.

What seemed to be an eternity, the dog came to his feet, wagging his tail and showing more excitement than Ty had ever seen him show. The door opened and Mrs. Casey walked toward Ty carrying a small bundle wrapped in a piece of blanket. Holding the package in both her hands, she said, "Ty I want you to keep this for me, please don't open it, I will ask when I need it back. If anything should happen to me," She paused, patting Tuff on the head and as her eyes went back to Ty's, she added, "I want you to have it."

"Now that we are here we won't let anything happen you're safe with us. There is something that we have to talk about what ever happened in the past is wiped clean, you can start over. You are a young woman and have a long life ahead of you. I will take you anywhere you want to go, if it's back to your farm, to Westport Landing or whatever. We will pack up today and head back, get you away from this place."

"Ty, I have often thought of you and wondered what you were doing. I never pictured you out here, but I do remember that you talked about it." As she talked, she was constantly trying to smooth her hair down; her hair was just too short to lie down. "I can't go back to those places there are too many memories that I want to forget. You remember when I told you that Charles had inherited that money from his Mother."

Shaking his head yes and starting to say that he had remembered but with a small nod of her head, he shut up. She must have something important to say, so he let her continue.

"I wondered then what we had done with it, I could not for the life of me, figure out where we could have spent it all. Well the night that Charles returned I found out he had hidden it in a can under the maple tree not wanting me to spend it. He would rather I starve to death than spend his damn old money. That night when he dug it up he laughed and showed me, said it was right under my nose and told me that I was to damn dumb to find it. He used dirty word that I had never heard before and that was just the beginning."

"The funny thing that happened was with old Tuff here." A sudden smile formed on her lips and her eyes were the eyes that Ty remembered, starting to chuckle, "Charles had never liked Tuff and Tuff never liked Charles, shortly after his arrival he ordered me to tie the dog up. 'Tie him up or I will shoot the son-of-a-bitch,' he said."

Throwing me a piece of rope, I tied him to the post that was near the barn, Tuff didn't like that but I tried to convince him that it wouldn't be for long. Charles and his buddies ate the rest of the beans and corn bread. I just had time to get my money jar down and give it to Charles. He had come in and threw me an old pair of men's britches said that we were leaving and to put these on."

Wanting to stop her from telling her story because Ty thought it to was painful for her, "Mrs. Casey don't scrape up old memories, let 'em stay in the past all we got now is today and the future anything else ain't important."

"Ty I got to finish this, it won't take long."

Nodding his head and glancing to his left, he saw Rocky step around the shack, shaking his head no, Rocky disappeared back to where he had come from. "Go ahead Mrs. Casey, we got plenty of time."

"Ty, I think that you can call me Wilma you have earned that right."

"I'll try, but it does sound disrespectful, do you remember when you called me Mr. O'Malley, I sure didn't feel like a Mr. then, and I'm not sure about now."

"They had an extra horse and a pack mule; I had to ride astraddle which I had never done before. I was very embarrassed and just hoped no one would see me. We hadn't gotten to Garrett's place when Tuff came running up, barking and jumping at Charles's legs, he had chewed through the rope I knew that he would, he had done it before. Charles tried to kick him and finally did but the dog was smart enough to know when to stop and he stayed behind us the rest of the night. When we camped, one of the others asked Charles why he didn't shoot the damn dog that was when I found out that they were deserters. Tuff was always near I could see him from time to time but he always stayed out of sight of Charles. I thought that I would never see him again when we boarded the Yellowstone. I could see him running along the bank of the river; slowly he disappeared in the trees and shrubbery."

"One last thing and I will shut up, Ty for me this is like a confession I have to get it off my chest knowing in my mind that I will never forget it."

In the corral Rocky was busy saddling the horses, loading the packhorses and occasionally looking over at the two people talking.

Tuff was at the side of Mrs. Casey, she slowly caressing his ears and neck. Starting again, she began, "For several days we only traveled at night until Charles thought it was safe we changed. One night we were camped in a grove of trees with a small stream passing by. We had ridden well after sundown and I was busy fixing supper of salt pork and can beans. when out of nowhere came a voice asking to share our fire. Charles's friends disappeared in the trees and the stranger was welcomed to come on in. He was a big man, walked his horse in and tied it near ours. As he stepped into the dim glow of the fire I saw that it was Mr. Goodnight, you know the banker in Jamesville."

"Charles invited him to eat with us and when he sat down; he looked at me and said, "Aren't you Mrs. Casey." And before I could answer, Charles shot him, I screamed and fell to the ground. His companions came rushing in just in time to see Charles pulling me up and handing me his pistol. I didn't understand what he wanted but I found out soon enough. Mr. Goodnight desperately tried to drag himself away from the fire, he was sobbing, and trying to talk but nothing came out, blood was coming out of his neck or up there somewhere."

Charles said, "Shoot the bastard."

"I dropped the pistol, it was so heavy and it felt dirty. Slapping me and forcing the pistol in my hand, aiming at the dying man, he pulled the trigger and the sobbing stopped. "There you bitch; you're as guilty as we are you just shot your first man." I couldn't control myself and again fell to the ground, I was hysterical, I didn't feel Charles hitting and kicking me, all I could see was the blood pouring out of the man's body."

Like in some sort of a trance, Mrs. Casey went on, tears streaming down her cheeks and she was continually wiping at her running nose. Several times Ty tried to stop her but completely carried away with her story and between sobs and sniffles, she went on.

"Charles pulled me up by my hair, he slapped me for I don't know how long, yelling, cussing and telling me to shut up."

"Break camp," he says and in the next breath, "Empty his pockets boys let's see what he is worth."

"Mr. Goodnight was stripped down to his underwear, his money belt handed to Charles along with what ever was in his pockets. He didn't take time to look inside until morning, when he did he placed the gold coins in stacks, he looked up and said, "We can eat and drink a long time on this."

"How much?" the one that was called Bill said.

"You boy's share comes to about fifty dollars, twenty five a piece, I took a little more cause me and the bitch here did the killing, I took her share too any questions?" Charles stared at them till they both shook their heads no. "I know that the money he kept for himself was at least three or four times as much as he gave the others."

"We had left the body laying there; I still can see it when I close my eyes. That was the first of I don't know how many killings, someone died everywhere we went. I used to think it was for the money but it was the killing that they liked."

Finally, she stopped with her head in her hands and her knees pulled up to her chin, she cried, shaking and sobbing as she sat there. Tuff licked at her face, all the while wagging his tail, trying to tell her it was all right.

Ty thought that she should be left alone till the tears stopped. He went to the horse enclosure; Rocky had stopped what he had been doing and stood at the railing. "I couldn't hear but it wasn't hard to know that she was pourin' her heart out to you, she goin' to be all right?"

"Just have to wait and see."

"It can't be easy bein' around all the killin's and stealin' that was goin' on. Most likely never had a day of peace or a time when she wasn't scared to death."

"She sure as hell been through a lifetime in the last year or so, a damn tough life for a lady like her. She's livin' with this pack of bastards and her own husband didn't say a word what a son of a bitch he must have been."

"She say what she wants to do?"

"I told her to think on it some."

"Ty, I'm leavin' this mornin', want too get as much country under my belt by sundown as I can."

"I guess the only thing to do is ask her, out right and maybe push just a little."

Looking at where he had left her and seeing her gone startled Ty. Quickly he surveyed the area around the shack, worry creased his forehead and a sense of concern crossed his mind.

"Rocky she's gone did you see where she went?"

"Seen her get up and head for the shack just a minute ago."

Crawling through the rails of the enclosure, he had just started for the door when Mrs. Casey turned the corner. "Mr. O'Malley may I speak with you and your friend, Mr. Rocky?"

Lost for words he looked at Rocky first and then back to Mrs. Casey. "Ma'am, anytime you want to."

Both he and Rocky met her at the fence, Ty and her stood on one side and Rocky on the other.

Without hesitation, she began. "I have been thinking about what choices I have and what I should do. I have thought about staying here where most likely I could not provide for myself. If I go back, the only friend I have is Mrs.

Simpson at the Landing and that would only remind me of the past, which I want to forget. There is nothing back at the farm for me, again just memories. I want to go west and I know that I will need some help, so I am asking you both if you will help me, I will not slow you down I am sure. With Charles, we had to move from spot to spot very quickly, I have been taught well."

"Where west do you want to go, there is a lot of country out here and it is all west."

"Just west as far as I can go, where no one will know me and where I can maybe salvage the rest of my life."

Rocky spoke to her, "its mighty hard country out there. I know for a fact that it is damn hard on most men, let alone a woman, what would you do?"

"I know that there is talk about a railroad that is being built and where there is a railroad there are men that need fed, their clothes washed or just need company." With that, she lowered her eyes and became silent.

Looking at each other, Rocky shrugged his shoulders at Ty and looked away. Letting the silence hang in the air only briefly Ty said, "There is a lot more to do at a railroad town besides what you mentioned. There is always stores and shops that will need help, before you were married, I seem to recall you worked in a store of some sort. If you can sew, there will be millenary shops or just plain old mending. Knowing that you are educated better than most, people are always looking for someone that can keep books and such. Don't sell yourself short life is better than you're use to."

Rocky had gotten up and started to readjust the saddles and the packs coughing; he never looked at the couple behind him but started to tell Mrs. Casey what she had to look forward too. "West of here is a mighty tough country. A lot of people think that it can't be much different than back home. Most places ain't even real towns there is no law, people do what ever they can get away with; it ain't a good place for women and a single one at that. I ain't sayin' that you should go or not but you got to know what you are walkin' into. I know that your life these past months ain't been good but why walk into somethin' that could be just as bad? I never thought much of education, I can't read much and don't have much use for writin'. Ifin' I was you I would go to a place like Omaha, just north of here we could take you there and get you settled and later if things get better you can always move west. At least Ma'am, you will be around civil people. You can start over and most likely no one up there will know you."

Waiting for her to answer, for what seemed like a very long time, Rocky thought that maybe he had said too much. He added, "If its west you want to go, that's where we will take you just give it some thought. We will head northwest out of here any ways; you'll have some time to think on it."

Rising to his feet, Ty said, "I'll help you get whatever things you want to take and we can get moving."

"Ty you and your friend, I know, want only the best for me you are afraid that I will bite off more than I can chew. If you will let me accompany you today, I will promise to give your words deep thought, Mr. Rocky. I know that I cannot stay here and I know that my life is not over. It is not going to be easy to move on but I know that I must. I have told you, Ty, about my life the last year I want to forget it ever happened, I will not talk about it again."

Her eyes moved from Ty to Rocky as if to get their approval her expression told both that today was a new day and that the past forgotten.

"It will only take a minute to get ready there isn't much here worth taking."

Turning her back, without another word, she walked toward the shack. Almost immediately, she reappeared carrying a small cloth sack, a shotgun that Ty recognized as the one she had at the farm and a bedroll. She was wearing a buffalo coat that had seen better days and a floppy felt hat, making her look very much like a young man.

All the while Tuff never left her side. Ty said to himself, "Old dog you never was anyone's dog, but hers now you got to take care of her."

"I left the door of the chicken coop open hopefully they will be all right. I am worried about Rosie here; we can't just leave her, can we but I don't know how we can take her." As she patted the milk cow side, she waited for an answer.

Before Ty could answer, Rocky said, "We'll take her and give her to some settler, were sure to run across one up yonder."

With a smile as wide as the country that they would be crossing she said, "Mr. O'Malley will you give me a hand up?"

Making a saddle with his hands, she placed her left foot on it and mounted her horse.

Rocky lead the strings of pack animals, all four of them, out and left the three remaining horses for Ty, tied neck to neck hoping that they followed him out of the enclosure. Duke stood at the rail fence and waited for Ty to get Rosie in the mood to move out. Slapping her on the butt and giving a shout convinced her it was time to go.

Crossing the narrow stream, they rode to the top of the small hill just north of the shack. Mrs. Casey stopped and looked back and then silently rode on.

CHAPTER 9

The smoke from the small fire drifted slowly in the air and disappeared in the shadows of the evening. The dancing flames reflected in the eyes of the three people as they sat quietly within their private thoughts. Each was holding a cup of fresh coffee, too warm to hold and too comforting to put down. Without speaking, each knew the others thoughts, the smiles and the thanks were still present in their minds and would most likely last a lifetime.

The young couple had homesteaded less than one year ago happily accepted Rosie and the three horses. The woman, her hands across her stomach told them that she was expecting soon and the extra cow would come in handy when the baby was born." Her husband couldn't take his eyes off the horses he repeated over and over again that, it couldn't be true. Three fine horses like these would take forever to acquire; yet here they were.

Both Ty and Rocky had assured him that they weren't stolen, just that their previous owners would not need them any longer.

Gratefully the young woman prepared an apologetic meal, within which the limited larder would permit. The venison stew was lacking in vegetables but the freshly baked bread made up for it. Washing it down with a cup of cool milk, Ty thanked her for the fine meal, explaining that they had a ways to go today and that they had better get started.

The lonely couple enthralled with hearing voices not of their own making, tried desperately to convince the three to spend the night and leave on a full stomach come morning.

Knowing that there was little enough left to feed themselves, let alone three more, they begged their leave. They rode off very much satisfied with their brief encounter with the young couple, and knowing that the new livestock would have a good home. It just might make the difference in the success of the isolated homestead.

The sound of Mrs. Casey's voice shattered the silence, "How much further do you think it is to the river?"

Ty looked first to Mrs. Casey then to Rocky. Rocky's eyes looked to the northwest and giving it some thought said, "Three, maybe four days hard to say we lost some time followin' that raw hider to your old cabin, took us more north than I wanted and then Rosie slowed us down some. I'm hopin' that we will come to the river right where it turns northeast a couple of days East of Fort Kearney."

Squatting on the ground and with his finger drew a line with a big loop on the right side. "This is the Platte, it runs pretty much to the southeast till about here, and then it loops toward the North, a good distance. It drops back to the Southeast and dumps into the Missouri. Fort Kearney is just west of the start of the loop, about here."

"Only been there one time and I came in from the West, mind you, I'm just guessin' on how long till we get there."

Before he could finish his thoughts, Mrs. Casey said. "I'm going on West, I've been thinking about this since we left the young couple's place. I want to start a new life and away from all that might know me. You tell me we will be following the river or maybe the railroad, if it's built, I'll find something somewhere." With that, she got up and disappeared in the darkness of the night, not waiting for their response.

The men looked at one another as if a bomb had exploded. "God Dammit Ty, the west is no place for her, what in the hell is she thinking about? It don't feel right taking her any further west, it is not the place for a lady. The only woman that goes out there are whores and dance hall girls, unless their married or something. I was thinking that when we got to river we could talk her into going east to Omaha that's the place for her, not out west." Standing up he too disappeared into the night, taking his coffee with him.

The still surprised Ty sat where he was; he tried to figure out an answer to what had just happened. Rocky was just beginning to accept that she could carry her own weight now she has put him back in the box again. She has raised his hackles and he ain't going to back down without a fight, not to a woman anyway.

I got three ways to go, convince her to go to Omaha and maybe wait for the railroad, which I know that I can't. Agree to take her a little further west and hope to find a place for her. Last and most likely Rocky and I will have to split, he is mad now and I don't see him getting over it soon. I sure as hell can't just leave her on her own, Rocky's right; she has to see that there is a better way.

Deep in thought, Ty did not see or hear Mrs. Casey return to the fire. "I'm sorry Ty; I can't go to some place where someone might know me. After the life that I had with Charles, I can take care of myself, I can blend into a community and no one would ask where I came from. I have made up my mind and I do appreciate what you and Rocky have done for me, I hope you understand."

Both sat as if the other did not exist, the crackling of the fire seemed loader than usual and the chill of the slight breeze cut deeper.

"You're sure this is what you want; I can't tell you what your walkin' into, cause I don't know. Rocky's been out there, I know that it has changed since he was there, but I still have to think that the right place for you is in a town that has some order to it. If we find that the railroad is further west than I think, it is we'll talk on it again, I don't want to dump you just anywhere. Railroad towns are tough places, mostly men don't give a damn for tomorrow and only live for two things, payday and tonight, no place for a lady like you."

"A lady like me, Ty you just don't know."

"I got to sleep on this, you know what you would do out there?"

"I can sew and cook and I could open a boarding house or a store, I have some money, which I didn't think I would ever need it. The way we lived, we did not need much, always out of sight. What did we need money for; we didn't spend it on any thing, never so much as a new dress, a bonnet, or a damn pot or a pan. Oh, Charles got a new shirt and a new pair of boots once, but otherwise he just hid his money for what I don't know."

"Money's not a damn bit of good if you ain't around somewhere to spend it. If you end up in some old town that you can't go out for fear of harm, what good is it? Mrs. Casey there is more to living than just money, I want to ask you to think on that some more, I won't pretend to tell you what is best, but think on it real hard. Rocky is only thinking about what is best for you, when we left Westport Landing, I agreed that Rocky was the teacher or the leader and that I would do the followin', that ain't changed. I'll wait till mornin' and see if the three of us can come to some answer, one that will work out for the best."

"I know that I should have approached this differently, I did not want to cause trouble. I hope Rocky and you will understand what I want, at the most, what I think I need. I want to go as far away as I can, I don't want even a slight chance that I might meet someone that might know Charles or me. Talk with Rocky." After a hesitation she went on, "Explain to him what it is that I want and what I think it is that I need, Good night Ty, I'll think on it some more but I can tell you that it is all that I have done for the last few days."

"Good night Mrs. Casey."

Watching her unroll her robe and crawl inside, Ty thought some about how she deserve better than she has got. I'll just wait for Rocky and put it to him as she did to me, black and white. Let him make up his own mind, Hell, even if he did decide to go his separate way, he can't make any better time than we are, we can stick together till the trail splits.

Tuff came in from the darkness and went directly to Mrs. Casey side making a complete turn; he stretched and lay down at her feet, Ty knew that he would remain there for the duration of the night. "Wouldn't want to be the one that threatened your mistress old dog, you would chew me up and spit me out sooner that I could say stop. To have a friend like you is really something, even if you're just damn old dog."

Rocky still had not returned so Ty made up his mind to go look for him. He had not gone far when a voice out of the blackness stopped him in his tracks, "I heard what she had to say and I don't think that she really knows what she wants; she is scare't of the past, hell she may never see another soul that she has ever known before. Sometimes when you think that you are clean away from everybody and no one can find you that is when some son of a bitch will walk right up to you. She can't hide the rest of her life, at some point; she has to start to live, if we don't take her, she will find a way on her own. I'll go along with it as long as she understands that we ain't goin' to dump her just anywhere, think that she will agree to that?"

"Thanks Rocky, I think that she will."

"Let's get some shut eye and see how it goes in the mornin'."

The darkness of the night had not lifted when the fire came to life and the smell of coffee was hanging in the cold air of morning. Each one went about the routine of preparing for the day, making breakfast fell to Mrs. Casey, Ty and Rocky saddled the horses and loaded the packs. Mrs. Casey was squatting near the fire with a stick in hand, stirring the coals, and watching the bacon sizzling in the iron skillet. Rocky finished with what he was doing and helped Ty with the packs, one man could handle them but two made it much easier. The last one hung from the wooden saddle frame when Mrs. Casey announced, "Come and get it before it gets cold."

Ty broke a cold biscuit in half, soaking half in the hot grease of the skillet and loading the other with bacon and without a word, they proceeded to eat the sparse meal.

Chewing on the biscuit and bacon, Ty thought to himself that Mrs. Casey was trying to stay away from her wanting to go on west. If she don't bring it up, I'm sure as hell not going to, I think that we should just let it ride and see what develops.

Rocky lead off, Mrs. Casey next and bringing up the rear was Ty with the string of packhorses strung out behind him. If things went as usual, there would be very little talking or exchanging of words, the silence would only be broken when something needed pointing out. They would ride this way until midday and after a short break stop to give the riders a chance to stretch their legs and letting the horses rest and graze, hopefully near a stream or a pond of water. It never took them long to eat their piece of cold jerky, this was also when the silence of the day would be broken and the conversation would go from one subject to another. Most generally, it would start with something about what they seen during the ride that at the time didn't seem important or a lighthearted exchanges made to pass the time and today was no exception.

The next four days were a repeat of the day before and the day before that, cold nights, bright mornings and a late afternoon rain shower that never was hard enough to slow or stop the small party. For Ty each day was full of new things to see and different sounds to hear, he never showed any sign of disappointment or of getting tired of the trek west.

They saw wild game, deer, a few small buffalo herds, rabbits, prairie chickens, coyotes and a chicken like bird with a crown of feathers on its head, Rocky called a fool hen. He said that they tasted terrible and were not good for anything. Rocky said that the Indians feel that every living thing had a place on this earth, but he could not figure what the fool hen was good for.

They ate a lot of rabbit and prairie chicken but never a deer and Ty asked Rocky why, was it that he didn't like deer meat, the answer that Ty got surprised him. The time Rocky spent with the Indians taught him not to waste anything. Rocky said, "No way can the three of us eat a whole damn deer before it spoils and we ain't got time to make jerky out of it. I just figure that a chicken or a rabbit or two is enough. If in' we kill us a deer and can only eat a hindquarter, we'd leave the rest for the varmints, makes us just like other white men and I don't think that I want to be that way."

As the days passed, Mrs. Casey drew more into her own thoughts and at times, she was very short when asked a question, by either Ty or Rocky. At breaks or resting periods, she stayed by herself and seemed to eat less and less.

To respect her privacy, the men did not say anything that might drive her deeper into herself. They both knew that the trip was harder on her than on them; it was not easy to ride all day, with only short breaks to rest the horses. The past many days consisted of sleeping on the hard ground, eating breakfast on the run, riding, resting, making camp, eating and starting all over again tomorrow, not the life a woman would choose.

Rocky spent his days watching the horizon and the endless grass for signs of trouble. He spent his breaks checking the horses and the packs that they carried and when he finished, he would stand off by himself and look off into the west. His need to get to the mountains was always on his mind and the hurt for leaving Evening Star seen in his face.

Riding into a shallow draw, Rocky turned in the saddle, "A good place to stretch our legs and rest the horses."

Still setting in his saddle he added, "Can't figure out where the big herds are, the few scattered bunches that we've spotted can't amount to very many. I keep expectin' to run into the main bunch anytime, but they sure ain't around here."

"I ain't even seen any tracks to speak of." Ty added.

"Must be a reason they ain't here maybe we are still too far east."

The bridles were removed and as the horses started to graze, the small group went about doing the chores that had become commonplace. The meal consisted of jerky and a hefty drink of water.

Walking to the top of the rise, a short distance from the other two, Rocky raised his head, took a deep breath and followed with, "Do you smell that?"

Ty looked at Mrs. Casey with confusion and she looked back just as confused, both walked to Rocky's side, sniffed the air, and looked at Rocky.

"I smell the grass, the damn horses and our stinking bodies, that's all, what are we suppose to smell?" Ty answered.

"What about you Mrs. Casey, anything jump out at you."

"No.'

"It is a damn good thing that you're not deep in Indian country and had to depend on your wits to survive. When smells change out here you had better know what it is or your scalp will be hangin' on some bucks belt. Take another sniff and think on it."

Taking in deep breaths and looking skyward, as if for divine help, both seemed like idiots, with Rocky smiling like a cat that had just eaten a mouse.

"The air seems heavier is all that I can tell," Ty said.

"I can't even tell that." a confused Mrs. Casey lamented.

"Ty your damn close, you want to think on it some more?"

"Just tell me and let me rest my brain."

"What would make the air smell heavy?

"Just before a rain or maybe just after a rain, hell, the sky is clear there's not a cloud to be seen it sure ain't going to rain today."

"You don't smell the river?"

"Hell is that what it is, I just didn't figure on the river."

Mrs. Casey was now excited, "How much further is it Rocky?"

"Not far I'd guess its real close; we will be sleepin' at the river tonight."

"What are we waiting for, let's go." Mrs. Casey said as she rose to her feet,

"What's your rush it's not goin' to go anywhere, it will be there whenever we get to it, the horses need to graze and the little rest won't hurt 'em." The now reclining Rocky answered.

Mrs. Casey excitedly asked, "The sooner we get to the river, the sooner we will head west, I've been waiting for that and it will make me feel that we finally are heading in the right direction. I will be leaving my troubles and don't want to ever go back again."

Ty understood what she was saying, he looking at Rocky and hoped the subject of her going west would go by the way side. Rocky never stirred, just gazing off into the distance as if he hadn't heard a word that Mrs. Casey had said, he was in his own world. He was most likely thinking of Evening Star and kicking himself again for leaving her.

The trance broken Rocky said, "I'm with you on that, it's tells me that I'm headed to the mountains. We'll turn west there and follow the river till it breaks north. When I get to the fork, it will mean that I'm gettin' real close to where I want to be, I know that I will most likely never see this part of the country again, at least I don't plan on it." Pausing momentarily then started again, "Mrs. Casey we will find you a place west of here, not just any place but one that you can live in and start a new life. What you got to understand is that what happened is not your doin' it was Charles. If you should ever run into an old acquaintance, you have nothin' to be ashamed of; Charles and his bunch did the killin'. I think most people will figure that out, don't spend your time lookin' over your shoulder, a new day is here and the past is gone. The sooner you get the hate and the misery out of your heart; things are going to be better. Promise me that you will forget the past and lets all start planin' our new lives, Ty, you're livin' your dream, goin' west, I'm headed home to see what has happened to my woman and you Mrs. Casey are goin' to be your own boss and do what ever it is that you want. Tonight we will let our hair down we'll will have a song or two and a party it will be."

"Thank you Rocky, I'll try, a new life is what I want but the past is hard to forget, but I will try." Raising her eyes and turning toward Ty, she continued, "Some things I don't want to forget, the good times I'll remember, only the time with Charles, after his return from the war will I want to forget." With that, she got up, walked off a short way, and started to cry; this time the tears were tears of happiness, not sorrow.

When she returned, with a big smile on her face, she announced, "I'll start soaking some beans tonight we'll have a hot pot of 'em. I have that bacon rind I'll throw in for seasoning, it will start to mold if we don't use it, how does that sound?"

She was out of her shell and as she placed the beans in a canvas bag, she hummed a song.

The next few miles lasted forever and while she rode, following Rocky and just ahead of Ty, thinking of what she might want to do with her life. It seemed to her that it had been ages since she felt that a new life was possible, now was just days or weeks away. She had time to look back at her life and was very surprised when she realized that she was only remembering the good times, maybe a new life was possible.

A line of trees indicated where the river was well before they actually seen the water. Rocky started to rein to the left and as he rode, he studied the area for any signs of tracks or anything that might look out of place, finding nothing he reined Satan to a stop. Wait here and keep your eyes open I'll go take a look-see wait for my signal, then come on in. He rode into a grove of huge trees and after dismounting, he looked around and then signaled his companions that it was all right.

"Looks like a good place to camp." He studied the surrounding areas and the ground for any signs that might indicate recent visitors. After a short time, he announced that this was where they would camp.

Cottonwood trees surrounded the campsite and the sound of the river was faintly audible. The spring run off had swelled the flowing water well above the banks and was slowly receding back to its regular width. The lush grass was greener and higher than the short prairie grasses and the horses took little time before they were eating their fill.

"Mrs. Casey you watch the stock so that they don't flounder on this here feed, eat too much and we will have a bunch sick horses on our hands. This grass is too green and will bind their guts into knots."

"Ty you and me will build our camp there by that big old tree, just on the east side. It will give us a little shade and if it should rain it will give us some place to hide."

After the packs were arranged where Rocky wanted them, you could see his reasoning, they surrounded the fire pit and provided a bit of protection in case of any surprises. Trees that were staggered around the campsite blocked the other openings; anyone would have to be mighty close to get a clean shot.

"Are you sure you weren't a military man in an earlier life, you picked our camp as if you expected trouble."

"Another lesson, you can't be too careful always plan for the worst, It don't take any more time and it's a hell of a lot better to be right than lucky."

As the pack carrying the food supplies was unpacked, Rocky suggested that a dip in the Plate River would be in order. "It will be a chance to wash the trail dust and dirt off us and ifin' I am guessin' right it will cool us down some."

Mrs. Casey you can go first and I promise that you will have your privacy we won't peek or nothin'. But I want to tell you that river is runnin' fast so don't go into it too far and keep a watchful eye upstream you never know what might be floatin' down. This time of year I've seen whole trees come down smaller rivers than this."

"I don't like water all that much but I haven't had a good bath since the Landing, I'll take you at your word about my privacy and give it a try. I can't figure out if I should wear my clothes in, wash them first or get myself clean and then wash them."

Ty said, "You take a blanket with you and hang those clothes on a tree to dry, better yet, bring 'em back up here to dry."

Looking at Rocky and with a big grin on his face he said, "It's better to be safe than lucky."

Rocky was holding a small ax in his hand and holding it up, pointing it at Ty, "Watch yourself son, what goes around comes around."

All three had a good laugh and the men continued with the campsite, placing the bedrolls between the packs, still rolled up. A ring of large rocks and stones, placed to contain the fire and as Ty was removing the taller grass and weeds from the outer edge, he asked, "Thought we would cross the trail used by the families heading west?"

"We'll be comin' into it right soon I'm not sure if it's this side of the Fort or the other, know its west of here some. We've been east and north of it since we left the Landin'. When we cut north a-followin' that raw hider, it took us a far bit further north and east than we had planed on. Charles's shack was, I'd guess, was about a two-day ride east of the trail, close enough to raid the wagons but far enough away to stay out of sight. When we get to it, you'll know the ruts are hard to hide."

"Stayin' away from the known trails like we have gives us a better chance of not runnin' into any more raw hiders, as big as this country is, you can still come across other riders. On the trails, the chances are a hell of a lot stronger that you will, we don't need anymore visitors."

Wrapped in her blanket and carrying her wet clothes, Mrs. Casey returned to the camp with Tuff right behind her, soaking wet. His coat was matted and for the first time you could see that his muzzle was white. "Hoped you would have had the fire going by now that water is a might cold, I looked for ice but didn't see any. I don't know who enjoyed the bath more, Tuff or me, he is good swimmer and I thought I had lost him once but he showed back up. The river had taken him down stream a ways didn't seem to bothered him, he went right back in."

"He looks a hell of a lot smaller wet still I wouldn't want to mess with him wet or dry."

Rocky agreed and said, "Hold your horses; I'll have a fire goin' in no time at all, these buffalo chips will heat you through in no time and you will be wantin' the chill back." The fire sprung into life and small pieces of cottonwood was added to supplement the chips.

The fire was very pleasant and dried her garments in no time at all. While the men were at the river, she hurried and dressed, started the beans and in short order they were boiling. As the time passed and they had not returned, she began to worry about them, wondering what could be taking them so long. As soon as the thought crossed her mind, Ty's voice was heard. "Are you ready for us to join you, the fire is going to feel real good."

"Come on in I am dressed and got the supper going."

Dressed in their buckskins and after first hanging the wet underwear on a limb, they approached the fire.

Rocky was following Ty, walking very slowly.

"You boys were gone so long that I thought you might have drowned was just starting to worry some, as cold as that river was, I couldn't believe that you could stand it this long."

"Cold it was but when your havin' fun, time just flies." Rocky answered.

Ty commented, "For Rocky being a mountain man, he sure can't swim very well, then again he can always just stay away from deep water." With his face beginning to turn red, he burst out laughing unable to control it any longer.

Rocky's voice joined in while he too had a good laugh. "You couldn't keep your mouth shut could you, you heathen."

Watching all of this and wondering what had started it she said, "Don't keep me in the dark any longer, what happened?"

Trying to tell her but unable to stop the laughter, he pointed at Rocky and then he would break into another burst of laughter. Finally after many attempts he started by saying, "Rocky sure ain't safe in the water by himself, he don't pay no attention to his own advice. No sooner had he got in the river, when the current grabbed him and sent him tumblin' down stream, a rollin' and a twistin', head over teakettle he went. I was a yellin' at him to grab a limb of a tree or somethin' and slow himself down but I guess that he was way to busy keepin' his head above water." Pausing and shaking his head from side to side, he started to laugh again.

Not wanting this to go any further, Rocky said, "I got hung up on a river snag and had a bit of a time gettin' loose let's just leave it there, alright."

Looking at Ty and giving him the look that the fun was over but then he couldn't help it and broke into another round of laughter, after seeing Ty with tears in his eyes.

"Did you get hurt?" Mrs. Casey asked.

Again, this caused Ty to get up, stamping his feet and beating his hands together. Roaring with unbroken laughter he finally got the words out, "Don't ask to see his wounds." And with this, he fell on the ground and continued his uncontrolled laughter.

"With friends like you, I sure as hell don't need enemies."

"Yes to answer your question, Mrs. Casey, I did get a scratch or two. I'll be alright just have to ride real careful for a day or two."

Blushing slightly, Mrs. Casey was lost for words, wanting to change the topic and not knowing just how to go about it she picked up a long spoon, stirred the beans and said, "It is going to be awhile before these are done. I think I will make a pan of mush, if I can find the right sack, I'll have plenty of time."

"That sounds real good it will taste right good with a hot plate of beans. It just might take our minds off our little aches and pains, don't you agree Rocky?" With that, a big smile crossed Ty's lips but he did not laugh, enough was most likely enough.

Lying back with his back leaning on a pack, Rocky said, "We'll be headin' almost straight west from here on. We should run into the trail tomorrow or the next day, I'm thinkin' were still ahead of any wagons, it's a little early yet."

At times like this, I wish we had kept the old cow a glass of milk with Mrs. Casey's mush sounds mighty fine.

"Well we haven't any milk, wish we did, what trail are you talking about?" Mrs. Casey asked

"The Pilgrim Trail, some call it the Oregon Trail, comes up out of Independence and runs pretty much next to the river. It's on the south side and the trail that they call the Mormon Trail runs on the north side."

"We won't be crossin' to the north side for some time. The families that cross this wild country to find a new place are just like the ones that crossed the big ocean to settle in a new land. Takes a lot of guts and nerve to leave all that you got and head into the unknown, its not bad for a man but hell these folks bring everyone, wife, kids, their moms and dads, everyone. They don't know what they are going to find out here but they're willin' to gamble all they have on someone else's word and on what they might hope to find."

All three people were silent, the sound of the burning wood, the boiling beans and the feeding horses were the only things that broke the silence. The peace and quite was so different from other campsites that they had built, normally they were in a hurry to get the camp set up but today was different. Today there was plenty of time to do nothing but relax and enjoy the company of friends, appreciating the rest.

Mrs. Casey looked at Ty and then Rocky, sure that they were both sleeping. At that instant Rocky said, "Think I'll break out a bottle, for medicinal reasons only, you know." All three broke out in laughter with Rocky being the loudest.

"I think that would be a good idea you most likely will be need something a slight stronger than coffee. Hell lets have us a party old Tuff will be on watch, nothing will get by him."

The bottle opened and Rocky first offered it to Mrs. Casey at which she kindly declined, then to Ty. Taking a long draw from the brown bottle and making a terrible face handed it back to Rocky. After a long drink of the dark liquid Rocky sat it down at his feet, smacked his lips and commented how good it tasted. Ty knew better and smiled to himself he had only wet his lips and swallowed very little of the rotgut, Rocky could have more that way and Ty would feel better tomorrow.

Rocky was singing a Scottish song and halted the tune from time to time for an occasional drink, then pick it up again as if never interrupted. Ty would take the bottle when offered and pass it right back to Rocky.

The mush was cooking and Mrs. Casey was saying how much better it would taste if she only had an egg or two, milk would help too. "It will taste more like cooked corn crumbs but we can pretend it will be yellow like mush anyway."

"It will be fine old Rocky there will never know the difference that is if he slows down enough to eat."

"I'll be eating youngster, don't think I won't, this medicine is just the right ticket, my hurts are feelin' real good right now and after I get a belly full of those beans and mush, we are goin' to have a real party, I'm just warmin' up."

The hot meal was ready and placed in tin plates. The beans seasoned with strips of bacon rind and the smoky flavor of the rind added a back home taste to the broth.

Ty and Mrs. Casey had stopped eating; they were watching Rocky trying to eat his beans with a knife. The rotgut that he had drank, made eating a real challenge, placing a few beans on the blade and having them fall off before reaching his mouth.

"Rocky, why don't you use a spoon or just pick your plate up and drink your supper, it's alright. Afraid you might starve fighting those little buggers with your knife; it looks like they are winning the battle."

Rocky made a couple of more passes at them with his knife and then wiped the blade on his buckskin leggins. Picking up the plate, he took a mouth full; lowering the plate away from his mouth with a rind hanging between his lips, with a slurping sound, the rind disappeared from sight.

"Spoons are for greenhorns. A mountain man only needs his trusty knife to eat with, and besides never used a damn spoon in my life, was raised usin' a knife, always worked for me."

"Have you ever seen a mountain man starve himself because he was too stubborn to use a spoon?"

"Only one and he was tryin' to eat soup with his knife, done wore him self out tryin'."

"Son you were getting close to doin' the same thing."

"You making fun of me?" and with that, he started to laugh, Ty and Mrs. Casey joined in The laughter ended and Mrs. Casey expressed how disappointed she was with the way the mush had turned out it was dry and crumpled at the touch. "I was afraid it wouldn't work without an egg or some milk to put in it. While it was cooking, I was wishing we had some sweet butter to put on the hot mush, now if we had it, you couldn't get it on the bread with out it falling apart anyway, I guess it does make a good filling or for soaking up the bean juice."

"Tastes might fine anyway you made it, a hell of a lot better than eating dry old jerky. It's been a long time since we had food like this; my bellies not used to eat-ins this good, I have already eaten so much now that all I want is a nap."

Having said that, Ty looked at his friend that was now lying on his side, sound asleep, the hot food and the rotgut whiskey had the best of him. "Looks like our party is off for now, old Rocky is down for the night."

Helping Mrs. Casey put the cooking supplies back in the pack and leaving the last of the beans just off of the fire, Ty got up to spread the bedrolls, placing Mrs. Casey's between his and the sleeping Rocky.

"You can turn in anytime you want, I'll take the first watch and if I can't wake the Mountain man here," pointing at Rocky, "I'll just trust old Tuff to watch for us, he never sleeps apparently and always is on guard."

"Ty, can we walk down near the river, it will just take a moment but there is something that I want to tell you."

"Sure I think that the old man will be alright."

Sitting on a bent tree stump, Mrs. Casey began to tell Ty what was in the blanket bundle that she had given him. "Charles kept his ill gotten gains hidden in the soddy; he had no idea that I knew where he kept it. I knew that he had two hiding places and he loved to get it out, when no one was around and count it, he would put it back, smile and talk to himself. He seemed very proud of his gains but I never had the nerve to get it out, afraid that he would somehow find out if I did. You know that I feared very much for my life and as I told you, he was a mean person, and I would put nothing pass him."

"Well the bundle that I gave you was his spoils, I never took time to count it, I just placed it in the blanket and gave it to you. I did not know Rocky and I hate to say it, I did not trust him. There is a lot of money in there, money that I thought, at least on that morning, I would never want or accept under any circumstances. The only reason I took it was because it is what Charles was so proud of, when I placed it in the bundle, I had the feeling that I was taking the one thing that he prized most. I didn't want to leave it there, thinking if for any reason he would come back, it would be gone. I even knew his was dead and buried it still made me feel like I was denying him of something. "

She stopped and looked at the river for short time. Ty knew that she was trying to decide just how she was going to continue. She was wringing her hands together and rocking back and forth. What ever she had to say was very important to her and she wanted to say it right.

"Ty, what would you think of me if I said that I am glad that I brought the money with us. When we ride along, with nobody talking, it gives me a lot of time to think, I think of the life that I thought that I wanted. I think of things that have happened to me, good and bad and I always come back to two people. You and Mrs. Simpson back at Westport Landing, you remember her don't you, such a fine lady. She offered me sanctuary and I was just too afraid. that Charles would not hesitate to kill her if he felt like it; I knew this and it was part of my reason for not staying."

Ty looked back at the campsite, nothing was changed, Tuff was lying next to the fire pit and Rocky's feet, partially hidden by a tree and it was still plain that he was still sleeping.

Mrs. Casey looking back at the camp went on, "Ty, as I think on it, I want to build a boarding house, somewhere along the railroad line. I want a house that will keep the rain out and the heat in, a place I can set a table, I don't have to worry about dirt from the ceiling falling into my food, and I can have curtains on my windows. I want to go as far west as I can and someday I might be able to offer help to someone that needs it just as Mrs. Simpson did me."

"Like I say I don't know how much money is in that bundle, I think that there is enough for my boarding house with some left over for you to start a new life, if you want. If you continue west, I'll understand but remember the offer will always be there."

"I'll get the bundle if you want, I know you can trust Rocky; I will go so far as to say that money means nothin' to him. He is set on findin' his Evenin'

Star, nothin' is goin' to come in his way of doin' that. I have trusted him with my life and would do it again; he is a good man just in a hurry to find the Blackfeet Indians."

"I don't want the money yet; I want you to keep it until I need it. I was just worried that you might think different of me, I felt the money was dirty and I knew that it was obtained with a gun. A lot of innocence people killed but as I think on it, I don't how to return it to its rightful owners; it would be stupid to throw it away, I can't see how that would help. Oh, for a while I thought of doing just that, I have had a few days of peace and I have been thinking on my future. I know with the help of you and Rocky I will find my place in this new country, I'm starting to dream again Ty, and it feels good."

Ty didn't say anything for several minutes but as he sat there, he thought that what she said made sense. He didn't see anything wrong in her plans at least now, she was thinking about her life. A boarding house was a safe business, there always will be people looking for a good clean place to stay.

"One more thing Ty, I can't stop smiling when I think of using Charles's money to build something for me. He wouldn't even buy me a new dress or a decent pair of britches. He was always saving his rotten money for himself; I just get happy thinking about spending his money."

"I can see why you feel that way, kinda like gettin' revenge."

"That's it exactly."

"Don't think I'll be needin' any of your money, I thank you for the offer but when we found that dead raw hider, we found all that money on him. Most likely was from the sale of the stolen stock of their last raid, guess that maybe it is rightly yours and you can have it if you want. Rocky says that there is not much need for money where we are goin', I plan on sendin' most of it back home if there is a post office at Fort Kearney."

"No, that money is yours and Rocky's, I don't need it, like I said, I should have enough for what I want to do. I have no idea what it is going to cost if I have to build new, I'll worry about that when the time comes."

"Just tell me when you see a town or somethin' that looks good to you, we'll stop and you can check it out, don't know how far from the Fort the first one will be, guess it don't matter."

"How far do you think they are with the railroad?"

"Depends on how early this spring they got started laying tracks, they can move real fast if the weather gives 'em a break. This country is so flat, so that shouldn't slow 'em down and I don't know if they have to cross the Platte or if they can stay on one side or the other, anyway we'll know soon enough."

The sun had set and the darkness would be setting in very soon, a slight breeze had come up and there was a definite chill in the air. The bed roles lay out and the only thing left was to be sure that the fire was dead and the remaining beans were secure from varmints, foxes and skunks were noted for robbing a campsite.

"Better turn in before we won't be able to see, it's going to be dark soon. I'm ready for tomorrow, a new day and maybe Fort Kearney you never know."

Rocky was still sleeping like a baby and Ty decided to leave him where he was. He could pull the robe over himself when he got cold enough, wake him now and the party might last all night.

Checking the fire and seeing that the heavy lid was securely on the beans. Mrs. Casey had told Ty that she would like a little private time before turning in so while he waited on her return, Ty went to where the horses stood hobbled and talking lowly, he assured them that everything was going to be all right. He patted them on the neck and rubbed their muzzles, bending down he checked the hobbles of each horse assuring his self that they would still be here in the morning.

Meeting Mrs. Casey at the campsite, they proceeded to get in their bed roles, it had been a long day and even the hard ground felt good.

"Good night Ty, you know that when we arrived here this afternoon, it seemed as if all my worries were over. Tomorrow is a new day and I can't wait for it to get here and I hope poor Rocky will be alright."

"He drank his fill and it didn't take him long to do it, he might be a little sore and maybe a little slower come morning but next time he has the chance to let his hair down, he'll do it again, never learns his lesson. Good night, I'll set here till I can't stay awake any longer and then I'll turn it over to Tuff, he won't let anyone or anything get close to us, especially you. Now you get some sleep."

A light rain woke Ty it was hitting him in the face and it must have just started, more of a nuisance than anything. He rolled his robe into the ground sheet to keep it as dry as he could and he placed in the protection of one of the big cottonwood trees. Checking on Mrs. Casey and Rocky, they both had covered their heads and apparently were still sleeping, the bottle of rotgut was setting next to Rocky's side.

Starting the fire before he went to relieve himself and then he checked on the horse, when he returned to the fire, both Mrs. Casey and Rocky were up.

The gray morning had a chill to it but the sky showed a clearing trend and the rain most likely would soon stop. The sun would warm the air, and then beat down on the riders, making them wish for the rain to come again.

The first thing that Mrs. Casey said was, "What a beautiful day it is going to be, this rain is just a little delay in what I know will be a perfect day. I feel that it is the beginning of something special, like the rest of our lives. I can't wait to get on our way I know that each day will bring more joy and happiness to us."

The boys nodded their heads and Ty winked at Rocky, as the new Mrs. Casey moved to the fire pit.

"Do you want bacon and biscuits to eat or finish up the beans?"

"Beans is fine with me, what about you Rocky?"

"Beans is ok, but I don't know why you're both screamin', I have a pain in my head that won't quit."

"I bet that it feels like you got kicked in the head by a bottle of booze, they tell me that it really hurts when that happens."

"Ya, something like that." he answered with a slight smile on his face. "Did I screw up the party, I don't remember much of anything after our swim but I do remember that the damn hurt is still there. How was the hot mush, I know that beans can't be messed up very easy."

"Without you the party was pretty quiet, the mush was a little dry, still it was better than cold biscuits Ty ate his like he liked it, but I knew better."

"They were good, they sure filled me up."

While they ate the warm beans and the rest of the mush, Rocky said, "Old Tuff here looked so damn small after his swim yesterday but look at him today, his old fur has dried and fluffed up some, it makes him look a hell of lot bigger, even bigger than before."

"It's kinda like he is wearing them frilly buckskins you telling me about." Remembering that Mrs. Casey hadn't heard Rocky tell the story, he began to explain it to her. "Rocky here told me that the Indians wear those buckskins, like these we got on. The strips of leather hanging down from their sleeves and leggins is to mess up their enemies, makes 'em look bigger than they are. The other guy don't know where the frills begin and the body ends."

"Makes sense, I never had given any thought to it, I just thought that the fringe was for design or for looks."

"The Injuns can teach us a lot, like I was tellin' Ty, some people call 'em savages and heathens and maybe to some they are. But we got just as many white folks that we can call the same thing, hell, you know that, look at Charles and his kind, something made 'em that way, same as for the Injuns. No, we can learn a lot by just thinkin' on how they seem to find a way to survive."

"I have never been around the Indians, so I can't say anything good or bad, I have heard stories and I can say that they scare me. It is strange that up till now I have not worried about them it's hard for me to realize that we are not still back east."

"Don't do you any good to worry about 'em all you got to know that they are real and be on your toes all the time, if you find sign, then you can start worryin'. Were goin' to try to stay a step ahead of any trouble that comes up."

It's nice here but I don't want to root here, we better get moving before we do. Hell it will be night fall before we shed ourselves of this place." Ty said, looking at Mrs. Casey, "Starting to sound a lot like Rocky don't you think."

"I ain't been in no hurry to get in the saddle, kinda worryin' some on what it is goin' to feel like but I guess the time has come to see first hand. You lead out Ty, just follow the river but stay south of it, just out of rifle shot, don't know what might be in these trees." With a big smile he said, "Better safe than sorry."

"Why do you want me to take the lead, you're the leader and our master."

"Just do it, I'll be in the back nursin' my wounds, no sense to give you anything more to laugh about, now is there."

"Sure you can ride?"

"I'll ride, don't you worry your little butt about me."

Mrs. Casey stayed clear of the conversation as she went on getting ready to move out. She was the first to hit the saddle and sat waiting for them too mounted up.

At the mid day rest, Rocky never sat down, he ate his jerky leaning against a tree.

"Think I'll go take a dip in the river might help my hurt some." With that, he walked toward the river. "I won't be long."

After he was out of ear shout Mrs. Casey said, "What do think about stopping for the day, do you think Rocky would go along with it, a half a day isn't going to make a difference when we get to Fort Kearney, is it?"

"I'll put it to him, but his pride will most likely get in his way, he could be nearly dead and he would keep goin'. If it was one of us he would do it in a minute."

"Did you see the wound, was it very bad?"

"It was bleedin' damn good, didn't look at it so close as to tell how deep it was but it looked bad. When he got out of the water, he packed it with mud, to stop the bleedin', I guess that he should have got in the river before he started today, the dirt can't be easy on the sore spot and the ridin' most likely just rubbed it in."

On Rocky's return, Ty mentioned that this might be a good place to camp the rest of the day and get an early start tomorrow.

"What's this, you want to stop for the day, what in the hell for?"

"Just thinkin' that it might be for the best, it's a good spot and with you, healin' and all we thought that it might help to wait a day. One more day ain't goin' to hurt us none, give us and the horses a chance to rest up some"

"Hell one day ain't goin' to help me none, the sooner we get to Fort Kearney, the sooner we can find what's happenin' ahead of us. I spect that most of the Injun trouble is west of Fort McPherson at least that would make sense to me and that's still a couple of three days ride west of here."

"Rocky we know that it is very painful for you to ride, Ty and I were just thinking that it might be better to rest up another day. Were all in a hurry for what ever reason but one day is not going to hurt, is it?"

"Won't hurt but I don't need any nurse maidin'; I can soak away my trouble in the river when we stop. Thank you Mrs. Casey, but I will be ok, I've had worser hurts than this and still carried on."

"If that's the case then let's ride, you still want me to lead out?"

"Might as well."

They hadn't ridden far when two deep ruts running side by side appeared, they came from the southeast and were headed nearly straight west.

"There is the trail; we're not far from the Fort now, figure we will be there tomorrow."

"Don't know what I was expectin' but somethin' more than this." Ty added."

"It's only a trail that a whole lot of wagons have cut their mark in, a lot of oxen and mules have walked here. They say that for every mile the trail runs, there is a grave to mark the way."

"Just follow that trail and you will find the Fort."

The afternoon of the second day, Fort Kearney came into view located away from the river and surrounded by large trees, the only trees seen, except for the ones along the river off to the north. They also saw that a group of buildings that could only mean that a new settlement or new town had sprung up just north of the river.

Pulling up his horse and waiting for Rocky to come up along side, Ty asked, "I see the fort off to the south; I think it is anyway but what place is that over north, you never mentioned that there was a town so close to the Fort."

"Damn if I know, weren't there when I was here last."

No sooner out of his mouth, than a whistle of a train broke the stillness; it came from some distance off to the east.

Looking at Ty he said, "I'm guessin' that it is a railroad town, didn't know that the tracks were this far west, but then again how would we know. The damn country is goin' to hell in a hand basket; the rails will bring more pilgrims to this side. They will start tearin' up the damn ground and there ain't goin' to be room for a man just to go where he pleases and such, be bumpin' into all kinds of critters mostly bad, I'm thinkin'."

"It's a big country, there is room for everyone that wants to come, the railroad will only make is easier. You say that they intend to build it clear across the land from ocean to ocean it is hard to believe. I wonder how they are going to get across your mountains. Rocky, I don't think that the railroad is going to be bad for the country, you will still be able to live where you want and do what ever it is that you want to do."

"Mrs. Casey, I hope you're right, it makes me sick when I think about the Tribes and the changes they will have to make. This has been their land for as long as any of 'em can remember. The iron tracks are goin' to change a lot of things just you wait and see, it's goin' to cut the injuns world in half. Look long and hard at our passin', we might be the last ones to make this trip and see what we see."

"As the tracks are laid folks are goin' to start farming right along side 'em and the buffalo will be the first to go, can't have 'em tearin' up the fields and all, can we. The Injuns count on the buffs to survive, the Buffs go, and the Injuns will be next. I don't want to guess what will be followin' that."

Ty said, "You think that this is goin' to change all of the west, sure it won't just change the time it will take to cross it. The tracks are headin' west not north, think it will change the country you're headin' too."

"This is just the beginin', it will take some time but it is changing. Everything will be different from now on and I'm thinkin' that it's goin' to rile up a hell of a lot of the tribes, there will be some pretty mean Injuns. White folks out here are in for a big awakein' I'm thinkin'."

"Hell you didn't talk this way back in Missouri."

"We was in civil county then, they can build all the damn tracks they want; it's their part of the world but this side of the river is different, it ain't ours. There is others that got a claim on this side and it sure as hell ain't white."

"I don't see the difference, chimed in Mrs. Casey. You and a lot more have been trespassing for some time, aren't we trespassing right now? Are you saying that we should only let certain people come into this country and keep others out?"

"I wish we could, you weren't here and neither was I when Louis and Clark crossed this wilderness, it might have been one of the greatest opportunities a person could ever hope to take apart in. Then again, if you look at it from the other side of the coin their adventure just might have turned the lives of the Injuns upside down, it might have destroyed a part of this country that will never be the same again. Right now, a soul can still get lost on this side, only way you will find him is if he wants to be. I don't know how long it's going to take, but a day will come where that can't happen, there will be folks everywhere, fences, houses, and people in ever nook and cranny.

Mark my word, maybe not in our life time, but the day will come, just wait and see."

"Enough of my thoughts on a subject that I can't change and don't know anyone that can. Do we go to the Fort or north to whatever they call that place, there must be a river crossin' or maybe a ferry to get us across."

"When you came through here last did you leave anything that you need to retrieve, if not I vote to go north?" Ty said.

"I'll go along with that," Mrs. Casey answered.

Without another word, the three reined their horses to the right and headed for the river. The three rode side by side, with Rocky in the middle, and the noisy pack animal behind them. Tuff walked off to the left as he most generally did. Rocky laughed and said, "This change in plans most likely saved me a lot of hurt."

"Why is that?"

"A few miles west of the fort is a place called Dobytown, I was thinkin' on stopping., seein' if there were any old timers there that might know what's goin' on west of here, maybe even somethin' about the Blackfeet country. Then ifin' things would go like I think that they would. I would start by havin' a drink or two and stayin' up half the night garnerin' all the rumors and such. Probably get drunker than a skunk doin' all of that, the next day I would hurt real bad, besides I got enough hurts now, I'm guessin' that I don't need more. Besides that place is not for Mrs. Casey, it's damn rough. All the hellcats hang out there, yes sir, its no place for Mrs. Casey or for that matter, for us, I think that it's better to just stay away."

"Don't sound like it's a place that you would want to stay away from. The stories you've told me about how rough and tough the mountain man is, I'd be thinking that you wouldn't want to miss seein' who might be there. Never know but what you might run into some one you knowed from your last trip."

"I ain't got time to socialize with anyone any how, ifin' there is any of my friends there I'd be guessin' that they wintered there. Most likely don't know what's happenin' west and north of here anyhow. They most likely been too drunk all winter to care and it would just slow us up."

Mrs. Casey reined her horse and stopped, the others followed and turned in their saddles to find out what might have happened.

She said straight out, "I am no longer Wilma Casey, my name is Katherine Kelly and you may call me Kate."

The two men looked at one another appearing slightly confused, finally, Ty asked, "Been thinkin' on this long?"

"Yes, I want to start a new life just as I told you and with a new start, I have decided to change my name. I hope that I never hear the name Casey again. I have been worried that out here, at some point, I just might run into someone that knew Charles. He may have told them his wife's name was Wilma; I just don't want to take a chance. As Rocky has said, it is better to be safe than sorry." And with that, she smiled and kicked her horse forward.

Ty started to laugh and looking at Rocky said, "See we all listen to you, you're the boss."

"Go to hell O'Malley."

After a short time Rocky added, "I'm thinkin' that it is a good notion, all we got to worry about is screwin' up. We knowed Mrs. Casey longer than we have Kate and it might be hard to forget her, what do you think?"

"I'm with you and I sure as hell don't want to be the one that screws up, she just might kick us in the ass if we do and your ass is kinda tender, ain't it."

Shortly they rode into the trail that ran between the new settlement and the distant fort. The trace was not worn into the ground as the big trail was and every indication was that it had not been used for very long.

Topping a small rise, they saw riders coming toward them, reining in Rocky said, "Ty be on your toes don't know who they are but by the look, they could be army. Be on guard but don't be jumpy."

It wasn't long until the faded blue shirt of the first rider could be seen and behind him were five more riders with shirts of bright blue. The five didn't look old enough to be in the army and their leader looked like he was to old to be a soldier.

Nearing them, the first rider held up his right hand and the group came to halt.

"Howdy," said the leader.

"Howdy Sergeant," replied Rocky.

The Sergeant looked at Ty and then Mrs. Casey, if he recognized her as a woman he did not show it.

"Been ridin' far?"

"A ways."

"There has been some savage's attackin' folks round these parts, hit and run for the most part just wondering ifin' you had any run ins."

"Just turned north a bit back, been ridin' west for couple of days ain't seen or heard nothin'."

"Headed for the railroad?"

"Headed north, don't know of no railroad."

"There is a new one just across the river, that's what's stirring up the Injun trouble; they don't seem to care much for what were doing to their land. Don't seem to understand that they can't win this fight but for all I know about them red heathens they ain't goin' to give up easy like, it will get worse before it gets better. I worry some on how the Army is going to stop the damn ruckus look what they send me to try and make fightin' solders out of kids, nothin' but damn wet ass kids."

"Know what you mean, got a couple that I'm workin' on myself.

Ty raised up his head and wanted to ask just who Rocky was talking about when he called us kids, he said to his self, "I should tell the Sergeant about Rocky's swimin' ability."

"Sergeant I could set here all day and tell you story's about this here crossin' but I real have got to get this here bunch to the other side, is there a crossin' up ahead?"

"Ya, the Army built one, Goddamn I don't know many loads of rock the Army hauled and dumped into that damn muddy river. It's got a good bottom now, but it's damn hard on the horses. Ifin' you cross up a head be slow about it, takes a little time but it's a solid crossin'."

"Looking to stock up before going on, there a place where a fella can do that?"

"The damn Sutter at the Fort moved most everything he had to the new railroad camp, railroad workers got more money to spend than us Army people, I guess. Can't miss it, it's the biggest tent there and tell the old man that Sergeant Alpine sent you, he might just treat you better than most but watch him he can be damn mean at times."

"Thanks for the word Sergeant, best be headin' that away."

Again, the Sergeant held up his right hand, with a forward motion swung his troop to the right and rode toward the fort.

"Kinda neighborly weren't he?" asked Rocky.

"To hell with neighborin', what's this shit about us kid's givin' you fits. The way I see it you gave us a fit or two between your swimin' and your hurtin', you've been a hand full, don't you agree Kate?"

"Well you got to remember that without old Rocky here we might not of been able to find the river or for that mater the Fort. I'll forgive him for his calling us kids."

"Thanks, I was just makin' small talk."

Ty sat for a minute before saying, "Your forgiven, guess I can forget about it." Then he added, "Sounds like we might have been lucky, at least so far."

"Maybe with us ridin' quiet like we been didn't hurt us none, better be safe—."

Mrs. Casey, Kate, and Ty said together "Than sorry."

All three laughed. "I'll remember that till the day I die, I'm sure I will." Said Kate.

"Let's go take a look at this new place, just might find a big plate of fried potatoes and maybe an egg or two." Ty added.

CHAPTER 10

The new settlement was nothing more than a Canvas City; most every building had canvas somewhere in its construction. The lack of order to the structures and it was obvious there was no thought to making this a permanent settlement.

It was a railroad camp, like the ones that Ty and Rocky had lived in back in Missouri. Few men were in camp at this time of day but north of the tented area were the tracks and there was activity there, a line of wagons lined up along side of the tracks. The lead wagon, loaded with rocks of all sizes, driven up on a raised platform and men with shovels and gloved hands were busy unloading the wagons, placing the material in an open railroad car.

"Ballast for the track bed, glad that those fellas are doing that back breakin' job and I'm just sitting here watchin'. Done my share of that dirty damn job, ain't enough money in this here whole damn world to get me to do it again, it ain't even any fun watchin'."

"Come on Rocky, you know that you miss it."

"Lets not even talk about it we'll get what we need and shed ourselves of this place." He looked at Ty, "I didn't leave anything here either."

"Can't we see if there is a cook house that we might get a plate of eggs and tators, ain't you ready for some real cookin' that don't include cold biscuits or jerky?"

"Got time for that I'm guessin' won't hurt to have a break from trail fixin's."

Hitching their horses to a wooden rail in front of the largest tent in sight, they dismounted Ty stretched his legs and said to Kate, "Want to stay here or go on in?"

"I thought that I might go in and see what they got if you think that it is all right I'll stand near the door and keep Tuff out of trouble. I don't see anything that might tempt him, but you never know. "

Looking to Rocky for his advice and seeing him nod his head, "Don't see anything wrong with that but I'm thinkin' maybe it would be best ifin' you don't talk, no sense in lettin' on that you are a woman just yet, most likely you are the only one in camp."

"I understand."

Entering the dark interior, the only light in the place was the little sunlight that crept in through the rolled up sides. A big man, in a dirty apron stood behind a plank counter. The planks were resting on wooden barrels spaced well apart from each other and sitting on the planks were jars of pickled eggs, pickles, coffee and near it was a red grinder. Tobacco and a jar of horehound candy was crowded on the near end. The counter placed in the center of the tent with boxes and crates stacked on either side and most likely, only the big man knew what was in them.

Above the counter hung a slab of bacon, blankets, a sack of onions, some dried red peppers, and a multitude of shirts and pants. At the very end of the rough counter laid three new rifles, at first glance, they looked to be Winchester carbines, but longer.

"Welcome gents." The big man said.

"Howdy." answered Ty, "Know of a Sergeant Alpine, he told us to look you up."

"I know him he is so full of bullshit, more than anyone I know, my name is Glenn Denning, I own this mercantile or whatever you want to call it."

"They call me Rocky, this here is Ty and over there is K—Kelly.

"What can I do for you folks today?"

"Need a few things, that all the bacon you got?"

"How many slabs are you asking for?"

Rocky turned to Ty and asked, "What do you think, two?"

"Sounds right."

Turning back to the counter he said, "Need maybe two."

"I can do that, anything else."

"We'll take a sack of those onions there, maybe a sack of taters and a bag or two of coffee, same with sugar, have you got any biscuits and jerky?"

"Both, got some hard crackers too."

"Give me a taste of the jerky don't trust the taste of some, had some that I couldn't swallow."

With his knife, he cut the piece of jerky in half he handed Ty a piece and then one to Rocky. Rocky put his half in his mouth, chewing it for a considerable period and seeing Ty nod his head, he said, "Give us a goodly amount of all three."

Rocky looked to see where Kate was standing and seeing that she was near the front, leaning forward he said, "I see you got shirts and such, do you have any long johns?"

"Yep."

"Throw in a pair, and maybe a bottle of the good stuff you got behind the counter there," Pointing to about a half a dozen bottles of amber colored liquid.

Ty could not help but grin.

"What you think Ty, anything else?"

"Thought you was goin' to stock up on rifle powder and remember that canteen of yours sprung a leak, think you should replace it."

"Forgot that, I'll need a pound of the best you got and a canteen."

"I'm out of canteens but I got a canvas water bag, cheaper too."

"Give me one of those and I'm thinkin' that's about it."

"I just got a new bunch of canned peaches and tomatoes, west of here you won't find many places that will have them."

With that, he turned to a wooden crate and removed a can with a white wrapper that just said "peaches"; he sat them on the counter.

"Hell you can throw a half dozen of them there peaches and the tomatoes too we'll eat 'em at the next party we have, alright with you boys?"

Shaking his head in agreement, smiling he said, "Ya I'll go for that."

"Sure that this is all that you'll need, some tobacco, maybe a pair of real to God Injun moccasins?"

"That should do it for us but just give me a minute will you."

Walking up to Kate, he asked very quietly, "Anything that you need, a new pair of britches, maybe a shirt or two didn't mean to leave you out of it, forgot we told you not to talk."

"That would be nice and Rocky; do you think I could get a new pair of those moccasins?" Turning her head to the side and in a near whisper added,

"A new pair of long johns for me would be real nice."

"Couple of more things, I just thought about, I'll need a pair of those long johns and a set of leathers and moccasins for Kelly over there, he don't talk much and I forgot he was here. He is kinda on the small size so nothin' to big."

"It will take me a minute to dig a set out, Railroad workers don't buy many leathers, but I got 'em. Do you want to wait here for your stock or come back later, either way is fine with me. It will take a little time to put this all together, say an hour or so."

"We'll be back."

"Say take a can of these peaches, have a snack while you wait for me to fill this here order, the peaches are on me."

Handing the can to Ty, and said, "Appreciate your business."

Stepping out of the tent, they walked to the horses. Tuff got up from his resting-place at the tent opening and followed. Ty tossed the can to Rocky who pulled out his knife and began to open the metal can. Making a ragged hole in the top, he tried to press down the sharp edges. Doing what he could, he handed it to Kate and said, "Have to eat it like I eat beans, with your knife and then drink the juice. Don't cut yourself on them there rough edges could be neater but best I could do."

Between bites and with sticky peach juice running down his chin, Rocky said, "I just about did it to you Kate; started to call you Kate and remembered at the last minute. I did remember your name was not Mrs. who ever you were, that part I got right."

"That's why I chose Kelly for my last name, you did real well, I'm proud of you."

Having finished the peaches, they sat the empty can next to the tent. Rocky turned around; he stopped and said, "Son of a bitch, sorry Kate, Ty is that who I think it is?"

Following the direction of Rocky's gaze, "By damn its Mr. Perry from the railroad, ain't it?"

Nearing the three and looking up, he stopped, tilting his head to the right and with squinted eyes, he barked, "Buntrock is that you, it sure as hell is I couldn't forget you."

Walking towards the small group and sticking out his hand to welcome his old employee.

"Hell, are you here looking for work or just passing through?"

"Howdy Mr. Perry, I'm done with that damn back breakin' work, you was lucky that I stayed as long as I did."

Shaking his head in agreement, answered, "Headin' to the high country, are you, can't believe that I would run into you way out here."

Looking at Kate and then at Ty, he paused for just a short time and looked back at Rocky. Turning to take another look at Ty he finally said, "You can't be Ty O'Malley are you?"

"Hello Mr. Perry, thought you were goin' up north when you left Missouri, how you been?"

"Fine boy damn near didn't recognize you with all that hair on your face. I guess you were serious about comin' out here and I see you got a partner to boot. My job offer still stands I'll put you on the job this very minute, if you say the word."

"Mr. Perry I thank you for the offer but I'm still wantin' to see the mountains that my friend here has told me about. Were only part way there and still have a ways to go."

"Well I tried just to let you know the name I would like you folks to call me is Bob, the Mr. Perry is fine for some but to my friends, I like Bob better."

Knowing that he should introduce Kate to him and unsure just how to go about it. He trusted him and knew that he would keep their secret, would Kate see it that way?

"Boys stay right where you are, I will go get the tobacco that I came for and if you have time, we'll go to my office. We can have my cook fix us some vittles and maybe a drink if it's to your likin'." With that said, he walked away.

Ty didn't waste anytime he faced Kate and Rocky, "We got to cut Mr. Perry in our secret about Kate ifin' we don't it could come up a little sticky if he found out. I trust him Kate, want to tell him that you're a woman and friend of ours; I don't think we have to tell him more. Rocky knows what kind of a man Mr. Perry is I bet he will go along with tellin' it right up front, what do you think?"

Before Kate could speak Rocky said, "Ty is tellin' it true; Mr. Perry will understand and never say a word till you say so."

"I was thinking that we had to tell him something seeing as how you are all friends. If you trust him as much as you say, I'll go along with your decision, we don't have to mention Charles do we?

'No just that you're our friend and we're headed west together."

"As you were talking to Mr. Perry I was thinking, you remember I was worried that somewhere or some time, someone would recognize me; you know connect me to Charles? The very first thing that happened is that someone you have known walks right up to you. We are in the middle of nowhere and a friend has found you, I hope it doesn't happen to me."

"Not likely Kate, Charles didn't make many friends I'm guessin' and the ones he met are most likely dead, he seen to that." Rocky added.

"Your probable right, but I still worry."

"I'll just go tell the store keep where we are, tell him we'll be back before too long."

As Rocky left, he met Bob on his way back with a brown sack in his hand, "Just give me a minute, this won't take long."

Leading the horses, they arrived at the rail car that was Bob's office. It was in need of a good coat of paint and at least one window had beet broken, a piece of red cloth was stuffed in the ragged hole to help keep out the cold and the rain.

"You can put your stock here in the corral, the other horses won't mind. There is some hay over there you can feed to 'em, should be a fork there somewhere, might want to pump a little more water."

"Come on in you can stretch your legs and set on a real chair for a change. Whatever you're hungry for, I'll get Chan in here to fix it for you; we got most everything even some fresh milk."

Care if the dog comes up hate to leave him by his lonesome he likes Kelly's company."

"No, he is welcome too."

The interior of the office was very clean and neat, several chairs with arms, sat along one side and a settee along the other. A large desk sat in the far corner with a leather chair with wheels setting in the desk well.

A little yellow-skinned man appeared at the far end of the coach, he was wearing what appeared to be a dress covered with some sort of an apron, his black hair combed back and ended in a braid. Bowing to first Bob and then to Bob's guests, he spoke in a dialect that brought a smile to Ty's lips.

Bob turned and said, "This is Chan, my friend, housekeeper and cook just tell him what you want to eat and he will it have set in front of you in no time."

Ty looked at Kate and to Bob he said, "Bob could I talk with you, it won't take long?"

Stepping back to the doorway Ty explained to Bob about Kate. Without a question, Bob turned to Kate and said, "Why don't you start."

Kate asked if she could have a couple of eggs, some fried potatoes, a slice of bread and a glass of milk.

"You want a piece of buffalo steak with those eggs, just shot fresh yesterday?"

Kate responded with a yes and added "Just a small portion please."

Ty and Rocky went along with Kate's order with the exception of the size of steak and number of eggs.

Chan left the room and Ty asked, "What kind of words was that fella usin', never heard that kind of talk before."

"Chinese, a lot of his kind are working on the western end of these tracks. Hard working people, work for a little of nothing. I hear that they will actually work until they drop, no quit in 'em. Chan was working for the old superintendent and I just sort of inherited him, don't know what I would do without him."

"He didn't seem to have any trouble knowin' what we was sayin' does he know English?"

"As well as I do, don't know why he won't speak English in front of strangers. He and I talk all the time when were alone."

Taking a piece of bread Ty wiped his plate clean, leaned back and rubbing his stomach said, "Best food I've had since I left home I forgot how good a cool glass of fresh mile was. All this reminds me of Mom's cookin'."

Lighting a pipe of tobacco, after offering some to Ty and Rocky but first, he asked for Kate's approval. Bob crossed his legs and asked, "Goin' north from here or what's your plans, reason I'm askin' is tomorrow I'm headed west to the end of the line takin' supplies and those horses out there. The Indians don't like what we are doin', buildin' these tracks and all, they either kill or steal every head of stock we take out there it's their way of slowin' us down. Poor souls are fightin' a losin' battle but they don't seem to care. What

I was goin' to say was that if you are headed the same way, you can load up and I will save you a lot of saddle sores?"

"How far west do the tracks go?" Ty asked.

"Rocky you might know the ground west of here. You know where the south fork is?"

"The south fork of the Plate ya I know, that's where were headed, when we get to the fork we'll head north and west some."

'Well west of the fork itself, about two or three days is a camp that is called the Forks. Don't know exactly why they called it that but I guess it was that well before the railroad ever started west. We are crossin' the north fork just west of where they come together, gettin' closer to the camp every day. Ridin' a train is a hell of a lot easier that settin' a saddle and sleepin' on the ground. Be leavin' before first light tomorrow and can have you there by night fall, maybe three days short of the fork."

A smile crossed Ty lips as he thought about riding the train and saving Duke's legs, wouldn't hurt to give the horses a rest anyway. While Ty was busy thinking about the horses, Rocky had another thought.

"Sounds mighty fine except for a thing or to, Kate here is looking for a place to put down roots." A quick look at Kate and he continued. "Was kinda hopin' that she would change her mind and go to Omaha but don't look like its goin' to happen, she is determined to go on west. If we ride the train it ain't about to stop at every whistle stop and we just might miss a decent place that she could be happy livin' in, Bob do you know of any place between here and the fork that would be safe for her?"

Before Bob could answer Kate broke in, "Rocky and Ty are worried that I might not be able to handle myself out here in the west. I think that I am perfectly capable of doing just that, I have not had an easy life, what I have been through has prepared me for the worse. I am looking for a place that I can either build or buy a boarding house. Not just a nice quiet place where I can provide a room for the school ma'am and a couple of widows but a place that will grow with the town, I am not afraid of hard work."

Puffing on his pipe and scratching his right ear, Bob thought for a while before answering. It was oblivious that he was giving his answer some real deep thought, after what seemed to be forever, he spoke. "Most places are like this camp, here today and gone tomorrow. The railroad will bring shops and business to this part of the world at sometime but where is the question. This place might last and grow because the Fort is just south of it, move or close the Fort, anything could happen. Fort McPherson is the same, no guarantee that either one will last. With the river right next to the tracks, water is not a factor and Ty you bein' a farmer know that the soil around here is just waitin' for the plow; it's the same all the way to the Fork. Towns can start up anywhere and will mind you, just don't know where or how long they will last."

Looking at his pipe and then looking at Kate.

"What I'm about to say might not set right with you boys, but you asked and I'm answerin'. The place that I think you are lookin' for is at the Fork itself. The tracks are goin' straight through for now, but come a year or two there will be a track, breakin' off to the southwest goin' to the town of Denver in the Colorado Territory. I think the tracks will branch off at the Forks and if that's the way it works out, there will be a big switchyard built there. In addition, a trail that comes up from Texas called the Western Trail comes right to the Forks on their way to the Montana Territory. I think that the herds will still come and the cattle can be shipped east on the Union, the railroad is gamblin' the same way. Goin' to build a big stockyard there that will handle a thousand head a day. Plannin' to start even before the tracks get there. Ain't much there now, but I'm bettin' it will be a real busy spot before too long."

Rocky asked, "Been there?"

"Nope, but heard about the area from the surveyors, plenty of farmland and there is grassland near there that have supported a million head of buffalo for a thousand years or more. According to the surveyors, it's just the start of real good cattle country; they think it's got all that you need to make a real good spot for a town. Farmers and Ranchers will need some place to buy their supplies and socialize with their neighbors, most likely it will need a good boarding house too."

"When I was there it looked just like Injun land to me, course I wasn't lookin' to start no farm just tryin' to keep my hair."

Deep in thought, Ty sat there listening and thinking at the same time. When he had what he wanted to say sorted out in his mind, he said, "Don't sound like it's ready for settlein' just now what happens if the tracks stop before they even get that far? The railroad could go belly up and just stop, run into some real big problems with the Indians and the Indians win. I'm thinkin' there is a lot that can happen between here and there it might leave Kate high and dry."

Shaking his head in agreement, Bob said, "Your right Ty, all those thing might happen, but they ain't goin' too. Don't think for one minute that this track is goin' to fold up, its goin' to connect with the far end, as sure as I'm sittin' here today. Too much money is involved the whole country is just waitin' for this job to be done and folks are ready to move this away. All this land is opened for homesteadin' and this railroad is makin' it possible. This country is prime for settlement and even the Injuns aren't goin' to stop it, hells bells look at the folks that already have risked all they ever had to settle in California and Oregon. They had to walk all the way, they fought the Injuns, weather, and sickness of all sorts, yes this track is goin' through, no doubt about it."

Kate had listened to all that they said. She had let the men do the talking but she had smiled to her self-knowing that she would have to make the final decision. All the questions that were on her mind except for one had been asked, was there anything there now and was the land there for the taking? Just as she finished her thought, Ty asked Bob the exact same question.

"There is a man that has a trading post there now been there some years. I'm told he served mostly the cattle people; it was extra business for him when the railroad surveyors got there. The surveyors set up a camp and the Railroad Company sends a wagon train with supplies every two weeks. Matter of fact we got a hell of a load of stock for the post and for the railroad people that's there now. There is also a large group of buffalo hunter's doin' their thing and they protect the camp from the Injuns. A saloon or two I understand have been set up in tents and last I heard another young man was trying to open up his own mercantile there, it's going to grow I'm sure of it."

"Part of the deal between the U. S. Government and this here railroad was that when the tracks were built the land on both sides of the tracks would be deeded to the rail company. You pick out a spot and the land will be transferred to Kate here or to anyone that wants it, the more business's that are opened the more people will settle near them."

Rocky had sat quiet like thinking not being able to hold himself back, he interrupted. "You mean the heathens that are slaughterin' the buffs for their hides and tongues. Didn't think that they were this far west, sure, as hell didn't think, the railroad would be helpin' 'em. The damn Bastards, sorry Kate, are no good to anyone, you know that Bob, hell if I was an Injun and seein' 'em shoot and skinin' the buffs I wouldn't stop at killin' or stealin' the damn companies stock I'd kill me as many white men as I could. Hell they just leave the meat to rot it's a damn sure way to start an Injun war. The buffs are one thing that keeps the tribes alive." With that said Rocky got up and left the rail car.

"I say something that I shouldn't of?"

"No Bob, it's just that Rocky has a fondness for the way things are. He don't like what he sees comin' and I think that he would have liked to be born an Injun, he told me that their way was the honest life. Poor bugger was too late in finding his true feelings, I'm thinkin'."

"Must be why he is in such a hurry to shed himself of civilization. Hope he can see his way clear of any buffalo hunter he might meet, they're a tough bunch, drinkin' and shootin' is all they know, maybe I had better throw in fightin' too."

"Don't know if in' anyone could stop him if in' he went after one, he's his own man and don't ask for much help."

Standing up Ty said, "Think I will go check on him then the two of us will go see if Mr. Denning has our stuff put together, be back shortly."

"If you want, there is a hand cart at the other end." Bob raised his right arm and pointed to rear of the car. "Just load your things on it and bring 'em back here, no sense in takin' a horse and buildin' a new pack you can do that at the end of the line."

Ty stepped out on the platform and looked to see where Rocky might have gone. On the far side of the corral, leaning with his back to the fence rail stood his friend, approaching him Ty asked, "You alright?"

"Just got a little pissed off about them damn savage's killin' the buffs. Ain't no one that can get it through their damn heads that they are the one thing that the Injuns need to stay alive? It's like the damn whites that don't give a shit they know that if the buffs are gone, soon the Injun will follow. The damn whites have got to get it through their heads that the injuns ain't the only damn savages, a hell of a lot of what the white man does is just as bad."

Looking off to the west, he started again, "Ty I ain't one to talk, I've killed an Injun or two, it was me or them and I might have to again, but I sure as hell won't starve 'em to death. People can't seem to figure out that there is a difference between one or two Injuns and a whole way of life. We take away how they have lived for hundreds of years and try to change 'em to goin' our way is wrong. When a man's pride is taken from him, watch out. We expect that only life he has ever knowed has to change, has to be like the white man's way of thinkin', wait and see there is goin' to be a damn passel of trouble."

Turning to look at Ty, he shook his head, "Why in the hell do the damn people think that our way is the only way, most have never seen or been around a real Injun. All this land out here and we can't seem to want to get along with people that ain't just like us. Ifin' I wasn't so damn mad, I think I would just give up and cry, I'm damn ready to shed myself of these hypocrites, yes sir, I am."

"The railroad people want to rid this country of the Buffs so farmers and such can set up their places. If the Buffs stay, they won't leave crops and such alone, that's why they are encouraging them damn hunters."

Ty waited for Rocky to continue and when he didn't, "You were just born to late my friend; you should have been out here years ago. You can see both ways and can judge 'em, I can't, your words are all that I can go on. I know that your words are true but most folks are damn scare't of what they don't know about. They don't know what you have learned, so they will fight cause they don't know no better."

"Hell Ty, there won't be any Injuns left by the time they get to know 'em that's what scares me."

"You're most likely right old partner, but like you told me back at the Landin', this land has been changin' hands for many a years maybe it's time again."

"Maybe it is, but I want no part of it, the way it was, is fine with me."

Slapping Rocky on the back Ty reminded him that they had supplies to pick up. "Bob said that there is a two wheel cart that we can use and load it on his car till we get to the end of the line."

"Might give my mind a rest and get me thinkin' about gettin' to where I'm a headin', the sooner the better."

The bacon slabs were wrapped in a brown wax paper and tied with white twine and the balance of the order sat on the rough wood counter next to the coffee grinder. Denning bent over at the counter and was writing on a piece of brown paper, looking up he said, "Got your order put up and was just figuring the cost, you think of anything else you need?"

"Nope," Ty answered, "Those peaches hit the spot tasted mighty good, want to thank you again."

"Just take a minute and I'll have this figured, makes me feel like a damn crook, chargin' these prices, everything is gettin' so damn expensive don't know how a person is goin' to make it. The Army and the railroad don't pay a decent wage and that's where my business is, I guess when a man is hungry he'll work for peanuts. People take advantage of that that's why I work for myself."

With a smile on his face Rocky said, "Tried workin' once, didn't like it, man can break his back, workin' no sir, work ain't for me."

Putting the pencil back on his right ear, he looked at Ty and then Rocky, "Gave you the best price I could on the leathers, jerky and the bacon. Can't do much with the price of the rest, I have to freight all that in. I just threw in the biscuits, my wife makes 'em and if I say so myself they're the best that there is."

Rocky spoke up, "Hell we want you to make a livin', ain't askin' you to go broke on the count of us? What's the damage?"

"I ain't goin' to go broke but I sure wish I could lock this place up and go west with you. My wife would kill me if I ever said I wanted too, I just get tired of the same shit day after day. Never havin' in stock what people ask for and havin' to listenin' to all the folks complain about the weather, it's always too hot or too cold, too wet or too dry that goes for every damn one I serve. The total comes to 27 dollars."

Rocky opened his pouch and handed the storekeeper two twenty dollar gold pieces. "Mr. Denning I want you to keep the rest of this money and when a man tells you that he is down and needs a hand up, just take the price out of this."

With the coins lying in his palm and looking Rocky in the eye he said, "First time this has ever happened to me, I've heard of generous folk's doin' such a thing in the city but never out here, you sure you want to do this?"

"Where were headed, we won't be needin' much money."

"Well if you're sure I'll put the extra money in a safe place and use it as you say."

"Use it any way you see fit, might help some poor, out of luck soul and change his life."

"You know, when you walked in here this mornin' I just had a feelin' that you boys were a cut above most and now I know that I was right, it's been a real pleasure to meet you."

Offering up a big smile, Rocky answered, "Thank you for your words, Mr. Denning my mother would have been proud to hear you say that, thank you again."

Lifting his apron, he placed the two coins in pouch hanging from his belt, smiling at them he said, "Safest place I know of right now, later I'll put them away proper. Didn't hear you ride up, did you bring your pack horse with you?"

"No we borrowed a cart from Mr. Perry down at the railroad. We're goin' to be ridin' with him when he heads west in the mornin' we worked for him once back in Missouri."

Coming around the counter the storekeeper started to load the cans and bacon in a wooden freight box. "Just load this on that cart and if you can leave the box, I'll pick it up later. They charge me for the damn things, which don't make sense, I pay enough for what they put in the damn thing, let alone for a damn empty box. They get you comin' and goin'."

Ty carried the large box out of the tent and loaded it on the cart. "I carried it out so you can push it to the train." Turning he shook, the storekeepers hand again and he thanked him for his kind words and the peaches.

"Boy you don't tell me what to do I might and again I might not push the damn thing at all. Thought I might open one of these bottles right here and now find a quiet spot and heal myself. But then again Bob might have some more of that cool milk and that sounds better that the rot gut. Sorry Glenn, I know that your stuff is better than I'm use to but all whiskey is rot gut to me."

"Suit yourself old man it would most likely of tired you out pushin' this cart and I wouldn't want that to happen, now would I.

Glenn asked, "This the way you two always act?"

"Nah, been tryin' to teach this young pup the ways of the world, but like my mommy always said, "You can't make a silk purse out of a sow's ear"

I' m hopin' that he will at least learn enough to stay out of trouble."

Ty added, "It's always hard to teach, when your student is smarter than the teacher."

"Bullshit boy, who said that you knew anything at all?"

"I got you this far ain't I?"

Rocky moved his head back and forth in wonderment while Ty moved to the cart with a big smile on his face. Turning he said, "Hope to see you again Mr.Denning, you comin' old man or do you want me to come back with the cart and get you."

"That will be the day you pipsqueak."

They left with the storekeeper laughing and waving goodbye.

Stepping up on the platform, they could hear Kate and Bob talking, when they opened the door, they abruptly quit talking. Bob asked, "Must of have had everything ready your back sooner than we thought."

First looking at one then the other, Rocky asked, "We interupin' somethin'?"

Kate spoke first. "No not at all, Bob was just telling me more about the forks. He made an offer to help me get set up."

Nodding his head, Ty said, "Got those leathers you wanted and the other things too."

With the excitement of a young girl, she stood up and said, "Do you think that they will fit?"

Ty handed her the brown paper package, "Try 'em on, we'll know soon enough."

Bob added, "You can use my compartment, first one on the right."

Moments later, she returned all giddy like and said, "First new things that I have had in a very long time, how do they look?"

They fit just fine, makes you look just like Rocky but that ain't a good thing."

That brought a laugh and Bob added, "You look cleaner than any mountain man I ever saw."

"Just got to get those new duds broke in, with a little dirt and grime you'll look just fine." said Rocky.

"They're very nice compared to my old clothes, but they do smell a little smoky but just the leggins."

"That's a good sign, means they were made and hung close to the fire. The smoke, or whatever helps shed the water and keeps 'em dryer, the real good ones are made out of the top most leather of their tipi or lodges."

Sitting down across from Ty and Rocky, Kate first asked Bob, "Do you mind if I tell them what we were discussing when they came in, I'll have to tell them sooner or later."

"No."

"Bob was concerned about me going on to the forks without a plan, to his knowledge, there are no women out there and that worries him. He told me that when this train reaches the end of the line there would be a supply wagon going to the forks the following day; he offered to take us along. I then could look the place over and decide if it was something that I might be interested in, if so, I could make a plan for my boarding house and I could return with him, back to the end of the line then on to Omaha. I can then look for someone to figure out what I am going to need and if I'm happy about everything, I could then order it. Bob offered to ship it back to the forks or to the end of the line. His point and it is valid, there is little I could do out there until the line reaches the forks."

"What is there to think about?" asked Ty.

"I am not sure that I want to stop at the forks I might decide to go on north with the two of you."

Rocky's face and neck turned immediately red, he had started to stand up, when Kate started to laugh. "Rocky sit back down I am not serious, I just wanted to see if you were listening to me. No, Ty, I real don't know what there is to think about, I'm sure that it is the best way. I just wanted you and Rocky to know how much I value your opinion."

"I will take good care of her boys I just don't want her alone out there with all the riffraft that is there. We talked about her bein' a lady and we most likely will have to tell everyone that she is. When a lady travels with a bunch of men, it's hard to hide the fact that she a woman if you know what I mean." Bob said.

"It sure takes a load off my mind knowin' that Bob will be there to help out till you get settled and I know that Rocky is pleased too."

"It settled then, we do as we talked about."

Kate answered Bob, "I might be a distraction to you as I have a strong will, are you sure you want to get involved with my problems?"

"I think I can handle it, by the way, I took the liberty and asked Chan to fix a special supper for us, I think you will enjoy it. It will be a big leap from trail rations and it should be ready anytime. If you want to wash up you can."

They dined on roast buffalo, fried chicken and ham along with potatoes, gravy and a piece of hot apple pie. A pitcher of cool milk and a loaf of hot bread with fresh butter rounded out the meal.

Leaning back in his chair Ty thanked Bob for all of the fine food and added, "If I knew that you ate like this every evenin', I would have agreed to that job you offered."

"If I thought that fixin's like this would change your mind I'd say we would."

"Thank you, but I still plan to see those mountains that Rocky and others have told me about. I've came this far and seen things that I had never seen before and I'm anxious to see more."

"Come work for me and I will take you clear through your mountains and I'll show you the Pacific Ocean as well."

"Don't think that it would be the same Bob, I want the feel of bein' there; you know ridin' the valleys and goin' to the top of a mountain, kinda pretendin' like bein' where no one has been before."

"Don't blame you son I'd feel the same way if I was younger, I get a similar feelin' when we build a new track, goin' somewhere or doin' something that no one has ever tackled before makes a man feel down right good."

Rocky sat quiet, listening to Ty and Bob, thinking to himself that the one thing that neither one is saying is, how scared a man can get when you tackle something alone. He thought, "I have been to those valleys and to the top of the mountain and many a times some company would have been alright. You only feel real good after you have completed what you have set out to do. Who is the bravest man, the one that is first and shows the way or the man that stays in one place and makes things better?

"While Rocky was deep in his thoughts, Bob was saying, "Kate could sleep in his compartment and the three men would sleep out here. We will be leavin' before sunrise; it's goin' to be a long day's ride best we turn in a little early. Chan will wake us up and give you boys a chance to water your stock and get them loaded. We'll eat our breakfast on the move."

Well before first light, Bob wakened by Chan, rose up from the settee and was surprised to see Ty and Rocky busy rolling up their bedrolls. "Chan wake you before he did me?"

"No, heard the stock being watered by your boys, thought we had better get our stock separated from yours, before they get loaded."

"We'll put your horses in one of those car that have a fence in the middle. You can tie them to the side rails if you have a mind to or they will ride just fine loose. The saddles and packs you can load into this here car, bring 'em in from the other end they won't be in our way."

"Might need a little help gettin' Satan loaded, the damn hammer head can be damn persnickety at times."

"Check with the head wrangler he goes by the name of Hank, tall lanky fellow. You can't miss him, hell I'll just go with you and tell him myself that I want to load your stock first."

Light to work by provided by fires built in large barrels surrounding the horse pen. Hank was crawling through the fence rails as the three men arrived.

"Hold on will you Hank?"

Hank stood just inside the enclosure as Bob said, "Hank these fellers are friends of mine, this here is Ty O'Malley and Rocky Buntrock they are goin' to ride with us today. I would like to load their stock first if you don't mind."

"I wondered where those extra horses came from, all six of 'em yours, I noticed 'em last night when I put 'em to bed."

"There must be a hundred horses in this pen and you know that there was some strangers mixed in, that's hard to believe. You know each and everyone, most likely you've names for all of 'em too." Rocky said.

"I name some, horses are better than most men I ever met. You get to know a horse and you can trust it, not many men you can say that about."

"If you can put them six in a fenced car, I would appreciate it."

"I can do that, Mr. Perry."

Rocky said, "We'll give you a hand, if that's alright, that pinto of mine can be down right mean at times."

"I'll take all the help I can get let's get started, we'll get your horses in that loadin' chute and be ready when they get the cars in position."

Surprisingly Satan followed his traveling partners into the waiting car without a fuss and shortly all the stock was loaded and the train nosily headed west.

Chan served breakfast and after eating their fill, they sat back and watched the unchanging plains fall behind them. An occasional conversation would break the silence but the rolling of the car and the clicking and clacking of the wheels as they pass each joint of the tracks made all four just want to set quiet.

Mid day came and past uneventfully, off to the north Kate saw a group of riders, coming toward the train. She brought this to the attention of Rocky and was surprised when he announced that what she saw was a band of Indians. Calmly Rocky picked up his rifle, stepped out on the platform and kneeled down on one knee, waiting for Ty to join him.

"Just play it safe like they ain't goin' to hurt us none, not that they don't want to but they can't catch up to us. It's their way of blowin' off steam and makin' a show of it."

A few puffs of smoke told them that they were shooting but none of the shots came close.

"You told me that they were good horseman but I didn't really believe it till now. They are riding with the rein in their teeth and usin' both hands to shoot at us, never seen that before and at a full out run to boot."

"Like I told you they live to ride, it's their grab at freedom."

First one and then another pulled up, then they all came to a stop, they could still see the puffs of smoke but the train was well out of range.

Bob said, "It's a damn shame that we can't convince them how important these tracks are, I know Rocky that it is their land but some how we got to learn to live together. A few stray bullets and an occasional tearing up of the tracks ain't goin' to stop it."

"Just like you or me Bob, if it was our people or land that was threatened we'd fight back, I know that I would and I bet you would too. That's all they are doin', fightin' back."

Shaking his head in agreement Bob said, "You're right but there must be a way."

Just before dusk, the train's whistle sounded and the feeling of the train slowing prompted Bob to said, "Must be at the end of the line, we just took on water a short time back, shouldn't be dry this soon."

The end camp was no different from the ones in Missouri, tents and stacks of ties and rails were neatly located near the tracks. Temporary stock pins were off to the north and slightly to the west. As the stock was unloaded each horse was lead off the car separately and walked to the pins.

Ty and Rock lead all six of their horses to the pin, placing them inside of the enclosure and then tied them to the fence rail.

"We won't have to spook the whole damn bunch in the mornin' when we get ready to ride out."

Ty agreed and asked, "We ridin' west with Bob and his bunch or takin' off on our own?"

"Might as well start with 'em if it starts to drag we can take off on our own."

Returning to Bob's car they seen Bob talking with two big men, dressed in leathers and both carrying a bullwhip, the two turned and walked away. Bob seeing Ty and Rocky approaching said, "Those two are the wagon masters and they tell me we are just three long days out of the forks. Indian trouble seems to be pickin' up but right now, they seem to be happy with just hittin' and runnin', no one has been hurt yet. I told them we would be leavin' at first light so they will have to work most of the night to get things loaded and ready to go.

"Kate inside?"

"Yes and she tells me she wants to talk to you Ty. You go on in and let us know when we can join you; I'll have Chan hold off on supper till you give the word."

Kate was pacing back and forth she stopped when Ty entered.

"I asked Bob if I could see you alone for a short while, we might not get another chance to speak in private and there are a couple of things I want to tell you. Some I have already told you about but I want to tell you again. You are a very big part of my life when I needed someone you have been there. Ty I am most grateful for all you and Rocky have done for me and I will thank Rocky myself before we get to the Forks. In three or four days, we may never see each other again. In the very short time that I have known you, there has never been a man that has affected my life in a good way, as you have. When we first met, you talked about your Mother with such respect; I know that she is very proud of you. You are a very kind and caring person, I love you for that. Since the return of Charles and the life, he chose for us, they took advantage of me at every turn. Charles didn't seem to care how his so-called friends treated me. I didn't think that my life would ever change and had resigned myself to that. When you and Rocky freed me from that terrible life, I was just as leery of Rocky, never you, I was afraid that things would not change. When we part and you go on with Rocky I just want you to rest assured that everything will be fine. I have my mind made up, I am positive that things will work out, Bob will be a big help, and he is a very nice man. Ty I know that it is not for a lady to say this but you are very special to me and I'll never forget you." And with that said she ran to Bob's compartment and shut the door.

Ty waited long enough to digest what she had said and then walked to the closed door, preparing to knock, he hesitated, as he heard her sobbing. He thought back to the time, sitting on the blanket and watching her cry. It had been over a year and he still didn't know what to do.

Kate didn't join them for supper and this bothered all three as they ate in silence.

"She goin' to be alright?" asked Rocky

"She'll make it she has toughened up a lot in the past year. Just a little scared I think about startin' her new life. Give her a little time, she knows she going to be leavin' you boys, you've been a big part of her life. She is not sure how things are goin' to work out but Kate puts on a good show of how tough she has gotten, I think that most of it is just a way of assurin' you that everything is goin' to be all right. I'll stick close by and help in any way I can."

"Thanks Bob, it will make us feel better about leavin' her alone.

"Still don't like it one damn bit."

"Rocky we tried but what in the hell are we suppose to do, I guess that we could tie her up and send her back to Omaha with Bob. Then she would be mad at him and not have a friend at all."

"I know but I still worry we got her out of one mess and don't want to see her get into another. Watch her real careful like Bob, she is a pretty special lady."

"You got my word."

CHAPTER 11

The sun was directly over their heads when they arrived at the settlement, it was larger than what Ty had expected. Tents and lean-to shelters were on the north bank of the south fork, not very far from the river, which gave them only three sides to protect in the event of an attack. A stench of dead and rotting meat was in the air and off to the north of the camp there were the sounds of rifle shots.

"Stinkin' damn bastards and their damn hides, don't know how a man can stand to fill the air with that fowl smell. We ain't even in camp yet and it will get worser when all the damn idiots come in from the day's hunt, they'll smell as bad as the damn hides. It won't be long before we start to smell that away too, if it weren't for Kate I'd just keep on a goin'."

"We'll be gone before you know it, Bob said that the wagon train would be leavin' sometime late tomorrow. Kate will have to make up her mind in a hurry, can't see her bein' to proud of this place the way it stinks and all."

"Can't see her playin' it safe either and she won't change her mind, she'll build here. I know it; she is smarter than you and me, she is goin' to look a hell of lot further down the line than we would."

"Guess with Bob's help we won't have to worry much longer, Kate will figure out what is best and Bob will help her."

As soon as the wagons arrived, the unloading began, first, the supplies that belonged to the railroad and then the balance were off loaded at two large tents.

In short, order, Chan had set up two living tents side by side and a third tent, just behind the other two, Chan's cooking supplies went in that one.

When Bob returned from his visit with the head surveyor he said, "Boys if it is alright with you, we can share this tent and Kate can use the other. I'll post a couple of men to guard her tent tonight, don't trust these damn people out here."

"I was just thinkin' about that and thought I might do the guardin'. I'll just put my robe down and sleep in front her tent for tonight make me feel better about it." Ty said.

Kate interrupted, "I got Tuff, if Bob puts a guard outside I should be fine. I know that you men worry about me but soon enough I will have to learn to take care of myself. Tuff and I will be just fine, besides it looks like rain again and if it rains like it did yesterday you won't want to be out in the open."

"If you're sure about this, we will play it your way." Rocky said.

Ty wasn't sure and decided that he would do it his way, he would wait till everyone was asleep and then he would set up his own watch. It worried him that when Kate would return to the Forks, without Rocky, Bob or himself what would happen? He thought on it for a time and then decided that Kate should hire a couple of trustworthy men to protect her. At least till the place got some sort of law. Before they parted, he would advise Kate to do just that.

Chan had brought fresh hot coffee and as they sat on camp chairs in front of Bob's tent, the conversation had come around to Kate's decision. The talk had centered on what she was going to do. Her voice had a distinct sound of fear and worry in it as she said, "This place is just as Bob described it, maybe it is a little rougher than I thought and I will be honest, it scares me some. I know that the smell will disappear in time and it would be nice if there were other women here, I'm sure in time there will be, it just bothers me to think about being here alone."

"Ty and Rocky you were most likely right when you tried to talk me out of this, I wonder if your advice wasn't what I should have followed. I think about staying here and then I start to worry about going back east, I don't know who might know me back there. Bob has assured me that he will find some men, which I can trust. Once I get the boarding house built, I know it will be all right, it is the time in-between that bothers me."

Ty and Rocky were silent as she continued. "Bob thinks that the best location for it would be right here on the north side of the river. The railroad will be on this side and Bob will find out from the surveyors where the depot is to be. Being near by, my business would have a good chance of getting the travelers first."

Bob added, "It will be a while before the place can be built, I think the Forks will change a lot by then. I'm thinkin' that by that time, my office will be set up here at the Forks and I can keep an eye on her. I can't say that I don't have some doubt about her bein' way out here but damn it boys, I think we have to trust her choice."

"I have till tomorrow to make up my mind, I guess until I actually start to build I can back out at any time."

"I think that we should go get the surveyor and pick out a spot, I will have him stake it out and mark it on his map, we got to start some where."

Walking through the maze of tents and nearing one of the largest one they could hear a loud commotion up ahead. As they rounded a tent, there us a small crowd gathered to watch two burly men kicking a man lying on the ground.

Ty watched for just an instant and when he didn't see any of the onlookers attempting to help he said, "Rocky hold my rifle and watch my back, I'm goin' to stop this now."

Gripping Ty's arm, "Ty it ain't our fight best we move on."

"I'm makin' it mine the poor bastard can't even protect his self."

Stepping up to the back of one of the men Ty said, "I think he has had enough, why don't you back off?"

The man whirled around and without a word swung a huge right hand at Ty's head. Ty ducked and as he came back up, he buried his left hand into the man's belly, the man gasped and bent over. Ty lifted him back to an upright stance with his right hand, the crack of the blow on the man's chin inflicted a bloody cut across it.

Ty heard a rifle shot and Tuff's bark, then a steady growl and he heard Rocky say "Stand where you are, I got a dozen more shots in the rifle and I don't miss very often, they don't need any help."

The big man wiped his chin with his right hand, he looked at Ty with a snarl on his bloody lips and said, "You picked the wrong man this time you bastard I ain't never been whipped and it's not goin' to happen today."

Not waiting for the man to finish or take another swing Ty hit him with a right cross. He sidestepped the roundhouse right of the man and Ty hit him again with a glancing blow but followed it with a strong left hand to the mans right cheek The big man staggered back a step or two and regained his balance.

Ty watched the man shake his head as if saying, you son of a bitch I'll get you one way or the other and about then the hunter hit Ty hard in the chin with a right hand. Hitting the ground, he saw the man charge at him, the big man left his feet, leaping for Ty's prone body but Ty neatly raised both of his feet and planted them soundly in the over size belly of the diving man. Stopping his fall and with a quick extension of his legs, tossed him over his head, back on his feet, Ty waited.

With an effort, the man got to his feet, he attempted a feeble right which missed by a foot or more. Ty moved in and hit the man three times, he was ready to hit him again when the man fell on his ass. He sat for a moment before he slowly tumbled backwards and laid still.

A jolt hit Ty in the back of his head moving to his right he turned to find the man's partner preparing to swing again. The man's fist hit Ty on the cheek and knocked him down, regaining his feet so fast that the second man was caught off guard and not prepared to hit him again. Ty circled to his left and waited for his opening, the man rushed at Ty with his arms out stretched and Ty neatly stepped to one side and hit the man in his kidney. Staggering to his left, he turned and rushed Ty once more; again, Ty neatly stepped aside and punched him in the face. This blow visually rocked the man, figuring out that he must stand and fight he slowly approached Ty. One wild swing and the fight was over, Ty had hit him with a solid left hand and had followed that with a stinging right. The man fell on his side, with blood streaming from his nose and there was a nasty cut on the man's lower lip. His face now covered with blood, he made no effort to get up.

The first man looked at Ty, shaking his head and sitting up and looked over at his partner, "You whip us both or did you get help with Cy?

Ty did not answer.

He spit a mouth full of blood on the ground. "It's no matter, seein' that your still standin' and Cy and me are on our asses."

"This is the first time that I have ever been whipped in my life, it ain't much fun tellin' you that but I'll will give you your due. You kicked the shit out of me fair and square, I don't hold no grudge and my friend won't either, I'll see to that. It's none of my business but do you mind tellin' me what you go by, folks call me Joe and they never see'd me this way."

"Names O'Malley."

"You Irish?"

"Ya."

"Me too, I guess if your goin' to get your ass kicked it's better by another Irishman than some other son of a bitch."

Ty stuck out his right hand and offered the man a hand up, grasping the open hand Ty pulled him to his feet.

"What did the man do that he deserved a beatin' like you were givin' him?"

"Didn't like the way we smelled and told us so. Didn't like us killin' the buffs and told us that too. Besides, he is a goddamn Davis lovin' son of a bitch Reb from Texas, figured to teach him some manners, he a friend of yours?"

"No, never saw him before."

"You're either goddamn sure of your self or a damn fool, I'll just figure on the first."

Rocky and Bob was kneeing beside the beaten man and was asking questions.

Rocky turned to Ty and said, "I think he has a broken arm and maybe a broken leg. Bob is goin' to take him to Chan's tent, see what he can do for this feller. He said his name is Edwards, John Edwards."

The crowd still stood where they were a couple of men was helping the second man who was still down.

Bob said, "I'll get a wagon so we can move him, it might take a while but I'll be back."

A short while later Bob returned with a wagon and two more men, they carefully lifted and placed the injured man in the wagon then headed for Chan's tent.

Bob said, "Chan is pretty good with healin', knows a hell of a lot more than I do."

Kate had tears in her eyes, she told Ty how worried she was but was also very proud of him. Placing her fingers on his left cheek she asked, "It is so red, does it hurt?"

"No, I'll be fine."

Before they removed the man from the wagon, Chan was busy gently pressing up and down along John's arm. At times, a grimace would cross John's face but he never said a word.

Chan turned to Bob and in nearly perfect English, said, "Its broken right here," Pointing to his forearm, "Have to put a splint on, it's going to hurt bad when I pull it back to set it."

Bob asked John, "You want a drink or two of whiskey to easy the pain or maybe a stick to bite on?"

Looking up and with a smile on his face said, "Maybe just one drink, I think I can stand it."

By this time, Chan was checking his leg for breaks and as he went about his business, he reported that he didn't think there were any breaks but there was a lot of cuts and some real bad bruising. "Going to be pretty sore for awhile, might hurt to walk, his ankle looks the worse, but it can wait, we'll fix his arm first."

With an ax, Rocky cut a piece of firewood into two flat boards and asked Chan if theses would do for splints.

"They will be fine."

John had taken a long pull on the bottle that Bob had brought and with his eyes shut said, "Let's do it."

Ty hanging on to John's shoulders and Rocky on his legs, with Bob and Chan, pulling in opposite directions, gave the arm a long slow pull. With tears running down his face John just laid there, grimacing, but silent.

Chan checked the arm again, shook his head up and down, he then proceeded to place the rough splint and wrap the arm with strips of cloth. When he had it as he wanted, he stood up; "He will need a sling, but it will be as good as new in a month or two."

John asked if he could have another pull on the bottle and with a great effort tried to set up. Ty helped him as Bob brought a camp chair and helped Ty place John in it and then they placed his leg on a round piece of firewood for support.

John said to Ty and Rocky, "You the ones that got me out of that fix I was in?"

Rocky answered, "He's the one, I just watched."

"Well son I want to thank you, I've been in tight fixes now and again but most times I get out by myself. Guessed wrong this time didn't expect that the two of 'em was goin' to go at me the same time. Hate to say it but two was more than I could handle at once."

Ty looked at Rocky, "Thought you were goin' to watch my back, how come you let the second one come after me?

"Just wanted to see what you could do, I had a hell of a time holdin' Tuff back he wanted to help but I thought that I would see if you needed it first."

"I got pasted along side my head and it didn't feel very damn good. Expected you to keep that one and the rest of the bunch off my backside, can't seem to trust you to do just simple little job."

"Hell son, I kept 'em off till you was done with the first one, thought that was the least I could do. I was thinkin' to see if you could go another round or two, I wouldn't of let 'em hurt you real bad. Hells bells I wasted a shot as it was just tryin' to help."

Bob was listening to all of this and decided to chime in. "Just like the old days only this time I got to watch, you fair the well laid a hurt on those two, never a doubt in my mind that you might need help. I did think old Tuff was goin' to bite off Rocky's leg or arm tryin' to get to one of 'em, he didn't like it for one damn minute, bein' left out of the fight."

"The second one just caught me by surprise is all, wasn't expectin' to be let down by someone I thought was my friend."

"I'll try not to let it happen again."

John sat quiet and listened. "You know son, when I was your age I didn't think that I could be whipped either. Thank god, you was here today, I think they just might of killed me if in' you hadn't of done what you did. I'll always be in your debt; I owe you a lot, Thanks."

"Wasn't right what they were doin', just couldn't stand there without helpin' some. You don't owe me nothin', just curious how it all came about."

"I came down to the Forks to get some supplies; we left my spread with two teams and a couple of my cowpokes, about two weeks ago. We made it all right, no injun problems but my boys decided that they were goin' back to Texas and took off on me. Was busy most of the last three days tryin' to hire some one to replace 'em? When the wagons got here today, I loaded my supplies, all except for my chickens and a fella told me that those two that you already met, might be interested in goin' on north. When I told 'em what it was that I needed the big one said that I talked funny. Told him I was from Texas, that didn't seem to matter, then he said something about Jefferson Davis that I didn't like and told him so. He called me a goddamn Rebel and I said that he stunk of dead buffalo. That's about it, he wanted a piece of me and I guess he got it, with help from his friend. Something hit me in the back and next thing I remember is bein' on the dirt, gettin' the shit kicked out of me."

Rocky said, "Ain't hardly enough to get crippled over now, is it?"

"Didn't think I would be, thought it was just a disagreement between two people. Now I'm in a hell of a shape, can't hardly harness and drive two four-horse teams at the same time. With one arm, it's goin' to be damn tough shootin' a rifle, ifin' I have too. I really got to find some one today, got to be headed back come mornin'."

Bob said, "I'll see what I can do, you ain't in any shape to be walkin' around, where you headed and what is it worth to you and is two all you will be needin'?"

"Hell I'd settle for one just to get me back to my spread might have to tie the wagons together, kinda like a train. The place I'm headed is north of here a couple of week's ride. I'll pay a dollar a day or maybe two if need be, got to get back to my cows and the rest of my boys, if they're still there."

Bob got up and said that he would be back; he first asked John if he wanted his teams and wagon's over here or left where they were.

Shaking his head yes he said. "The outfits are still over at the mercantile tent it would be nice to have it over here, most everything I got left is tied up in those supplies."

Rocky said, "I'll go with Bob and help get 'em over here, anything I need to know?"

One wagon has black leaders and the wheel horses are pintos, the second wagon has a mixed pair of big sorrels and grays. Both canvases' has seen better days, shouldn't be hard to find 'em, they were the only ones there earlier."

Chan kept their cups full of hot coffee while Kate and Ty talked with John.

"What's this spread your talkin' about?" Ty said, "Never heard of that before."

"It's where my stock is; back home in Texas it would be called a ranch.

The prettiest place you ever did see, wouldn't trade it for all the gold in Californie."

"Been up there long?"

"Not quite a year but figure on being there a damn long time.

Rocky returned first and unhitched the teams, he watered them and then he tied them along side of his own horses. He made sure that they had plenty of hay and after getting the second team taken care of, he joined John and the others. At that time, Bob walked up shaking his head, "Ain't one man that was interested, they make too much money shootin' buffalo. I passed the word around maybe someone that comes in from the hunt tonight might look us up."

"Thank you for tryin'; I got the same answers when I was askin'. Don't know what I am goin' to do come mornin' but I got to head back. I'll give the team a try and ifin' that don't work I guess I will leave my supplies here and ride one of the horses back and get help."

"With that ankle you got it is goin' to be damn hard even gettin' into a saddle." Bob warned. "You must need those things or you wouldn't risk the trip down here."

"Need all of it but ifin' I have to I guess they can stay here another month or so."

Rocky asked, "If you don't mind sayin', where is your place?"

"I was tellin' Ty and Miss Kate here that it is north of here, up in Dakota country. The prettiest valley you ever did see, high rock walls to protect the stock with plenty of water and grass that don't end, I was just damn lucky to find it when I did."

"How'd you happen on to it?" Bob said.

"Last fall I was pushin' a herd of cows north, tryin' to get to the gold fields up in Montana. We got a late start but I wasn't worried I had a good crew and they all knew cows. When we started, we had a shade over three thousand head and was movin' real good, lost a few, crossin' rivers and such. When we hit the Forks, we just kept on movin'; a week or so later we thought we was on the Bozeman trail but must have been east of it some."

"We got hit by an early storm, snow and wind like I never did see, lost about two, three hundred head in that one, just driven away by the damn wind. We held up for a few days and rounded up what strays we could find.

Had been movin' just a couple of days when my cook warned me that another storm was blowin' up, guess his bones told him so? I had seen the hills and trees off to our right and we just crossed a small stream that looked like it might go all the way to the timber. Decided it would be best if we could find some protection for the cows and men. I followed the stream and near sunset, I found this valley, right then I knew that I had found something that I had been lookin' for, a long damn time. Without dismountin', I headed back to the herd, we moved the stock as hard and fast as we could, right through night, pushed 'em into the valley just before the storm hit us. That's about it; decided then and there I was never leavin' it again. Made up my mind to wait for this railroad and start a new ranch, figured that I could ship my stock east."

"Any other white men up there."

"Only one that I ever see'd.

"Know who the man was?"

"Not at the time, he was just passin' through said he was a lonesome child, I thought that his sayin' it was funny, complained that the price of beaver had gone to hell and all the folks he had known had crossed over, didn't know what it meant, but he told me. He was headin' west away from all the shit that was about to happen in this part of the country?"

"He told me that the name of the river that we was settin' on was the Cheyenne and the name the Injun's called the valley was The Valley of the Ancient ones. There is a little, fast movin' stream that joins up with the river on the east end, he said that the Sioux call it the river of singin' death. He seemed to know a lot about the area, even more about the Injuns. Said that the Injuns stayed away from the valley cause the place was bad luck, too many old spirits live there."

"He told me that the Chief of the Cheyenne tribes was a feller that goes by the name Red Cloud and another Chief was Runnin' Horse. The old man had wintered with Runnin' Horse's tribe, said he decided to move on when he got wind of this here railroad."

Rocky asked, "Tell you his handle?"

Asked him, he said that he was a bastard child of a Grizz and his Mommy was a she lion. After he drank some, he did say that he favored the name Fitz, might have been his name, don't know. Stayed with us a better part of a week I'd guess and then one day he was gone."

"Knowed a man once that went by a handle just about like that, he was a squatty fella, white hair and his face covered with hair the same color."

"Sounds like him." John answered Rocky.

"Notice his trigger finger?"

"Short the first knuckle, but that's about all."

"That was Joe Fitzsimmons, met him at Bridger's the year I went back east, he told me then that I would not like the other side and he was right."

Rocky went on, "Mean lookin' fella on the outside but ifin' he took a shine to ya, a better friend you'd never see'd. He liked what he called the little mountains in Dakota, the injuns call 'em the Paha Sapa, in Sioux it means the Black Hills. Told me once that he knew where there was a lot of gold, yours for the takin' he said but I never believed him."

"He was nice enough to me and the boys; he did tell us that he always figured that the valley was his. Said that we could have it for he weren't comin' back this way."

"Hell he has got to be near eighty, if he's a day."

"He did say that he first came to the valley in '26, finest place on earth he said. He warned us about the little creek and told us a story that many years ago a tribe of Sioux was camped on that creek. One night a wall of water washed 'em all away and killed most everyone, the ones that made it never went back, that's where it got the name, Singin' Death."

Tuff stood up, curling his lips and sounded a low snarl, a voice from behind the tent was heard saying, "Hello the camp."

"Bob responded, "Come on in."

A tall, broad shoulder men stepped up to the fire, "Is there a man that goes by the name of O'Malley here?"

The hair on the back of Ty's neck seemed to come erect as he stood and said, "I'm O'Malley."

"Name's James Adams, knew an O'Malley in the war, was wondering ifin' you were him, his name was James too."

"Got a brother named James."

"He from Missouri?"

"That's right."

"Might he have been in the 4th Missouri Calvary?"

"Think he was."

"Then I'm bettin' were talkin' about the same man, he was a friend of mine. Have you got time to talk, I have a couple of questions you might be able to answer."

Ty and the stranger moved off a short distance before saying anything.

"Heard about the fight today and when they told me, an O'Malley did it to old Joe it sounded like something that your brother James might have done. I just had to come and see ifin' it was him, you his younger brother?"

"Ya, my name's Ty."

"They tell me you made short work out of your run in with Joe and Cy."

"Didn't like the way they were beatin' the man they downed."

"That's what I would have expected from James. I'm guessin' you're a lot a like your brother."

"I think most anyone would have done the same."

"Don't bet on it."

Adams then asked, "Just wonderin' if James made it through the damn war, last I see'd of him was in Virginia, the battle of Seven Pines it was. Ifin' I remember right he had another brother in the war too, was his name Kevin?"

"He made it home a little worse for wear but he made it, had his arm and shoulder shot up pretty bad, but they was healin'. Kevin made it home a little after James, Mom and me was sure happy to have 'em both back."

"You've got a hell of a fine brother in James. He was a good friend and a damn good soldier, never see'd anyone shoot like he could."

"You make it through alright?"

"Except for some scars inside my head, I made it alright. Some nights I fight the damn war all over again, wake up a sweatin' and can't hardly breath."

"James and me stuck pretty close to one another for the most part, he kept the Rebs off my back and I did the same for him that is till we got separated that day. That fight was a hell of a mess; we rode right into it, never even knowin' the Rebs was there. Shot us up bad, they did, never seen James again."

"He ended up in a hospital in Pennsylvania after that fight, that's where he was when they told him he could go home."

"Glad he made it."

"You a hunter?"

"No, workin' for the railroad helpin' to keep the Injuns off the surveyors back."

"Accordin' to my partner that's better than bein' a hunter."

"Was that Bob Perry back at the fire, the superintendent of this railroad?"

"Ya."

"You work for him?"

"No, just a friend did work for him back home, before we headed west."

"You're not stickin' around?"

"No headed to the mountains north and west of here, my partner Seth Buntrock has been there before; he was kind enough to let me come along."

"Always thought that I might head that way, but there is a piece of ground east of here that caught my eye. I did some farmin' in Iowa, Paris Iowa it was, before I went to Missouri to be a damn coal miner. Didn't plan on doin' anymore minin' and that was final and after seein' the land out here, decided to take up farmin' again. If in' you're ever back this away again, look me up. The place that I got my eye on is a day's ride west of Fort Kearney and just north of the river, you can't miss it. When the surveyors got there, they put up a big sign that says it is the 100th meridian, that's how they mark off the ground or something."

"Don't know what my plans are goin' to be after I get to the mountains, right now old John has got a problem that we are tryin' to solve. He needs help getin' his wagons back north and Rocky and me might have to help, ifin' he don't find someone. If I get back this way, it shouldn't be too hard to find your place if they leave that sign there."

"You say you guard the surveyors, had a lot of run-ins with the Injuns so far?"

"A few times, they hit us, then turn and get the hell out of rifle shot and maybe come back two or three times a day, we knock a couple off their horses and they pull out. We all carry Henrys and there is ten of us most of the time we can lay down a hell a barrage of hot lead, in a big hurry."

James went on, "If I didn't want that piece of land back yonder and didn't have to honor my agreement with the railroad to get it, I'd help that friend of yours, I'd like to see what's up there."

'You serious about helpin' old John out cause if you are I'll talk to Bob, see if there is anything that he can do about your agreement."

"I am."

I'll see what Bob can do."

The subject was changed and it went back to the war. Adams talked about his friendship with Ty's brother and the longer they talked, the more Ty came to like this man. He was just an everyday person that had a dream just like his, maybe his dream was more practical than Ty's and maybe safer. After the mountains, it might be nice to settle out here, bring Ma and the boys out to help work it.

After more small talk, the two shook hands and Ty asked James if he would like to go with him when he talked with Bob.

Arriving at the camp, they were greeted by Rocky, "Everything alright?"

Ty introduced James to the group by saying, "James here was a friend of my brother in the war, they had been separated and he has worried about my brother's well bein'. He might be willin' to help John out ifin' we can work something out, with Bob's help."

Bob stood up, shook James's hand and asked, "What can I do to help?"

"You go ahead James and explain the problem."

"Well Mr. Perry you see I work for the surveyors, guardin' their backs while they do their job. When I signed on with this railroad, they told me that if I stayed to the end of the line, I could pick any quarter section of ground that I wanted. I found that piece of ground back there a ways, right at the 100th meridian. The surveyors laid out the lines and marked it on their maps as the one I wanted. I told Ty here that I would like to help Mr. John but don't want to loose my land, if there was something you could do to help me keep the piece of land, then I would sure help get his supplies up north."

"I think I'll go talk with George, he is the head surveyor and see what he can do, James why don't you stay here till I get back shouldn't take long."

Smiling from ear to ear John spoke to James, "I thank you for kindness even if you don't know if it will work out. You look like the kind of a man that I have been lookin' for; hope Bob can find a way out with the head man of your crew."

While John and James were talking, Rocky motioned to Ty to follow, they moved off a short distance.

"You need to talk to me you damn traitor," Ty said with a slight grin.

"If my old friend has time."

"Anything for you, you old goat."

"Ty, as far as time goes, we haven't known each other for very long but I think we both understand one another's thoughts pretty damn well. I've had something on my mind every since we talked with John and clear down in my toes I think you have had the same thought. It's about the fix John is in, he has to get back to his place, which is north and we is headed a little northwest. I'm thinkin' that we could help him out, not havin' to go far out of our way, mind you, I know that it's goin' to be slower than what we could do alone but I'm thinkin' that maybe it is the right way to go."

"Dammit it that's pure frightin' havin' you thinkin' you know what's in my mind and all. Goin' to have to stop thinkin' bad things about you but you are right I have been thinkin' on a way to help John; I was hopin' to say something. Didn't know just how to go about it, I know how important gettin' back to Evenin' Star is to you and I sure didn't want to slow you up. For just for a minute, when James showed an interest in helpin', I thought that the problem was solved. Then I figured that John ain't goin' to be able to handle that team by himself with his arm that away."

"Then that's settled, let's go tell John that we will leave at sunrise."

John and James were still talking, Bob had not returned yet.

Ty stepped up to where John was sitting, "How's the arm and foot feelin' some of the pain goin' away?"

"I've had worst hurts but don't remember just when."

"Where's Kate?"

"Went to her tent seemed to be down on her feed or something, she was really quiet."

"I'll go see if there is anything wrong, John, Rocky and me have decided to go take a look-see at your place up north. It ain't far out of our way and you can show us that pretty valley of yours, we'll leave at first light if it's alright with you"

With a smile big, enough to break his jaw John started to get out of the chair but instead decided just to shake Ty's hand. You boys get me out of more fixes than I could shake a stick at, thank you very much I'll be ready. Have to send word to the mercantile so he can get my chickens over here, he built me a basket out of chicken wire and reeds so I could carry 'em under the wagon, damn this is good news. By the way, James the offer is still on ifin' Bob can work things out."

James said, "I hope he can I'm ready to see some new country."

"Better go see if anything is wrong with Kate, I won't be long."

Going to his pack, Ty got the blanket wrapped bundle, for the first time he realized how heavy it was. Stopping just short of the entrance to her tent Ty asked, "Kate you alright?"

A moment of silence, then, "I'm fine Ty, just a little melancholy come in if you like."

Kate was sitting on the edge of her canvas bed and she motioned for Ty to sit in the only chair in the small tent.

A pretty smile was on her face but it was obvious that she had been crying, her eyes were red and she kept wiping at her nose.

"Why so blue, Kate your dream is just about in sight, the location is picked out and all that is left is to build your boardin' house."

"That part doesn't bother me; it's loosing you and Rocky that hurts. I've come to respect you both and I have relied on you for protection, advice and friendship; I'm going to miss that."

"You'll be alright you've been through a lot and that has toughened you up, you can whip anything that comes along and I know you will."

"Thank you Ty it is just another change in my life I have been so happy the last few weeks I just hate to loose that feeling again."

Just remember that you will have Bob and old Tuff, they will stand by you."

"That's the other thing taking Tuff back east with me, I am not sure that I should, he is so protective of me that I just don't know what will happen when we start to meet other people. He just might take a leg off, you never know."

"I'll bet that Bob will keep him for you while your makin' the arrangements for your buildin', he seems to like him."

"But Bob meets strangers every day, can Tuff be trusted to be on his best behavior while I'm gone? You yourself said that Tuff likes to fend for himself, kill chickens and hunt rabbits, he most likely will get shot if he is ever caught."

"You're right about that if he does hold true to form; he will most likely take off huntin' for you like he did before. I think you will have to take him along with you and put him on a short rein, a collar and a small chain might do it, I don't see any other way out. You know that he is your dog and I know that he don't want to loose you again."

"I don't want to loose him either for a long time he was my only friend, till I met you, I'll just have to try to control him the best that I can."

"I did want to tell you that Rocky and me are plannin' on leavin' at first light we are goin' to help John get back to his place and then move on. I brought this to give back to you." Ty handed the package to Kate. "Just about forgot that I had it."

Laying the blanket parcel beside her she said, "I am going to miss you so very much; you and Rocky mean so much to me." With tears welling up in her beautiful eyes, she went on, "If I live to be a hundred years old, I can never repay you for what you have done for me, I owe you so much."

"Now don't go gettin' mushy eyed on me you know that I don't know how to handle that."

"I can't help it Ty, I am going to feel so alone without my two bodyguards here with me."

"Why don't we just go outside and join the others and have us a good time, Chan will be fixin' supper before long and I'm as hungry as a bear."

"I'll be out shortly just let me dry my eyes and regain my composure."

Bob was back and was busy talking to James, with John and Rocky listening in, seeing Ty, he stopped and said, "I got a deal worked out with the surveyor that James is goin' to work for me, kinda like a scout or something. I'm thinkin' about sendin' him north for a month or two, just to look around, he won't loose his land that away and while he is goin' north he might as well ride with you John."

"Bob, me and Rocky have decided to ride along with John and James, want to see that valley of his, we thought we would leave come sun up."

"Figured you might, knew you two wouldn't leave John in the lurch."

Standing up James slapped Ty on the back, "I guess John's got his hands full now, you, Rocky and me is goin' to be a whole mess to handle at once."

With the smile still on his lips, John answered, "Hate to say this to your face and all, but I'm thinkin' that you three are like little kittens to what I am used too."

Rocky answered, "Don't mix me in with these two I'm thinkin' that I'm a whole hell of a lot better than their kind, don't you agree John?"

"Just have to wait and see, sometimes it takes awhile to trail break a maverick., thinkin' I'm up to tryin'."

"Better go get my gear and say my goodbye's, I'll bring 'em over here and be ready to leave in the mornin'. Ain't got much, but Bob invited me to supper and Rocky says that I wouldn't want to miss it." With that, James left camp.

As soon as he was gone, Rocky asked, "She alright?"

"She'll be out in a minute she was takin' stock in her situation afraid to go east with Tuff and afraid to leave him with Bob. She might be thinkin' about us leavin' her too, takin' stock in her bein' alone for a change, I told her to come on out and we'd have a party or something."

Bob said, "She don't have to worry about her dog, we'll think of something. Might have to build a box for him to sleep in, do you think that he would fight that?"

"Sorry Bob but I don't think all of us could put him one, he's a free sprit. Don't like to eat other peoples food, lessin' he kills it him self. With Kate it might be different, but I'm thinkin' he still won't like it."

"I think your right Ty." Rocky added, "Hell as much as he likes you, he still wants to fetch to his own vittles."

"We'll handle it," said Bob.

"You talking about me?" Kate asked and then she continued, "I'm just a little down in the mouth knowing that Ty and Rocky will be leaving tomorrow. We've been close for quite sometime, I am going to miss you both. You did live up to your end of our bargain you seen me west and found a place for my dream, for all you have done, I thank you; I'll never forget either of you."

She walked over to Rocky and kissed him on the cheek and he turned as red as a fresh raspberry. Turning to Ty, she did the same and got the same response.

"I decided to say my good-byes early and not wait till morning; I think it would be a lot harder then. If I am not up when you leave you know that I love you both."

"Now that has been done, lets act like it isn't going to happen tonight is just another night and tomorrow is just another day."

The camp was still and no one knew what to say to break the silence.

Just as James returned John said, "Bob, I have something that I would like for you to give to your friend Chan. It ain't much but I would like him to have this here injun arrowhead that I cut out of me years ago. I've kinda been carryin' it for good luck and it sure as hell worked for me, at least for the most part. A man with his talents might not need a good luck charm but I would feel better ifin' he had this."

Handing the little shaped stone to Bob, he added, "Don't figure that I will be needin' this anymore."

Bob tried to talk John out of giving it away too no avail, then he added, "Chan will treasure this I know he will, I'll go give it to him right now."

All through the meal, Chan paid special attention to John, his cup never went dry. As far as Chan was, concerned supper was not over till John leaned back from the table and shoved his tin plate to the center.

Darkness fell and two burly men appeared out of nowhere. Bob introduced them to the group as the men that were to stand guard at Kate's tent. He asked the men, "You know what I want, no fallin' to sleep, no drinkin' and keep your eyes open. Miss Kate here is important to all of us here; we don't want anything to happen to her, can you make it through the night without sleep? I'm a light sleeper and will check on you from time to time mind ya."

Both men assured Bob that they could.

Kate retired to her tent and a sadness that Ty had rarely felt before settled down on him, he had to swallow many times before he could speak. He thought to himself that a big part of his life had just left; he may never see Kate again and looking over at Rocky, Ty sensed that he was feeling the same.

Bob broke out a bottle of whisky and this time Ty did take a big swallow. After the bottle had made two or three rounds, they all turned in. Bob and James went to Chan's tent. Rocky and Ty helped John into theirs.

The whiskey had made Ty very sleepy, his plan to wait and then move to the front of Kate's tent soon vanished as sleep over came him.

In the darkness of the morning, a candle threw enough light so the remaining supplies could be loaded, the horses saddled and the teams hitched to the wagons. Chan had been up well before any of the others and the breakfast meal was ready in no time at all the men ate as if it might be their last. Ty kept looking over his shoulder hoping to see Kate.

They lifted John into the lead wagon while James, with the horses tied behind, crawled into the second. Ty and Rocky was busy thanking Bob for all that he had done and giving him final instructions about Kate. Ty reminded Bob that she would need some protection when she returned to the Forks, and told him not to let her talk him out of it.

Ty asked Rocky if he wanted to rest his butt some more and drive the first wagon or should Ty plan on being the skinner.

Rocky slapped Ty on the back and attempted to kick him in the ass at the same time. "My ass is well rested so I'll just scout ahead of this wagon train; try to keep you youngin's out of trouble, if that's possible"

Still looking for Kate and not seeing her Ty climbed up along side of John. With Duke and Pat, following behind Ty shouted to the leaders and slapped the wheel horses on their butts with the reins.

Just as the wagons were pulling out of sight, Ty looked back seeing Kate and Tuff standing with Bob. Tuff was looking up at Kate his head tilted at an angle as if to say, "Why aren't we going along?"

Tuff would jump a few feet ahead of Kate and then would look back. Then he would run a few paces after the wagons and again look at Kate, this went on until the wagons topped the long hill and were out of sight.

Tears streaming down her face she knelt down and hugged Tuff's shaggy head, "We're going to miss them aren't we my friend, in my heart, I wish we were going with them, I know you do too. Those two need the open life they would feel boxed in if they had to live in a dirty old town and I'm afraid that you feel the same way, I wonder if I am right in keeping you here with me. I don't know what I will do with you in Omaha or wherever I have got to go."

All the while, she was talking Tuff kept looking back to where he had last seen the wagons. Looking up at Bob, Kate asked, "Am I doing the right thing Bob, keeping Tuff here he acts like he wants to go with Ty and acts like he wants stay here with me too, what should I do?"

In Bob's usual way, he thought for a while, "Maybe you should let Tuff decide what he wants."

"How can I do that?"

"Turn him loose, let him know that he can stay or go."

"What happens if he decides to goes, what would I do without him?"

"Kate you just have to take a chance and know that whatever he does is the right thing. Your strong and you love him too much to hurt him by forcin' him to stay."

Turning and walking away, "It's your call Kate do what you think is right."

Pulling Tuff as close to her as she could and with her head lying on his she said, "Old friend I know that Bob is right but I hate to loose you too. What he said is true, I do love you and want you to do whatever you want, if you go with Ty, I'll understand."

That said she turned Tuff loose and Tuff looked up at her with eyes that were as sad as hers were and then looked back over his shoulder.

"You can go if you wish, old friend."

Tuff turned and dashed in the direction of the wagons, he stopped and came running back, rubbing up against Kate's leg, whimpering he turned and ran out of sight.

CHAPTER 12

It was a long and slow climb out of the Platte valley, up to the rolling plains above. The horses were blowing hard and needed to rest, the wagons were loaded heavy with everything needed to support a ranch, from dried beans, flour, coffee and sugar to bags of potatoes, onions and corn meal. New shirts and pants, building supplies like nails and a piece of glass for a window. Tools of all kinds needed for building a cabin, a barn or anything that might be required. Long handle scythes tied to the sides of the wagon along with shovels and axes, heavy chains that hung in big loops. A crate of chickens hung beneath the second wagon and tied on to the end of one was a roll of chicken wire, on the other wagon a steel plow.

Half way up the ridge, the grass changed to the short buffalo grass, quite a contrast from the tall lush grass that grew near the river. The sweet yellow clover that was so abundant along the river was gone, plants up here seemed to be stunted like the grass. Clumps of thistles with their sharp spears, some with purple flowers attached, were everywhere. The plant was more like a cactus but in place of the thorns, there were razor sharp edges that ran along the tall spears.

Letting the horses rest while the men stretched their legs and relieved themselves, Rocky moved a short distance away from them looking off into the west. "Ty, that dog out there belong to you?"

Ty whirled around and saw Tuff, setting on his haunches and looking back at him. Ty said, in a voice that sounded choked up, "Nope, that dog don't belong to nobody, not now anyway, guess he didn't want to go back east and decided to head north same as us."

"Looks like he ain't goin' no where till you move, I think he's yours now."

"He is a strange animal that dog is, I'll be happy if he decides to tag along."

After a short while, the wagons moved on and the stench of rotting flesh was heavy in the air. Occasionally buffalo, seen grazing along side of the decaying flesh of their once majestic comrades, ignoring the passing strangers as if they did not exist. Coyotes feeding on the dead carcasses would look up and run with their tails between their legs, coming to a stop after running a short distance, checking out the new disturbance, before returning to eat their fill, as the wagons passed, they were back stuffing themselves.

With rags tied across their faces, trying to keep the rotten smell out of their lungs, they rode north. The horses pulling the wagons plodded along, their heads lowered and with ever step, the wagon rocked in a monotonous manner. A wheel would fall into a rut or run over a rock, the jolt would bring a string of profanity out of John's mouth the like that Ty had seldom heard.

Rocky rode a head, still wearing his buffalo coat while scouting for the easiest path and watching for any thing out of the normal. The wagons would come to a stop every so often to permit the horses to rest and Rocky would come riding back just to be sure that nothing had happened. After a drink of water, he would ride out again.

At the midday rest stop, the men ate jerky, cold biscuits and drank from the barrel that hung from the side of the wagon...

John was shaking his head in wonderment, "Dammit Rocky the way your drinkin' that water, we ain't goin' to have any left.

"Just tryin' to lighten your load, ever little bit will help these poor horses."

"Why don't you take off that damn fur coat, you might not get so thirsty?"

"I'll tell you a story why, I once knew a man that lived in these parts, it was a pleasant day but it got a little warm so he took off his coat and he tied it and his rifle to his saddle, shortly there after his horse spooked and threw the man to the ground. The horse, he ran away with all the man owned includin' his coat and rifle. If he had just had a hold of his rifle he might have shot, the damn horse and saved his supplies. The man nearly starved to death and then fell to sleep; he froze to death the next night. I'll just keep on wearin' my coat and hangin' on to my old rifle."

"Shit, thought that everything was bigger in Texas, ain't ever heard such a damn tall tail in my life but you do what you have to do son, never mind me."

Late in the day, a camp was set up in a grove of trees, near a small pond of water. Tasting the water, they found it to be stagnate and brackish so they watered the horses with the water they carried. The horses were on picket ropes tied to the wagon wheels, the wagons were side by side and it was between the wagons that James scraped out a spot for the fire while Rocky gathered some firewood. Ty hung an iron pot over the fire, boiled some water and added beef jerky, an onion, a couple potatoes and their meal was cooking.

The men drank the soup out of tin cups and waited until it was all gone, never saying a word until Rocky said, "Sure as hell miss Chan's cookin'."

"Might never again taste anything that good for the rest of our lives, that man could sure make a man smile with his fixin'," answered James.

"Only sat at his table twice but I sure as hell won't forget it." John said.

"Something wrong with my cookin', I thought that it was mighty tasty."

"Oh, nothin' wrong with it at all son just might have tasted better with a carrot or two in it is all."

"Ya and maybe a piece of fresh beef." Added James.

"Could have went and cut us a chunk of buffalo off one of those dead beast a layin' out there but maybe a loaf of fresh baked bread would have please you more."

They all laughed. John spoke for them, "Son you just leave that rotten meat out there. Just to let you know, I have ate worse than your fixin's."

At sunset, the men were ready to call it a day Ty and Rocky spread their robes on one side of the fire, John and James on the other. John had volunteered to take the first watch, Rocky would be next, then James and Ty was to have the last watch.

Rocky reminded them that they had better watch the horse's real close, "Injuns can sneak up on anything and never be seen or heard. They can steal a horse right out from under you and you won't know that the damn horse is gone till you drop on your ass and hit the ground."

"Your right, we need those horses bad, hate to have to carry this shit on our backs." John added.

Just at dusk, Tuff came into camp; he went directly to Ty's robe and laid down at its foot.

Ty patted his head, "Proud to have you come along, feel sorry for your mistress, she must be kinda sad right now. Old dog you know that your free to go back any time you want."

It felt good to have the dog lying next to him, first, it reminded him of Kate, and second he just felt safer.

Ty woke up in a panic it was nearly light and he hadn't woke up for his watch. As he got up the first thing Ty noticed was that Tuff was gone. Walking over to where James was leaning against one of the wagons. "Dammit James I'm sorry I didn't get up when you tried to wake me."

"Didn't try, John, he took two watches in a row, he didn't wake Rocky till maybe three hours ago."

"What did he do that for?"

"Don't know you'll have to ask him."

Hearing the rattle of a pan and the tin cups, Ty saw John standing at the fire pit. "Dammit John what's the idea of takin' two shifts last night?"

"Hell just thought that I would let one of you sleep a little longer is all. With this arm in a sling, I don't do nothin' all day, thought I could make up for it that away. I can doze all day ifin' I want with you and James a doin' the skinin' and all."

"Weren't necessary, but thanks."

A quick breakfast and the wagons were back on the trail.

The morning turned hot as hell, the pulling horses, covered with a white foaming sweat, that sapped their strength by the added heat. John said, "As hot as it is we will have to rest the teams more often it will slow us some but it is better than losin' a horse."

At every rest stop, the horses drank water out of a canvas bucket, giving them plenty of time to catch their breath, after a quarter of an hour, they were ready to go again.

When the sun was at its highest, the teams were unhitched and watered from a nearby stream. With a sharp eye on them, they were allowed to graze a way from the stream; too much water at one time could make them as sick as hell.

Rocky and Ty, using the canvas bucket, filled the water barrels. "Hope to hell this makes old John happy, there will be water for another day anyways. Maybe he won't yell when I get thirsty again."

"I think that John worries more about his horses that us but then again I sure as hell would hate to lose any of 'em. Don't think old Duke is up to pulling a load like we got, like he said, hate to carry this shit on my back"

Taking another drink of the cool stream water, Rocky said. "Surprised me we ain't seen any sign yet, figured we might see some here. As John said, we'll be crossin' the North Platte and another river up north and in between several smaller streams. If we don't find sign out in the open, we'll find it near the water."

With the barrels full, the two returned to the small fire, James was busy frying bacon, the coffee pot was steaming and with his good arm, John dumped in a hand full of coffee grounds.

Ty said, "After a few days of smellin' that rotten odor it feels good to breath clean air again. Figure that the damn hunters would have hunted up here too. Don't get me wrong I don't like seein' the dead animals, they don't look very good without their skins."

Rocky joined into the conversation by saying, "They're a damn bunch of cowards afraid to go out this far, might have a run in with some mad Injuns. I guess I have to give 'em their due, they just wait and take advantage of the lack of fear the buffs have and just let 'em walk right into their sights."

"It's a damn shame that they are that dumb. If the people back east don't get their fill of buffalo tongue and robes soon, there won't be any left, that's a damn shame of it. Now if the damn easterners would just get a taste for snake, any kind of snake, I'd go along with that, I hate snakes.

"Your right James, I ain't never see'd another creature on this earth of ours that as big and grand as a bull buffalo. Makes a man want to hide a few just so they can out last the damn hunters and that's just what I plan to do. Then again, I never see'd nothin' as ugly as a damn snake, I never thought about your idea about gettin' rid of the 'em thata way. Maybe some day they will take a likin' and do just what you said."

Rocky asked, "You got buffs on that place of yours?"

"Not many but a few head, maybe a hundred or so. They don't seem to bother my cows none, so what's the harm. I think my cows can get along with 'em, they don't mix but that might change. And If it does, I'll just move 'em to another part of the valley."

"You might end up with the last of 'em."

"That would be a shame ifin' that's all that is left, I figure that the railroad is to blame for what is happenin' to 'em. They got to feed the workers and the buffs are handy. They need folks to move out here and settle, damn hard to convince 'em if the buffalo comes in and destroy their crops and then the railroad wouldn't have anything to ship back east."

Rocky looked at Ty as if to say, "See I told you."

"Rocky thinks the same way he told me the same thing, I didn't believe him at the time, I sure as hell do now it's a cryin' damn shame what's happenin'."

By mid-afternoon of the next day, the clouds were starting to build in the western sky, turning a dark gray, the wind was steadily getting stronger, and the smell of rain was in the air.

John was half-asleep when Ty said, "The sky sure as hell is lookin' bad, think we had better keep an eye on the weather and if need be, find us a camp site early."

John sat up straighter, look around the canvas and replied. "Don't look good, that's for sure, you're right, we had better start lookin' for a place to ride out the storm."

About that time Rocky came riding back, "You want to camp early tonight; there is a spot just up ahead. There's some trees to shelter the horses and it is not on high ground, I'm thinkin' that there just might be some lightning along with the rain."

"Just thinkin' the same thing, let's do it."

Amongst the scrub oaks and stunted ash trees, the horses were hobbled and left to graze. The wagons pulled in side by side and a ground sheet placed between them slanting from the top of the wagon box to the ground. With a shovel, James dug a small trench around the high side, placing the dirt just under the bottom edge of the tarp. The trench would catch the run off of the tarp and surrounding ground and divert it away from beneath the shelter.

They built a small fire just as the rain started, before long they were drinking hot coffee. A portion of a cured ham was sliced and placed in the skillet and Rocky opened two cans of peaches, "I'm thinkin' that we're goin' to be here for a while ducking' the rain and tryin' to stay dry, we might as make the most of the rest."

The rain got harder and the wind picked up, driving the rain against the tarp. Two of the men were squatting under the shelter; the others were lying under Ty's wagon, with tin cups of hot coffee in their hands. The chickens were quiet, all huddled together in one corner of the cage, afraid of Tuff who had taken up a spot next to the cage.

"The rain at least quieted the damn chickens all day long; I can hear 'em over the noise of the horses and the wagon." James said.

"They might be noisy and stink of chicken shit but I sure as hell like their eggs." John added, "And they ain't bad fried up either."

Rain, driven by the wind, blew in under the wagon. Drops of rain falling from the shelters edge formed small puddles, quickly turning into mud. Each time the wind increased, the men would fall silent and look up to see if their temporary protection would blow away.

"If this keeps up, I think we are in for a long night, won't have to worry about takin' our watch cause we will be awake anyways."

"Think your right John out here, the damn rain might last all night and then could be over before we know it."

Just as Rocky said that, a crack of lightning lit up the sky and moments later a rumble of thunder crashed through the noise of the howling wind. The horses, nervous and frighten by the thunder, reacted by jerking against their tie ropes.

Ty left the relative protection to go out and quiet them, assuring each of them that everything was going to be all right.

"Son of a bitch that was close it sure as hell scared the hell out of me, never was one to like that shit, I say let it rain but don't make so much noise about doin' it."

"I agree with you James, what is worse is to be sittin' on top of a damn mountain and watchin' that shit hit a tree and see it explode into a fire ball, now that's damn scary." Rocky said.

"When your drivin' a herd of cows, the last thing that you want is lightnin', spooks the damn cows and can start a stampede in a wink of an eye. The herd starts to run and the cows they can trample a cowboy to death ifin' he gets in the way. If you don't get 'em turned back on themselves they will run forever. Then they spread out and it can take days just to round what's left of 'em up. Been in a few and don't look forward to doin' it again."

During his brief statement, lightning interrupted John three times and each time a huge clap of thunder followed, it made hearing anything else impossible. With each bolt of lightning or clap of thunder, the horses would whinny and pull back on their ropes and Ty would dash out to calm them and be sure none broke away.

After the third time, Ty shook his head, "Think you guys are right, it's goin' to be a long night."

"I'll go out the next time." Rocky said

"No need for two of us to get all wet, I'm soaked now, can't get any wetter."

The noisy storm kept up for nearly the whole night and after the thunder and lightning ceased, the wind died down. A stead rain followed and just before dawn, the rain stopped, as the men dozed, Tuff went looking for his breakfast.

Stepping out of the shelter, Ty was surprised that where he thought there would be nothing but mud, the ground look dry. The only evidence of the night's rain was puddles of water that stood in the low places.

"I sure as hell didn't think that we could move out this mornin' figured that the mud would stop us. Back home a rain storm like that would keep us high and dry for two, maybe three days."

"Out here the country don't see all that much rain and when it does rain the ground really soaks it up in a hurry."

The breakfast was finished, the horses hitched, and the small wagon train headed north.

Ty sat on the wagon seat and thought, "This is damn near as bad as walkin' behind old Buck only I get to ride rather than walk. You get to set a little higher and can see more and instead of lookin' at the ass of one mule, you are lookin' at four horse's asses at the same time. His thoughts about Buck and plowing brought him to think of Kate. I wonder if she is in Omaha now buying, the things that she would need to start her business and had Bob hired a man or two to protect her? She most likely had bought her self a new dress and a hat, bet she looks like a grand lady now.

Brought out of his thoughts by John saying, "The Platte should be right over the next rise, when I crossed her last she was runnin' a little high, plenty of crossin's though, shouldn't be hard for Rocky to find one."

The river was wide but not deep, the sandy bottom made the wagon horses work but the crossing went well.

Just on, the other side of the river they came across the ruts made by the immigrants heading west. Maybe a mile further on, Rocky came riding back and told them that there was unshod pony tracks up ahead and made sometime today.

"How many, could you tell?" John asked.

"I counted six all together, might be a scoutin' party or a huntin' bunch."

"What do you think we should do, hold up in them trees or keep on goin'?"

"The thing that bothers me", Rocky answered, "Is the horses, their like gold to an Injun, we could hold up and maybe hide some of 'em in the trees but ifin' we start hidin' every time we see a track, it will take us forever to get to your valley. I say we should keep on goin' and let the chips fall where they might."

"Sounds right to me." John said.

"How you goin' to handle it ifin' we meet up with 'em?" James asked.

"Been thinkin' on that too, the way I see it is we have to protect the horses first then set up to fight 'em ifin' we have too."

"What's your plan Rocky?" Ty asked. "Think I know what you will say, about stayin' out in the open and away from the trees. What do you think about pullin' the wagons up side by side, like we do when we set up camp, only further apart leave room for the teams in between and the others too? We can each take a corner and try to save what we got."

"Sounds good to me," James said. "We could tie the ridin' stock to the sides of the wagons now, won't have to move 'em."

"Might work, James when you come up along side Ty's wagon, you come up on the right just drop the traces and leave 'em harnessed." Rocky added.

John said, "Lets do it, Rocky why don't you leave your Hawkins here in the wagon and take one of my new Henrys it will give us a hell of a lot more firepower. We can load the others I have and we can sure as hell lay down some lead in a hurry."

"Won't hurt I guess ifin' you got plenty of ammo."

Replacing his rifle and taking one of John's he said. "Wish I had time to sight this one in guess I'll just have to wait and see where it shoots."

After the sun had started on it's way down, Ty relaxed figuring that the danger was over but topping a small rise Ty pulled to a halt and said, "Damn it there they are, comin' right at us."

It was obvious that the Indians had seen Rocky or the wagons at the same time. They sat their horses and the two parties although a mile apart, stared at one another.

Rocky sat Satan a short distance in front of the wagons and he motioned them to come forward. Easing the horses forward they pulled along side of Rocky. "Don't look like no war party, most likely hunters?"

James had pulled along side of Ty's wagon and started to get down. Rocky, without taking his eyes off the Indians said, "Ty, you and John get down all three of you bring your rifles and come over here, they don't look like they want to start any trouble and I think we will let 'em make the first move. There is six of 'em and we will let 'em see that there is four of us."

The wait seemed longer than is was and after a short time, the Indians moved forward at a slow walk. As they got closer Rocky said, "Only see one rifle and the rest look like they got bows I'm guessin' that they want to have a meetin' and check us out."

About half way there, the small group of Indians came to a stop, the one in the middle raised his right arm and with his rifle across his lap started forward by himself.

"It's my outfit, want me to go out and meet him?"

"Don't really want 'em to know just how bad your arm is, four rifles is better than three. If it is all right with you, I'll go, I know a little Sioux and hand signs are all about the same."

Riding toward the lone Indian, Rocky too left his rifle across his saddle, he raised his right arm, leaving a short distance between them. Rocky nodded his head at the Indian and in response, the Indian made a hand sign first with his index finger, he pointed back at himself, then wriggled his fingers and then gently laid his open hand across his chest and said, "Hi Wowahwa." {"I come in peace."}

Rocky shook his head up and down in agreement sure of what the Sioux had said; he repeated first the Sioux's words and then said in English, "I come in peace, too."

The Sioux then went on. He raised his right hand, with two fingers pointed at his eyes. He moved his eyes back and forth and then placed his two wrists on his temples. "Wanasa pi." {"We hunt for buffalo?"}

Again, Rocky moved his head in acknowledgement and signed that the buffalo was gone.

The Indian pointed at Rocky "Kute tatanka." {"You shoot buffalo."}

"No we don't shoot the buffalo, others do, bad white people do that." {Sica wasicu econ he.}

Nodding the Indian answered, using sign and words, "Yuha niye maza caku." {"Have you seen train tracks?"}

Scratching his head, trying to figure just what he had signed, he thought for an instant then using the symbol for railroad tracks and the Sioux nodded yes and he took his hands showing that he would break it in half.

During the confrontation, Ty had moved to his left until he had a clean line at the Indian, just in case. He wanted to protect Rocky and as Ty moved so did Tuff, standing at Ty's side and watched what was happening.

The Indian looked at Ty and then back at Rocky. "Kutkel niye iyaya? Niye wanasa pi?" {"Where are you going? Are you hunters or trappers?"}

Pointing to the north, Rocky had to think how he would answer the question, he knew the Black Hills were sacred to the Sioux and he didn't want to anger the Indian. Remembering that John had said that there was another river north of here, he said with his hands the sign for river and shook his head no, they were not hunters or trappers.

Seeming to understand, the Indian dismounted and squatted on his haunches and with that, Rocky did the same. With his finger, the man drew a line on the ground with another line going southwest and connecting with the first. "Pakesha wakpa."

Understanding Rocky said, "The Platte River?"

The Sioux knew the name, "Ha." {Yes.}

He then drew a line north of the others, wiggling and well past the actual fork of the Platte. Looking at Rocky he said, "Niobrara wakpa." {"Niobrara River".}

Then with his finger, he made a mark a short way north of the river, "Wowapi." {"Post."}

Rocky shrugged his shoulders signaled that he did not understand.

"Chartran" {"Chadron."} and he drew a square with just one opening into it. Another wiggle line drawn west to east, which Rocky took as another river? The Indian did not seem to have a name for the river so it must not have been anything major.

"Trading Post"

Nodding in agreement, he pointed first to Rocky and then to the square on the ground. "Niye iyaya he?" {"You go that one."}

Rocky thought that it was as good as any and shook his head yes.

Placing his hand, flat on the ground, between the two rivers he said, "Ogala Sioux." {"Ogallala Sioux."}

Pointing north of the second river he said, "Lakhota Sioux." {"Lakota Sioux."} He looked up at Rocky to see if he understood.

Rocky said, "Ha." {"Yes."}

The Indian grunted and smiled, he then pointed to himself and said, Mitawa caje Gleska Sukawaka." {"My name Spotted Horse."}

Rocky had no idea what the Indian said and shrugged his shoulders again, he thought that sukawaka was Sioux for horse but was not sure.

Spotted Horse pointed at Satan and then himself, then he repeated his name, "Mitawa caje Gleska Sukawaka." {My name Spotted Horse.}

"Oh, is that your name?"

Shaking his head in agreement, he then pointed at Rocky.

"My name is Rocky," Not wanting to complicate the situation with his whole name.

The Sioux was confused and showed it by using Rocky's jester with his shoulders.

Rocky looked around and found a small stone, then repeated his name. Smiling he said, "Iya," {Rock.} and pointed to the stone.

Rocky answered, "Iya." {Rock.} And pointed back at himself."

Looking over at Ty, "Tuwe Wicasa tuwe mani kici sumanitu taka?" {"Who man who walks with wolf?"}

This Rocky understood and he answered by doubling up his fist and flexing his muscle saying, "He is very powerful, wasake." {"Strong."}

Grunting, he shook his head yes. He looked at the wagons where John and James stood both holding their Henry rifles, "Haska kute mazawakan?" {"Long shoot rifle."}

Nodding Rocky said, "Ha."

The old Hawkins that now leaned across the Indians knee had seen better days. Brass nails studded the stock and an eagle feather tied just in front of the trigger guard. Up against a Henry it was not much firepower, let alone against four of them.

Holding up his rifle, he offered it to Rocky and held his other hand out to receive the Henry.

Rocky shook his head no. The Sioux pointed to his horse and rifle, again reaching out his hand for the Henry.

Again, Rocky said no, the Indian wanted to trade, in his world, when you made a friend it was the thing to do. Thinking of something that would save face for his new friend he offered to trade him coffee, {"wakalyapi"}, for his rifle.

Shaking his head, no he asked for some wakalyapi. {"Coffee."} Without hesitation, he then asked for some cahapi {"Sugar."} He removed is his necklace of bear teeth and arrowheads strung, on a leather thong and handed them to Rocky.

Rocky shook his head that it was a deal. Turning to James, he told him to bring a sack of coffee and a bag of sugar.

Receiving his prize the Indian told James that his name was Gleska Sukawaka {Spotted Horse.} and pointed to James.

Rocky told James that he had said that his name was Spotted Horse and wanted to know James's name.

"My name is James," As he pointed to himself.

"James?"

Rocky said, "Just say Ha that is yes in his words."

"Ha."

The Indian grunted, shook his head yes and then pointed to John who was still standing at the wagon and keeping an eye on their back trail just in case, there was a sneak attack from the rear.

Rocky answered his name is John Edwards and this time giving the whole name so as not to confuse John with James.

"John Edwards, I will go now he said in sign and added iyaya el wowahwa, Iya." {"Go in peace, Rock."} Looking at Ty and Tuff one more time, he raised his hand to them and with the ease of a dancer; he mounted his pony and rode back to his friends.

"What did he say James asked?"

"I think that he said to go in peace and my new Indian name is Iya it means a rock or a stone."

"Hell and he just called me James, don't seem fair."

Back at the wagons, John was as nervous as hell and told Rocky so. "Didn't know what in the hell was goin' on out there, caused me to worry some. Couldn't hear a damn thing you was a sayin', but it looked friendly enough."

"It was, his name was Spotted Horse and they was out lookin' for buffalo, ain't found any. Wanted to know if we were hunters and I told him no, mad as hell with the damn hunters, he was. Wanted to know where we was headed and he told me there was a tradin' post up north, he called it Chadron or something like that. He also said the name of the river up there was the Niobrara. Didn't want to say we was headed for the Paha Sapa's, they think they are sacred so I told him we was headed for a place on the river west of where he said the fort was. Nice enough to me I think we made a new friend, he wanted to trade for my rifle, but settled for the coffee and sugar. I got this medicine necklace I don't think we have to worry about that bunch, but won't hurt to keep our eyes open. I told James my new Injun name was Iya, you should hear what he called Ty, he called him Wicasa Tuwe Mani kici Sumanitu Taka, and you want to know what it means."

Ty said, "Hell yes."

"It's Man Who Walks with Wolf, I guess he thought that Tuff was a wolf, pretty damn impressive comin' from a Sioux injun."

"I'm more interested in the necklace what kind of teeth are those?" James said.

"Bear."

"The arrow heads just for looks or do they mean something?"

"Most likely used to kill something special might have been the bear that once had these teeth."

"Lets build a fire; eat a biscuit and a cup of coffee give 'em time to move away." John suggested.

"Sounds alright to me." Ty said.

The next several days were uneventful the ground had turned sandy and off to the west small hills of sand and tuffs of grass could be seen. That evening they were told by Rocky that there was a river just up ahead. "I found us a crossin', it's not very wide but is deeper than the Platte was, thinkin' it's the Niobrara."

"Were gettin' close damn it, I would like to just keep on goin', been forever since I see'd my valley."

"We'll cross it in the mornin' but we had better find a new place for your chickens, might just drown 'em if we leave 'em where they are."

"While we cross we can put 'em in James's wagon, cage and all."

"Why my wagon?"

"Won't have to carry the cage as far that a way." John said with a smile on his face. Then he added, "We got one more water crossing, it ain't much of one then we are only a step or two from my place."

"That must have been the stream the Spotted Horse said the fort was built on."

"Most likely is, where I crossed it on the way down you could just about jump across it."

"How far you think your place is from here?" Ty asked.

"With good goin' like we've had, less than a week. When we get there, we'll roast a calf over an open fire and I'll break out some of the booze that I bought at the Forks, hell we'll eat and drink till mornin', you ever eat Texas roast beef.

They all shook their heads no.

"Ain't nothin' like it, the out side is cook done and the inside is bloody red, any way you like it, we'll have it."

The crossing made and James complained about the stinkin' damn chickens' way after they were back under his wagon. He told John that it was a hell of away to treat a man, after he had given up a damn good job just to help a fella out.

"Hell, I'll make it up to you before it's over, when we get to my ranch, we can be friends again, I'm a hell of a ramrod but a damn good friend."

"I'll think on it, you old reprobate, by the time we get to your damn old ranch, none of us will want you for a friend, you keepin' the whiskey locked up like you have."

"Well son just to keep your friendship I'll break out a bottle right now and you can get as drunk as you want but remember we leave at sunup."

They all got a good chuckle out the exchange between the two, James went on, "I guess it can wait, don't want you to go diggin' in your damn wagons and all."

For the third time in three days, Rocky had ridden back to report seeing pony tracks. In each case, they were not fresh and made maybe two days earlier. There was never more that six or seven ponies and Rocky was sure that they were hunting parties.

Early one morning Rocky came riding back and informed them that a string of trees were up ahead. "Be a hell of a nice place to hide for an ambush, can't see shit in them trees. A whole tribe could be in there and we would not know till it was too late."

"What you think we should do?" asked Ty.

"I thinkin' we should check it out before we get the wagons too close. If you agree, I'll take Ty with me you and James can stay with the wagons, if you see anything back here, like maybe an attack from behind us, fire a couple of shots we'll come back as fast as we can."

John said, "If you don't want to go Ty, I'll go."

"I'll go it will give me a chance to ride Duke again, it's been a while."

They rode separated by about twenty paces; their eyes were constantly moving searching for any sign that might give an ambush away. Once they got into the trees, they each went a different direction, Ty to the right and Rocky went left. After about a mile, they turned and retraced their trail they met just about, where they had separated.

"Seen some old tracks and that's about it." Rocky said

"There is an old camp back here a ways, fire ring and some old horse droppin's, everything looks quiet." with that said, Ty added, "Better to be safe than sorry, right?" and broke out in a little chuckle.

Glaring at Ty, in a funny way, he said, "Kate would be proud that you ain't forgot and I'll bet she ain't either."

They camped in the trees, near the narrow river, the water was good and the barrels filled first, then the stock was watered. Securing the camp, they settled in for the night and the light rain started just after dark. A cool breeze rustled the leaves and the swaying branches made just enough noise to leave a comfortable quiet over the camp.

Ty had the first watch and as he moved about the camp, he would stop at each horse, rub their necks and pat them gently on their shoulders. Grass was plentiful, the horses quietly grazed, and the only thing heard was their chewing with an occasional shiver to shake the excess water off their backs.

Tuff never left Ty's side, when Ty stopped so did Tuff, suddenly Tuff's low growl caused Ty to stop in his tracks, standing as if he were a statue, he looked around slowly but mostly in the direction of Tuff's gaze. By this time, the horses all had their heads in the air and they too were looking out to the open ground, getting more nervous as they pulled on their picket ropes.

Kneeling beside Tuff he asked very quietly, "What do you see out there old dog, I can't see a damn thing, the damn clouds are blockin' out the moon and it is black as hell. You go wake Rocky I don't want to leave the horses so the job is up to you, go get Rocky fella, I'll be alright, go get Rocky."

Tuff turned his head and looked at Ty and Ty took the dog's front shoulders a pointed them back to the camp, gently slapping him on his rump, "Go get Rocky."

Tuff silently moved away from Ty and when Ty heard a noise off to his right, it scared the hell out of him, turning he saw Rocky with Tuff heading his way.

Walking up to Ty, "What's goin' on?"

"Don't rightly know old Tuff and the horses are gettin' a little nervous."

"I woke up John and James told 'em to stay with the wagons."

"What do you think is out there?" Ty asked

"No idea could be anything but I'm thinkin' that if it's Injuns, they're after the horses they don't normally like to fight at night."

Tuff suddenly barked and started to run after something, grabbing at the dog but missing, under his breath Ty said, "Damn it dog what's got into you?"

They stood there, listening to the barking dog until the sound was faintly audible.

Rocky said, "Thinkin' now it was a big cat, a wolf or a bear would have stayed and fought, cats as big as they are, they don't like dogs."

Rocky and Ty went among the horses settling them down and as they completed the job, John silently walked up, "What in the hell is goin' on, we heard Tuff a barkin', could tell he was a chasin' something."

"Rocky thinks that it may have been a big cat, Tuff sure as hell chased him off."

They decided that they had better stay with the horses just in case something else was out there. Tuff came back and laid down just in front of Duke, his panting was rapid and with his tongue hanging out, the panting drowned out the rain. Apparently, he was convinced that there was no other danger.

The rain stopped and the wind subsided, the rays of the moon again lit up the black night. Shortly after midnight, Rocky took over the watch and sent Ty back to camp. "Think what ever it was, is gone you might as well get some rest and I'll wake James when I get tired."

Ty took a step toward the wagons and looked back at Tuff, he laid where he was and was in no hurry to leave Duke's side.

Before dawn, the camp was awake breakfast hastily put together and the wagons were ready to start their daily grind.

"Better wait for full light before we cross, ain't wide but I want to see where we're agoin'." John said.

"I want to go out and look for tracks, be sure just what Tuff scared off; I'm still bettin' it's a puma cat any one want to place a small wager that I'm wrong?"

"Hell no Rocky I wouldn't bet you if I knew for sure what it was. You would most likely make a damn track just to be right." Ty said.

Rocky and Ty hadn't gone far when Ty stooped over, "Ain't never seen a cat's paw this big in my life."

"I was right; it was a damn old puma cat, just the way old Tuff chased the damn thing off, I figured it had to be one. They're a sneaky breed of cat then as I think on it, all cats are. Still I don't want to come up on one unexpected like, they do have a way about 'em that can scare the shit right out of a brave man."

The next few days they were in and out of small stands of pine trees. The country got rougher and the flat ground disappeared behind them. It was further between sources of water now, an occasional creek or small reservoir of trapped water satisfied the stock.

The stead plodding of the pulling horses brought then to the top of a long climb, pulling in on the reins Ty said, "Better let 'em blow that was a hell of a rise."

"Ty see those hills of in the distance, those are what we have been lookin' for these pass two weeks. my place should be just inside of them hills."

James had walked up along side of Ty's wagon and had heard what John had said. "Hell we are just a day or two away from the first of 'em."

"They sure as hell look black from here. When I heard, you say the Injuns call 'em the black hills, I didn't figure that they really looked black." Ty said.

"With any luck we will find my place and crew before night fall tomorrow. Rocky came riding back, "Must be your mountains over yonder?"

"Damn right they are."

"See now why old Fitz called 'em his little mountains they ain't very big."

"Biggest I ever seen." Ty said.

"Just wait son till we get a little further west and you'll see mountains."

As they rode northwest, the blackness of the hills changed to dark green and individual trees were visible. The terrain steadily got rougher and the horses worked harder. John would stand up in the wagon box, trying to find landmarks that would tell him just where we were. Rocky would look back from time to time and John would signal with his hands as what direction Rocky should ride.

Midday John got real excited, "There it is, the bend in the river that I have been lookin' for. The crossin' is just west, right over there. We cross it once and then we have to cross it again to get into my valley." He pointed to his left, "We'll be across the river in no time at all, damn it feels good just hope the boys are alright."

Rocky had seen John's hand signs and had veered to his left, riding out of a long draw, seeing the river up close for the first time. He suddenly pulled Satan to a stop; holding up his arm to stop the wagons, up ahead stood a rider less pony grazing on the lush grass. Rocky studied the surrounding area, seeing nothing out of the ordinary neither could he see a rider.

Ty came up on Duke, he started to ask what the problem was and then he too saw the pony. "What do make of it?"

"Don't know, thinkin' it might be an Injun restin' or sleepin' in the trees, lets spread out and go take a look."

Coming in from two directions Rocky and Ty neared the lone pony. As they drew closer, the pony spooked and moved away. Speaking soft words, in Sioux Rocky approached the skittish pony.

Ty stayed mounted his eyes constantly moving checking the trees and the area around them. Rocky dismounted and approached the pony taking a hold of the chinstrap that hung to the ground. Rocky patted the pony's neck and the first thing that he saw was that the left side of it's back was covered with blood, some was dry but fresh blood was also visible. "His rider must have been hurt bad there is a hell of a lot of blood."

"The rider must have fell off a ways back. Must of been hurt bad or maybe he just died and fell off. Think I'll backtrack it a ways, see if I can find him and see if he is still alive."

"Want me to go with you?"

"Won't hurt, just stay your distance I'll try to follow the tracks, here you bring the pony."

They hadn't gone far when, lying next a bush was a lone Indian, he laid still and not knowing if he was dead or alive, Rocky approached him carefully. Kneeling down next to the man, "He's alive but been shot up pretty bad, looks like he was hit in the chest and left arm. He's got a hole that goes clean through from front to back. His arm ain't bad but he's got a hole in it too, come here and give me a hand."

"He's lost a lot of blood it don't look good. Give me that water on my saddle horn I'll wet his lips."

Picking up his head, he placed it on his knee; Rocky poured a little water across his mouth and the Indian blinked his eyes, tensed and tried to rise up, fear was in his eyes as he focused on Rocky.

"Hold on partner, I ain't goin' to hurt you just lay still."

Placing the canteen to his lips, the Indian swallowed a small amount of water. With this done, his eyes relaxed and he settled back against Rocky's knee.

His eyes watched Rocky's every move, when Rocky turned his head to say to Ty, "Go get the wagons and see if John has got an old shirt or something to patch this man up with. The Indians eyes went to Ty and then right back to Rocky.

"Don't look very old."

"They grow up fast out here, maybe not as old as you, but every inch a man."

While Ty was gone, Rocky pointed to the Indian and then said, "Niye oyazoye sica." {"You hurt bad."}

His eyes went first to the right and then to the left but said nothing.

"Tuwe kute niye" {"Who shot you?"}

Again no response.

Pointing at the man, "Niye Lakhota?" {"You Lakota?"}

This time he shook his head yes.

"Wasicu kute niye?" {"White man shoot you?"}

His eyes told Rocky that it was a white man that shot him.

Taking the water and giving him another drink but his time Rocky had to pull it away, "Not too much just yet, old fella."

The wagons pulled up and the men got down, Ty held a piece of cloth in his hand and when seeing this Rocky began to clean, the chest wound with water and his hand. When he got to the wound itself, he tore a bit of cloth and soaked it with water. The Indian started to resist and Rocky just went on about his business.

John and James wanted to know how this happened and Rocky told them that a white man did it.

"Why?"

"Don't know just yet, might take some time to find out."

Ty helped hold the man up while Rocky placed the clean cloth around his chest and arm, then he drank a little more water.

"Now that you got him fixed up, what we goin' to do with him, take him with us or what?"

"We can't leave him here by himself, if the fever don't kill him, some animal will."

John said, "We can put him in the back of my wagon and haul him to my place, wait and see if he makes it."

"Think we got time to boil up a pot of coffee, might help if we get something hot in him, soup would be better but coffee might do it. Most Injuns like their coffee with a lot of sugar, shouldn't hurt him none."

"Got time for that, people have helped me at times; one or two have saved my life least we can do for this poor fella."

Ty said, "If you think he needs soup, I can most likely shot one of those prairie chickens over there, won't take long to clean and boil 'em up."

"John what do you do you think, coffee or soup?"

"Take a little longer for soup but let's do it."

Walking off a short distance, with Tuff at his heals, Ty shot once and then again. Tuff ran over, sniffed at one of the chickens, and carried it back to Ty. Over his shoulder, he heard Rocky say, "First time I ever see him miss, damn boy is loosin' his touch."

About then Tuff ran off again and brought back a second bird, Ty turned and said, "Did you say something about my shootin' old man?"

"Should of knowed better, sorry."

"I just thought that we might like some of soup or maybe a piece of chicken."

James walked over, "You shot 'em so I guess I can clean 'em." As he picked up the first one and then the other he added, "Hell you shot the heads off both of 'em. I told you that your brother James was the best shot that I had ever seen, guess it runs in the family."

All the while this was going on the young Indian would come in and out of conscience's. When he was awake, his eyes never stopped, the fear had returned, it was helpless to do anything about it.

Rocky got a half cup of the hot soup down but the Indian could no longer stay awake. They lifted him into the wagon and placing him on a bed of buffalo robes, making him as comfortable as possible.

The river was wide but for the most part the water was only ankle deep. The riverbed was full of sand but the bottom was solid. Both crossings made, they entered a green valley with high rock cliffs of multi-colored stone that rose nearly vertical, started at the south bank of the river, then continued to the southwest as far as Ty could see. Off to the right, cattle with extremely long horns were grazing. The horns curved slightly up and then outward to what looked like very sharp points.

Shortly John said to turn left and up the incline and as they topped out of the pull, a group of men was setting waiting for them.

"Howdy Boss, glad to see ya, looks like you got a bad arm," Said a long legged man setting on a black horse. Flanking him were nine others, all smiling from ear to ear. Rag tag bunches if you had ever seen one, shirts were tore and their trousers had holes all up and down their legs. Most had loose fitting leather leggings strapped to their waist and around their legs. Some had hand guns stuck in their waste bands and some had them in a leather pockets attached to their belts, all wore boots and on them they had, spurs strapped to theirs heels.

"Howdy Tom it's better now, how has things been?"

"Busy.

"Any problems?"

"Nothin' we couldn't handle."

"Looks like you're a little short handed, where's the rest of the boys?"

"Willie, him and his crowd decided that there was more to offer in the Montana gold fields, they left the same day you left. Damn near before you was out of sight, by the way I don't see Donny or Sonny?"

They thought the same as Willie I guess, they left me high and dry at the forks. Headed back to Texas but I found some new friends. I want you to meet Ty O'Malley, Rocky Buntrock and James Adams, got me out of a fix back at the Forks. Thanks to these gents, they gave me a hand and that ain't all but I'll tell you the whole story later. Would have had a hell of a time gettin' these things back here with out 'em. We got a hurt Injun in the wagon, shot up damn bad, we found him just south and east of here, you have any trouble with 'em?"

"No, ain't even seen one on this side of the river, a couple of times we see a small party come up to water their horses but never came across."

"Might as well get aquatinted, I hope these fellas will stay a day or two."

Every one said hello and a few shook hands, the introductions made and forgotten as quickly as water off a ducks back.

"Get anything done on the cabins?"

"Both are up, just waitin' for the saws and nails so Larry can finish the doors."

"Let's see 'em."

There were two buildings, both made out of rough logs and windowless with a wooden corral built next to the larger of the two. The smaller one sat by itself, under a large pine tree and again, the only opening that seen was the doorway.

"Lets get the wagons unloaded and put the young buck in my cabin he has a fever so be sure he is covered. want to keep him warm. We'll put the soft stuff in my cabin and the rest in the bunkhouse. Be damn careful, of my window, if it didn't break getin' here, I sure as hell don't want it broke unloadin' it." Laughing he said, "The whiskey goes in my cabin too."

"Dammit Boss, we ain't had a drink since, hell, I don't even remember, be nice to welcome you back in style, like havin' a party or something."

"Boys that comes tomorrow we'll all dress in our new outfits, that I brought back, and have us a party. I told the boys here that we would kill us a young calf, put it on a spit and drink a bottle or two, give you something to look forward too."

The wagons were unloaded and the young Indian moved to the cabin and made comfortable. He slept through the transfer only stirring when Rocky placed the edge of the robe under him. A couple of the men started to dig a pit and several men started to carry wood for the fire. One of the wagons topped the plateau and in it was a dead yearling calf, skinned and gutted. The lifeless body of the calf, placed on the spit and the roasting began.

John said, "Boys if you want to wash up in the river do it now, I'll go get the new duds for you, then you'll be ready for the party tomorrow."

CHAPTER 13

After a long night, Rocky stepped out of John's cabin, the sun was not yet above the high canyon wall and already it was damn warm. The smoke rising from the fire pit went straight up into the still air blinking his eyes against the bright sun light, he stretched, raising both arms over his head and uttering a small grunt. The sick man had made it through the night and as the light of day entered the cabin, the young man had looked at Rocky then he closed his eyes and went back to sleep.

Ty and John was standing at the end of the cabin heard the grunt and walking over to Rocky, Ty asked, "How's our new friend doin', still got a fever, when I seen him last evenin' he seemed to be restin' alright."

"Fever is still there, been forcin' water down him and had a hell of a time keepin' him covered up. He is sweatin' like a stuck pig, hope his fever breaks soon he looked up a minute ago and then seemed to run out of strength closed his eyes again and went back to sleep. I think he is a fighter and that should help some, only time is goin' to tell if he will make it."

"Worryin' about the young man might throw a crimp in the party for you Rocky. I think we will place a watch over him, change every hour or so. Don't think we should leave the lad alone, he needs someone to doctor him back to health." Laying his hand on Rocky's shoulder he went on, "You can't sit by his side all day and all night, you got to get some rest."

"Good idea John, Rocky why don't you go get some sleep I'll watch for a while." Ty said.

"Afraid that if he wakes up and sees a strange white man it will scare the hell out of him, he's seen me and you Ty, nobody else. Think it will be up to you and me, I'll rest up some and get back so as to not ruin the party for you."

"Ain't worried about no party, you know me better than that. We can do both I'll stay with him till you wake up and we'll go from there."

"You go in the cabin and get some sleep; we'll take care of the boy. I'll go get the whiskey now. the boys are chopping at the bit to get started"

"Might take a pull or two before I give up the ghost."

"Ifin' you want you can cut a piece off that steer over there it might stave off your hunger, it's been cookin' all night and its lookin' mighty tasty."

"Sounds good, think I will try it, I like my meat bloody but when you're as hungry as I am, a fella can eat it any way."

The crew was standing near the smoking pit each one had a knife in his hand with a piece of the hot meat stuck to the end of it. Nodding his head to the group, Rocky pulled his bowie knife; he sliced a good-sized chunk off the reddest part the calf. With it stuck on the tip of his knife he said, "Is it as good as it looks?"

Tom, the big ramrod answered, "Beats the hell out of all the damn deer meat we've been eatin' I can tell you that."

"All these cows out there and you eat deer meat?"

"Can't eat your stock, back in Texas we might eat a neighbors beef from time to time, but never your own. Up here, its different ain't got no neighbors, so we have to eat our own."

"I figured that's all you cowman would eat is beef but now I see what you mean."

Finished with his breakfast he returned to the cabin, Ty was sitting near the sick man, "He's awake, but ain't said nothin' and I think his fever has broke, he ain't sweatin' any more."

Rocky stepped over to the prone man seeing his eyes were open said, "Tokel misu?"

Ty said, "What did you say?"

"How's my brother?"

The injured man spoke for the first time. In a weak voice, "Tokala Luta, Lakhota." [Fox Red, Lakota.}

"Okahnige." {Don't understand.} Rocky shrugged his shoulders.

His raised his hand up from his side and with his shaking finger pointed to the red bead on Rocky's leather shirt.

"Red."

"Ha, Luta. {Yes, Red}

"Is it, Red Deer, Red Horse, Red Buffalo, Red Sky, Red Cloud, Red Fox, or?"

With the last name the young brave said, "Ha." {Yes.}

"Red Fox is your name?"

"Ha, Tuwe niye?" {Yes, who are you.}

"Iya."

Repeating the name, he then pointed to Ty.

"His name is Wicasa Tuwe Mani Kici Sumanitu Taka." {Man Who Walks with Wolf.}

Again repeating the name and with a slight nod closed his eyes, opening them nearly as soon as he had closed them, he tried to move. Rocky putting his hand on his side, "Rest, we want to help you, asnikiye." {Rest.}

Relaxing back against the robe he appeared to be in deep thought, then in English said, "I speak your tongue."

"Dammit why didn't you say that sooner, are you hungry?"

"My mouth needs water first."

With the canteen, he gave the man enough to wet his lips and then he followed that with just a small swallow.

"Ty will you go get the bloodiest piece of meat that's out there I just want him to suck on the meat for now, he can eat some latter."

While Ty was gone, Rocky gave him some more water, a little at first and then he let him drink several swallows.

The wounded man understood Rocky when he handed him the meat, he chewed and swallowed the juices, spiting out the chewed meat. With each piece given him, he seemed to get stronger.

"That's enough for now, there is plenty more out there just let this settle first."

Ty asked, "You know who shot you?"

"Many white men."

"Where were you when they shot you?"

"Looking for Tatanka, I think they too must be looking for Tatanka, they see us and bang, bang they shoot, my friends killed." A tear formed in his eye and dripped down his cheek, his eyes closed he went on, "And I was hurt and ran away."

"Hell son, nothin' wrong with savin' your own skin if your friends were already dead, not much a wounded man could do, just get the hell out of there and live to fight another day."

Looking up at Rocky he said, "Must return to my people and tell them what happened, the mothers will be worried."

"Who is your Chief?"

"Running Horse."

"Where is your people?"

Not wanting to say and give their location away, he shook his head no.

"Son we will get you back to Runnin' Horse, but we got to know where he is. We don't like the man that shoots your Tatanka, their spirits are bad."

Ty asked again, "Is your people close?"

His eyes darted back and forth between Ty and Rocky; it showed that he was confused and scared.

Rocky and Ty waited and after a short time the young brave said, "They are at the big turn of the river, where it turns to the sun."

"What river?"

"The Cheyenne."

'You say the Cheyenne?'

A confused look crossed his forehead and he shook his head yes, "Ha, the Cheyenne, are we close?"

"Yes were sittin' on the Cheyenne."

A smile formed on his lips and he tried to raise himself up.

"Steady their son you'll be up before you know it but first you need rest."

"I think the worse is over, we'll let him rest some and then decide what to do. I think the best place for him is to be with his own people, let his medicine man heal him."

"You know best, but what does a medicine man do."

"The ones that I have seen most generally carry a bag of things that will suck out any infection. Other things they use for healin' the wounds, stuff like herbs, grass's and weeds that only they know what they do. They use drums, rattles, sweat lodges, chants and more but in fairness I have seen 'em heal a hell of a lot of people with all kinds of ailments. They use tobacco, cedar chips, sage and sometimes feathers; they burn some and waved the others over the sick, can't say it don't work, cause it does."

"How soon do you think we can head that way?"

"Maybe tomorrow, don't want to wait more that a day or two."

The Sioux brave was lying with his eyes closed and seemed to be sleeping soundly. Rocky said, "I'm goin' to have me a pull on one of those bottles out there, then do the same that our friend is doin'. Don't think that you have to stay here, he'll be sleepin' for a while might as well join the party."

Lying in the shade, leaning against trees or the wagon wheels the cowboys were busy drinking and chewing on the tender roast beef. Ty joined them and John asked, "Everything alright?"

"He was awake for awhile, his fever broke and he is restin' damn good considerin'. Surprised me that he speaks English damn good and told us his Chief was Running Horse. His people are somewhere the on the river." he pointed north towards the Cheyenne. "Rocky wants to find 'em and take him back to his people."

"Rocky think he is ready to travel?"

"Not yet, but the way he sounded, soon."

"Well let's get back to eatin' and drinkin' Tom tells me that the calf crop is in good stead and all the stock is fat and sassy. The grass and water seems to be doin' wonders for 'em, I'll take you out and show you part of what I got here."

"Maybe Rocky can come along, depends on Red Fox."

"Get yourself some of that steer and I'll share my bottle with you."

"I'll get me some eatin's and save the bottle for later then I'll have a drink or two but too much of that shit and I fall a sleep."

As the cowboys ate and drank, mostly drank, the louder they got, a couple showed off their skills at dancing and rope tricks. Soon it got around to who was the best shot and four empty whiskey bottles were set up about thirty paces away from the cooking steer. A cowboy called Shorty challenged another that he called Claude to a shooting match; each man had a navy colt, Shorty had wagered a dollar that he would break more of the bottles than Claude would.

"There is not a chance in hell that you can out shoot me, you little pipsqueak, any of you boys that want to make your wages that John gave you grow, bet on me."

Several of the drunken men shouted their bets and the contest began.

With the first shot, Rocky came running out of the cabin, rifle in hand, "What's goin' on out here, Injuns?"

"Sorry Rocky," John said, "The boys are just havin' a little fun, didn't mean to wake you."

Waving his hand as if to say that's all right, he went into the cabin but within minutes, he was back, joining the crew at the fire pit.

"How's Red Fox doin'?"

"Sleepin', don't know how with all this shit goin' on."

"We're just havin' a little shootin' contest, want to place a wager?" Shorty asked.

"I'll pass."

Shorty took another shot and missed, Claude laughed and after careful aim, he shot and he too missed. After both guns were empty and none of the bottles was broken, both men went back to the bottle. Before long, Claude was sleeping and it brought a chuckle from the rest because he was sitting on a log and very gracefully tipped over, feet in the air, half loaded pistol in his hand and snoring.

Tom carefully removed the pistol and grabbed the open bottle of whiskey before Claude could spill it.

"Damn kid, can't hold his liquor worth a damn, a drink or two and he's out like a broken lantern, but I guess that leaves more for us." Shorty commented.

The cowboys all carried guns, most were not very good with them, but many thought they were better than they were. It was only natural that the same bottles, set further out and then rifle shooting matches broke the silence of the peaceful valley again.

"Boys you had better save that ammunition just in case, we won't be havin' a chance to replace it before this fall. I'm thinkin' that by then we might need it for our protection, you never know when some thievin' whites or maybe a mad Injuns or two might show up. By that time the injuns should be damn mad at the railroad and for the white's killin' of their buffalo." John warned.

The quiet restored, the cowboys had drank and ate their fill, they settled back and one by one, they fell to sleep.

Tom said, "Look at that, they are all sleepin' even the ones that brag about all the whiskey they can drink."

"Not sure who is sleepin' and who is passed out but they are a quiet bunch right now." John added.

Ty and Rocky would take turns checking on Red Fox when he was awake, they would feed him red meat and plenty of water. As soon as he finished eating he would drop back to sleep.

John and Tom had been talking about what needed done before the round up and things that they should wind up before the snows started. A barn or at least a shelter had to be put up for the milk cows and the chickens. "It would be nice if it was big enough for a few horses and to store some hay." Tom said.

John was more worried about his chickens right now, by using the new wire, a pen for the chickens would have be built tomorrow and nests would be needed for the eggs that the chickens would lay, John wanted a lean-to built to cover the nest.

Tom asked, "When you want to start the round up, you said it took you a little over two weeks to get back and it will take us longer to push the herd that far."

"I'm thinkin' that we got maybe forty five or sixty days, it will take us the better part of a week to gather up what we want to sell; mind you, I don't want all of the yearlin's to go. There is plenty of grass and water in this valley to run five or six times what we got now. Sell enough to buy supplies to get us through the winter and pay the men is all that I'm lookin' for this year. I told Sid, the storekeeper at the Forks, what I needed and about when we would get the herd there. I told him to look for two more wagons, we will have to take a couple of more teams with us and buy new harnesses."

Ty and Rocky listened to the two men talk and the thought of driving a herd south over the same ground that they had just crossed, did not excite them. Ty mentioned that to John and he just laughed.

Before John could answer, James said, "Think I will stay and help you with the herd Bob didn't say just when I had to be back and I'm always interested in doin' something different ain't ever been on a cattle drive."

Tom said, "We can sure as hell use every man we can get, with Sonny, Donnie, and the others gone, we'll be short handed as it is. We got to leave some of the boys here at the place so we ain't goin' to be long on help."

"I've been thinkin' that away too, another reason for not takin' a big herd this year." John said. "And Ty, you don't know what you are missin'; on a trail drive you get just enough to eat and sleep to keep you goin'. All the dust and cow shit you can breath, ridin' watch for half the night and then you get to sleep on the ground in the shit and mud. The only time you can wash up is when it rains, yes sir you don't know what you're missin'."

That brought a chuckle from the five men and Rocky asked. "How many head do you mean when say just enough?"

"Talkin' maybe seven, eight hundred head, some of the steers and the older stock that's gettin' past their usefulness."

"Out of all the damn cattle you got out there, how in the hell can you know what ones are worth keepin', what's to let you know the ones are past their prime?"

Tom spoke up, "A good cattleman knows all his stock, he knows 'em so damn well that he could name each and every one of 'em, ifin' there was enough names to go around."

"You're shitin' me?"

John said, "No, that's the truth of the mater, them cows are kinda like your kids you get to know 'em all. Hell, I think we still have time to show you part of my valley before it gets dark; you want to go for a ride, it might take me a little while gettin' into the saddle, my ankle still is a little weak."

"I'm sure that we can get you in the saddle, if you need help," Said Tom.

'That will be the day, when I need help gettin' on my damn horse; I'll quit ridin' and buy me a buggy, I appreciate your offer but no thanks."

Saddling up and kinda excited to be doing something more than just sitting around, Rocky said, "Dammit, I clean forgot about Red Fox, I can't leave him alone I'd best stay."

James asked Rocky, "You think that the kid would be scared of me, I don't mind stayin' and I'll have other chances to see the valley. "

Looking at Ty and getting nothing but a questionable look back Rocky said, "I'm thinkin' that he will sleep for the rest of the day. If you don't mind James, I would like to see some of this here valley."

Riding down off the plateau, onto the floor of the green valley, they rode among grazing cattle with horns larger than Ty had ever seen. "I see why you call these longhorns, ain't never seen any thing like 'em."

Some of the cows had calves at their sides and still others looked as if they could cave out at any minute. A short ride brought them to a herd of horses that were grazing and not bothered by the intrusion of the men.

"Those all yours?" Ty asked.

"Yep, everyone of 'em, durin' a round up or a drive a cowboy might go through six, seven horses a day and every damn cowboy has his favorite, some for ropin' and others for cuttin' or herdin'. Next to the men themselves, a rancher's horses is the most important thing he's got goin' for him."

Ty's head was constantly on the move, turning from one sight to another. The high walls of the canyon and the many little streams that were flowing down to meet the Cheyenne seemed endless. Dams made of sticks and mud was on every small waterway, and John told Ty that they were beaver dams. The Cheyenne slowly moved to the center of the valley and shortly a fast running stream, out of the northwest, flowed into the bigger river.

"That's the river of Singin' Death at least that is what the man told me, looks peaceful enough, don't it?"

"Sure as hell ain't very big but I think it has more water in it than there is in the Cheyenne, runnin' harder too. Looks like a man might be able to drink that water, sure as hell, don't want to take a drink out of the Cheyenne. I was goin' to ask, where do you get your drinkin' water; don't figure its river water?"

"Just south of my cabin is a spring, they're all over the valley, some places it just bubbles up out of the ground. The one at the cabin just runs right out of the side of the cliff, damn good water don't you agree, part of the reason we built there."

They rode further and the cattle were everywhere, a herd of buffalo was seen off in the distance but they were on the north side of the river, away from the grazing cattle.

Later on, another herd of horses, grazing in the distance and Ty asked, "More of yours?"

"Nope, wild ones when we get caught up with the place, we will see if we can break a few of 'em. Looks like the young ones have had good breedin', seen the head stallion and he is something to see. There he is now, back there in the trees a big gray brute if you've ever seen one. Some day I'd like to try ridin' that one, but I guess I'll just have to wait and see."

The valley seemed endless and Ty said, "How much further to the end of your valley, John?"

"From here I would say another day's ride, if you start from the cabins. You got to get started before sunrise on a summer day if you want to see the other end before dark and that is if you don't dilly-dally around and you're on a good horse. Figure that at the widest part it is maybe three, four miles across. We got a hell of a lot of room to raise cattle and those rock walls on both sides gives 'em a lot of protection. The Cheyenne and most of the dams froze up last winter but the singin' river and most of the springs flowed all the time, a cattle man can't ask for more."

The south wall was like the one at the cabin, multi-colored and looked as if it were made out of individual stones stacked one on top of the other. The north wall was gray but as they rode, bright twinkling spots would appear and then be gone. Trees lined both sides and part way up the walls of the valley. Pine, spruce and trees that looked like birch, with their white trunks, were growing in clusters or in big groves. The floor was not flat, rolling hills and smaller valleys were everywhere. Occasionally along the rock walls, side canyons would go back deeper into the wall and on the other side of the opening the wall would continue.

Tom said, "John that box canyon over there is where we got the bulls pined up, had to get 'em separated or we would be calvin' all winter, might have to anyway."

It was without a doubt the prettiest place Ty had ever seen, it was no wonder why John had fallen in love with the place. Ty said to himself, "If there is a nicer place on this earth, I wonder where it is."

The sun was starting to close out the day when they turned and headed for the cabins.

Tom said, "I'll put the horses in the corral you boys go and check on your friend"

Entering the small cabin, James stood up, "The boy woke up about the time you went for your ride, me and him have had a good talk. Ain't ever talked with a real Indian before, had a lot to ask him. Surprised the hell out of me that they think about the same things that we do, he's worried about his family and what they are doin' and he wanted to know if we had found his pony. Don't like the idea that the railroad is crossin' the country and all the buffalo bein' killed. Said that he had his eye on a certain female and he thinks she likes him too. He sure as hell changed my mind about Indians, got to thinkin' that maybe they ain't all bad, when you take him back to his people, I sure would like to go along."

Speaking to Red Fox and then to James, Rocky said, "Guess that can be arranged, don't know what we might run into the way it sounds Runnin' Horse looks out for his people, he will most likely let us ride on in before he does something foolish."

"I asked him and he said that he was ready to go, I don't think he can ride a horse, seems to damn weak."

"Think you're right, James we can put him on a travois and see if he can handle that."

"What is a travois?" James asked.

"Take two long saplin's and tie 'em to a horse let him drag it. We'll wrap a robe between 'em, it's like a movin' bed he just has to lay there and his horse does the rest. That's the way his people move their things from place to place, been doin' it forever."

"Can't hardly drag him through the river, can we?"

"Nope we will have to hang the sticks between two horses, till we get across."

"Red Fox, you think you can ride a travois tomorrow?"

"I want to ride into my village, not go in as an old woman would."

"How about you startin' out on the travois and if you feel stronger later then you can ride your pony."

"I am strong now, I'll ride."

"Suit yourself son, we'll leave at first light."

Outside Rocky told John that they were leaving at first light and if everything went alright, they would come back to the valley and stay a couple of days. "Could you have one of your boys cut us two of those jack pines over there and have 'em striped down to the wood."

Rocky explained the purpose of them to John and Ty said, "Thought you agreed to let him ride out of here, what do you need those jack pines for?"

"He can't no more set a horse let alone ride it and if I'm right I want to be ready to haul him home."

Before dawn, they were up and ready to leave helping Red Fox to his feet, he tried to make it to the doorway of the cabin, on very wobbly legs. Standing along side of him Rocky and Ty let him try on his own to mount his pony after three tries, he admitted the he was too weak and that he needed help.

Rocky sounding like a good father, "Let's do it my way for awhile at least till you feel stronger."

Nodding his head, they helped him to sit down on the log.

They tied the poles to Red Fox's pony and loaded Red Fox on the robe. Using Rocky's packhorse, they raised the poles and strapped them under the packs onto his front shoulders. "We'll go this way till we get to more even ground, don't want to break open his wounds."

The crossing made with no problem and Rocky thinking he knew the answer, ask, "Which way from here, up stream or down?"

Red Fox looked left at the green hills and pointed to the northeast, "Don't follow the river but go this way."

Several times, they stopped and tended to the injured man giving him water and some of the red meat, they had brought from the roasted calf. Each time Red Fox would tell them when he was ready to go. The hardest part was when he had to relieve himself, finding a tree or large stone that he could lean against was not easy at least not when they needed too; they would help him to it and wait until he was done. Each time the effort would take a little more strength out of the young brave as soon as he was placed back on the robe, he would fall into an exhausted sleep.

Mid afternoon, the same day Tuff sounded a warning growl and the hair on his neck stood straight up.

"Think we got company and before that was out of Ty's mouth, they were surrounded by Indians on horse back, they seemed to come out of nowhere. Sitting on a very large brown and white pinto was an equally big Indian, he was adorned with several eagle feathers tied to his long black hair and on his chest was a vest of colored porcupine quills. He carried a Winchester carbine across his thighs and he sat on a red blanket.

He held up his right hand and greeted the men with, "Hemaca Iyankapi

Sukawaka, Le makoce sahiyela." {I am Running Horse, this land Cheyenne.}

Rocky said, "I think he said his name was Runnin' Horse and that this land is his or something."

Raising his arm in a sign of peace, he said, "Hemaca Iya." {My name is Rocky.}

Pointing at Ty and then James he said, "Le Wicasa Tuwe Mani Kici Sumanitu Taka, le James. Unkis hi wowahwa." {This is Man Who Walks with Wolf, this is James, we come in peace}

"Ka Luta Tokala." {That is Red Foxes pony.} Pointing to the pony.

"Iye wayazo. Unkis yuha iye." Rocky said, {He is sick. We have him.} Pointing behind him.

While this was taking place Tuff, stood next to Duke, the hair on his neck was still standing up and his eyes had never stopped moving. It was obvious that he did not trust these new people but he would bid his time until something happened.

Running Horse dropped from his horse, watching the three men he walked to the travois. Showing no emotion, he touched the face of Red Fox and gently turned it toward him and after seeing that it was Red Fox, he motioned to one of his braves to come forward. The man went to the side of the Chief and looking down, his expression changed to smile, the only sign of recognition.

With a nod of his head, the Chief walked back to Rocky and with a sober face said, "Unkis waste." {That is good.}

He mounted the huge horse with an easy leap and with his arm motioned the band to fall in behind the travois.

The brave that the Chief had brought to the travois, rode next to the wounded man, Ty assumed that it was most likely Red Fox's father. He rode along and at times would look down at the young man, with pain showing on his face he then would look up, with a straight back, pride in his eyes and a tear on his cheek. He rode as only as a very proud man could do, showing the love in his heart.

Rocky, in a very low voice said to Ty and James, "Don't look around and don't act like you give a damn where we are going, I don't want 'em to think we are worried or scared, just ride lookin' straight ahead."

The journey continued without stopping for any reason, finally the brave that had been riding along side of the travois rode up to Running Horse. After a short conversation, the Chief called a halt and he rode with the brave back to the injured man, as Running Horse rode past Rocky he said, "Iye kikta." {He wake.}

Pulling Satan around, Rocky followed them back. Red Fox was awake, he looked up to Running Horse and the other brave, his eyes betrayed the excitement that he felt. After a quick smile that lasted a very short time and said, "Iyankapi Sukawaka is lila waste el tiyatani." {Running Horse, it is good to be home.} He then added, "Atewaye ki is waste el wayate niye." {Father it is good to see you.}

"Mitawa Ciks, nitawa ina kasna niye." {My Son, your mother misses you.}.

Red Fox moved his eyes from his father, looking over his right shoulder saw Rocky, Ty and James, all sitting their horses just ahead of his pony. "Lena oyate okiye miye, epi mitawa ciyewayas." {These people helped me they are my brothers.}

Running horse said, "Ha." {Yes.}

"Taywapi caje is Iya na James." {Their name is Rock and James.} Pointing to them, he added with what sounded like pride, "Le Wicasa Tuwe Mani Kici Sumanitu Taka." {This is Man Who Walks With Wolf.}

Again, the Chief said "Ha." {Yes.} He looked at Ty, nodding his head, before he looked down at Tuff. "Tanka, sumanitu miye sni wayate sni hani." {Big wolf. me not see before.}

Indicating with his hand, he told Rocky that this was his Chief, Running Horse, then that his father's name was Big Arrow. Each time he repeated what he had said in Sioux.

Rocky told Running Horse, in staggering Sioux that Red Fox said a white man shot him, he went on by telling him that he did not know where. They had found Red Fox a short way south of the Cheyenne. The Chief looked at Rocky and shrugged his shoulders and said, "Okahnige." {Don't understand.}

Red Fox repeated what Rocky had such a hard time saying then Running Horse nodded his head, "Niye kute Luta Tokala?" {You shoot Red Fox?}

Red Fox shook his head no and said in Sioux, "Others, they kill all my brother warriors, I was hurt and ran away."

Looking the Chief directly in the eye, he waited for the response that was slow in coming. Running Horse dismounted, placing his hand on the shoulder of Red Fox and said, "Niye econ waste. Hemaca iyokisice kici ukitawa teca ohiti ke. Niye patan, ukitawa oyate tawaci un iyuski niye lel. Niye tawaci iyotake oceti hahepi ki. " {You did good. I am sad for our young braves. You are safe, our people will be happy you are here. You will sit at the council fire tonight}

He told his friends what the Chief had said, first in Sioux and followed it with English,

"Chief Running Horse, my father, I don't want our people to see me come into our village riding like this. If I am to sit with the elders tonight, I should ride my pony like a brave warrior, just as I left days ago."

"Ha." The Chief said and shook his head in agreement.

Ty had smelled the faint smell of burning cottonwood and figured the village could not be far and he said to Red Fox, "How far are we from your village, can you ask your Chief?"

Running Horse pointed to the near hill and with a dipping motion indicated that it was just over the rise.

"Think you can ride if your Father hangs on to you?" Rocky asked.

"I can ride."

Rocky looked at Big Arrow and signaled with his hand that he should hold on to him.

Ty and Rocky started to lift Red Fox but a loud remark stopped them. The Chief said, "Inaji, unkis tawaci econ is." {Stop we will do it.}

The sound of his voice brought a growl from Tuff and Ty told the dog that is was all right but the dog did not relax and stayed ready as he always was.

Backing off they watched the Chief and Big Arrow carefully lift the young brave off the travois. A brave removed the travois and attached it to Rocky's packhorse while another held the chinstrap of Red Fox's pony. It took all of his strength to sit the pony but he eventually sat straight up and looked every inch a conquering hero triumphantly ready to enter his village. Following the Chief, Big Arrow and Red Fox stopped at the rise looking at the entire village lying below them. There were at least two hundred tipis with small fires in front of most. Men, women and children stopped what they were doing to watch as the party descended the rise. Off to the east, very near the river was a herd of horses, there must have numbered in the thousands. Barking dogs came running towards them.

Tuff's growl and his strut meant to be a warning to the on coming dogs and as they got nearer, Tuff took several steps out to meet them. Ty warned him to come back, but the words were useless. The pack of approaching dogs stopped, they too were ready to fight. The bravest, a large shaggy haired one, walking stiff legged, was about to challenge Tuff but like a lightning strike, Tuff charged the leader. and before he had taken a half dozen steps, the shaggy animal turned tail and was headed home. A few of his friends continued to stand their ground and when Tuff did not stop but continued toward them, they too put their tails between their legs, yelping as they followed their leader back to the camp. Tuff strutted back to Ty as if to say, "Nothing to worry about, I handled it."

Entering the village, people lined up in a solid line and shouted their welcome. Red Fox rode as if nothing was wrong, riding with a straight back and looking neither right nor left. The whole camp knew that riding beside the Chief was a special honor. In the center of the village Running Horse dismounted, lifting Red Fox off his pony and with no help, he carried him into the largest tipi in the village. When the Chief came out, he went to the side of an old man who was holding a long stick with feathers and bright colored ribbons tied to it and he talked very low to him. When they were through the old man went into the lodge and the Chief approached a group of women that were nervously rocking and singing in a very low voice. The group gathered around Running Horse and after a few words from Running Horse, the singing got louder and the women moved, away separating they went to their own place of mourning.

Running horse announced to the tribe that Red Fox had returned but had been hurt, he hesitated and he said, "Heci tawaci un oceti hahepi ki." {There will be a council fire tonight.}

He then told the gathering who Ty, Rocky and James were. When he mentioned Ty's name most shook their heads in acknowledgement. The wolf was a spiritual figure in their eyes and any man that could walk with one, as he was with Tuff, was indeed important. Ty's size added to the mystique and the presence of the dog standing next to Ty was even more impressive. Running Horse went on saying that this white man did not hurt Red Fox, they only found him and made medicine over him, these were good men. The tribe would honor them and they would join in the council.

The Chief said something that Rocky did not understand but several women left the crowd. Big Arrow motioned for their guests to dismount and a young brave took the reins of their horses. Ty looked behind and saw the brave following them with Big Arrow lead the way. He stopped at another tipi, a short distance from the Chiefs, two warriors each with their weapons stood guard at the lodge. One of them opened the leather flap that covered the entryway. The covering was made of cured skins and stitched together, paintings of buffalo, horses, and many symbols of religious meanings, in every color, decorated the outside.

The young brave leading the horses moved to the side of the tipi and tied them to a wooden post he then went about the work of removing the travois, he folded up the buffalo robe and placed it inside.

The circular like enclosure was about seven pace's wide and was slightly oblong from front to rear. The floor covered with buffalo robes and in the center was a small fire pit, a flickering of the flames showed it already was burning. The smoke slowly rose and exited out of a hole at the very top and the pleasant smell of sage and pine was in the air. The west side of the skinned structure was rolled up a short distance from the ground for ventilation.

Big Arrow motioned with his hand for them to stay, he left but the young braves remained at the entrance.

"We prisoners?" Ty asked.

"In a manner of speakin', I guess we are they let us keep our rifles so we ain't in a whole lot of trouble just yet. We can leave most anytime we want but we won't go alone, those braves out there will get all the help they need to keep an eye on us."

"The Chief didn't seem to be mad or upset with us, why the guard?" James said.

"I'm thinkin' that they want to sort out what has happened, at the council meetin' tonight we'll learn more. All they know right now is that some damn white man shot Red Fox and to most of them, out there, all white men are the same, kinda the same as what white people think of the injuns. It will be up to Runnin' Horse to decide if they will take it out on us or not."

Ty said, "You remember tellin' me about how fair Injun justice is, startin' to wonderin' about it now how will old Runnin' Horse make up his mind?"

"He'll listen to Red Fox's story, find out what Big Arrow has to say and the elders will speak, everyone will have their say. Most likely, there will be talk of war and it wouldn't surprise me if they don't talk about the railroad. Maybe we might get to state our piece, but that is unlikely, it's more to my thinkin', that the Chief will just ask us questions."

"You know Sioux well enough to understand what he might ask, don't want you to say something and find out later that you answered the wrong question, old people do that sometimes," Joked Ty.

"You know me better than that, if I don't know the words I'll ask Red Fox what he said."

The entrance to the tipi darkened and low mumbling outside, an older woman entered with two younger women behind her. One carried an iron pot and hung it on a metal hook that she pushed into the ground; the second had a birch bark platter with what looked to be fried bread. The older women said, "Iyankapi sukawaka wote." {Running Horse said to eat}

Using their knives, they dug into the thick soup, spearing pieces of meat and cautiously tasted it, Rocky was the exception he took a chunk of meat and ate it without hesitation. After tasting the meat, James commented that it was good and Ty agreed. With the fried bread, they sopped up the juices and in the process, they found that there were wild onions and turnips along with green leaves of some kind, Rocky called it sheepshank or something like that nonetheless it tasted good.

The pot licked clean, James said, "Fed us better than I thought they would, that was mighty tasty. Don't know what it was, couldn't figure out what kind of meat they had in it, do you know?" Looking at Ty and Rocky.

"Reckon they like us better than I thought, it was puppy."

With that, both Ty and James gagged and James stood up, "I think I am goin' to be sick."

Ty followed with, "Damn it Rocky, you knew it from the first taste, didn't you and you just kept your damn trap shut till we got done. I'd puke too if it weren't for it makin' you happy. First at the Forks and now here, don't know if I will ever trust you again, you son of a bitch. How could you let us eat puppy and set there and not say a word?"

"Hell boys I was just so damn happy to see that it was puppy, I was so excited that I couldn't talk."

"Why it make you so happy, you bastard?" James asked.

"They only feed you puppy if they like you, it's a delicacy to 'em. Only have it at special occasions and we must be special, don't you think?"

"You might of warned us."

"James, if I had told you would you have eaten it?"

"Most likely not."

"You would have insulted these people the one thing that an injun expects is that their guest appreciates what they do for 'em. Feedin' you puppy is their way of sayin' thanks; eatin' is our way of sayin' thank you, next time I will let you piss 'em off."

'Didn't think of it that way, sorry but your still a son of a bitch you could have warned us, so we wouldn't make a fuss over eatin' a little puppy."

"Damn, you learn fast son, your stupid as hell but a fast learner." Rocky said with a smile.

The same woman returned with an armload of small twigs and a few larger pieces of wood. She placed the armful next to the opening and stepped over to the pot. With a smile so large that smoothed out her wrinkled checks, they heard her say, "Ha.waste." {Yes good.} And picking up the empty pot she left the tipi."

"Made her happy."

Shortly after the woman left, Big arrow entered, with a hand sign and a simple, "Hi." [Come.}, he led them out

Tuff followed but did not enter the lodge; he lay just outside the door, which brought nervous glares from the two guards that stood at the opening.

The council was held in a very large tipi with a fire burning in the center and around that, more than a dozen people sat crossed legged, all looking up when Big Arrow and their guests arrived. They were shown their place, Ty first then Rocky and James. Red Fox sat at the right of Running Horse, the old medicine man that appeared to be sleeping, sat at his left. Ty sat just to the right of Red Fox, not knowing he had just received a high honor.

Nothing was said until Running Horse stood up, holding a long stemmed pipe in his hand, it was decorated with carvings and a single eagle feather hung near the red bowl. Bending over he placed a small stick into the fire when it ignited, he held it to the bowl and within a very short time, a sweet smelling smoke filled the tipi. He pointed the pipe upward, downward then to the four winds, each time taking a puff and slowly exhaling. Each member of the council handed the pipe and each took a puff, including their three guests, slowly exhaling the smoke through their mouth and nose. With the pipe back in the Chief's hands, he once again went through the opening ritual, he sat down and in Sioux he said, "Red Fox has returned to us. All though brave, all of the others the white man killed. Red Fox tells me that these white men did not shoot him or kill his friends." He nodded at Ty and went on, "They found him and made medicine over him. As you can see he is hurt, but he will heal. For his meeting our enemy and for his safe return I will present him with an eagle feather."

"Tonight we welcome Red Foxes brothers, Man Who Walks with Wolf, Rock and James. These are brave warriors, they come to us in peace and the will go in peace, Running Horse has spoken. Man Who Walks with Wolf has received a good name and I have decided to give James an Indian name, it will be Flying Hawk for today I see a hawk flying over our village. Today Red Fox returned. It was a good omen. Rock's name will be Swift Bear for he wears the skin of a bear and it's medicine around his neck, his bravery must be like that of a charging she bear."

"Red Fox has something to say."

All of the words that Running Horse said, Red Fox repeated in English.

He began telling the council how they were attacked and how brave his friends were. "Our arrows could not reach as far as their bullets. We fight till all are dead." He lowered his head, "All but me I did not know what to do I was bleeding and very weak. My pony carried me away. Man Who Walks with Wolf found me and they gave me water. They gave me hot soup to drink. I did not know it but they took me to the valley of the old sprits. They kept me warm and fed me red meat. The sprits watched over me. These are my brothers, Man Who Walks with Wolf, Swift Bear and Flying Hawk."

Looking at Running Horse he added, "As brothers they should be welcome into our village forever."

"It is done."

The old Medicine man said, "I will prepare the sweat lodge for Red Fox. When he is healed I will sing a song to honor his friends and their courage."

The members all in unison said, "Ha." {Yes.}

During all of this Big Arrow sat straight and tall, very proud of the words that the Chief and the Medicine man had to say.

The Chief looked at Ty and said Niye slolye Wiyaka Ite? {"You know Feathers on Face?"}

Waiting for Red Fox to repeat the question, he looked at Rocky and back to Running Horse, "Feather on Face, Fitz, the mountain man?"

Rocky wrinkled his brow and thought, the kids is fast.

Ha, iye el mnikaoskkokpa wanagiyata?" {"Yes, He in valley of the sprits now?"}

"No, he is gone."

The chief would speak and Red Fox would translate it.

"He is a good friend of the Lakota. To old for war, he leave before the killing starts. He say he might go to big mountains and die. He did not want the war that the whites will start if the railroad does not stop. You see what they do to our country? It is our lands that they take and our buffalo they leave to rot."

This time Ty said, "Ha." {Yes.}

"They kill buffalo soon no more buffalo. We all die better to die fighting than of hunger."

"What they are doin' is not right maybe the buffalo will come back"

"No."

"You stay with us?"

"No, at sun up we will leave."

"Ha." {Yes}

The chief looked around at all of his assembled council and not getting any indication of them wanting to speak said, "Go, the council is finished."

Back at their lodge Rocky said, "Boy, these people like you, think it's the name old Spotted Horse gave you that makes 'em respect you. You got to sit in the place of honor and the Chief; he only talked with you, that's a good sign. Thinks you are the boss of this here outfit, he just don't know that you're just a kid, me and James here are the real leaders."

"Didn't know what to think when he asked me about old Feathers on Face, lucky I remembered old Fitz's name."

"You did pretty good with that one, I'll give you credit for it, yes sir you have had a good teacher."

Before sunup they were waken by the old serving woman, she had started the fire and had a pot on the iron stake. As soon as she had wakened Ty, she left.

Sitting up, seeing Rocky and James sitting as well he said, "How in the hell did she get in here without us hearin' her, hell Tuff didn't even growl."

"Told you they could steal a horse out from under you, didn't I, Tuff most likely knew she wasn't goin' to hurt us and just let her in."

Checking the pot James questioned, "Suppose it's puppy again?"

"Most likely not," Rocky said, taking a piece of the bread, he dipped into the broth and tasted it. "It's buffalo."

"The puppy was good but Dammit it I think I like buffalo better."

The sun had just risen when Big Arrow entered the lodge; he signaled them to follow, standing there, was the entire village. Running Horse held three horses, a beautiful gray gelding he presented to Ty, a black, with a white face and stockings, he gave to Rocky and James received a pinto, cream in color with white spots. He said, "Lena kici niye mi tawa ciyewayas. Epi yuha niye heta okokipe kici el niye cin hena. Niye wicoti. Nitawa unkis tawaci ataye ake. {"These are for you, my brothers. May they carry you safe from all danger, for as long as you have a need for them? You are welcome in my camp. We will meet again."} With that, he grasped Ty's wrist and gave it a shake, he repeated the jester with Rocky and James.

Another brave brought Duke, Satan and the other horses. Digging in their bedroll, all at the same time, they presented the Chief with all the coffee and sugar that they had.

With a nod of his head and after saying, "Ha' he turned and opened a path for them to ride out.

When they had reached the outer limits of the camp, they saw a large group of mounted riders. The riders followed them for a distance and with a very loud yell and a few shots fired into the air, the riders pulled to a stop. They held up their rifles and bows in a jester of good by…

"That made me a might nervous, seein' 'em sittin' there and it bothered me a little more when I see'd 'em followin' us, didn't know just what to think." James said.

"Their way of showin' respect, we apparently made us some new friends."

Ty added, "Can't never have too many of those."

"You think these horses are broke?"

"Doubt they ever had a saddle on 'em but broke to bareback ridin', I'm thinkin'."

'Damn pretty horses, to be givin' away, you would think that they would be the pride of any string a man would ever own. You think they belonged to Running Horse?"

"I'm thinkin' maybe one was Big Arrow's and the others Running Horse." Rocky said.

"Strange how they would just up and give us each a mighty fine horse, all they got was a pound or two of coffee, don't seem right." James said.

"Been tellin' Ty here that is the way an injun thinks, nothin' is too good for his friends. Would give his shirt right off his back ifin' he had nothin' else, we made some good friends let's not forget 'em.

As they rode, Rocky seemed to be a long ways away, he might be riding next to Ty and James but in his mind he was somewhere else, James and Ty were busy talking about their visit to the Indian camp. Rocky had not spoken for sometime and he appeared to be in a deep thought, Ty had seen this before, most likely thinking of Evenin' Star.

The dark green of the pine trees made the distance hills look black. Ty made a comment as to why the Sioux camped out in the open when they could just as well set their camp up in the hills. "Think it would be cooler in the summer and warmer in the winter."

"Seems strange don't it?" James answered.

For the first time in a very long time Rocky spoke. "Cause of the buffalo, most everything that the Sioux does hinges around the buffalo, one way or another. Like Runnin' Horse said, the Paha Sapa's are scared, when they need to make medicine, they go into the hills. North of here, maybe four, five days ride is a mountain that looks like a sleeping bear, their name for it is Mato Paha, means Bear Hill or Mountain, that's where they go when they need big medicine. There's another place not far from here they call Kata Wiwila Mni. It's a hot water spring, Red Fox was tellin' me about it. he said it makes the old feel young; it's a place for healin'. Thinking maybe that's where I should be, wouldn't hurt to feel a little younger, now would it?"

"Kinda got a feelin' that old Runnin' Horse was bein' nice and tellin' us stay away from those hills." Ty said.

"He was but you know me I don't always listen."

"How far is it to that hot spring?" James asked.

"Red Fox says there is a trail that starts a little north of the river, it will lead you a little northwest into the hills, from the crossin', he said it was only a day's ride. We're not quite a day's ride from the crossin', so I figure it to be about two days ride from here."

'Think you can find the trail" Ty asked.

"Won't know till we try."

"Hell I'm game for it, be something to talk about a few years from now." James said.

That night they camped in the Paha Sapas, in the shelter of an over hanging rock formation. They built a small fire and roasted a pair of prairie chickens that Ty had shot. Waiting for the meat to get done, James started to talk about his family. He admitted that he was older than most people thought, he was married to a hard working woman and had two grown sons and a daughter named Hattie. When the war ended and he returned to Iowa, he found that his land had been taken for taxes.

The boys were working in a coalmine near Kirksville and his wife Elizabeth did laundry and some mending of worn out clothes. He wanted to rebuild their lives and the best place for that was on a farm besides, he wanted the boys out of the mines to many young men had died of lung ailments working in those dark, damp mines.

After being separated for four years, due to the war, he didn't relish the thought of leaving again but the deal the railroad offered was just too good to pass up.

Rocky was back into his thoughts and he barely heard what was being said. "Rocky, you still with us, you seem to be damn far away, thinkin' about Evenin' Star?"

""What, you talkin' to me, Ty?

"Ya, but it was nothin'."

The meat eaten as it cooked, cooking from the outside in, they would cut off a leg, a wing or a piece of the breast and followed it with water. "Should have kept us a little of the coffee we gave the Chief it would taste good right now." Ty said.

"Was thinkin' about breakin' out a bottle but think I will save it for tomorrow night have us a party, old John is too damn stingy with his whiskey, best drink while we is away."

Following a trail, which ran near a rapid stream, they came up to several pools of steaming water. Huge semi flat boulder that over the decades, were covered with sulfur, which was hardened by the sun and smoothed by the wind. Testing the water first and finding it very comforting and extremely warm. Soaking in the water and lying on the flat rocks, to dry, they spent most of the day. Eating jerked venison but this time, they chased it with the burning brown stuff that Rocky called whiskey.

Ty asked, "Wonder if this here stream is the same one that runs into the Cheyenne back in the valley its got to go somewhere, didn't see it out on the flat."

"Thinkin' it is." Rocky said.

A half a bottle later Rocky came to life. "Remember our talk back at the Landin'." He asked Ty.

"Most of it, we talked about a hell of a lot of stuff."

"You were tryin' to talk me into takin' you west and I said something about me bein' the boss, remember?"

"Ya."

"Said I would teach you what you needed to know about stayin' alive out here, well I think I have done that, it weren't hard. You learned damn fast, even taught me a thing or two. Stead of me bein' the boss, I figured we shared that job; we got out here in one piece. I don't think I had anything to do with teachin' you what is important in this world, I feel you knew that. Been to a real Injun Camp and they figure that your something special and I think you are too."

Ty tried to interrupt him but Rocky held up his hand and went on, "You can take care of yourself, don't know of a time you ain't knowed what to do, ain't see'd you scared of nothin'.'

"What's this leadin' too, I know there has been something on your mind the last day or too, you goin' to tell us what it is."

"I'm gettin' to that, I'm goin' to pull out of here got to see if Evenin' Star is alright, Ty, I'm goin' alone, think it is better that way. Been figurin' on how I'm goin' to pull this off and one man might just be able to sneak up to the Blackfeet camp without bein' caught, two of us is only goin' to get in one another's way."

"Thought we were partners, I signed on knowin' that it might not be easy to get Evenin' Star."

"We are partners, damn good partners, couldn't of ask for a better one. This is something I figure I got to do myself, I've got things worked out in my head how I'm goin' about it. There are things that I don't know, is she alive and if she is, she's most likely married by now and maybe has some youngin's. Hell, she might just love her man, if she's got one. The biggest question is will she want to leave with me, no way of knowin' till I get there."

"While you figurin' all that out I could watch your back, two guns are better than one, if it comes to that. Hell we come this far, don't see any reason to change now."

"Knowed you would feel that a way but I've made up my mind, this time one is better than two. If I can get her to leave, we'll be on the run for, hell, I don't know how long, I know there will be a hell of a chase that I plan to win. Told you once the damn Blackfeet don't take kindly to whites and their women, I'll leave come mornin'."

"That's all there is to it, your mind is made up, what about trail supplies you got it all in your pack?"

"All but my Hawkins, want you to keep it for me."

Through all of this, James never said a word. He could feel the disappointment in Ty's voice; it wasn't easy to loose a friend. He hated to think how many he lost in the damn war. He thought of Ty's brother James and he figured he had lost him too, thank God; he had made it home safely.

The bottle was empty before the fire died out and Ty drank his share, the whiskey helped him forget about the morning. As he slept his thoughts centered around the day, he had left home, only this time in his dream he had turned around and went back.

James had the fire burning when Ty woke up; Rocky had left some time in the night.

Ty asked James, "Was he gone when you got up?"

"Yep, he must have snuck out of here real quiet like, left us some bacon and a biscuit or two."

"That son of a bitch, he must have been afraid to say goodbye like a man."

Nothing more was said and the ride back to the ranch seemed longer but it gave Ty a chance to think back on his friendship with Rocky.

They had been a good pair; Rocky had said they thought alike, dammit, he was right except for this time. Still can't figure why he had to pull out alone, the son of a bitch just might fall a sleep some night and not have me there to cover for him.

A sad smile crossed Ty's lips as he remembered that night they had the run in with the raw hiders, then the whole journey west came into Ty's mind, finding Mrs. Casey, the homesteaders, seeing the river for the first time and just happening into Mr. Perry. A lot of miles and plenty of time to get aquatinted with his friend, no sir, I couldn't of found a better partner.

Crossing the Cheyenne, he broke the silence; he repeated his thoughts to James. "Couldn't have found a better friend than old Rocky, hope he finds Evenin' Star." He started to choke up and after swallowing a few times he added, "I'd like to see the old fart come a ridin' up right now, James, bein' in the army like you were, I think you will understand what I'm feelin' right this minute. Him and me, we think alike, somehow I knew what was on his mind and he knew mine, it will be a long time till I can say that about another. Guess all I can do now is keep him in my mind and wish him all the luck in the damn world."

"Know what you're goin' though, felt the same way when I got separated from your brother, it's a hell of a feelin' not knowin' if they are all right, kinda makes a man empty inside."

"Hell I'll worry about the old coot till I see him again and I hope it's damn soon.

CHEYENNE CROSSING
The Valley of the Ancient Ones
Book 2

With
Wicasa Tuwe Mani kici Sumanitu Taka
"With Man Who Walks with Wolf"

CHAPTER 1

Ty was quiet on the trip back to the crossing after leaving the hot springs they rode to the over hanging rocks where they had camped earlier. Supper consisted of roasted rabbit, shot earlier in the day. It was not a time for talking; Ty was still feeling like he had let his partner down and in his mind he figured there had to be more to Rockys leaving than what he said. Did I do something that pissed him off or upset him to the point that he no longer wanted my company? Dammit, for the life of me I can't figure what I done, I should have ask him more questions when I had the chance now it's too damn late.

He seemed to have forgotten James completely and he acted as if he was alone, riding like a dead man, not caring or seeing anything around him. Since first meeting Rocky and deciding to pair up with him, Ty knew that getting Evening Star away from the Blackfeet was the reason they headed for the Montana territory in the first place. The man must love her very much to spend most of his waking hours thinking of her as he did. Apparently, at some point Rocky decided that it was better that he go on alone, he said, 'Hell, Don't even know if she will leave with me she might be married and have a passel of youngin's by now, might even love the buck she is with. I'm thinkin' it is better if I look the situation over and if need be make some fast decisions. If we both go it just might slow me down some, ifin' I have to move quick like, I don't want anyone but me to worry about.'

Ty remembered Westport Landing; they had become best friends and in addition they became real partners. They met while they worked on the new railroad from Saint Louis to the Landing. Ty, challenged by a man named Zack to fight over the job Ty had and Zack wanted. As the fight, progressed Zack pulled a knife on the defenseless Ty, Rocky, a complete stranger tossed an equally large knife to Ty to defend himself. The fight ended when Ty broke Zack's arm with the hilt of his knife. This was the start of their friendship

On the outside, they were like two peas in a pod and at one time Rocky had told Ty that they each had developed the knack of knowing what the other was thinking then he had added, "Makes for good partners."

Breaking off a leg of his rabbit and speaking to James for the first time in a long while said, "Damn it James I still can't figure him out, what in the hell did I do to make him go out on his own like he did?"

For the entire day James had respected Ty's silence; he rode with Ty quietly letting him have the time to wrestle with his disappointment about not going with Rocky. The ride had also given James time to think on what he would say when the time came. In his heart he knew what was going on in Ty's head, it had happened to him in the war many times but never quite, as bad as when Ty's Brother James and he separated. As Ty and Rocky had done with the raw-hiders on their journey, so had they protected each other from the Rebs during the Civil War. Not knowing what had happened to James was worst at night when you had time to think about your loss. Lying there, just before sleep overtook you pictures of the time you last saw your friend would creep into your mind. James's pictures of his missing friends were as dead men, lying twisted and cold.

"You didn't do anything, you just happen to be his best friend and he don't want you to get killed or hurt. He thinks a hell of a lot of you I know, because he told me so. Part of what he told you about his plan to gettin' Evenin' Star away from the Blackfeet was true; I'm thinkin' that he knew it weren't goin' to be easy."

"He was thinkin' hard on what might happen when he got to Blackfoot country, spent most of the time after leavin' Runnin' Horses camp thinkin' on it. He never heard what we said and he didn't talk at all for two days, think he was a worryin'. Don't think that he held much stock in gettin' her and makin' a clean get away, I'm only guessin', mind you, but I don't feel that he wanted to risk you too."

"It should have been my call, the old fart has got only one thing on his mind, I see'd that way back in Missouri. He'd get to tellin' a story and all sudden like he would get real quiet, most generally he would be lookin' off to the northwest. On one or two occasions, I'd see his eyes get a little damp. She's mighty important to him but for the most part, he just wants to know what kind of life she has. Ifin' she's happy stayin' there, he'll be back, ifin' she ain't then only the Lord knows what might happen."

"Ain't known him as long as you, but he strikes me as a man that knows what he wants."

Ty was silent as he chewed on the tough meat of the hind leg. Over the time he had been on the trail with Rocky, he had learned never to stare into the fire; tonight he forgot his lesson and watched the dancing flames, catching himself he said, "Rocky told me that it takes your night vision away in a damn hurry." Throwing the bone into the fire, he continued to watch it burn. "You know James; on the trail out here I learned a hell of a lot. One thing that always struck me was never to get in the old man's way. There is something about the man that says he's goin' to get what he goes after, might have to go through or over you but he was goin' to get there."

"Son, there's nothin' that I can do to ease your bein' separated from the Rocky but I can tell you what helped me get over loosin' of my friend's durin' the war. I'd wake up from dreamin' about seein' all their dead bodies, just a lyin' on the damn ground it always took me a minute or two to get the picture out of my head. The easiest way, at least for me, was to spend the rest of the time rememberin' 'em like they were. Take your brother James, hell to this day I remember his eyes and smile; he looked at life as if he could whip most anything. He was a damn fine soldier and a real friend; somehow I figured he would make it, think Rocky will too."

The second day Ty was more relaxed leaving the pine trees behind them they headed for the crossing, trading the isolation of the hills for sagebrush, short grass and open spaces. Watching Tuff run out ahead of them brought back memories of Rocky, causing him to speak out load several times expressing his thoughts aloud. James ignored them for the most part, again respecting Ty's privacy but on one occasion, Ty blurted, "The son of a bitch better watch his backside."

"He will; he knows what he's up against, he's been there before."

"Hell, I always watched it before, might forget I ain't there and get himself in trouble."

"Think he will?"

"Nope, guess I just want to worry about him, he ain't smart enough to do it."

Before making the crossing into the valley Ty said, "Hoped he would come a ridin' up before we got this far, was wantin' him to say he needed my help, he might not know that he needs it, but I do."

It was late in the day but there was things going on everywhere Ty looked, two men were sawing logs into lumber, stacking the flat lumber in one pile and the support pieces in another. Two more were busy making shingles out of short blocks of cedar, one man would place the broad ax on the block and another would strike it with a mallet, making each one about the same thickness. They were working on the footings for the barn, the temporary chicken coop was built and the chickens were busy scratching for worms and seeds.

John was going from work site to work site, checking and giving directions. His arm still in a sling, but the absence of the splints and bandage no longer interfered with the use of his arm. All that remained of the roasting steer were small strips of meat drying out over red-hot coals. The strips most likely had been soaked in salt water and maybe pepper to make jerky. Before winter sets in many pounds of the dried meat would be stored for the cowboy's meals when out on the range.

"Hello the camp, were comin' in." shouted Ty.

John turned and waved his hand, "Glad you're back, Red Fox make it alright?"

"Their camp is not far, a shade better than a half days ride. He rode into the village like a returnin' king or something, still a sick kid but you would never know it when he rode in."

"You stayed a while, where's Rocky, they keep him?"

"Nope, he took off for Blackfoot country. On the way back we took a ride up in them hills." Ty pointed to the northwest. "Red Fox told Rocky where there was a place that the water is damn hot year around, we camped there one night. That's where he told us he was leavin' and while me and James was sleepin' he rode out, pissed me off but maybe it was for best. We've been through a lot together since I tied up with him at the Landin' in Missouri. Hell, we traipsed across the corner of Kansas and clear across Nebraska without gettin' mad at one another, we even had a run in with some damn raw-hiders and got Kate out to the Forks with no problems. Thought we were goin' to the Montana Territory to get Evenin' Star away from those Blackfeet but he changed his damn mind. He told James and me that he figured it was best he went on alone; felt he might stand a better chance of gettin' her on his own."

Ty paused; thinking of loosing his friend brought more memories. "Dammit John, I always figured that we were good for one another, hell, I knew what he was thinkin' before he did. James figures that he didn't want to get me killed or something, I'm afraid I won't ever see the bastard again, only hope that he knows what he's doin'."

"Kinda had a feelin' this might happen, he talked with me one time about what he was thinkin'. He knows that the odds are against him in gettin' Evenin' Star I think he only wants to see her to be sure that she's all right, you never know he might show up here one of these days."

Before Ty could answer he said, "Where in the hell did find those horses?" John had stepped around the riders and was checking the new horses. "Don't look like ones you might come across just runnin' loose on the prairie?"

"Runnin' Horse and we think the boy's father gave 'em to us, they were real glad to get Red Fox home, treated us real well, they did, even feed us puppy meat and all." Ty said.

"Puppy meat, you mean dog meat?"

"Yep, that's another thing we're pissed about, the son of a bitch let us eat it before he told us what it was. James and me thought about killin' him but we found out he had a good reason for not doin' it, if you can believe the bastard. Said that they only serve it to the people they really liked, it's their way of welcomin' you and eatin' it was our way of sayin' thanks, didn't want to make 'em mad."

"What did it taste like?"

"Kinda sweet, but real tender, can't say I want to eat it again."

"When you think about eatin' puppy, kinda gives a man the shivers." John replied.

"Kinda made us want to puke, ain't that right James?"

"Your damn right it did."

"They let you ride right in?"

"Running Horse and his bunch met us just outside of camp. We made some friends, even told us that we were welcome to come back, ifin' we wanted. Maybe better than gettin' the horses was the Chief givin' James and Rocky new Indian names, I want you to meet Flying Hawk and he gave Rocky the name of Swift Bear. Got that name cause of the bearskin coat and the medicine necklace that he wears. We told the old bastard he was damn lucky that he didn't have skunk skin cap on."

"Stead of Swift Bear it might have been, Stinkin' Skunk, or something like that." James added.

"You men sure got busy when we left, got a lot done ain't anyone out watchin' the cows?"

"We got Tom and a couple of the boys out, they're checkin' the bogs and mud holes, the damn critters will walk right into a hole and get stuck, have to pull 'em out most ever day."

"Looks like your movin' right along."

"Ya, I'm in a hurry to make this a real ranch, got to get the barn up and build a place for a blacksmith shop, can't run a ranch without one and you might want to ask Walt to fire the forge up and shoe these new horses."

"We got time before I leave to have it done, there is no hurry."

Looking back at the cabin he went on, "Decided to re-do the roof on the cabin and bunkhouse, get a heavy snow this winter and afraid the flat roof will cave in. Want to put rafters up and shingle 'en to let the snow slid off. Doubt that we will have time to put us up a cook shack, be nice if we had one this winter the bunkhouse will have to do. I got the chickens taken care for now but before winter we'll move 'em to a warmer place, maybe into the barn. James would be disappointed if they all froze to death."

"The way things are lookin' you'll have this place lookin' real nice long before winter." Ty said.

"Why don't you put them horses in the corral and we can talk sitin' down, have us a cup of hot coffee and put our feet up. You know the more I look at that gray the more he looks like that wild one out there." and John pointed to the west, "Both big for bein' range raised."

Placing the horses in the corral and rubbing them all down Ty said. "Think I'll see what he thinks about havin' a rider on his back." Grasping the mane with his left hand, he swung his right leg over the gray's back and before he could settle on to the horse, the gray decided to object by bucking, forcing Ty to dig in his heals and hold on. After about three crow hops, the horse must have figured out that the rider was there to stay and stood quiet. Patting the neck and talking gently to the animal, he swung back down, still talking to it, he again mounted and this time there was no reaction at all.

Rubbing the horses muzzle and saying "Got to come up with a name for you horse but none come to me just yet. It's got to be special but I promise it will be a good one."

James mounted his with no problem and as he faced Ty, "Think the gray is the youngest, I think mines been ridden more."

The coffee drank, with more of John's desires discussed, Ty said, "Think I will go on west, like to see those mountains I heard so much about."

"Why don't you wait a day or two, you can give me and the boys a hand. Rest your horses a bit and it will give you time to see how the gray is goin' handle under a saddle."

"Guess a day or two won't hurt got to have time to find me a place to winter, dig me a hole or put up a shack, ain't lookin' forward to sleepin' out in the open?"

James, you ever think about ranchin'?"

"Hell I'm a farmer, don't know anything about raising this many cows at once. I can handle a few at a time but it looks like it's a hand full to raise more."

"Takes time to learn to do anything, wouldn't be long before the farmin' was clear out of you and the range takes over, be nice to have you for a neighbor. If you change your mind, I'll give you some stock to start out with and you can pay me back whenever. As you have seen, there is plenty of good grass land on the north side of the river."

"I'll have to think on that."

A team of horses topped the rise dragging a half-a-dozen logs. The teamster was riding standing up on the top log and bringing the team up along side of the already huge stack of logs, he released the chains. With just a wave of his hand, he turned the team and was out of sight in no time at all.

"John, you got more shit goin' on, I don't see how you're goin' to keep up with it all. You got stock to care for and you've got to get ready for the drive to the Forks, think you're goin' to able to handle it all?"

"That's the fun part of ranchin', James, you ain't ever done, if I live to be a hundred and never stop workin', there will still be things that need doin'. We just do as much as we can, when we can and leave the rest for later. We still got a few weeks before we have to start separatin' for the drive and it will take some time to trail brand and castrate the calves that we missed this spring. After that, it will take the better part of six weeks to get 'em there and back. We'll still have some time this fall to put some of the finishin' touches on what is really needed."

"Thinkin' about your offer, I decided to stick to farmin', when the snowballs start hittin' you in the ass, you can set inside and watch for the most part sounds like ranchin' is a year round job, thanks for your offer but no thanks."

James heard a commotion at the corral and seen that the pinto was busy kicking at the rail fence. "Better, settle that damn horse down or you won't have a corral left, might even hurt him self."

"I'll give you a hand."

James caught the horse and tied it to the snubbing post in the middle of the enclosure, taking a little time to settle it down while becoming better acquainted.

John was setting where they had left him. "If you want our help gettin' things done around here John, you better tell us what you want us to do."

"Hate to put my guest to work, why don't we just sit here and shoot the breeze, the boys will get things done. They know that there is more rotgut in the cabin, wages up here don't mean shit to these boys but a bottle of hooch sure as hell gets their attention."

"Sitin' around never was my thing, druther be doin' something there will be time this evenin' to chat, where you want me to start?" James asked.

"Well I need to start haulin' some of those flat rocks for the foundation of the barn. Ifin' you want to do something and you don't mind what, take that black team over there. Just down off the hill and about a mile to your left is a hell of a pile of 'em, there's been a wagon or two there already, just follow the tracks. Bring 'em in and dump 'em right over there." and he pointed to the open trench.

"Looks like you got plenty of those rocks right over there be a hell lot shorter haul."

"I know your goin' to think I'm crazy but I don't want to disturb any thing up here at the ranch grounds. A higher power made this plateau up here and I don't think that I can improve on it's beauty. Want to leave it just as I found it except for these buildin's and the ones I'm goin' to build. These here ones are only temporary; I have a plan in my head to make the new ones blend in. What we're puttin' up now ain't goin' to be the way it's goin' to end up."

"It's your place John, do it any way you want, I agree ain't seen any place nicer than here." Ty said.

"I'll get Archie over there to help you, got something else for Ty to do."

James hitched the Blacks to the wagon, the canvas had been removed and he and Archie headed down the hill into the valley.

Ty started to get up and asked John what it was that he wanted him to do. John put his hand on Ty's arm, "Sit a spell longer, got something that's been on my mind and I guess that there is no better time than right now to say it."

Sitting back down he waited for John to start. After a long wait John said, "Been tryin' to figure out how to say what I want to say, it's damn important that I get my words the way I want 'em. Ty, I've been thinkin' on this for a hell of a long time, damn near since I first met up with ya. I've learned a hell of a lot about what kind of a man you are and ifin' I had a son, I would be damn proud if' he was like you. Don't have no family, been to damn busy tryin' to make a dime. I did have me a girl once, she got tired of waitin' on me and married some one else. The only thing I know about women is what I've learned out back of a saloon."

He lapsed back into silence and scratched his head for a moment before he went on. "Ty, you see what I got here, could be the biggest break I've ever had. A man can build himself a place he can be proud of but it ain't no small undertakin', it will take a lot of sweat and blood, I ain't afraid of that. The one biggest thing that a rancher has workin' against him is the weather. and I ain't worry none about that either, God he built this place and I think he's goin' watch over it. It's him that controls the storms that will hit us, same with the rain and sunshine that a man needs to raise cattle. I'm thinkin' that he would not have put so much effort in makin' this valley ifin' he wanted to ruin it latter; the beauty of this place is goin' to last well past our life time."

"Now mind you, I ain't no bible thumpin' religious lunatic but I do believe that some one with a hell of a lot more power, thought and love built this here place. I'm thinkin' there ain't another like it on the face of the earth. Ty, I think that same power led me here, right to this here valley. Like I told you boys just a short time ago, I don't want to change any more things than I have to, I'm here but I feel that is still his valley. Some day I want a house and barn built out of the same rocks that are in the cliffs over there." Looking off to the east, he went on "Hope to build me a bunkhouse the same way. The house is goin' to be right down here in front of us and the barn and bunkhouse will go over there. Put me a white fence around the house and a porch to sit on, come evenin'. I'm even thinkin' maybe about add' in a tree or two for shade. Are you startin' to think I'm crazy yet, sometimes I think I am?"

He went on, "Ain't a young man any more but I still got years left in me and a hell of a lot to do, intend to stay right here and make myself proud. When my time comes, I want folks to remember me and have people talk about what I built out here. I'll need someone to carry on and visit my grave, on occasion be best if them folks could feel that they had a part in makin' my dreams come true."

He pulled a plug of tobacco out of his shirt pocket; with his pocketknife, he cut himself a chew, holding it out and Ty refused it, he put it safely away. After several chaws and a spit or two, he settled it into his cheek and looking Ty in the eye said, "Son, this ain't the way I planned to say this but I don't know no other way. Words ain't ever been my long suit, so here it is in a nutshell. I knowed that you had plans to go north with Rocky, figured you might still go to the high mountains. I don't want to stand in your way of that but what I'm askin' is that after you seen the mountains; I would like to have you come back this way and consider workin' with me to build this place up.

To go a step further, ifin' I could write I'd put it on paper and put my mark to it, sayin' that half of everthing I own would be yours. I'm guessin' that you will just have to take my hand and word on it. I ain't in no hurry to get your answer but before you leave would you let me know?"

John silently worked on the wade of tobacco; he spit a stream of the brown juice at an unsuspecting horse fly as it flew by. Ty also sat there thinking of what to say, moreover just what to say. John's words about him and the son he never had brought thoughts of his mother and then of the father that he never really knew, it brought a feeling of pride that Ty had never felt before. John had said things that he knew his father and mother would very proud to hear and in his case it was an offer that he hadn't expected, one that had set him back on his heals. When Ty had first seen this valley, he had fallen in love with it, it would be a place that he could bring Mom and the boys out to and experience the peace the valley had to offer.

"Hell you drop a blanket over my head John, never expected this is what you wanted to talk about and don't know what to say. Hope it's not because of that thing back at the Forks, that's over and done with. Told you back there John that you don't owe me nothin' and I meant it."

"Has nothin' to do with that, well maybe that's when I got to thinkin' that here is a man to walk the river with. I ain't met many men in all my years that I could respect more; no this is a business deal, I'm goin' to need some one that thinks like me and can back up what he thinks, that's all there is about it."

"It's a hell of an offer John, something to think about but I'll have to give it time to sink in."

"Don't say anything just now Ty, think on it a while." John interrupted.

"Oh, I'll think on it, are you sure you have given it enough thought I don't know a damn thing about ranchin'. You got Tom workin' for you and he seems to be a real nice man, you ever think about offerin' him this deal, he knows ranchin' and you have known him longer than me."

"Knowed Tom for the best part of four years, he's a true and loyal friend. I would trust him with my life and I have but no, I haven't made him this offer. I will tell you why, Tom wants to go back to Texas, his family is there and that's where his roots are. Bein' the man he is, is all that is keepin' him here. He said that as soon as this place is up and runnin' he wants to go south, nothin' that I could do would make him change his mind, yes sir he's loyal to a fault that man is."

"Let me tell you this Ty, I did ask Tom's opinion of you, I asked him to keep an eye on you and let me know what he thought. Ain't asked him what he has found but he did say that if Tuff here trusts you like he does, you can't be bad, dogs seen to know people better than most folks do."

At the mention of his name the dog looked up, decided that ever thing was alright and lowered his head to his front paws.

Ty said, "The dog has walked a long ways, from home to here, guess he needs his rest."

The rock wagon returned and Ty was helping to stack the flat rocks, when the sound of a horse, ridden hard, came from the edge of the plateau caused everyone to stop and look. Tom, riding a lathered up horse, came to a sliding stop just short of John.

"Boss we got trouble."

"What kind of trouble?"

"Some one is drivin' our stock and they ain't pushin' 'em this way. I tracked 'em to a canyon at the far edge of the valley."

"Injuns?"

"If that is who they are, there're ridin' shod ponies."

"How many do you think there are?"

"Figured it to be about seven, Willie left here headin' for Montana with his six buddies and I recognized a couple of the tracks I followed 'em them all the way from Texas, they're Willie's."

"That son-of-a-bitch, as long as he was ridin' to Montana he decided to make it worth his while."

John yelled to his men, "Put the saws and axes down boys grab your guns, saddle up and bring along an extra mount, someone is stealin' our stock. That goes for all of you except for Walt and Henry; you two stay here and watch the place. Tom here thinks that it's Willie and his bunch."

Walt fired back, "Dammit John, I want in on the action that god damn Willie, I always hated that gutless son-of-a-bitch. Let me go and some one else can watch the place."

"Walt I need you here, know that you can handle this place short handed.

You never know, you may see more action than we do, take care of the place."

"Your welcome to come along but it ain't your fight." John said to his friends. "Might take us a day or two to tree those bastards but we will do it."

A quick glance at James was all that he needed before he answered John. "Count us in."

Ty saddle Duke and gave some thought to the gray but not knowing how he would react to a saddle he settled on Pat. James choose his packhorses as well, which had been Kate's riding horse, with no need for it she had given it to him.

Mounted up and each man leading a spare mount, they headed down the slope at a hard gallop. Shouting over the noise of the galloping horses, John said, "Got a hell of a ride ahead of us ridin' hard like this we won't get to the far end till just before dawn. Tom, you sure you can find that canyon again?"

"Ain't hard to find, a grove of them aspen trees blocks it and right in the middle of the aspens is a big old spruce a blind man couldn't miss it."

The thunder of the horse's hooves and the rattle of the bridle chains sounded through out the night. The full moon shed an eerie light on the thick grass and dark shadows of the scattered trees fell across the rider's path. John called a halt somewhat after midnight and the tired cowboy's switched mounts. The tired lathered mounts left to rest and graze near the slow moving river. A bite of jerky, a drink of water and the race was back on.

As they rode Ty's thoughts were about Duke, he didn't want to leave him at the river but the horse was tired and need rest. It was the first time Ty had ever left Duke on his own but before he could finish his thoughts, the horse on Ty's left went tumbling down. The rider thrown ahead of the falling horse, head over heals he rolled. When the tumbling ended, the cowboy jumped to his feet and went directly to the dazed a horse. Ty pulled hard on the reins and dismounted before Pat had come to a complete stop. The horse was standing straddled legged with its head down, his eyes bugged out and seemed to be extended. His nostrils were flaring in and out, as he fought to get air into his lungs. He would lift up his right front leg up off the ground and set it back down so that is where the man started to check the horse's leg. Starting at the horse's hock the thrown rider slowly checked the apparently injured leg, never once seeming to care that there was blood on his face or that his injurer might be more serious than the horse.

"You alright fella?" Ty asked. "Know what happened?"

Rubbing the horse's leg just below its knee, he said, "Don't feel any broken bones and his tendons seems alright."

The horse put his weight on its bad leg and stood on it. Leading the horse a short distance the cowboy said, "He's goin' to be alright, just stumbled, I'm guessin'."

"Want to leave it here and ride double with me?"

"No, you go on with the others; I'll take it easy for a while and catch up after a bit, hate to turn him loose, he's too damn good of a horse."

"Sure you're alright, looks like your bleedin' on your forehead."

Wiping his forehead with the back of his hand and checking the results, "Scratched is all, ain't much, my damn pride is hurt a hell of a lot more, maybe if I had been payin' more attention, he might not of stumbled."

"If you're sure you're alright, I better get a move on."

"Yep. See you up ahead."

The others were long gone by the time Ty got started but the trail wasn't hard to follow, Ty figured that there was very little chance of catching them unless they pulled up. He and Pat moved through the night and as the first light of the new day was starting to break into the valley, he seen John and the crew bunched together next to a stand of jack pines.

With just enough sound to his voice so that it would carry he said, "Comin' in."

Dismounting and walking up to the group when John asked, "You by yourself, did you see Rusty?"

"His horse went down but Rusty is alright. He checked the horse out and decided that nothin' was broke he's comin' but most likely it will take him a spell."

John went back to talking with the crew. "Tom says that the box canyon is just past them rocks over there, maybe a half mile, no more. On the east side, he tells me, there is an openin' that they run the cattle trough, don't know how far back it goes after it gets in there a ways it breaks back to the west. Don't have any idea if there is another way out or not but we'll play it like there ain't. Tom, what do you think about us just bustin' in there and maybe catchin' 'em asleep?"

Kicking at the dusty pine needles that laid on the ground, Tom thought for a minute or so, "Don't know what we might be ridin' into, ain't ever seen beyond the trees that block it. Hate to have us go ridin' in like a bunch of damn Comanche's and get all shot to hell. If in' there is another way out, they will know about it and maybe out run us, our horses are done in and theirs are fresh. I'm thinkin' that we had better go a little slower to start with; find out what were up against."

"It's gettin' lighter and before long the way we're bunched up it won't be hard for 'em to see us, think we had better spread out and take to cover, boys keep your eyes open and try not to make any noise. Don't let anyone come from in there and get though our line, tell 'em once to stop and then shoot their ass off if in' they don't. Remember they're damn rustlers, nothin' more, some of you might have been friends to Willie and his boys, but remember they turned against ya. They're goin' to try to save their necks and if in' they have to kill you to do it; they're in the wrong, not us. Lets get spread out and move real slow to the tree line, any questions?"

Ty stood there not knowing if he should say what was on his mind or just keep quiet. He looked over at James, "Think you and me could injun up and scout the canyon, gettin' a quick look will sure help our chances and might get a better idea of where they have camped; see if they got any watches set up."

"Think you got a good idea, but it's up to John, it shouldn't take us long unless they're back in there a ways, knowin' that would help too, I'm thinkin'."

John, holding his bad arm, slowly rubbing it to restore the circulation said, "If you want to try it, be damn careful, don't want either of you to get shot, just look around and don't start anything on your own. Better figure some sign so every one will know it's you a comin' out."

"If we can get in there without bein' seen, we sure as hell can get out, don't worry we ain't goin' to get ourselves shot." Ty said.

'We'll do it your way Ty, we'll give you and James a head start but after you get in those trees, we're comin' in. We'll do it slow and spread out, alright with you?"

"Let us get far enough in to see what's there and then come on in."

"Where do you want to start, left, right or down the middle?" Ty asked.

"It's was your idea, you pick."

"Most likely if they posted a lookout it would be to the left, near the openin'. I say that we go right up the middle and let the chips fall where they may, no sense it dragin' it out."

"Let's go, John if you hear shootin', come a runnin'."

Taking advantage of what night shadows remained, they moved to the distance grove of trees. Without saying a word, they moved apart several paces, each watching for any sign of a trail that might indicate the possible movement of the rustlers. All they seen were cattle tracks, all moving into the trees. They crossed the meadow and at the edge of the aspen grove, then joined up once again.

In a low voice James said, "Think the best way is keep goin' straight in, we can keep our eyes open and go slow."

Ty commented that he was surprised, "Expected that there would be some one up here watchin' must feel right at home not postin' a guard."

Catching a slight movement off to his left, he whirled around and brought his rifle to his shoulder at the same time. Sitting on his haunches and slowly panting to cool himself down, was Tuff. With a hand sign, he signaled James but he had already seen the dog. With a shrug of his shoulder and a quizzical look at Ty, "Son as long as that dog is around; you are never goin' to be lonely."

"Didn't think that he came along, hadn't seen him."

"He took a short cut or two, look at the damn cockleburs won't be easy to get them bastards out."

""We're this far, want to keep goin' ahead or spread out again? James asked.

"Stay separated but in sight of one another and keep goin'" Ty said.

The smell of smoke was first and then the sound of the cattle gave the camp away. Staying hidden behind trees and shrubbery, they crept closer and at the edge of the tree line, the floor of the box canyon started a gradual rise, large boulders and rocks that had fallen from the surrounding walls were scattered across the open area. Around a dying fire with a ribbon of gray smoke, disappearing before it could rise in the air, were sleeping men. The camp surrounded by large rocks and a more that adequate defense against surprise attacks.

Beyond the camp, was a fence made of shrubbery and rails. The restless cattle were constantly moving and the clacking of their horns and the lowing indicated how crowded they must be. Seven horses were tied a short distance from the fence and several more seen within the cattle enclosure.

A low growl from Tuff brought their attention back to the fire two men had stood up and stretched; one threw a couple of pieces of firewood on the smoking fire, checked the coffee pot and then followed the other man into the brush, away from the camp.

The two men returned and started to go about waking the rest the heavier of the two said, "Let's get a move on dammit, we want to be out of here by full sun-up, we'll eat on the move. There is hot coffee on the fire, drink it fast and saddle up, I want the herd movin' in ten minutes, lets hit it."

Some rolled up their bedrolls while others relieved themselves just a short way from where they had been sleeping.

John along with Shorty crept up to Ty and James and in a very low voice John said, "That's Willie's bunch alright seems like we got here at just the right time, they're gettin' ready to move out, ain't they?

"You're here now John; it's your show how do you want to handle it?" Ty asked.

"Most of 'em are good men its that god damn Willie, he's the problem ifin' I could just get him alive, I'd hang the son-of-a-bitch. Make an example out of him and the rest I think would fall in line."

Ty asked, "What's Willie look like?"

"Wears a cow hide vest, kinda average height, a little stocky and has a bushy mustache."

I think the man you call Willie and another went into the brush over there earlier, most likely to relieve themselves when they got back they stated to yell at the others to get a move on."

"Think you're right, I seen him too." James said, "They don't know that we are here yet, so the first play is ours.

"I'm goin' to try to talk some sense into those kids, see if they will give up Willie to save their hides they're all Texans, so I doubt that they will."

"Want to get their attention?"

"Might as well, what do you have in mind?"

Ty said, "Show them what they are up against at least make 'em think a spell. See those two cups settin' on the fire ring and the pot hangin' on the hook?"

"Yup."

"James, you take one of the cups and I'll shoot the bail off the pot, show 'em that we can hit what we aim at."

James said, "Sounds good to me, let's do it on three."

John started. One—Two—Three and one of the cups went flying and at the same time, the pot dropped into the fire.

"The game is up boys, this is John Edwards and I want you to lay down your guns your surrounded and got no place to run."

At the first sound of John's voice, the outlaws headed for cover, diving behind the rocks and at least one of them started to shoot at the sound of John's voice.

"Dammit boys, you ain't got a chance, your out numbered and out gunned, and you got no place to go but down, think on it. All I want is your leader; I'm thinkin' that it's Willie. Give him to us and the rest of you are free to go where you want, you all know me; I'm a man of my word."

"Go to hell you old bastard." A voice said. "We're leavin' together and it's goin' to be over your dead ass, right boys?"

There was no response and Willie tried again, "We're stickin' together, ain't we boys."

This time there was a couple of affirmative answers barely audible beyond the camp.

"It ain't worth it boys, those cows are mine and I aim to keep 'em. Stay and fight, the only thing that it will get you is a ticket to hell, what's it goin' to be."

"You want these cows, come and get 'em." Willie answered and with that, he fired a shot into the grove of aspens.

The rustlers fired a couple of shots and one came near Ty. Standing next to a tree for protection, Ty took a bead on dark headed man that was shooting at anything and everything. Easing his finger back against the trigger, the Henry bucked into his shoulder and the dark headed man shouted and ducked out of sight. He said, "God Dammit, they near shot my ear off."

Ty heard him and answered, "That's where I was aimin', throw down your gun and come on out, next one will be between your eyes."

"He means what he says and he can do what says, Pete, don't want you to get hurt anymore bring the boys and leave Willie to us." John added.

Willie shouted back, "I'll shoot the first one that tries to leaves, we're in this together and by God we'll fight our way out this."

There was silence in the outlaw's camp before a voice said, "Willie no need for you to say that, if you want to shoot me it don't have to be in the back, I'll face you straight up anytime, what's it goin' to be." He waited for an answer and not getting one, he went on, "Boys this is Wesley talkin', I'm leavin', old John said he wanted Willie, I believe him, any of you want to join me?"

Again, silence had fallen across the camp, a man stood up and with his hands in the air, left the protection of a large rock.

"Hold your fire boys, that's Wesley."

A shot rang out; Wesley spun around and fell to the ground.

"I told him I'd shoot, anyone else want to leave?"

A new voice from behind a rock said, "Willie you just pissed me off, there was no need in killin' Wesley, he was a hell of a better man than you will ever be. I'm goin' to back out of here and ifin' you want to shoot me you will have to do it facin' me. One more thing, you had better get me with your first shot, there won't be time for a second."

As a man appeared, with his back toward them John said, "That's Stan."

Backing up with his pistol poised to fire, he suddenly stopped and fell to one knee, the smoke was seen before hearing the sound of the shot. Following the first shot, several more sounded and then nothing but the moaning of an injured man.

"Stan you got him, I don't think he's dead, but he's on the ground hurt." An unknown voice said.

John said. "Stan you ok?"

"Ya John, I'm ok, I'm goin' to check on Wesley tell the boys not to shoot."

The four remaining rustlers were all standing, two walked to the edge of the brush to check on Willie.

"John, this is Billie, Willie is hurt bad but he's alive."

Stan said, "John you said we could go our own way ifin' you got Willie, does it still go?"

"I gave you my word, I haven't changed my mind."

"You might as well come on in we ain't goin' to give you any shit, the fight is over."

John went first to where Wesley laid a crease that ran from his right ear to above his right eyebrow. Blood had cover the whole side of his face but he looked up at John, "My Daddy always said if you walk the road straight and minded your own business, you can always look anyone in the eye and know you did right. John, I kinda fell off that straight path, don't know why it had to be you, you always was a fair man. Willie just made everything sound so damn easy, I'm sorry I did what I did but can't blame Willie for it. Ifin' I wasn't interested I could have kept on ridin', reckon you can do what you want with me, I did what I did, what ever you do, I'll understand."

The rustlers, all except for Billie and the wounded leader, were standing nearby. They were all listening to Wesley and when Wesley had finished, Stan said, "I think we all pretty much think the same way John, we weren't to bright doin' what we did, like Wesley says, it sounded so easy. We're all sorry we did it to you we'll get our bed rolls and be out of your hair."

"Boys you're free to go where you want. I know my friends will call me an idiot and that I was lackin' in brains, I most likely am. You all know the penalty for stealin' another man's cows, I don't mean one or two, hell, everybody does that but a whole damn herd is different. Back in Texas, you'd hang on the spot and I gave my word, all I wanted was Willie."

Billie walked up and said that Willie was dead. "Died in a hell of a lot of pain, he was gut shot and had couple of holes in his chest. The last words out of his mouth was that he could have been rich, then he grabbed his gut, curled up with pain and died."

"Dammit, he died too damn easy; a rope would have made me feel better then again I ain't sure he was worth a rope."

"As I was sayin', I'm buildin' me a ranch up here in this valley and I'm goin' to need some help in doin' it. You boys made a hell of a mistake and you all know it. A man that has all his facilities would send you down the road a packin' but what I'm sayin' is ifin' you think that you want to help build a ranch second to none and stay loyal to the brand, I'm willin' to go along with givin' you another try. Mind you, the next time there will be a rope around your neck and I will put it there. Think it over, we got work to do."

Leaving them standing there, he walked over to where Willie laid. Looking down at the fallen man he shook his head and said under his breath, "You sorry bastard, you don't know it but you proved a point that I've been thinkin' on every since I hired you. I didn't trust you then and I should have listened to my head. I should have the boys put you under the ground to protect the coyotes but to hell with 'em, you don't deserve a grave." and he walked away.

"Were headed home, those that want to ride for the brand, your welcome to come along. Tom get the cattle movin', we'll meet you back at the ranch. The rest of us will go find our ridin' stock.

Tom said, "I need five of you to stay and put these cows back on the range." Looking around he added, "Whose it goin' to be?"

"Think that the ones that put 'em here should take 'em home, Pete you and Wesley go on back get your selves fixed up." Stan said.

"Need one more, how about you Shorty?"

"Better than sawin' them damn logs."

Mounting up and heading out of the aspens they saw a red headed cowboy leading his horse. Riding out to meet him John said, "Rusty you alright?"

"I'm fine boss but old Brownie is a little sore and I decided to give him a break, so I walked, sorry I didn't get here sooner, everything work out?"

"Sure did Rusty you can ride Willie's horse, he won't be needin' it, let's go home."

Printed in the United States
48332LVS00003B/109-129